Modern Wicked Fairy Tales: Complete Collection

By Selena Kitt

eXcessica publishing

Excessica LLC
P.O. Box 127
Alpena MI 49707

To order additional copies of this book, contact:
books@excessicapublishing.com
www.excessica.com

First Edition December 2011

Table of Contents

BEAUTY

Jolee could never stay out of trouble for long and being locked in the trunk of Carlos's black BMW was no exception to that particular rule of her life. She'd given up trying to kick the side of the car to make noise—luxury car makers practically sound-proofed their trunks. Who knew? She wondered if engineers considered scenarios like this one—after all, any rich husband might have to enlist his hit men tie up and toss his troublesome wife into the trunk for easy disposal, right?

Besides, her feet were secured with zip ties, as were her hands, which stretched painfully behind her back. They didn't use duct tape—too easy to wiggle out of—except for the pieces over her mouth. And even those weren't just slapped on—they'd used the roll to wrap the silver stuff around and around her mouth and jaw in layers. Carlos's guys knew exactly what they were doing. Of course they did. It was their job.

There was just no way out of this bit of trouble. That realization finally hit her in the darkness, the car's wheels crunching gravel a long time now, off the highway, she surmised, the suspension bouncing her violently up and down.

This was going to be the last batch of trouble she ever got herself into in the whole expanse of a life that seemed suddenly very short.

She'd been so focused on escaping or finding a way out since Carlos's goons had grabbed her out back—zip-tied and duct taped before she could even raise the snow shovel she'd been using—that this final realization hit with such terrifying force Jolee actually wet herself, urine staining the crotch of her jeans with spreading navy blue darkness.

She was going to die.

"No," she whispered, feeling herself giving in at the same time as she denied the notion. "Please, no."

She had no one left to mourn her. Her mother had been gone since she was a baby, her father dead for years, killed in a logging accident. And her husband—Carlos was the reason she was facing this end, a betrayal she still couldn't wrap her head around. But for the first time in her life she was glad for the miscarriages, that she had no baby or child to leave behind. Her only real regret was that she had never really loved a man who truly loved her back.

Jolee wailed, a muffled cry that wouldn't have been heard over the pounding bass of Ted Nugent through the car's speakers even if they'd been stopped in traffic somewhere, but they were far from civilization. She knew where they were. Not exactly, but they'd driven a long way on this back, bumpy, winding road and there was no doubt in her mind they were in the middle of nowhere, deep into the wild, far from the logging camps, but still on the thousands of acres of land Carlos's father had left him.

That was where Carlos buried the bodies.

Jolee thought of her husband, the way he sucked on a Wintergreen Lifesaver and tied his tie in their dresser mirror every morning as if he was going off like any other man to a regular job living a regular life, the way he ruffled her hair and called her "chickie" and kissed her cheek before he left. How could that man be the same man who had ordered her kidnapped and killed?

As much as she wanted to deny it, she knew it was the truth. Her husband killed people. No, he had people killed. If they got in his way, if they threatened him or his little empire, Carlos had the money, the power and the influence to simply make them disappear. She hadn't wanted to believe it, for years she had suppressed her intuition. But when proof had arrived in her mailbox, when she had confronted Carlos with the information and he had petted and placated and pacified her, she had still denied it, hadn't she? She'd believed his lies. Because she wanted to? Because she had to? What woman wanted to believe her husband would have her father killed?

It had been over a week since the blow-up, since the unstamped white envelope with proof of Carlos's crime had shown up in their mailbox with just her name—Jolee Mercier—scrawled onto the front. She'd thought things had gone back to normal, that Carlos had forgotten, that they could live out their lives as they always had, separately together. How could she have let herself sink so low? How could she have believed for one moment that the man she married wasn't the monster he'd been revealed to be?

But she had found that living with something, day in and day out, numbed you to its power. Now she was going to pay for that denial, with her life.

"No!" She didn't know where she found the strength. Maybe it was the thought of Carlos telling his next conquest that, sadly, his last wife had run off on him. Maybe it was the injustice of being interred beside her father somewhere in the middle of nowhere, a mass grave for Carlos's enemies—men who had defended the union, women who had turned him down, people who had made Carlos's life uncomfortable. How many bodies were buried out there, she wondered? If he would order his own wife killed—who *hadn't* he gotten rid of?

Jolee wiggled around in the trunk. There was nothing back there—made more room for bodies, she assumed dismally—just a tire iron and a jack and a set of jumper cables. All great weapons if she could have gotten her hands free, but the zip ties were drawn so tight behind her back the circulation had long ago disappeared from her fingers. She could still feel her feet though, and that was what she used, slamming both of them against the latch of the trunk.

There was no way to disguise what she was doing. She knew the guys would hear her. The music stopped blaring almost immediately. She was probably denting the hell out of Carlos's car. The thought, *he's going to kill me*, crossed her mind and she gave a strangled, crazed half-laugh, kicking again, again, again.

"What the fuck? Bitch! Knock it the hell off!" She recognized the voice. One of the guys who'd grabbed her, an older man, her father's age, someone she remembered seeing around the logging camps and later, at her husband's office.

She heard him yelling but didn't stop. If they pulled over now and shot her in the head it wouldn't matter. This was her one chance, her last chance, a last gasp for a final breath.

When the trunk popped open, Jolee screamed in triumph behind her duct tape mask. She had time to see a gun metal expanse of winter sky and fat flakes of snow still falling outside, her nostrils flaring as she filled them with a sharp, cold intake of air, before the car stopped.

But it didn't just stop. The impact was so sudden Jolee was tossed toward the front of the BMW, hitting her head against the car jack. She felt something floppy on her forehead, wetness flooding her eye, stinging, but then she was flying and couldn't think about that anymore, thrown out of the open trunk into a foot of heavy snow.

The landing was hard, so hard she couldn't breathe, but her head hurt the most and the last thing she remembered was hearing a scream, a wild animal cry of pain and death and horror, and she wondered briefly if she was making that awful noise before the world went black.

* * * *

Silas had been following the animal for over a mile. His father taught him long ago that hunting should be something a man did honorably, so tracking in the snow seemed a bit unfair, but he was carrying a bow, not a gun, and the elk had a good quarter mile head-start. Besides, the animal was a thousand pounds and bulls were known to charge any hunter forced to get too close. Silas was careful to stay downwind. He had two arrows ready—elk often ran, even after a kill shot, and he was ready to track it for the second if he needed to—but it turned out he only needed one.

The first shot was good, clean, a chest hit, surely puncturing the animal's lung, possibly piercing the heart. And still, the big bull ran, bellowing as it bounded through the trees, heading for the old logging road. It wasn't much of a road at all, just a two-track, and very few people knew about it—most of them dead. His brother, Carlos, only had it plowed or graded for "special occasions."

It all happened far too quickly for Silas to do anything but bear witness. He heard the animal cry, a horrifying, sorrowful squall, but by the time he'd reached a clearing near the road, following both the elk's tracks and the blood trail, events had already been set in motion. The first thing he noted, setting aside a rising anger at the sight, was that the two-track had been freshly plowed. The foot of snow they'd received overnight—nothing compared to the two more they were supposed to get over the next few days—had already been cleared from the narrow road.

The elk had bolted across the gravel path, not afraid or cautious of anything that looked like a road this far from civilization, and probably too weak from the arrow to jump far out of the way of the oncoming vehicle. Instead, it had tumbled sideways onto the hood of the BMW, its huge rack—calcified this time of year and sharpened to dangerous points on tree bark—shattering the glass, puncturing the air bag, and skewering the driver of the vehicle to his seat.

The other airbag had either malfunctioned or was nonexistent, because the passenger had gone airborne through the windshield, his body sprawled over that of the elk on the hood, limp and unmoving. There was so much blood Silas couldn't tell from an immediate assessment which was human and which was elk. But the elk was still alive, the arrow rising out of its side as it struggled to free itself, the pulling and tugging of its head making the driver do a bloody dance in his seat.

Silas moved to the front of the car and raised his bow, making it quick and fast, easing the animal's suffering and silencing its cries. He surveyed the scene, understanding immediately. He monitored the old two-track regularly, even though it was miles from his own cabin, knowing Carlos's penchant for using it, but he hadn't been down this way in a few weeks. He recognized the two men as Carlos's, in spite of their disfiguring wounds.

Probably the same men who had taken Isabelle, he thought, a slow heat burning in his chest as he assessed the damage. The memory of his wife was always close to the surface, and although his life out here was full and far from idle, it was also quiet and lonely and left him a great deal of time to think about her. He couldn't help imagining them carrying her out of his house while they left him, drugged and duct taped to a chair, in their burning cabin. What had they done with her? Where was she now?

There was no movement from either body, and they were probably dead—or would be soon if they weren't already—and he was glad. He might have killed them himself if he'd found them barreling down this road, off to carry through with Carlos's orders. God only knows what he had them doing.

He ran a hand over his own marred cheek, self-conscious—an emotion he didn't feel much out here—reminding himself that at least he'd lived through his ordeal, although there had been plenty of times he'd wished he hadn't. Slowly, he had discovered purpose in his life again—to protect his father's land and to find his wife's body. He was sure they'd killed her. He prayed they hadn't raped her. The thought of these two men anywhere near his wife made his chest burn with rage.

Silas slung his bow over his shoulder, circling the vehicle. He would have to extract the buck and get it back to his cabin. But what to do with the car and the two bodies? His train of thought was completely derailed as he came around the trunk, seeing it popped open. The woman had been thrown clear of the vehicle, but she was lifeless on her side, a pool of blood melting the snow around her head.

He went down to one knee beside her body, checking her throat for a pulse and finding one, strong and steady. Then he checked her for wounds, finding only one, a gash on her head that was bleeding profusely, but it wasn't deep or fatal. He couldn't tell if she had any broken bones, but the head wound needed to be addressed first.

Unzipping his parka, he peeled up his layers of clothing until he got to the long underwear closest to his skin. Using his hunting knife, he cut a solid piece away out of the front, folding it up and pressing it against the woman's head. She didn't stir or cry out at all. He opened one of her eyes with thumb and finger. Her pupil retracted in the fading light of the sun and he sighed in relief as the other did the same when he checked it.

She looked young, a good ten years younger than he was—maybe early twenties. It was hard to tell with all the duct tape wrapped around her mouth, but there were very few lines in the skin around her eyes and none across her forehead, and her hair was dark and long and lustrous, no hint of gray. She was exotic-looking—maybe Native American, he guessed, cradling her head in his hand and using his other to press against her forehead, applying enough pressure to get the bleeding to stop, and waiting.

It was quiet. The wildlife had scattered, frightened away by the accident. He could sense them quivering, watching—rabbits, foxes, coyotes, joined for the moment in silence as they waited for the outcome of this strange event. The trees above him creaked under the weight of the snow on their bare limbs. It had been hovering near the freezing point for days, making the precipitation heavy and wet.

Silas looked over at the car, noticing the vanity plate. It was his brother's BMW all right. Only someone as arrogant as Carlos would send men in a car with his own vanity plate on it to commit a murder. The car had stalled on impact but the engine was still ticking as it cooled. His brother would certainly wonder what had become of his BMW and his trusty sidekicks. Carlos would send someone to look for them. Perhaps he would even come himself. The thought of seeing and confronting his brother was tempting, but as he looked back down at the woman on the snow, he reminded himself of the reason he'd stayed hidden all this time. Isabelle first. Then he would deal with Carlos.

Long enough, he judged, peeling the cloth away from the woman's head to check, blood blooming on the material like a red flower. It was still seeping, but it had slowed. He worked quickly, using his hunting knife to cut the zip ties on her wrists and ankles, carefully, gently peeling the duct tape from her skin. When he had her free, he stopped to gaze down at her, struck by how like Isabelle she looked, all that dark hair, those red lips. She even had the same body type, tall and full-bodied. The poor thing didn't even have a coat— just jeans and a turtleneck—and his jaw tightened when he noted the dark stain between her thighs. Must have been terrified, he thought, trying not to compare this woman to his wife, trying not to think about her fate, wondering if Isabelle, too, had wet herself before they had killed her.

He checked the woman's wound again. It would need stitches, but he couldn't do that here. At least it had stopped bleeding. He used the remains of the duct tape to fashion a make-shift bandage, securing the material over the cut. The woman was cold, already far too cold. He looked around again, listening. Still quiet. Glancing up, he watched the snow falling around them growing heavier. There was no car coming after this one any time soon, he judged, and if they got as much snow as the radio had been predicting, there wouldn't be one for days.

The whole thing was a big mess. He could bring the snowmobile back for the elk, but he couldn't leave the woman here to freeze in the meantime. He unzipped his parka and wrapped her in it, zipping her arms in, making her an easy-to-handle bundle. She was dead weight but he lifted her easily, getting his head under her torso, using a fireman's carry as he squatted with her over his shoulders.

For the first time, she made a noise, and he wondered when she was going to come to. What was he going to tell her? At least she couldn't see his face from this angle, he thought, using the big muscles in his thighs to help him rise to standing. The girl over his shoulders sighed again and he stiffened, waiting, but she stilled. He wondered what the poor girl had done to arouse Carlos's wrath. Refused him perhaps? That's all Isabelle had ever done—she'd chosen one brother over the other. Of course, Carlos hadn't killed her over that, although Silas was sure it had been, at least in part, some of his brother's motivation. Carlos had killed her because Isabelle was Silas's only heir. She would have inherited all the land their father had left to Silas that Carlos had been determined to get his hands on.

He shifted the girl's weight, balancing her on his shoulders. There was nothing to do but take her back to the cabin and he couldn't get there by car. It was a mile on foot and the sun would be setting by the time he arrived home. He grabbed his bow and took another look around at the accident site, marking the location in his memory. It would be dark when he came back, and the falling snow would cover his tracks.

It was going to be a long night.

* * * *

She drifted in.

Her head throbbed. It felt too big on her neck, wobbling around up there, hard to hold up. The man in the camouflage hunting mask held her head, made her drink water. His face floated in front of her like a demon, and the first time she saw him, she screamed and tried to scramble away. It came out only as a whimper and a shuffling of her feet under the covers, but in her head she was running for the door. She choked on the water and it dribbled down her chin. The man wiped at her with a cloth and they tried again. He didn't speak and it scared her, but she didn't say anything either. Did she have a voice? She tried to vocalize and just croaked, an unintelligible noise. He shook his head and wiped her mouth once more, offering her water. She shook her own head, and the movement sent shards of glass rolling around through her skull.

She drifted out again.

* * * *

It took Silas almost a full day to clean and dress the elk. He started in the early morning as the snow came down heavily outside the shed, making it hard to even see the house through the little window on the side. He stopped every hour to wipe his hands on his apron and trudge back to the house to check on the woman, just opening the bedroom door a crack, too afraid to show himself, masked and blood-stained. She'd think he was a serial killer for sure.

She slept on. The room with its twin bed served mostly as extra storage. He boxes full of books and magazines stacked against the walls and tools littered the floor. He had thought about putting her closer, in his own room, but there was only the one bed, and she was already afraid of him. Not that he blamed her. The poor girl clearly had plenty to be afraid of, and he couldn't expect her to trust him.

There had been nothing to tell him who she was, no purse or wallet, no identification at all, and the woman was silent, like a beautiful ornament tucked away in his spare room. He had been forced to get her out of her wet clothes, undressing her quickly, doing his best to just take care of business, but he couldn't help his reaction. He'd almost forgotten he wasn't an animal, a monster living in the middle of the woods, but a flesh and blood man.

She was a stunning beauty, her tawny against the dark waves of her hair, her limbs long and lean. He checked them carefully for breaks, her skin almost painfully soft in his hands, like velvet. Her flesh was too much of a temptation and he was embarrassed by his raw, immediate response, glad when he was done and she was dressed and tucked back under the covers.

He took a break to try to feed her some turkey noodle soup about mid-day, but she just stared at him, her speech fuzzy, eyes glazed. He drank the soup himself instead, watching her drift off again and wondering if he should take her to the hospital. There was no way to get there that day anyway, he decided, even though he'd just winterized the Duramax. The snow was thick and heavy with ice and already another foot had fallen overnight. The main roads would be difficult and the back ones impassable, even with his plow.

Once the elk was taken care of, Silas took a shower, standing outside in the cold under the nozzle attached to the side of the shed. He could run the well on the diesel generator or use the hand-pump inside and there was a composting toilet and a sink in the bathroom in the cabin, but no shower. He'd never installed one, never saw the point. He got dirty outside, might as well wash off the dirt outside, he figured. Besides, the needling, freezing spray felt like good punishment, the warmth of the woodstove in the house a relief when he came back in, dripping wet, to dry by the fire.

Then there was another mess to clean up.

He tried feeding the woman again, but she just groaned and rolled over and slept. It was a gamble, but he decided to leave her. She probably wouldn't wake at all, he told himself, and if she did, who would be crazy enough to go out in this storm? Only him. He didn't take the diesel Arctic Cat—he made his own biodiesel fuel—but instead had gone on foot in snowshoes, not wanting to draw attention to himself if someone had discovered the accident.

The car and the bodies were where he had left them, undisturbed. The extra foot of snow now covering the two-track made it tough going. The BMW got stuck twice, and riding in the blood-and-gore-covered driver's seat left him in desperate need of another shower. He'd stowed the bodies in the back, both of them cold but the remains of rigor mortis beginning to fade, making them easier to move.

He drove twenty minutes before he found the spot he was looking for, a place where the road dropped off on the right into a ravine. It was thick with trees down there and a creek bed ran through in the summer. It was mostly frozen now. Silas put the car in neutral and pushed it over the edge. The front end crumpled, accordion-style, before momentum flipped the BMW onto its roof, wheels spinning.

It wasn't the best solution, but at least it looked like an accident, and there was no missing elk begging explanation. He covered his tracks to the woods and went back to the accident site. There was a great deal of blood in the snow and he did his best to cover that. They were going to get at least another foot of snow overnight again, and that would help. He covered his tracks again to the woods and started the walk on snowshoes back to the cabin.

He was nearly home when he saw a deer and thought of his bow, sitting in the shed. He had a gun in his belt—a good piece to take care of business, a .357 magnum, but nothing to hunt with. He faced the buck and its head came up when it heard him. The deer turned tail and bounded off further into the woods.

No sense being greedy, he thought. The meat from the elk would be more than plenty to feed him through the winter, along with the various turkey and pheasant and deer and rabbit in the freezer. *Feed us*, he corrected himself, walking a little more quickly as he neared the clearing where his cabin stood. He was careful to remove the camouflage hunting mask from his pocket and pull it back on.

The woman had been sleeping when he left to take care of the car and the bodies and he was sure she would be still, but he was worried. She still hadn't spoken, and although her pupils continued to be normal size and responded to light, he didn't like to consider things like concussions and brain swelling and hemorrhage, but he had to keep an eye out.

He went around the cabin, heading for the shed—and another shower—when he saw the woman standing just outside the shed door, still wearing his t-shirt. It came to mid-thigh and she was barefoot in the snow, staring at the mess inside. The shed was still full of blood and gore and tissue from butchering the elk. His heart sank when she turned and saw him, masked and bloody, and she let out a choked cry at the sight.

Her gaze darted quickly from him to the cabin to the woods, and he waited for her to run, but she didn't. He saw it beginning to happen and barely made it to her side before she collapsed, muttering something under her breath. Now they were both a bloody mess again. He sighed, looking down at the woman's bandaged head. *She's still sleeping,* he realized, seeing how her eyes moved beneath her eyelids when they closed. He hoped whatever dream she was having didn't involve bloody masked men. He lifted her easily and carried her into the house.

* * * *

She drifted in.

And this time she did scream. She was restrained, a makeshift zip-tie handcuff attached to her wrist, another looped around the bedpost. She pulled and pulled, thrashing on the bed, kicking off the covers. It was the first time she realized she was wearing a man's button-down shirt and nothing else. Where were her clothes?

The man in the mask appeared in the doorway, the light behind him making him loom like a god. He came swiftly to her side, his big hands pulling the covers back up, smoothing her hair. He could cradle her whole head in his palm. The man was a giant.

"Where am I?" she croaked, confused and horrified at his gentle touch. "Who are you?"

"My name is..." He hesitated, sighed. "Silas. And you're in my cabin in the woods."

She let that information sink in, trying to get the world to make some sense.

"Why am I tied up?" She pulled at the zip tie again, whimpering.

"You were walking in your sleep," he explained. "You went outside in your bare feet. It's snowing."

She didn't remember that at all.

"Who am I?" she whispered, reaching up to touch her throbbing head. There was a thick bandage there.

The man was quiet. Then he said, "I was hoping you could tell me."

She didn't remember that either.

* * * *

Silas couldn't deny his relief—she was getting better, eating now, getting up to use the bathroom—but she still couldn't remember her name or what had happened. He prompted her as much as he could, knowing head injuries could cause amnesia, that memory could recur any time, triggered by anything.

"You found me in the snow?" she mused, sipping the tea he'd made. It was good to see her sitting up, although she didn't do it for long and she still slept a great deal. Her head hurt her and although the wound was healing nicely, the bruises on her forehead were growing a deeper, angry purple by the day. He had taken the zip-tie handcuffs off since she seemed more lucid, but he didn't go far, never out of sight of the house.

"There was an accident," he reminded her.

"And you didn't take me to the hospital because..."

He nodded toward the window. The snow had drifted against the pane, a good four feet high. He had to use snowshoes everywhere now. He'd plowed out the driveway, but the cabin wasn't built near any real pavement or labeled roads, and the way out couldn't be called anything more than a path—room enough for one vehicle in and out. It was ten miles by car to anything resembling civilization.

"But how did I get all the way out here?" she mused, rubbing her bandaged head. She repeated that action often, as if her wound was a lamp and a genie might appear to tell her the answers she sought.

"There were two men in the car." He treaded this road carefully. He didn't know her relationship to his brother. "Do you remember them?"

She shook her head, frowning into her tea. "I remember snow. Shoveling snow. I remember a squirrel at our bird feeder. I chased him away. We feed the cardinals and blue jays that stay in the winter..."

"Who is 'we'?" he prompted gently. This was promising—more than she'd ever shared.

Again, she sighed, looking over at him with a helpless shrug. "I don't know."

He stood and took her tray. She'd graduated from soup to sandwiches and he was pleased to see she'd eaten almost all of it.

"The men...they were dead?" she asked again.

He nodded, waiting. She seemed to be considering this information as if for the first time, although they'd gone over it a dozen times at least.

"Will you call the police?" She put her tea on the night table, pulling the covers up high. "Take me to a hospital?"

"When the snow stops," he agreed. He turned to take the tray out and her voice halted him.

"Why won't you take off the mask?"

Her words made him cringe. She'd asked him this question before and he'd given his answer, trying to assuage her fears, but he found it hard to address the issue repeatedly. It was like piercing an old wound with an ice pick every few hours.

"It's for your own good." He hesitated, hand on the doorknob, balancing the tray. When he glanced back at her, he saw the hurt in her eyes and wished things could be different. "Trust me, you don't want me to take it off."

She usually argued with him, gave some sort of protest, but this time she didn't. Instead, she turned to look out the window. Snow was falling again and the world was white.

He shut the door behind him and when he went in later to check on her, she was sleeping, her tea cup empty, covers twisted around her waist. He pulled them up to her chin and, not for the first time, wondered what in the hell he was going to do about her.

* * * *

She woke screaming again.

She couldn't remember the dream, she just knew it terrified her. Silas stumbled in, feeling his way to the bed.

"Bad dream," she whispered.

He sat on the edge. "Do you remember?"

"No." It was hard to explain to someone how you could be so afraid of something you couldn't recall, but that overwhelming sense of terror wouldn't leave her limbs—they trembled under the blankets.

"Are you cold? Do you want me to put more wood in the stove?" He adjusted her covers in the darkness.

"No." She shivered. He started to stand and she grabbed his arm. "Please. Stay for a while?"

His weight made the little bed creak as he sat. She didn't let go, gripping the thick expanse of his forearm. They stayed that way for a few moments, quiet, their breath the only sound in the room.

"Would you talk to me?" she whispered, swallowing past her fear.

He shifted on the bed. "What about?"

"Anything." Her hand slid down, finding its way into his.

Silas cleared his throat, squeezing her hand gently, and she waited, her heart still trying to find a normal beat. Just his presence helped, but the calming sound of his voice was better.

"I saw a wolf today," he said finally. "She was really something."

"You did?" She half-sat, already interested. "How do you know it was a 'she'?"

"Females are smaller than males," he explained. "I wish you could have seen her. I was out back getting wood and I looked up and there she was, right at the top of the hill."

"Were you scared?"

"No."

She smiled in the darkness. "Are you ever scared, Silas?"

"Yeah," he admitted softly. His other hand moved over hers, petting her skin.

"Was she a gray wolf?"

"Black," he corrected. "Beautiful. She reminded me of you."

She felt warm at his words. "What did you do?"

"I just watched her."

She tried to imagine it, face to face with such a wild animal. She'd seen her fair share of deer and coyotes, even a bobcat once, but never a wolf. "Aren't you worried about her coming back and attacking us?"

"No. My father always said, anyone who's afraid of the wolf shouldn't live in the forest."

She frowned, something flashing into consciousness. It was brief, fleeting, a cross between déjà vu and the sense that something was right at the tip of her tongue, if she could just remember…

"You're safe here," Silas assured her.

"I've never been safe anywhere." The feeling was true even if there was no real memory to accompany it. She struggled with trying to remember anything about her life, even her own name. Again, it was that feeling, like it was all on the tip of her tongue, if only she could speak. Silas had been patient, prompting her often, but she could tell he was worried. She was worried too, but the snow falling outside kept them from making a much-needed hospital visit.

She turned toward the big man sitting on the edge of her bed, wondering about him. He seemed to have as much of a missing history as she did. He was quiet to the point of being laconic, giving her lots of space and privacy, although she had caught him checking in on her a lot in the past day or two. And the mask thing was strange, but everything felt weird, off-kilter, and he hadn't given her any real reason not to trust him, after all.

She gasped as a low, silvery flood lit the room from the window pane, a cloud moving from across the face of a full moon. The light was dim but she could see his profile.

"You're not wearing a mask." She reached out without thinking, but he grabbed her hand, shaking his head, turning away.

"Don't." Silas stood, his back to the window, his face in shadow. "I should go to bed."

The light dimmed, the moon playing hide and seek, as he moved away.

"Do you think the wolf will come back?" she asked as he opened the door.

"She was a lone wolf."

She nodded. "My father always said they were the most dangerous kind."

They were both silent, the air pregnant with the pause.

"My father…" She said the words again and they both let them dangle at the edge of comprehension. Her breath had turned to ice in her throat, her body moving from hot to cold and back to hot again. The world tilted up and down and back and she opened her mouth to speak, the first memory coming, the rest falling like dominoes behind it. It was a horrifying relief, that flood of memories, and all she could manage was a distressed cry.

Silas was by her side in an instant, pulling her trembling body into his arms.

"He killed my father," she choked, hiding her face against his chest. He wore a pair of white long-underwear and moved like a ghost in the darkness.

"Who?" he asked sharply.

"Oh my god." The tears came in a flood like the memories and she clung to him, feeling his arms tighten at her back. "Carlos killed my father! He tried to kill me too!"

He prompted her like he had been for days. "What do you remember?"

"Everything. *Everything.*" It was true. Her name, her life, her near-death, Jolee remembered it all in one terrifying, mind-blowing instant. "I'm so afraid." She quivered. "I want to go home."

He stroked her hair. "You're safe here."

"I don't have a home." She sobbed against his chest. This realization was the worst. For days she'd wondered about her family, the people who might be missing her, worried and waiting for her to return. Did she have a husband? Children? A mother and a father?

"Your father's dead?" he asked.

"Years ago."

"So where is home?"

"With my husband," she whispered, closing her eyes at the memory of Carlos, who he was, what he had done. Her emotions hadn't caught up with her brain, but they were coming—she could feel them lurking in the shadows, ready to spring her limbs and squeeze her heart.

Silas stiffened at her response. "But you said you don't have a home…"

"I can't ever go back there," she confessed, realizing the truth of her statement. Home wasn't safe. There was nowhere in the world that would be safe from Carlos.

"Why?"

She realized how cryptic and strange her words must be and tried to explain. "Because Carlos is my husband. He's the man who tried to kill me. Those men you found, they were his. He hired them, told them, to kill me." They both sat in silence, letting that knowledge sink in. "What am I going to do?"

He sighed, rocking her in the darkness. "You don't need to think about it now."

"You found me," she whispered, incredulous. He had been her rescuer from the beginning, but she hadn't understood just what he had saved her from, and clearly he hadn't either. It wasn't just the accident—in fact, the accident had been part of her salvation. "You saved me from those men. They were going to kill me."

"They're dead." His voice was like steel.

"If that elk hadn't come along…"

"But it did."

She tried to hide the sob rising in her throat and it came out anyway. He tried to hold her but she struggled, pushing at him. "I thought if I could remember, everything would be okay again. But it's worse. Everything's worse."

She twisted and buried her head in the pillow, still hiding her tears, although they were coming, whether she wanted them or not.

"I'm sorry," Silas murmured. She felt his big hand pressed against her shoulder. "You're welcome to stay here for as long as you need to."

She turned toward the window. The moon was a high, yellow, silver-lidded eye. "I guess I don't have anywhere else to go…"

Silas stood. "I'm sorry," he said again.

"I want to go to sleep." She closed her eyes. "I wish I hadn't remembered anything."

"Try to sleep." He moved to the door and then turned to ask, "Do you remember your name?"

"Jolee Mercier."

He stood for a long time. So long she turned to see if he was still there, framed in the doorway.

"Silas?"

"You should know." He cleared his throat. "Carlos Mercier is my brother."

Jolee gave a short, sharp laugh, but the man didn't return her mirth. He was serious. It wasn't possible, couldn't be true. Carlos's brother was gone, dead, that's what he'd told her, told everyone. But that was all she'd ever known about her husband's only sibling. She tried to remember more and couldn't.

"Goodnight, Jolee."

She tried to see him in the moonlight but could only discern his outline. "Goodnight, Silas."

Overwhelmed with the crushing impact of chance, she turned her face to the wall and closed her eyes, wishing again for oblivion.

* * * *

The woman was impossible.

He'd wanted to take her into a hospital when the snow finally stopped, but Jolee refused, too afraid Carlos could find the records, trace her somehow.

"There are privacy laws," he'd reminded her, but she just gave him a long, steady look and shook her head.

She did seem to be getting better, her cut healing, memory returning, but he would have felt better if he'd had confirmation from an emergency room doctor, or at least a few x-rays or an MRI.

Then he'd tried to take her into town for clothes. "You can't live in my t-shirts forever," he'd teased. But she didn't want to go. Even when he'd offered to drive three hours away, to a different town, she refused.

"He'll find me."

Silas didn't point out the holes in her logic. If Carlos found the car, if he discovered her body missing from the wreck, that would prompt a sweep of the area—and being anywhere near the accident site would then be the worst place to be. No, he didn't emphasize that fact at all.

But he did bolster his security around the cabin—not lights or alarms, but traps and snares. And he watched, and waited and tried not to leave her alone. But he couldn't always be there. He'd had to run to town for supplies, going three hours away, as he promised, getting them staples like sugar and salt, things he only had enough stocked of for one. He'd bought her clothes too, some jeans and shirts, both a little too snug—she seemed smaller to him than she was, apparently—along with underwear and socks.

"No bras?" Jolee had asked in wonder as she pawed through the bags.

Silas had flushed and shrugged and turned away to finish putting away groceries. What did he know about women's clothes? The truth was, he had looked at bras, lacy, strappy things, small and soft in his hands. They made him dizzy, and the woman who had come out to help him had just made him feel more uncomfortable, so he'd left. He bought underwear for her somewhere else, plain white cotton, the kind that came in a plastic package, the kind he didn't have to handle or touch. That seemed safer.

Of course, now the woman was walking around braless in t-shirts and driving him further to distraction. Lesson learned. But she'd really liked the oranges he brought home and had delighted in the bar of chocolate he'd splurged on. That alone made the trip worth it, in spite of her protest and worry and constant questions.

Silas wasn't used to living with someone—he knew that was part of it. And the mask was a bone of contention between them that wouldn't go away. He hated wearing it, she hated him wearing it, and yet he couldn't take it off. Revealing himself to her would be a mistake, he was sure of it, and so he tried to deflect, change the subject, make a joke instead. It didn't always work.

Just that day, she'd been eating her lunch in bed. He still made her take a mid-afternoon nap, even if she protested, like a child, "I'm not tired!" She always slept though, and he would bring her lunch on a tray. He liked seeing that sleepy smile on her face when she woke.

"What is this?" she'd asked, sipping from her spoon. "It's so good!"

"Elk stew." He'd had his before bringing hers, but now sat in the chair beside her bed while she ate to keep her company. The chair was a convenience for her nightmares, which came and went, but she liked to fall asleep after a bad dream holding his hand.

"My elk?" Her head lifted, eyes wide.

He raised an eyebrow. "I seem to remember having something to do with bringing him down."

"Oh sure, take all the credit." Jolee laughed, spooning another bite. "Just because you tracked him, shot him, dressed him…"

Silas smiled at her teasing. "I admit, it's the only thing I've ever eaten killed by BMW."

"Does food taste better when you've hunted it yourself?" she inquired, drinking her milk. Big Anna, his Irish Dexter cow, provided them with fresh, whole milk, and the three chickens, which the wolf had been eyeing, he was sure, when she showed up on the hill, gave them eggs for breakfast every day.

"I think it does." He nodded. "Wait 'til I make the chops."

"Mmm." Her eyes lit up. He loved the way they did that whenever she got excited about something. "I haven't had elk chops in years. My father used to make them."

"He was a hunter?" Silas had asked her as much as he dared about her family and the circumstances surrounding her father's death, although he'd been careful about what he, in turn, shared with her about his own life.

Carlos hated the unions, and it didn't surprise him at all to hear he'd been getting rid of loggers like Jolee's father who were organizing, although it made him furious. But most things about Carlos made him angry, although very little surprised him anymore.

Jolee smiled. "Know any loggers out here who aren't?"

"Good point," he conceded. He watched her eating and felt a deep ache in his chest. She looked a great deal like Isabelle, and he supposed that was one of the reasons Carlos had married her. That, and the fact that he'd killed her father and left her practically an orphan right out of high school. Carlos had created the perfect damsel in distress to rescue. Besides, his brother lived by the credo—keep your friends close and your enemies closer.

Silas noticed her looking at him and he let his gaze shift to the window, the pine trees sagging like a cluster of fat brides under the weight of the snow. He tried to keep himself from her as much as he could, to reveal as little as possible while still maintaining her trust, but it wasn't easy when she looked at him like that. He sensed the question coming before she even asked it.

"Why don't you want me to see you?"

"Jolee, please…" He held up his hand, shaking his head, and stood. This was the easiest way to end a conversation he didn't want to have.

"Just tell me why." Her voice was soft, pleading, and goddamnit, it made him want to relent. "Is it so much to ask?"

He tried not to carry the guilt of it, because part of him wanted to tell her, wanted to share his life—or lack thereof, anymore—with this woman. Then he reminded himself of their situation, that this was his brother's wife, a woman who was in serious danger, someone he now had to protect. Taking off his hunting mask and scaring her away wasn't going to do anyone any good.

"I'll be out back," he replied gruffly, heading toward the door.

"Silas, you don't need to run away."

Her words made him turn on her, in spite of his best intentions. He snapped. "I'm not running away. There are things to do around here. Food doesn't appear out of thin air you know. I've got wood to chop."

He heard her gasp when he slammed the door behind him.

It felt good to be outside and he stalked past the shed, around to the wood pile, grabbing the maul and swinging it at a piece of white oak already set on the block. He set about his task, easing into a steady, lulling pace, working hard, working up a sweat. He unbuttoned his flannel shirt, peeling it off, the cold air feeling painfully good against his skin. Picking up the maul, he got back to work, setting wood, swinging in a full, round arc, hearing that satisfying 'pop' as the oak split apart, flying to either side of the block. Lather, rinse, repeat. Splitting wood was like meditation, repetitive that way, giving his mind some freedom.

And he needed some freedom, because ever since he'd followed that elk onto the two-track and found Jolee in the snow, he'd been far too distracted. Life had taught him not to care, not to get too emotionally invested, but this situation had sunk him deep into something he wasn't ready for and didn't want. But what choice did he have?

Until this had happened, he'd had a purpose. Spring would be here before long, and his plans would come to full fruition. And he was sure to find Isabelle by then, he reasoned—although after so many years of looking, even he had to admit to losing some hope. There was a damned lot of land to cover, and he'd explored more of it than probably anyone in the history of the state.

But then this giant wrench in the works had come along…

He had his brother's wife locked up in his cabin—a brother who thought he was dead. Hell, Carlos might even believe his wife was now dead, if they didn't do too much investigation around the wreckage—at least until spring, when the way down the ravine was less treacherous.

We've got until spring, he told himself, swinging the maul again, aiming far past the point of impact, as if the top half-foot of wood didn't even exist. The result was a fine, resounding split, the wood flying apart, the wedge of the maul separating it cleanly. His father had taught him never to split wood with an ax. A maul did the job best, and a dull one at that. A sharp maul was no good to anyone—it just got stuck in the wood.

Silas swung again, thinking about his father, gone too many years now. The old man had taught them both all of the same things. He and Carlos had grown up side by side, their mother a distant, warm, sad memory from the time Silas was about six and Carlos fifteen. Maybe the old man had spent more time with his younger son, teaching him to set traps and track and hunt. Carlos had been doing older-boy things by then, dating girls and asking for the keys to the truck all the time. Perhaps the experience of their childhoods had been more different than he realized, Silas thought.

But the old man had done the right thing, the smart thing, when he finally succumbed to the cancer eating away at his esophagus—too many years of chewing tobacco, something Silas would never do—putting provisions in his will that one son receive all the land, the other son all the money. It was supposed to get them to work together, Silas was sure, although perhaps his father had known that was an improbability. Silas had been outspoken about the rape of the natural world taking place in the logging camps and strip mines, and had made it pretty clear what he would do if he got his hands on the land.

Still, had they parted ways amicably, it would have all been all right. According to the will, Carlos had the right to continue working on the land where he was already established—he just couldn't go any further or put up any new logging camps or mines without his brother's permission. There was plenty of money to be made still, and if there was one thing Carlos knew how to do it was making his money make money.

And Silas, who had never valued money and possessions in the same way his brother had, would have been happy protecting his land and the wildlife living on it. So maybe the old man had anticipated their split, had known the brothers would never see eye-to-eye, and had done the only thing he could think of to avoid trouble between them.

And it might have worked. If it hadn't been for Isabelle, maybe it would have turned out the way his father had imagined. Instead, his world had ended in fire and pain and death, while his brother…

"Silas?"

He stood upright, hearing the screen door creak on the side of the house. It was Jolee. His brother had gone on with his life, continuing with the business—even if it involved using Silas's land and making illegal deals and if someone got in the way, well, everyone in Carlos's world was expendable, after all…

And Silas had known all of those things, but the ultimate betrayal, the thing that made Silas's gut twist into knots, was the fact that his brother had gone on to marry a woman so like Isabelle it made him both wistfully nostalgic and furious every time he looked at her.

"I came out here to help." Jolee stepped around the shed and Silas quickly grabbed his shirt, buttoning it up, his back to her. "What can I do?"

When he glanced over at her, wearing jeans and her boots and one of his t-shirts—she still had a penchant for wearing them in spite of the fact he'd gotten her some that actually fit—and a hoodie pulled over that, he shook his head, more to clear it than anything else.

"Go back in the house." He kicked the maul aside, moving past her, heading around the shed. She'd broken his reverie and he was in a sour mood now. He needed to do something to steady himself.

"No." She followed him, watching as he withdrew his bow and quiver. "You said there was a lot of work to do around here. I can help."

Silas went back out behind the shed, ignoring her as she trudged alongside him. There was a target set up against a tree in the distance and he pulled an arrow, aiming, trying to focus.

"Wouldn't a gun be more efficient for hunting?" Jolee chimed in just as he let the arrow fly. It threw him off and he swore under his breath, drawing another arrow.

"Too noisy," he countered, pulling his bow again and breathing deep, centering himself. He could hear her stamping her feet in the snow next to him, bouncing a little to keep warm, her breath coming wispy white streams, and he found himself unable to concentrate. Putting his bow down, he turned to look at her, frowning.

"I'm sorry about what I said."

She pursed her lips for a minute, blinking those big dark eyes at him. Then she shrugged. "That's okay. You're right, if I'm going to stay here, I should help you."

"Maybe when you're all healed up." He nodded at the bandage on her forehead. It was smaller, but the wound underneath was still considerable and she was going to have a scar, no matter how many careful stitches he'd applied—he'd lost count after the fifteenth.

"Well there has to be something I can do." She threw up her hands, exasperated. "Besides, I'm going stir crazy staying in the house all day reading *Guns and Ammo* and watching you check in on me when you think I'm sleeping."

Silas flushed and was glad for the cold, an excuse for the roses blooming on his cheeks. "Well, there is one thing."

She followed him again as he headed to the truck parked in the driveway. His gun case was in the back and he unlocked it, pulled out the 10/22 Ruger, checking the safety and shouldering it. It was always loaded.

"I hate guns." She trailed him back again behind the shed.

He gave her a quelling look. "I can't be here all the time, you know."

He went out to the fence line, lining several targets up for them to shoot at that he'd picked up in the shed—three tin soda cans and a beer bottle. Then he went back to where she was standing, watching, arms crossed over her chest. Silas lifted the gun, let the safety off, and aimed.

"You're going to have to learn how to protect yourself," he said, pulling the trigger. One of the soda cans jumped and fell off the fence post. His shot was a good one, although he'd just clipped it—he was actually far better with a bow.

"The first rule of guns is to always assume they're loaded." He showed her the clip. "The second rule—"

"Never point the gun at anything you're not willing to kill." She held her hand out for it. Silas hesitated, frowning. "I said I hated guns, not that I didn't know how to use one."

He handed the Ruger over, watching doubtfully as she turned the safety on, checked the clip herself, and then unlocked it, shouldering the gun and aiming. The second and third soda cans fell, followed by the bottle, which shattered with her last shot. He gave a low whistle as she put the safety back on and handed the gun over.

"So you can handle a gun." He nodded, squinting his eyes at the carnage of bottles and cans left in the snow. It was pretty impressive. "But can you cook?"

Jolee grinned. "Far better than I can shoot. Where's that elk?"

* * * *

Jolee woke up Christmas morning feeling as she imagined most people felt on that day—excited, anticipatory and utterly happy. She almost didn't recognize the feeling. She heard Silas feeding the woodstove and smiled, wondering if he felt it too, rolling over in her little bed and glancing out the window. The sun was just coming up over the horizon, bleeding orange light into her room.

"Are you awake?" Silas whispered from the doorway and she turned to face him, grinning and kicking off the covers.

"I don't think I slept at all." It wasn't true, of course—she'd slept deeply, lulled by the sound of a hoot owl outside her window all night. "Did Santa come?"

She saw the flash of his teeth through the mouth hole of his mask. "I think there are some things under the tree."

She knew there were—she'd put a few of them there herself. Silas had bought her yarn and knitting needles and she'd found something else to do besides help him make their meals. She'd been knitting like crazy when she was supposed to be "napping."

Jolee bounded out into the kitchen, the smell of cinnamon drawing her toward the stove.

"Cinnamon rolls?" She dragged a finger along the top of one and groaned as she sucked the icing off. "Oh Santa has been very good us."

He put a roll on a plate and handed it to her. She curled up in a chair near the fire in the living room with her cinnamon roll and a big glass of fresh milk, drawing her t-shirt over her knees and admiring their Christmas tree.

Silas had dragged it home through the snow and set it up in a stand he'd made himself. They'd popped popcorn and strung dried berries and fruit—it was a truly an old-fashioned tree, no lights or sparkles, but in the glow of the fire it shined anyway, a magical thing.

She clapped her hands when Silas began handing out the brown packages wrapped in twine under the tree. Hers for him were more elaborately decorated in white butcher paper, stamped using nutshells and leaves and pinecones with a dark brown ink she'd made from boiling walnuts and vinegar.

There was an orange for her and a big bar of chocolate and she overdosed on sweetness as she unwrapped more yarn, thrilled at the bright colors he'd chosen. There was also a new pair of boots for her and a winter jacket, waterproof and warm. She blushed when she opened a package of delicate, lacy bras in a myriad of colors.

Silas shrugged one shoulder, reminding her, "You asked for them…"

"I did." She smiled, rubbing the silky material of one of the cups against her cheek. He watched her do this, his eyes dark in the holes of his mask.

"Open yours." She handed him the first, watching him unwrap the paper.

"It's beautiful," he murmured, spreading the wrapping out as he got it open, looking at the designs she'd made on the butcher paper.

"That's not your present, silly!" She unfolded the scarf, deep blues and greens. She wrapped it around his neck.

He fingered the edge of it, smiling. "Thank you."

"There's more." She handed him another.

"Someone hasn't been napping," he remarked as he unwrapped three pairs of socks and a pair of gloves, smiling over all of them. He stopped when he opened the last one, holding up the knitted thing in his hands, frowning.

"I thought, if you're going to insist on wearing a mask, maybe you'd like something a little more stylish." She showed him the way the eye holes were bigger, the mouth hole too. "Besides I'm sick of looking at that camouflage thing."

He turned his back to her, pulling off his hunting mask and putting the knit one on.

She nodded in satisfaction. "Now I feel like I'm being held captive by a crazed skier instead of a crazed hunter. That's an improvement, right?"

He grinned and she loved how she could really see him smile. "They say variety is the spice of life."

"It's made from very breathable yarn. How does it feel?"

"Pretty good." He rubbed his cheek through the black material, thoughtful. Then his eyes lit up and he stood. "I have something else for you. A big surprise."

She watched him heading toward the back of the cabin, still in his long underwear, always covered that way. She wished he would tell her, show her, whatever it was he kept hidden, but they had tacitly agreed not to talk about any of it, especially Carlos. They both had a history with the man that neither wanted to share.

"Are you coming?" He looked over his shoulder at her, waiting, and she hopped up, following him. He led her down the hall, past her room, past his, to a locked door at the end of the hall. There'd been a lot of hammering and pounding in there the past month or so, and whenever she asked him about it, Silas said he was making a "workroom."

"Did you make me something?" she asked, her eyes bright as he used a key hanging around a string on his neck to unlock the door.

"You could say that," he agreed.

Jolee peeked into the room expecting maybe something decorative made of wood, perhaps a rocking chair to sit in by the fire—he was quite an accomplished carpenter, she'd discovered—but the sight that greeted her left her stunned still and speechless.

"It's indoor plumbing," Silas explained, stepping into their new bathroom and turning on the water for the tub. "No more boiling water for sponge baths."

"How in the world did you do all this?" She stepped into the room, staring around in wonder. The tub alone was huge. How had he gotten it in by himself without her noticing? He knew how much she hated not having a warm shower, a real bathtub, and so he'd installed both, just for her.

"I managed." He shrugged one shoulder, half-smiling as he adjusted the water temperature. "Do you want to take a bath?"

"Do I?" Jolee laughed and clapped her hands. "I can't believe this! Silas, it's incredible."

"Merry Christmas," he said, standing up and nodding toward the towel rack where a big pink fluffy towel and a brand new pink robe were hung.

She moved toward him, putting her arms around his waist and resting her head against his chest. He was warm and solid and he hesitated just a moment before putting his arms around her too.

"Merry Christmas," she whispered, squeezing him tight. She went up on her tiptoes to kiss his cheek through the mask, the yarn soft against her lips.

"I'll give you some privacy," he said, taking a step toward the door.

"Silas." She called for him and he turned, his eyes bright through the holes in his mask. "This is almost the best gift ever."

He laughed. "Almost?"

"The best gift would be if you would take off your mask." She said it hopefully, breath held.

"You know I can't do that." Silas smiled sadly, taking a step toward her and kissing her forehead. Her bandage was gone, the wound healing. He'd removed each stitch carefully, tenderly. "Have a good bath. I'll make us a great big breakfast. Eggs and bacon?"

She nodded, smiling up at him. "Scrambled."

"Of course." He knew her well enough by now. He even made and canned his own version of ketchup and it was better than Heinz or Hunts ever thought about being.

Jolee waited for him to go and then stripped down and stepped into the tub, letting the warmth and steam envelop her, trying not to think about anything. It wasn't always easy, but she found it less difficult here, squirreled away with Silas in his cabin, than she had anywhere or any other time in her life. At first, she'd been afraid, always looking over her shoulder, worried that Carlos or one of his guys would show up, but after a while that anxiety had faded.

Now they both practiced a very zen life together, living in the moment, not talking about the past or the future. At first she was full of questions, but she found him less than forthcoming about his life, especially about his brother—not that she blamed him. Carlos wasn't a happy subject for her either. Silas had clearly chosen a different life and didn't want his family to know he existed. Whatever his reasons, they were his own, and who was she to question or argue with him about it?

She poured bubble bath into the water, watching the suds rise, delighted. Sponge baths were tolerable and got the job done, but this was pure luxury. She could feel layers of grime washing off her skin and she sank down into the tub, her hair spreading around her like a dark fan.

The thought of Silas doing all of this, the work it must have been, actually brought tears to her eyes. She'd never meet a sweeter, gentler soul, and she couldn't help comparing him to his brother, the two of them so opposite they could have been from different planets. Where Carlos was cruel, Silas was kind. Where Carlos was selfish, Silas was noble. She saw the similarities, too—their eyes, dark and deep, the curve of their mouths, that bright smile, their humor and charm. That was the thing Carlos had used to seduce her in the beginning, when she was just a young girl.

I'm not so old now, she reminded herself. Just twenty-six, hardly an old maid. But she'd been practically a baby when her father died, just turned nineteen, when Carlos had taken her under his wing and guided her life down a pathway to merge with his own. She'd been ready to take a scholarship to an out-of-state college, something her father had been so proud of, even if she had used her looks to obtain it—Jolee had entered and won Miss Teen USA, the prize a full ride to Boston University, that year's sponsor. Her father had insisted she go, had even packed her bags for her, even though she'd never been out of Michigan's Upper Peninsula in her whole entire life—and then the accident had happened.

It wasn't an accident. Of course, she hadn't known that then. She'd been a lost, grief-stricken child and Carlos had been waiting to swoop in and comfort her, convincing her to marry him and give up that scholarship so far away from anything familiar she'd ever known. She still couldn't believe her naiveté, how she had believed Carlos's lies through the years, listened to his excuses. And then, even when faced with the proof of her father's murder, she had allowed him to explain it away. She held the paper in her hand—findings suppressed at the hearing that the brakes on the logging truck had been fine after all—and had still denied it as truth.

She remembered it clearly enough. Her father had kissed her goodbye that morning, grabbing a thermos of coffee, stopping only to take a bite of the eggs she'd made for him. He'd been on his way to talk to one of the union reps and Daryl had pulled the chain outside on the big logging rig, informing the whole neighborhood that he was there to pick her father up.

Later Daryl tearfully told the cameras that the brakes had failed.

"I told the old man to bail!" he swore in his testimony. "He couldn't get his belt off. I tried to help him but I had to get out of the truck. What could I do?"

Watch her father sail off a ledge into a ravine, apparently. Daryl broke his arm in the fall, but he was alive. Her father had been trapped in the truck by his own seatbelt, and all those years she thought it had been a mechanical failure.

They said the brakes failed, but the brakes were fine. According to the report, they were just fine, and the handwritten note—*Your father was murdered- there was nothing I could do about it - he was a friend and a good man—your husband wanted him dead*—pointed the finger clearly enough. But Carlos had explained it away and she believed him. She had let him charm her once again, and had nearly paid for that mistake with her life.

Jolee thought of Silas on the other side of that wall, out there cooking breakfast for them. What did he know about his brother? He had certainly accepted the fact that Carlos had killed her father and had been trying to kill her as well, willingly enough. He had never questioned her assertions, not once. Maybe it was just because he trusted her—or maybe it was because he knew the kind of man his brother really was.

She looked at all the pretty shaped soaps and lotions and bottles of bubble bath Silas had left on the ledge, trying to remind herself not to think about it. Her father was gone, her husband believed she was dead. She didn't belong anywhere—but she had Silas, and he had her. It was enough for now.

* * * *

Silas gunned the Arctic Cat, the runners gliding along the hard-packed snow as he ducked his head to miss a low-hanging branch, realizing he was just five minutes from home now. He hadn't had that glad-to-be-heading-home feeling in his chest for years, and he knew it was because Jolee was waiting for him. Part of him hated leaving her, but there were things he had to do, in spite of her protest and questions—and Lord knew, the woman was full of both!

"Just tell me where you're going," she'd insisted as they both sat on side-by-side stools next to Big Anna while he attempted to teach her how to milk the old girl.

He'd considered lying to her, making up some excuse or reason he had to go, but instead had decided that being cryptic had worked so far, why stop now? Of course, Jolee had caught on to his deflection, and if that failed, his silence and refusal to answer.

"You are impossible!" She'd given up on both him and the cow, storming out of the old horse stall where kept Big Anna for the winter.

I'm not the only one, Silas thought, scanning the woods for wildlife, constantly using his peripheral vision, always practicing a high degree of situational awareness. He had instructed her how to do everything—when to turn on the generator, where he kept the extra fuel, how to milk the cow.

He'd been as thorough as he could, but he knew better than anyone that you couldn't plan for surprises. Anything could have happened while he was gone.

He gave the Cat another jolt, urging the machine faster. Dusk was settling though the snow-heavy limbs of the trees, casting long shadows. He'd promised he would only be three days and if he made it home tonight, he would keep that promise, although he hadn't been sure, yesterday morning when he'd been repelling deep into one of his brother's mines with four pounds of dynamite strapped to his back, that he would make it at all.

All's well that ends well, he told himself, seeing the house come into view over the rise of the hill. His heart raced at the sight of it, faster than it had been pounding when he'd flipped the switch and blown his brother's new sulfide mine, collapsing it into rubble. He was always careful to pull his jobs at night, when no one was working in the mines or at the camps. Carlos had them guarded now, of course—there were rumors around the mining and logging camps that they were being haunted and/or hunted by some sort of mythical "beast" who mangled trucks, equipment and even the sites themselves—but Silas could track so silently the guards were taken care of, passed out before they knew what hit them.

He didn't know who really believed the "beast" rumors, but he didn't do anything to discourage them. They were useful and kept Carlos and his cronies from turning their attention to the real culprit. They probably figured it was some overzealous activist from the EPA, Silas thought, and that was good. As long as he was careful and they didn't connect him to the millions of dollars of destruction and the months of set-back, he figured he and Jolee were safe in the woods until spring. And after spring, it wouldn't matter anymore.

He parked the Arctic Cat next to the shed and peeled off his helmet. The mask she had made him was breathable but it kept the wind off his face and he was grateful for it. She'd knit him several more, a small concession to his wearing them at all, in a myriad of colors. "At least give me something new to look at," she'd teased, handing him an orange one. "Besides, I don't want a hunter taking your head off out there."

He flipped open the storage container on the back of the Cat, removing two of the three rabbits he'd snared while he was waiting for activity to shut down for the weekend. The third one had met a different fate in the mines. He held the rabbits up in front of him as he stomped into the kitchen, calling for her.

"Slim pickins' out there, huh?" Jolee leaned against the door frame, frowning at his small game offering.

"We got plenty in the freezer." He took off his boots as she snatched the rabbits, tossing them next to the sink.

"I know." She turned to face him, arms crossed. "Which begs the question—where were you exactly? Because you clearly weren't out there hunting."

Silas shrugged off his parka and removed his gloves, the warmth of the room making his limbs tingle. He'd been on the Cat so long he'd grown numb to the cold.

"Did you miss me?" he teased. He glanced over at her drawn brow and pursed lips, looking for a hint of the truth. Had she missed him? He didn't like to admit it, but he'd missed her. He turned and headed toward his bedroom to change.

"There was someone here, Silas," she called.

He stopped, turning, his heart dropping to his knees, and looked into her eyes. They were bright with tears.

"Who?" he managed, his gaze sweeping over her as if he could assess, just by looking, if she was unharmed. "When?"

"I don't know." Her voice was choked and she wiped angrily at her falling tears, storming past him down the hall toward her room.

"Jolee!" He followed her, bursting through the door she'd just slammed behind her. "Talk to me!"

"You left me alone!" She sat on the bed with her accusation, looking up at him with such a dejected look he was instantly sorry. He wanted to scoop her up and make her feel safe again. Silas looked around the room, noting the difference instantly. Curtains—she had hand-sewn them, patch-worked from his old t-shirt material.

"Tell me what happened," he said flatly, going over to the window and pulling the curtain aside, somehow already knowing what he was going to see.

“I think someone was looking in the windows.” Her voice trembled and Silas saw the footprints in the snow, coming in from the woods and retreating again.

“Did anyone see you?”

“I don’t think so.” She sniffed. “I only went out to milk Anna in the morning and it was still dark.”

He considered this information. Whoever it was had been wearing boots, big ones. Definitely a man. He’d have to go out and investigate, see if there were any shell casings, arrows, signs he hoped he’d find.

“It was probably just a curious hunter.” Silas let the curtains drop, turning back to Jolee. “My land backs up to state land about five miles to the north.”

“What if it wasn’t?” Her hands twisted in her lap and she looked up at him helplessly. “What if he found us?”

“He didn’t.” Silas sat on the bed, feeling it sag under his weight, and put a comforting arm around her thin shoulders—she was actually quivering with fear. He told her the truth, in spite of her anxiety. “Carlos is no peeping Tom. If he’d found you, you would know it.”

“Maybe.” Jolee turned toward him, letting him comfort her, tucking her head under his chin. He could smell the sweetness of her shampoo and he let the heady scent envelop him.

“So did you see anything? Hear anything?” he asked, stroking her hair. She’d stopped having so many bad dreams and while he was glad, he missed holding and comforting her like this in the darkness.

“I heard something.” She pressed herself closer at the memory. “Last night, late. I thought it might be you coming home.”

The longing in her voice made him want to smile. “What did you hear?”

“I was sleeping.” She shrugged. “I heard something outside my window, but by the time I got up to go look, there was nothing. Then this morning, I saw the tracks.”

He nodded, hoping it was just a lost hunter, out too late, looking for somewhere to crash for the night. He’d been careful, backing his truck up into the make-shift garage out back so the license plate wasn't visible even if Jolee had gone in for something and forgot to shut the barn door. If one of Carlos's guys had stumbled on this place—and it was purposefully well-hidden dimly lighted—there was no reason for them to believe it was connected to him or to Jolee.

Unless one of them had seen her.

"You're safe." He said the words and hoped she believed them. Even if there was danger lurking, he had every intention of protecting her.

Of course, he'd intended to protect Isabelle too.

"I'm glad you're home." She sounded both relieved and truly happy. "I *did* miss you, you big lug." She went to pound her fist against his chest to emphasize the point and he caught it, stifling a laugh.

"So did you fix me dinner, woman?" he teased. She looked up and stuck her tongue out at him. That did make him laugh. "I smelled something good a mile away."

"Venison chili." She stood, picking up a skein of yarn and her knitting needles. "I used some of your canned tomatoes. I hope you don't mind."

"They're for eating." He followed her out, shutting the door behind him before heading toward the good smells in the kitchen. "What are you working on now?"

Jolee put her mass of flesh-colored yarn and needles on the counter, peering under a pot lid and stirring. The already delicious scent of food increased tenfold and Silas's stomach rumbled. He'd been living on jerky for two days.

"Another mask." She held it up. "I made my own pattern. Since you won't show me yours, I'm going to give you a face."

"Talented girl." He studied it—she only had a third of it completed, but he could see the image beginning to take shape in the stitches. "Keep it up and I'm going to need to buy you some sheep just to keep you in yarn."

"You should learn." She pushed the yarn toward him and let him finger it while she spooned bowls of piping hot chili. "It's a good skill to know out here. That way you can even make clothes for yourself when I'm..."

She didn't finish the sentence and Silas looked at her, his heart beating too fast, as she handed him a spoon. Of course she didn't have to finish the sentence. He finished it easily enough in his head. *When I'm gone.*

Gone.

He didn't want to think about that. He'd lost too much in his life and didn't want consider losing her too. They didn't talk about what might happen in the future, or what had happened to either of them in the past, and it was better that way. Thoughts of the past brought pain and looking into the future was too uncertain. Staying right here in the moment was the only thing that mattered.

Jolee was a surprise to him every day and he couldn't have expressed what a joy it was to wake up to the sound of her singing in the new shower every morning, how much he looked forward to stoking the fire in the woodstove at night so she could warm her feet while he whittled and she knitted and they played the "would you rather?" game.

Would you rather live in the country or the city? His answer was obvious.

Would you rather eat a bug or step on a nail? She made faces at him and refused to choose.

Jolee had introduced him to the game and he played with relish, seriously considering even the most ridiculous options, always giving her an honest answer. Of course, there were questions neither of them asked—they had a tacit understanding. But now a question came to mind that he didn't want to ponder.

Would you rather lose Jolee or Isabelle?

He couldn't choose. Isabelle was gone, and although he still searched for her, nothing was going to bring her back. But Jolee was here—safe and smiling at him from across the table, chattering on about how Anna had missed his big, warm hands and objected to her small, cold ones—and he wouldn't let anything happen to her. He would make sure of that.

He wasn't even going to let himself consider the alternatives.

* * * *

She tried to scream, but nothing came out. Opening her eyes, she saw only blackness. The darkness was suffocating, air like lead weight in her lungs—she could barely pull a breath.

She listened hard for something that would center her, give her a sense of location, and it took moments that felt like hours to discern the soft, hitching sound of Silas snoring down the hall.

The bed beneath her tensed limbs grew slowly familiar, as did the whistling of the wind through the pines outside her window and the sudden, startled call of an owl. It had just been a dream. She was safe. She was home. Rolling over and pulling the covers with her, Jolee willed her heart to slow, her breathing to return to some semblance of normal. It had been months since she called out for Silas in the middle of the night because of a bad dream, but she still wished for him upon waking, even if she didn't say anything.

There was something so comforting about the man, just his presence in a room made her feel more calm. Of course, that wasn't all it made her feel. Closing her eyes, she tried to drift off again, but the weight of the silence, the darkness, and her own loneliness were too great. The bed was too small, the sheets too rough. Nothing felt right.

Down the hall, Silas snored and Jolee couldn't help it. She pushed her covers off and crept toward the sound. She didn't know why she bothered—his door was always closed and locked, an unspoken barrier. She'd tested it a few times on her way by at night, listening at the door, hearing him breathing. His locking her out didn't surprise her.

What surprised her was finding the door open tonight. Maybe he'd gotten up to use the bathroom and forgotten to shut it? She felt her way in the darkness. The cabin had no ambient light and Silas left no outside lights on, so moving around at night was like being blind. She found the edge of the bed with her knees and stopped, hearing Silas snort, his breathing stop.

"Jolee?" He sat up, sounding wide awake. "Are you okay?"

"Bad dream." She crawled into bed with him, under the covers, and found him surprisingly, warmly nude, only the t-shirt she was wearing separating the two of them. He was always dressed, even on his way to the bathroom in the morning, usually head to toe in long underwear.

“Jolee…” Silas drew in a sharp breath when she snuggled in closer, tucking her head under his chin like she always did, her bare thigh snaking between his. They’d never been skin to skin like this. It was a shock to both of them.

“Someone was trying to kill me.” Okay, so she lied—she couldn’t really remember her dream—but it was a small lie. And to be fair, her dream could have been about someone trying to kill her because, after all, someone had been. Might still be, out there, somewhere.

Silas cradled her instantly and she let him, hands moving through her hair, over her back, soothing. Smiling, she rubbed her cheek against the solid expanse of his chest, feeling hairs tickling her and the rough edge of something. A scar? Her fingers moved up to explore it in the dark, finding her way, like a roadmap, to his throat. His skin was a surprise, smooth in places, rough and raised in others.

It wasn’t until she reached his chin and he grabbed her hand that she realized. “You’re not wearing a mask!”

“I don’t sleep in it,” he confessed, swallowing and shifting on the bed, placing her hand firmly on his chest—neutral territory.

“I can’t see you anyway.” She continued to follow the harsh terrain of his skin southward, finding the dip of his navel. “It’s too dark.”

“What are you doing?” His voice was choked, hoarse.

“Exploring,” she whispered, reaching a thatch of thick, wiry hair with her fingertips. She found what she’d been searching for, half-risen out of its nest, the wrap of her hand around its pulsing length bringing it fully to life. His cock was alive in her hand, throbbing against her fingertips, the skin moving under her thumb when she began rubbing the meaty shaft up and down. She listened, but he wasn’t breathing at all now.

“Silas?” She lifted her head as if she could see him in the darkness and heard him let out a pent-up breath.

“Shhhh.” His hand slid over her hip, finding bare skin under her t-shirt. “I’m dreaming. I don’t want to wake up.”

“Me either.” She felt his breath, warm against her cheek, and turned her face to his, their mouths pressed together for the first time. His lips were soft and they opened under pressure from her tongue, giving into her insistent probing. She sensed him holding back, restraining himself, one hand gripping her hip, the other fisting her hair as they kissed, and even the gentle tug of her hand between his thighs didn't move him.

"Jolee," he whispered as she slid a thigh across his belly, moving to straddle him. "What are you doing?"

"I have a job for you." She walked her way up his chest with her fingertips, stopping briefly at one of his nipples, feeling him shudder. Then she leaned in to kiss him, her breasts pressed against his chest, his cock trapped between them, steel heat, and felt his hands move to her hips, holding on.

"What job?" he gasped when she slid further up, pressing her breasts against his face. He groaned as if he was in agony but Jolee ignored his plea for mercy, peeling off her t-shirt, hips already moving in circles against his belly.

"It's a little repetitious," she warned as she put one knee on his pillow and then the other, straddling his face.

"Oh god."

She heard him swallow, felt the heat of his breath, and gave a little whimper of her own.

"Please," she whispered, reaching a hand down to spread her swollen lips. She waited—listening to him breathe, his chest rising and falling far too fast, just like hers, his whole body tense—waiting for him to refuse her, to tell her to go back to bed.

Instead, he gave a low, animal growl, wrapping his arms around her hips and pulling her in, his mouth and tongue pure heat, delving into her own. Jolee gave a squeal of surprise, her hands coming up to catch herself against the headboard, and then lost herself in the sensation. He attacked her flesh violently with his tongue, licking and sucking at her pussy, lapping at her slit, burying his whole face against her, making her burn with pleasure.

When he found her clit, almost by accident he was so lost in her flesh, drowning in her, he stayed there, sucking it first between his lips and then lashing it back and forth with his tongue. Jolee felt her thighs tense, trembling, her hips wanting to buck but stilled by the thick wrap of his arms around her, holding her in place against his face. His biceps were flexed, hard against her thighs and she arched her back, reaching behind to find the thick thrust of his cock, wanting to feel it pulsing in her hand.

It distracted Silas only for a moment. He gave a low moan, the sensation vibrating through her clit, and then redoubled his efforts. She heard him swallowing her juices, his breath coming almost as fast as hers. Silas made rough animal noises against her pussy, deep from his throat and chest, and still she tried to hold back. She wanted to do this forever, to feel his abandon, his wild lust between her legs.

But she was going to come. There was no stopping it.

“Silas,” she warned, barely a gasp, but he heard, he knew, focusing right on her clit, that tiny bit of flesh making her whole body shudder with anticipation. She screamed when he let go of her hips, letting her buck and writhe, so he could slide two fingers deep into her pussy. Her muscles clamped down immediately and she rode his hand, his mouth, mashing her flesh against his face as she came, her orgasm a bright flash of pulsing light through her body in the darkness.

She didn’t have time to breathe or think or even move. He had her rolled onto the bed in an instant, kissing her pussy like a mouth and then moving up to kiss her mouth, letting her taste herself. She licked at his lips and sucked his tongue and felt him parting her slim thighs with the hard flex of his, forcing them open wider. Reaching, she grabbed hold of his length, aiming and guiding him in the dark.

“Wait.” He took a deep, steadying breath, holding himself above her, poised and ready. She wanted him so much she was dizzy with it. Sliding her hands up his biceps, over his shoulders, feeling the uneven terrain of his scars, she felt his hesitation, understood it, and didn’t want to give him a chance to think, to second guess this.

“Fuck me, Silas, please,” she begged, sliding a hand behind his neck and pulling his mouth to hers, drowning in his kiss. She felt his body giving in as she drew his tongue in deeper, wiggling her hips up, attempting to bridge the gap. The tip of his cock teased her clit, sliding up and down her wet slit, but not in.

"Jolee." He groaned as she used her hand to grab hold of him, pulling, tugging, rubbing him furiously against the sensitive nub of her clit. "We can't."

She moaned in frustration as he rolled off her onto his back on the bed, throwing an arm over his eyes. The sound of their breath, both of them panting, filled the room. It was so hot it felt like a sauna in spite of the near-zero temperatures outside and the wind blowing tree branches against side of the cabin.

"I want you." Silas gulped, reaching over and finding her hand. He squeezed hard. "Don't think for a minute I don't."

"But…" She rolled onto her side toward him, feeling his body tense.

"But you're my brother's wife."

Jolee let out a tight little laugh. "Are you kidding me? Is that all?"

"I think it's enough," he said finally.

They hadn't talked about it, but it had been there between them from the beginning. She thought about her husband—this man's brother—and the idea that Carlos could keep her from one more thing in the world that she wanted filled her with a fierce, heated rage.

"Carlos hasn't been my husband for years. Not really, not in any way that counted." She sat up, hugging her knees. "I was something he could take around and show off. Something he could use, if he felt like it. I wasn't a person to him. I was a…a…thing. I was something he wanted for a while, but when he didn't want me anymore, when it got too inconvenient to keep me, I was disposable, like everyone else."

He made a small sympathetic noise. "That sounds like my brother."

"I never loved Carlos. I never really wanted him." She felt Silas's hand trailing down her spine and shivered. She turned to him, letting him pull her in and kiss her, their breath mingling, already feeling him relenting. Part of her had come here tonight knowing she wanted this, had always known from the first time he held her in his arms.

She reached up to stroke his cheek, feeling the scars there too, and he let her. "Silas, I want *you.*"

His silence stretched between them. Then he cupped her face in his hands. "Don't say that if you don't mean it."

"I mean it," she whispered, and he brought her mouth to his, the kiss fierce and full of everything they'd been feeling and keeping in for months. If she could have devoured him, turned herself inside out to feel him more deeply, she would have, but she didn't have to.

Silas gave her everything. There were no more boundaries between them and he took her without restraint. They rolled together on the bed, kissing, Jolee struggling under his weight, but protesting when he eased up, wrapping her legs around his waist, squeezing him between her thighs, rocking the hard length of his cock between them like an iron bar.

She protested, but not for long, when he rolled her onto her back and slid down between her thighs, his tongue working magic again. But it still wasn't enough and she whimpered and begged and reached for him until he finally gave in to her pleading, flipping onto his back and letting her crawl over him on the way to his cock, stopping her when her pussy reached the hungry gulp of his mouth and tongue.

Taking him into her mouth was a joy, feeling the slick silk of his skin moving over the thick length of his cock as she sucked him. His hips moved with her motion but his tongue never wavered, flicking steadily over her clit as his fingers explored her, sliding in deep and then retreating, rubbing the fat, swollen lips of her labia with his fingertips, tugging at the dark, wiry hair there. Jolee gasped and sucked him harder when he slid two fingers in, then three, really stretching her, making her moan and rock against his hand.

"Oh!" She rolled her hips, feeling him fingering her, deeper, harder. His cock slid out of her mouth as she felt her impending climax begin, rubbing the mushroom tip of him over her outstretched tongue, feeling his delicious pulse against her lips as she closed her eyes and gave into her orgasm. It started between her thighs, where Silas was working so hard to take her there, her pussy clasping his fingers in a fast, fluttering dance, and then spiraled outward from her center, making her grip his cock hard in her fist.

"Easy!" Silas croaked, gasping for breath beneath her. "Go easy, baby, please."

She let her hand relax a little, feeling a thick wave of precum flooding over her fist. He shuddered and moaned as she began to lick it off.

"Now will you fuck me?" she whispered, kissing the head of his cock, slapping it lightly against her cheek.

"You couldn't stop me if you tried."

She yelped as he grabbed her, not even bothering to turn her around toward the headboard before shoving her legs open with his big thighs. His cock found its way into her swollen wetness without her help and she cried out when he entered her, nails digging into his shoulders as she took him as deeply as she could, almost to the point of pain. She relished the sensation, burying her face against his neck and urging him on.

"Oh Jolee…" He settled himself between her legs, up on his elbows above her, face lost in the river of her hair. "Oh god you feel too good…"

"I can't believe you're inside of me." She actually felt tears stinging her eyes, realizing for the first time how much she had wanted this.

"You've been inside me since the beginning." He nuzzled her and she felt his scars. She cupped his face and he stilled, her fingers moving over his cheeks.

"I want you." She kissed his cheeks, his closed eyelids, his chin, the corner of his trembling mouth. "Please."

He began to move, his cock a swollen, driving heat between her thighs and a heady friction began to build again almost immediately. His breath was hot against her cheek and she slid her arms around his neck, pulling him closer, deeper. He curled himself around her as they rocked on the bed, the springs squeaking fast and hard, the headboard banging against the wall behind them, their breath coming in hot, short bursts. There was no one around to hear them and Jolee let herself go, moaning in pleasure.

"Fuck me," she panted, heels digging into his thighs. "Oh god, yes! Fuck me!"

Silas grunted and gave her more, making her scream with every deep thrust, her teeth raking his skin. His cock felt even more swollen somehow, filling her completely, and she felt him tense, the hard, flat expanse of his belly slapping against hers as he gave into his own lust.

"I'm going to come," she whispered into his ear, feeling the quiver of her pussy around the pounding heat of his cock. "Oh you make me come so hard. It's so close. I can feel it. Right…oh…right there…Silas…"

He groaned and thrust deep, her imminent pleasure forcing him to give into his own, his thighs spreading her so wide she thought she might break apart like a wishbone and still she wouldn't have cared. She'd gotten her wish. He cried out and called her name and buried his face against her neck. She felt every glorious pulse of his cock as he filled her with the white hot spurts of his release.

"Almost there," she whimpered, rolling her hips, arching up, and he moaned loudly and clasped her to him as her climax came in just behind his own, her pussy milking his still-spasming cock. Jolee threw her head back and let herself go, quivering beneath him, barely able to breathe, taking all of his weight and still wanting more.

"How did you get in?" Silas asked, still on top of her as they rested. He petted her, stroking her hair.

She wrapped her arms around him, as if she could get closer. "The door was unlocked."

He rolled them up in the covers like a cocoon, pulling her with him, impossibly hard still inside of her, and they stayed that way, joined together, Jolee sleeping on top of him. But it was still dark when she felt him carrying her naked to her own bed before she even knew what was happening. He tucked her in, kissing her forehead.

"Silas?" she asked sleepily, reaching for him. She kissed his mouth in the darkness, her body instantly remembering, wanting.

"Go to sleep," he whispered. "I'll see you in the morning,"

And then he was gone and Jolee found herself alone, wishing for his warmth as the door down the hall closed and locked her out again.

* * * *

Silas had never really been afraid of anything. When he was young, his father had labeled him "fearless," and he was. It wasn't always a good thing. He took risks others wouldn't, especially when an injustice was involved. Bullies ran the other way when Silas came along. Tyranny or inequity in any form raised his hackles, and often his fists. He'd discovered that fighting fire with fire, and fighting dirty if he had to, was a good strategy, even if it wasn't the most popular, honest or lawful one.

He'd faced down everything, from bullies to criminals to black bears. Once, in a bar, he'd taken a bullet that missed his spine by inches. It had been meant for a woman he didn't even know, but the man who fired the gun had punched her before pulling out his weapon—and that was all the information Silas had needed. He couldn't count how many times he'd faced death or the possibility of death, and even that didn't frighten him.

But he was afraid now. He was afraid of the hundred-and-twenty pound woman in his house, who had taken over his life and the way he lived it, in so many ways. She terrified him, that tiny slip of a girl. He hadn't thought about another woman since Isabelle, hadn't even considered the possibility. There was no reason to—Isabelle had been the perfect woman, perfect for him in every way, and you couldn't improve on perfection.

But Jolee had been thrown into his life, had found her way into his heart, and he couldn't deny it anymore. In the midst of protecting her, caring for her, guarding her against the possibility of his brother's harm—and he had to admit, part of him had been thinking about Isabelle when he was doing those things—he had fallen for her. The ghost of his dead wife had faded in the light of Jolee's smile, her quick temper, her soft hands and, last night, her lush, full body.

It wasn't Isabelle he thought about anymore when he neared home, a little extra speed in his step, carrying his bow over his shoulder. It was Jolee—the woman who had made curtains for the cabin windows and stuffed pillows to sit on for the wooden chairs, the woman who appreciated his subtle sense of humor, who teased him about his slow, fastidious ways, who spent a night with him in the stable when Anna was sick, petting the cow's head and singing to her in a native language he didn't speak but spoke straight to his heart.

He'd left early this morning, trembling at the thought of meeting her in the hallway, going off instead to find things to do outside—milking the cow, gathering eggs, straightening the shed, repairing his trap lines—too afraid to face her, too afraid to face what he might be forced to acknowledge.

Since Isabelle, he'd wanted to die, and when his survival instincts had gotten him out of the fire and he'd found her gone, he'd been determined to finish the job Carlos had started and join her—or, barring that, at least end his own suffering, although part of him still felt he deserved the pain he lived in for not saving her.

He'd tried to end it all several times after the fire. If it hadn't been for Abe, he probably would have. After the fire, the old Indian had found him crawling on his hands and knees in the dirt, calling Isabelle's name, and had made a litter to drag him back on. The time he'd spent at the Bad River reservation had been healing—and informational. They all knew about Carlos and the mines and the logging camps.

And, of course, Abe had passed on the information Carlos was telling everyone—that his brother and his wife had died in a fire. That was the darkest time of his life, when he'd realized that Isabelle was gone and he understood he could do more good dead than alive.

And it was his hatred that kept him going, in spite of Abe's efforts to sway him. The only reason he'd stayed alive was to thwart his brother's efforts to rape and pillage the land their father had left behind. And in the spring, he was finally going to get the chance to end it all—his brother's shady business and his own pain. Jolee had been a complication at first, but he only had to keep her here, safe until spring, he reasoned. Then she would be safe wherever she went.

Now she was far more than a complication and the plans he had so carefully and meticulously outlined seemed ridiculously simple—and horribly final—in a way they never had before. For the first time, he was questioning his decision, and Jolee was the reason. For the first time since Isabelle had died, life seemed worth living.

Well, he decided, hanging his mended lines in the shed and heading out, he didn't have to decide anything today, and he couldn't hide out here forever. Besides, he was getting hungry. The house was warm from the woodstove and the smell of bacon made his stomach rumble. He could hear her in the kitchen, singing to herself, and he smiled, stopping to listen. The words weren't in English—her father had been part Chippewa, she'd told him, and had taught her some of the language, many of the traditional songs—but they were lovely.

"Is that you, Silas?"

He heard the edge in her voice. Mostly she felt safe, he figured, but there was still a part of her on guard, waiting for Carlos to find her here—and there was always a part of him waiting for that as well.

"It's me," he confirmed, taking off his boots and coat, but leaving on his mask. The damnable thing was too warm inside, but in spite of his lapse the night before—how had he forgotten to lock the door?—he had no intention of taking it off in the light of day. Of course, if he hadn't forgotten, she wouldn't have come to his room, and he wouldn't have had the glorious opportunity to have her. Christ, just the memory of being inside her made his cock jump.

He stopped when he came around the corner, seeing her standing at the counter, plating up eggs and bacon—mountains for him and little rolling hills for her—wearing nothing but a pair of panties. She turned to look at him over her shoulder, her hair a dark waterfall down her back, and smiled, a new, shy smile he'd never seen before that made his heart lurch in his chest.

"Morning."

He'd seen her naked in the beginning, forced to undress her when she was unconscious, but he had tried to block it out, to not pay attention to her in that way. Not that it had worked completely. But in all honesty, he had never imagined she could be so beautiful. His imagination couldn't have stretched to those limits, even if he had, yes, okay he had fantasized and thought about her. In the darkness she had been all softness and heat. In the light she was long, tawny limbs and supple flesh and he found himself far hungrier for her than he was for bacon and eggs.

"Morning." He cleared his throat, trying to keep his eyes focused on hers. "Don't you think that's a little dangerous?"

"Cooking breakfast?" she teased, moving past him to the table. He followed both the scent of the food and the sight of the goddess in her plain white cotton panties bending over to put the plate down in front of him as he sat.

"Cooking breakfast…" he agreed, swallowing a dry lump in his throat as he now found himself on eye level with the fullness of her breasts, her nipples dark, the areolas lighter, a stunning contrast against her skin. "Naked," he finished faintly. "Grease has a tendency to splatter…"

"It does," she agreed, sliding a sleek thigh across his and settling herself into his lap. Silas kept his hands at his sides, knowing if he touched her, just for a moment, he was lost. "But I thought you could kiss my boo boos and make them all better."

His cock throbbed against his zipper, feeling the heat of her through her panties and he looked up into her eyes, seeing the lust there. God, he wanted her, more now than he had last night. Not touching her was killing him. She searched his eyes with hers, the only part of his face, aside from his mouth, that she could see, and he wondered what she was thinking.

"Do you regret it?" she asked, touching a finger to his lips.

"No," he admitted hoarsely. She made him tremble.

"Good." She leaned in and kissed him and he felt the rush of her breath through the knit mask, her tongue licking at his lips. When she reached down and grabbed his hands, putting them on her breasts, he groaned at the incredible weight of them, the shape and shift in his hands as she wiggled, making his cock swell. He couldn't believe they were doing this, that she wanted him, but everything told him that she did. He would never have initiated this, would never have crossed that line—even if he'd wanted to. And yes, he'd wanted to, but that was hardly the point.

"I want you," Jolee whispered, squeezing him between her thighs in the chair, her breath hot through his mask, her mouth next to his ear. "I touched myself this morning in the shower, remembering last night."

He made a small noise that, he had to admit, would probably be classified as a whimper by any objective observer.

"Do you want me?" she asked, leaning back in the chair, pressing her hands over his, mashing her breasts flat and then rubbing his palms over her nipples. They were hard little pebbles and Jolee moaned and rolled her hips at the sensation.

"Yeah," he croaked, watching her pull her lower lip between her teeth, her eyes half-closing with pleasure. "I'm just…afraid."

She stopped, eyes widening at his admission. He was glad the mask hid his flushed face.

"Afraid of what?"

"You." His hands were moving on their own, kneading her flesh, watching her reaction. He couldn't help it. "This."

"Why?"

He sighed. "It's complicated."

"Don't let this come between us." She reached for the edge of his mask, starting to lift it.

He grabbed her wrist, shaking his head. "Don't."

"What can I do to convince you that I want this?" Jolee frowned and then her eyes brightened as she slithered down between his legs, starting to work on his jeans. Silas groaned in protest, but his hips lifted when she yanked them down, freeing his cock for her mouth. He was scarred everywhere from the fire, even there, but she didn't seem to notice, her eyes never leaving his. Just watching the hot pink trail of her tongue around the head of his cock was a delight, but the sensation went beyond pleasure and bordered on pain, making his thighs tense and quiver.

She lifted her head, kneeling up and rubbing his wet cock-head against her nipples. "How do I convince you that I want *you?"*she whispered, leaning in and kissing his mouth, her belly deliciously soft, pressing his cock up against his own, trapping him.

"That's a good start." He smiled.

"Wanna feel how wet I am for you?" she offered, guiding his hand down between her legs. Oh Christ, Silas thought as she nudged her panties aside and let him feel. The soft, wiry hair, the swollen lips, the way they parted for his finger as he delved inside, was enough to make him crazy, but after last night, he wanted more. He wanted to see her.

Jolee squealed when he shoved the plate of eggs and bacon aside, reaching down and grabbing her hips, pulling her up and sitting her squarely on the table. It was solid and could hold her weight—he was sure of it, he'd made it himself—and it was going to have to hold a lot more than that in a minute. He yanked her panties down and Jolee lifted willingly enough at his insistence, spreading her thighs for him in the early morning light spilling across the kitchen table.

"You're beautiful." He couldn't help telling her as he took a seat in the chair again. The truth was, his knees didn't want to hold him upright. And besides, this way he could lean in and feather kisses up the slender, silky expanse of her thighs, moving slowly toward the thing he wanted most. He made himself go slow and Jolee squirmed on the table, her pussy visibly swollen already in anticipation.

By the time her pubic hair was tickling his lips, she was begging him, pleading, the sound of her cries only making him go slower, savoring it more. He snaked his tongue up the groove of thigh, skipping across to the top of her cleft, hearing her moan, her head thrown back and thrashing on the table. Her hands kneaded her own breasts, her palms rubbing her nipples, her thighs thrown wide. Silas let himself taste her, sticky and wet, moving his tongue back and forth against the raised flesh of her clit. Jolee moaned and lifted her hips in encouragement.

"Please," she whispered, reaching down to spread herself with her fingers, showing him, and he drank in the sight of her open for him like that. His cock throbbed at the thought of being inside of her and he grabbed it and squeezed as if he could send it a message—*easy, slow down, would you wolf down a gourmet meal in two minutes?*—but his cock didn't want to hear it. It had been starving for too long.

His tongue slipped lower between her lips, trailing down to really taste her, musky and hot. He remembered how she'd rocked on him the night before, mashing her whole pussy against his face. Glancing up, he saw her eyes were closed, head back, and he decided to chance it, pulling his mask up—not off, just up enough so he could open his whole mouth over her pussy.

"Oh god!" Jolee rewarded him with a trembling arch, writhing on the table as Silas sucked at her little clit, swallowing the hot, tangy taste of her juices, letting them coat his throat and then going back for more. He couldn't get enough of her, exploring her wet, swollen mound with his tongue and mouth and fingers, caught in a slick, pink labyrinth of flesh.

"Silas!" she gasped, rocking her hips, her toes beginning to curl. Just her saying his name that way, with the low, growly catch in it, filled his whole body with a blinding lust, but the words she followed it with sent him into overdrive. "Oh baby! Oh please, please, make me come all over your face!"

He fastened his mouth to her clit, working his tongue furiously, as eager for her orgasm as she was, holding desperately to his cock and trying to mentally reason with it. *Not yet, not yet. Soon, I promise.* Jolee was coming, her breasts heaving, belly quivering, her pussy spasming against the wet lap of his tongue.

"Oh god, oh god, oh my god," she moaned, rolling her hips from side to side. He couldn't tell if she wanted more of his tongue or was trying to get away from it. "Silas, please, I want you. I have to have you."

Struggling to sit, she reached for him but he was already half-out of his chair, cock in hand. He'd forgotten his mask was pulled up and she looked at him in wonder, seeing his jaw, his mouth still wet. He reached to pull it down but she protested, grabbing his hand, shaking her head, sliding her little hand behind his neck and pulling him into a kiss.

Silas moaned into her mouth. She sucked at his tongue as if drawing the taste of herself from him, her hand moving to take hold of his cock and guide him inside. She was over-wet, slick and hot as melting butter, and he slid in easily, his balls resting against the hard edge of the table, burying himself deep. Jolee held onto him, wrapping her legs around his waist, her arms around his neck, her mouth never leaving his.

He fucked her. He fucked her without thought or reason, thrusting deep and hard and fast, his cock feeling every delicious ridge and twist and turn of her body as they rocked together, the table shaking under their weight. Jolee wouldn't let him pull his mask down, keeping her mouth locked on his, their kiss hard and fierce and deeply probing, not unlike their fuck. Silas was past the point of caring, would probably have let her pull the whole damned thing off altogether in that moment, but thankfully she didn't.

Instead she climaxed, her heels digging into the small of his back, her nails raking his shoulders—he was grateful then he'd never taken off his shirt—and he felt every sweet flutter of her pussy around his length as he ground his hips and sent her flying. Jolee gasped out his name, begging him for more, begging him to stop, but he couldn't hear her, not really. He grabbed her hips, her ass, driving in as deep as he could, bottoming out with every thrust, making her squeak delightfully in his ear.

His cock swelled to bursting and then it did, boiling up from base to tip, erupting into the slick, hot sheath of her pussy. Jolee made a low noise in her throat as he exploded, almost a purr, sending shivers down his spine as her muscles consciously milked him. He continued to thrust, lost in the frenzied furor of his climax, as if he could empty himself completely into her and be utterly spent.

"Silas," she whispered, kissing his throat, the air blessedly cool on his neck and chin and jaw. Her lips caressed him, little feathered kisses, moving back from his jaw to his ear, murmuring words he was sure were in English, but he couldn't understand them at all. His mind was blank, his body verging on the edge of collapse, weak and helpless in her arms. She tugged gently at his mask and he would have let her then without a second thought. He was hers completely.

They both startled when someone knocked on the front door.

"Carlos," Jolee hissed, looking around for something to cover up with, and of course there were only her panties.

As senseless as he had been a minute before, Silas snapped into action, zipping his pants with one hand and reaching behind him with the other, grabbing the shotgun off the wall. He didn't think it was his brother, but you could never be too careful. Very few people knew about this cabin or its hidden location. The three knocks he'd had on his door in as many years had all been lost strangers looking for a way home.

"Bedroom," Silas whispered, nodding, but Jolee was already scrambling down the hallway. He didn't like her out of his sight, but he couldn't keep her behind him unclothed either.

His heart sank when he opened the door.

"There's trouble."

Silas looked at the old man, eyes dark and sunk into his leathered face, mouth downturned, and nodded. At least it wasn't his brother.

"Let me get my boots on. I'll meet you out back."

The old native gave him a nod and Silas shut the door, wondering just how he was going to explain this to Jolee.

* * * *

Everything melted, and Jolee melted with it. She tried to stay mad at Silas, for refusing to tell her anything, for leaving her alone in the cabin for stretches of time, but she couldn't stay mad at him long once he was home. She would melt and creep down the hall to his room, her breath held like a secret, and he would open up to her, the two of them free in the darkness to wallow in the blissful heat of one another.

And it went on like that, Silas masked in the daytime, quiet, often gone, but both of them unmasked and unclothed at night. It went on until the snow ran in rivers down the hillside and the leaves began to bud on the trees and then open and the forest around them teemed with life again. She knew it was fully spring when she saw a female deer and her fawn at the edge of the clearing while she was on her way to milk Anna in the hazy, early light of morning.

That, and the roses began to bloom.

She watched them open outside her bedroom window, growing up the trellis against the side of the house, a red carpet of flowers. Silas smiled when she exclaimed over them and started leaving one for her on occasion—on her pillow, or in a vase, or put across her latest knitting project, a budding reminder. She pressed them between thick books—heavy tomes about tracking and wildlife and growing mushrooms in the wild—and saved them in a dresser drawer, wanting to keep every part of Silas that he gave to her.

Yes, the world had melted and she with it, but it was the conversation she overheard outside her window that froze her again, breaking the spell, raising her hackles and making her curious once more. She had left the window wide open, letting the breeze blow in, and she was supposed to be napping—Silas still insisted and lately she'd actually been tired enough to sleep—when she heard their voices, low but clear enough.

"It's not your decision, Abe." Silas was angry—she knew what he sounded like when he was angry.

"There are other ways."

The old Indian had come around several more times and Silas had gone off with him. He wouldn't tell her, of course, what any of it was about. Jolee crept to the window to listen, ducking low so they wouldn't see her.

"You don't need to sacrifice yourself for this cause." Abe sounded sad, not angry or pleading.

"I'll decide what I need and what I don't need."

The old man sighed. "You can't wake someone pretending to be asleep."

"What does that mean?" Now Silas sounded really mad.

The old man countered with something even more cryptic. "Love beyond your fear."

Silas snorted. "Did you consult some Native American sayings handbook before you showed up today?"

Abe laughed. "Don't sacrifice yourself, friend," he said again. "The world needs more men like you, not less."

"I got work to do."

"We're going to the community board meeting next week," Abe called.

Silas's voice sounded further away. "I'm sure you'll get a lot done with the bureaucrats. In the meantime, I'll do it my way."

Jolee chanced a peek over the windowsill, seeing Silas heading off into the woods down a trail. The old Indian watched him go for a moment and then headed the other way.

She made a quick decision, running to the back door and pulling on her boots. She followed him as quietly as she could. Silas wasn't the only one who could track. Her father had taught her to shoot and hunt, how to track a deer for miles. Even when she lost sight of Silas in the distance, she knew the signs to look for on the soft ground, through the brush.

He walked a long time, going through parts of the forest that hadn't been cleared at all. She hopped logs, ducked under hanging branches. She was so focused on marking her way back and looking for signs of Silas's direction, she was startled when the forest opened up into a clearing.

She stopped, seeing Silas standing too, still, head down, in the middle of what was left of a house that had been ravaged by fire. He stood a long time amidst the charred remains, so long that she almost called out, went to him.

Then he went to his knees and made a noise that scared her so much she couldn't even think about moving. It started low, a keening wail, that grew into an intense, primal scream of rage so deafening she could have sworn the trees shook. Startled birds flew out of their nests, rabbits bolted, and Jolee stared, watching, terrified, as Silas began to sob.

I shouldn't be here. That was her first thought—to walk away and leave him here alone with his sorrow. Then she thought she should go to him, offer comfort, but how? The man didn't share much under normal circumstances. Why did she think he would in such a vulnerable state? She imagined him pushing her away, telling her to go home, and couldn't bring herself to risk the rejection. After following him for over two hours, she was just going to turn around and go home and leave him to his secret pain.

She stood, undecided, until Silas got slowly, heavily to his feet, rubbing his masked face on his shirtsleeves. He drew a few, deep, shuddering breaths and she thought she'd never seen anything so sad, the way his shoulders slumped and his arms hung at his side.

"Jolee." The sound of her name drew a startled gasp from her throat and she actually took a step back into the forest. "Come here."

He'd known. He had known she was following, had probably known the instant she was out of the house. She crept forward, wary, picking her way through the rubble, and came to stand beside him. They stood quietly like that until he reached over and took her hand, squeezing gently.

She found the courage to speak. "What is this place?"

"It was my home." He kicked at the ashy residue. "Our home."

She wanted to ask, but she was afraid to break the spell they seemed under. Silas was talking about his past? Was she dreaming?

"Who's we?" she prompted gently.

"Isabelle." He gave another great sigh. "I haven't said her name out loud in five years."

"She was your wife?" Jolee guessed. "What happened?"

"She was killed."

Jolee surveyed what was left of their home together, her heart breaking for him. "In the fire?"

"No." Silas's voice hardened, his grip growing tighter on her hand. "My brother took her and he killed her."

"Carlos?" Jolee whispered, incredulous. Although she knew what the man was capable of—she really shouldn't have been surprised. "But why?"

"Because I wouldn't give him this." Silas gestured toward the forest, to the hundreds of thousands of acres of land that lay beyond. "Our father left it to me, and I wouldn't let him destroy it."

Jolee leaned her head against his shoulder, her heart swelling with pride, knowing how much he loved the land, how he protected it, just as he protected her. But oh, god, how it had cost him. She couldn't even imagine his pain.

Silas glanced down at her, offering a small, sad smile behind his mask. "But really, he did it because he wanted her, and she wanted me instead."

Jolee's spine straightened. "I don't blame her."

He began to walk, slowly pulling her with him. "They left me here to die."

"But you survived," she countered, finally understanding his scars, the mask.

"My body did." Silas drew her around the rubble to a white fence, an old trellis there filled with roses. They had grown up wild from the ashes, thick and red, weaving their way up the trellis and blooming open toward the sun.

"So beautiful," she murmured, reaching to touch one of the velvety red petals.

"I don't know how they survived." Silas reached into his pocket and withdrew his hunting knife, a monstrous thing, and cut one of the stems. "These were Isabelle's roses."

She watched him, thoughtful, as he trimmed the thorns, talking the whole while. "Isabelle tried to play peacemaker between us. She invited Carlos to dinner. I should have known better, but I thought…I hoped…" Silas studied the flower in his hand. "He drugged us both. I woke up duct taped to a chair with the house on fire."

"Dear God."

He lifted the flower to his masked face, breathing in. "And Isabelle was gone."

"How do you know she's...I mean…" Jolee swallowed, almost not wanting to say the words. "How do you know she's not still alive?"

"I've looked for her body." He gestured toward the forest again. "It wouldn't have been the first time Carlos had someone killed. You know that as well as I do."

Jolee nodded, feeling sick.

"You were my last clue." Silas reached over and tucked the rose behind her ear. "If Isabelle had been alive, Carlos would have taken her, made her his. Instead, he had you."

"She would never have betrayed you like that."

"I don't know." He tucked her hair behind her ear along with the flower, shaking his head. "My brother can be charming. He seduced you, didn't he?"

She didn't have a response for that, didn't want to think about it. Instead, she turned to look at Isabelle's roses, wondering at their beauty in the midst of the devastation. There were no other plants growing, even after all this time, amidst the wreckage. The soil must have been completely drained after the fire. And then it occurred to her.

"Silas, she's here." Jolee knelt in the soil, her hands turning over the dirt, knowing somehow that she was right. "She's right here."

"I feel her here too."

"No." She looked up and met his eyes. "He buried her right here. With her roses."

Silas's eyes widened in realization. She saw the emotions passing, just in his eyes—the horror, the anger, the sorrow. And then he sank to the earth beside her with a howl of rage and pain so great it hurt her heart, tearing at the dirt with his bare hands. He'd dug down two feet, bleeding at his knuckles and fingernails, before Jolee located a shovel at the other end of the rubble. It was rusted through entirely at the handle, but the business-end still worked.

He accepted it with a grunt when she handed it over, making quicker work of the soil under his feet. She sat with her arms curled around her knees and watched him until he found her, still eerily preserved and recognizable.

Jolee knew Silas had forgotten about her sitting there. He was lost in his memory of Isabelle, the woman whose body he held and rocked, dead in his arms. *I'm not a part of this*, she thought.

So she turned and headed for home. She knew he would come to her, when he was ready.

* * * *

He couldn't have thought of a better resting place for her. He hated his brother for thinking of it, for burying her here. He couldn't believe he hadn't thought of it himself. All these years, she had been right here. How many times had he come back to walk this perimeter, reliving their life together? He could still see her pruning her roses, singing to herself. Now she was giving new life to the same roses she had so lovingly grown. Thanks to his brother.

Carlos had always taken whatever he wanted. Had she refused him? Silas knew she would, although what had he done to her while she was drugged? Or worse, while she was awake, by force? That thought burned and he tore two roses off the bush, breaking off the stems, ignoring the rip of thorns against his bleeding palms.

He had said his goodbyes, his final goodbyes, and buried her again under the roses. Now he stamped the dirt down under his feet and began tearing the roses apart, scattering the petals over her grave.

He stood a long time, thinking about his past, about his future. He hadn't realized, until he saw Isabelle's body, how much he'd hoped she was still alive somewhere. Now he had closure, and knowing she was really gone changed everything. His brother had taken her, had probably raped her, and then, when she refused to bend to his will, had killed and buried her. He'd imagined the scenario so often it had become truth in his head, but now he knew it was true, or at least, a close approximation.

He'd planned his revenge all along, sabotaging Carlos at every turn, but never going so far as to completely put him out of business. What had he been waiting for? Silas wondered. He could have gone to the police at any time, shown them where Carlos had buried other bodies—men like Jolee's father, people who had gotten in his brother's way.

I've been waiting to find her, Silas realized, squatting down and sifting his fingers through the freshly packed dirt, spreading the rose petals. And now that he had?

His plan to expose his brother, to sacrifice himself in the process, would hurt Jolee. She cared about him too, he was sure of it. Even if she could never really love him—who could love the monster he'd become?—his death would be a hard blow for her. She'd grown used to him, comfortable. He would be leaving her alone, unprotected, to fend for herself.

He thought about Isabelle, but he also thought about Jolee, who had followed him, who had witnessed his unabashed pain and who had been the one to realize where his wife was buried. She had come to mean far more to him than he'd realized.

There are other ways. Abe's voice came back to him. He'd worked closely with the old man, once they'd realized what Carlos was planning to do at the old White Pine Mine—re-opening it to get what was left of the copper with sulfuric acid, most likely poisoning the aquifers in the process, which included not only Silas's land, but the local Indian Reserve land next to it as well. Sabotaging the sulfide mine had set

Carlos back, Silas was sure, but it wouldn't stop him. Nothing would stop him, unless his brother was either dead or in prison.

Carlos had paid off all the mining safety inspectors to get the White Pine Mine opened again and had received all the necessary permits. While Abe and others on the Bad River reservation had been trying to draw attention to the issue, Carlos had been seducing the media on his own, telling them, "At this strength, sulfuric acid is a very diluted solution. This stuff is safe as lemon juice!" And, as Silas as pointed out to Jolee, his brother could be very persuasive.

But Abe had proof that the stuff was already leaching into the water. And Silas had dropped one of the dead rabbits he'd snared into a vat of the solution, watching the stuff eat away at its flesh, leaving it just a floating skeleton, in the space of a three minutes. The media wasn't listening, the local mining safety commission wasn't listening. The only way to get it all to stop was to use the media himself and get the EPA involved.

This spring would mark five years since Isabelle had died. That meant, this year, Carlos could have Silas declared legally dead and inherit all the land. Silas's plan of self-sacrifice, to martyr himself for the cause, to die like the rabbit in a vat of sulfuric acid on the day of the spring mine opening with cameras rolling, had seemed like a good one back before Jolee had been thrown into the mix.

Before Jolee, life hadn't been worth living. Silas had sacrificed far greater things than his own life, he realized, standing on his wife's grave. And it was a good plan. It would work. With Carlos exposed, the media would run with the story, the EPA would get involved. Silas had already provided Abe with enough evidence to give them after Silas' death to put his brother away for life—including plots of land where the bodies were buried and a long laundry list of detailed, illegal activity.

But for the first time since his wife's death, Silas had found something—someone—worth living for.

"Goodbye, Isabelle." He pulled his mask off and threw it aside, turning and walking into the forest, heading for home.

* * * *

Jolee should have known. Silas would have been on guard the moment he walked into the yard, she realized later as she bounced up and down, once again locked in her husband's trunk, zip-tied and duct-taped. *Right back where I started. Déjà-fucking-vu* .

But hindsight was 20/20, and she'd been distracted, worried about Silas. Should she have stayed with him? What was he going to do? Would he be okay alone? So she didn't notice the muddy tracks, men's shoes, not boots, on the wooden back steps. She hadn't noticed the tire-tracks either—definitely made by a car, not a truck—running up the rain-softened driveway. She hadn't even noticed that the back door was open. Because she'd probably left it open, in a hurry to run after Silas, hadn't she?

But she noticed all of those things on the way out, Carlos dragging her by the hair in a blind rage. She didn't know how he'd found her and it didn't matter. Silas was gone and couldn't protect her, and while she'd fought as hard as she could, even managing to stab her husband in the upper arm with a meat fork—she'd been aiming for his jugular—hard enough to impale it three inches, it had all been in vain. She was still locked in his truck heading toward her death for the second time in a year.

And she still regretted that she'd never really loved a man who truly loved her back. Carlos had never wanted or cared for her—to him, she'd been a trophy, something to win and display. And Silas? Did he love her? The last time she'd done this, she'd been full of thoughts of escape. This time, the ride was shorter, and she didn't have as much time to plan, but she thought about Silas almost exclusively.

Would he believe she got lost? Or worse, would he think she left?

Or would he realize what had happened and come for her?

Even as the car bumped down the old familiar two-track and she flashbacked to that day last winter, her pants wet with fear, her heart hammering in her chest just as it was now, she couldn't help hoping for the latter.

* * * *

Silas should have paid attention to his instincts. Miles from home, he thought he heard someone traveling on the old two-track. *Too wet out there,* he thought. *Gonna get stuck.* The rain had been heavy this spring, making everything soft and muddy. But he'd second-guessed himself as the sound faded.

Besides, he was changed, everything was different, his eyes just adjusting to a new light. He felt off-balance and was trying to get his bearings. Or perhaps he needed new bearings.

He'd buried Isabelle and now he was going to see Jolee. And he was anxious to be home. Even if she walked away after she saw his scars, he thought, stepping over a log and running a hand over the rough skin of his cheek—and some part of him was sure she would—he wanted to see her again, to tell her that he loved her, to give her that much, at least.

He saw the tracks in the driveway in the dappled afternoon sunlight as soon he stepped out of the woods, his senses immediately awake, telling himself it was a trick of the light and already knowing it wasn't. The man's footprints through the driveway, up the steps and down again—a second set of smaller tracks beside it on the way out—had his hunting knife unsheathed and ready as Silas slipped silently into the house. She wasn't in there, he was sure of it, but he had to be ready just in case.

Silas's assessment had been correct. The note on the kitchen table, written in his brother's handwriting, confirmed that much. It was simple and wouldn't implicate his brother in anything, of course, but it was clear enough.

Meet me at the White Pine. Bring the deeds.

And Jolee was gone. Her knitting was still on the table, another mask, this one black with a white skeleton face—for Halloween, she'd said with a grin, although he'd watched her making it and realized it would probably be his death shroud instead, because he didn't plan on being around in October.

Excerpt now he very much wanted to be here, and he wanted Jolee here beside him.

Silas worked quickly, not knowing how much of a head start his brother had. He would take the four-wheeler most of the way and then do the rest on foot, he decided. And he took several things with him—but the one thing he didn't take was a deed to any of his land.

* * * *

Kicking her way out hadn't worked this time. Jolee couldn't get the latch to pop and it did nothing except making Carlos even more pissed when he opened his now very dented trunk to drag her out. By the hair. She swore, if she got out of this, she was going to get it cut off so no one could pull her around by the stuff ever again.

"Fucking bitch! Look what you did to my car!" Carlos threw her to the ground and she sprang up almost instantly—the idiot had forgotten to zip tie her feet together—heading into a full-out run. He swore again and took off after her—he'd always been good about going to the gym and he was fast—catching hold of her hair and yanking her backward. She fell onto her back, hitting her head hard enough on the ground to make her see blackness and bright stars instead of blue sky and sun.

She was cursing the length of her hair again as he grabbed another handful and stalked off, forcing her to follow, bent over and panting, still struggling in spite of the pain and searching the ground for a weapon. There had been no jack or even a tire iron in the trunk, but her hands were zip-tied in front, not the back, and she could grab something if she could find it. She wondered, considering how sloppy he'd been, if her husband had ever really done this by himself, or if he'd always gotten one of his guys to do it for him.

"Carlos, please," she begged, trying to appeal to the part of him she knew must be in there. "Don't do this."

"Shut the fuck up." He shoved her through a door and threw her to the floor, kicking her in the ribs to leave her breathless and deter her from running. It worked—her side exploded, a bloom of pain, and she clutched it, groaning. "You don't tell me what to do. Nobody tells me what to do."

She looked up at him, seeing a gun in his hand, and she had a moment of panic, thinking of Silas, wishing he was here, at the very least so he could be the last thing she saw before her husband pulled the trigger. But when Carlos just stood there, her eyes skipped away from his hand, around the room, taking in her surroundings. A factory? There was a heavy, metallic smell in the air and it hung around them. It smelled like blood. A slaughterhouse?

She looked for an exit but the only one she found was between her and Carlos. He'd even left the door propped open and the light called to her like a beacon. The place was huge, full of strange looking machines with thick ductwork, heavy steel. She could get lost amongst them. That would be a start. She struggled to rise and he kicked her again, the other side this time, making her scream in pain.

"You were always way more trouble than you were worth," he snarled, unslinging a bag from his shoulder and dropping it down by her head. She saw the blood seeping out of it and screamed again, backpedaling from the sight.

He snorted, squatting down beside her and opening it up. "You think my brother's the only one who knows how to hunt?"

He pulled out a muskrat by the tail, its head half-gone from the shot that had killed it, and Jolee rolled away, shuddering. It wasn't the animal that made her sick, it was Carlos, the sneering smile on his face, the glint in his eyes.

"Wanna see something cool, chickie?" He grabbed her upper arm, still holding the muskrat with the other, and dragged her to her feet. She was doubled over in pain, looking around with blurry eyes for another exit, but she was forced to follow around the huge machine in front of them, down an aisle way.

It was dark back here, although the light coming from the doorway reflected against the ceiling, giving her some ability to see. Could she crawl under? Get into a small space and hide? But Carlos had a gun. He'd slipped it into his belt, but it was still there. Could she reach it? It was worth a shot. She took a step toward him, knocking him off balance, reaching for the butt of the gun, but he turned, shoving her backward onto the floor. She sprawled, hands thrown over her head behind her, hitting her head again, the other side this time, leaving a lump she could practically feel.

"Whoa!" He slammed his foot down on the zip tie across her wrists, making her howl in pain. He'd just broken her finger, at least one of them, maybe more. It hurt so bad she thought she might pass out, the world fading to gray. "Careful. Wouldn't want to fall in there. That would be nasty."

He squatted, turning her chin toward him and looking down at her. His face filled her vision, upside down, like a storm cloud. She tried to move her fingers under his foot and it brought more bursts of pain so she held still, letting the tears roll down her temples. Carlos was still holding the half-headless muskrat by the tail and she could smell its decomposing body. It made her gag, but not as much as what he did next.

Using his other hand, he yanked her t-shirt up, exposing her bra, his gaze burning over her flesh. Then he yanked her bra down too, his teeth showing in a sneering smile as he squeezed and kneaded her flesh. She turned her head away again, more in reaction to his mauling than to the smell of the dead animal, wanting to scream, knowing it would do her no good.

"I forgot how beautiful you are." Carlos tweaked her nipple and then twisted it, making her wince, but she didn't cry out. "And we've got time for lots of fun before we get down to the dirty work."

He had to stretch to reach her crotch, cupping and grinding his hand there. "I'm gonna fuck you so good."

"That would be new," she gasped, trying to twist away, the pain in her hands increasing enough to make her still. "Besides, your brother's been doing the job much better than you ever could."

He growled, bringing his fist down on her pubic bone, making her scream and curl up, turning fetal in spite of the pain in her hands. The hurt between her legs far outweighed that of her fingers. They were going numb, but her pelvis was on fire all the way to her bones.

"Cunt!" He stood, yanking her up again, dragging her by her mangled hands, keeping his grip on the zip tie between them. "Want to see what I'm gonna do to you?"

He let the muskrat drop, and Jolee heard a splash. In spite of the pain radiating through every part of her body, she turned her head to look. There was a vat sunk deep into the floor beside them, the liquid a good ten feet down. She saw something—a lid?—on the floor next to the hole, like huge manhole cover, that had been taken off.

Carlos sighed, looking down at the hole. "Would have been more effective if it had still been alive I guess."

"What?" Jolee glanced down again, still dazed and in pain, seeing something white floating in the liquid. She could hear a hissing noise, like steam escaping.

"Sulfuric acid." He grinned, meeting her eyes. "Gonna eat you right down to your bones."

She looked down again at the muskrat skeleton floating in acid and the realization rolled through her like thunder. She struggled, trying to get away from him, she didn't care how much pain she was in. She finally understood that he was going to put a world of hurt on her that she could never have even imagined—and that was all going to be before her sulfuric acid bath.

"Stupid bitch." He grabbed her, crushing her mangled hands between them as he tried to kiss her. She turned away and his lips mashed against her cheek, the corner of her mouth, and she tasted Wintergreen Lifesavers. "Why did you have to find out? I would have given you everything."

"You don't have anything I want." She spat the words out with his attempt at a kiss.

He had both arms around her and he squeezed her so hard she couldn't breathe. "Another few months and I'm going to be the richest man you'll ever meet. You know what's in this mine?"

She shook her head, letting out a little squeak of response, but she did know. She'd identified the smell, that thick bloody smell—it was copper.

"Silver!" he hissed, eyes bright with glee. "Do you know what silver is worth in today's market? Do you know how much it's going to be worth?"

She shook her head again, the world fading from gray to black and back again. She literally couldn't breathe.

"Millions!" He laughed, squeezing and twirling her around like they were celebrating something. "Billions!"

She caught a breath, her lungs burning, her side, both sides, aching with the expansion. "I hate you."

His eyes narrowed as he looked down at her. "Good. That will make dying easier."

She went on, in spite of herself. If she was going to die, she wanted him to know the truth. "I never loved you. I love Silas. He's more man, in every way, than you will ever be."

"We'll see about that." He shoved her backwards, grabbing hold and tearing at her bra. It wouldn't give, the hooks on the back holding fast. He frowned in frustration, redoubling his efforts, and Jolee saw the sudden widening of his eyes before she realized what was happening, the way his mouth dropped in surprise, jaw working with unspoken words.

Carlos tried to say something, but he just gurgled, his grip on her loosening. That's when she saw the arrow sticking out of the side of his throat.

"Silas," she whispered, pushing her husband away from her without thinking, already searching for her rescuer with her eyes. Carlos stumbled back, one hand reaching for the arrow sticking out of his neck, the other blindly grasping in front of him, and she saw that he was going to fall. There was no stopping his momentum—he was going to fall into the hole in the floor.

"Uuuhuhh!" Carlos choked, blood running down to stain the collar of his white button down shirt, blooming on the front like a rose. He had one hand on the arrow and was trying to pull but the pain was clearly too much. He pawed the air with his other hand and managed to hook his fingers through the front of Jolee's exposed bra again.

And she was falling.

His momentum became her own, and they were both going down together, falling into the darkness toward a roiling death. She heard thunder behind her, felt something hit the floor, but there was no time to turn. She could only see her husband's wide, frightened eyes and the white skeleton of the muskrat bobbing below.

Then a big, thick arm had her around the waist and she was watching Carlos fall, not falling with him. Silas, who had seemed to fly down to catch her, had been on top of one of the machines behind them, making for an easy shot—and the thunder behind her had been him jumping to the floor.

She turned away from the splash, ten feet below, and Silas pulled her in close, squeezing her so hard she couldn't breathe and didn't care. He whirled her away from the vat of acid and they both heard Carlos screaming, finally finding his voice in spite of the arrow in his windpipe.

Silas glared down to see his brother dying and snarled, "Don't worry, bro, it's as safe as lemon juice."

She was in too much pain to walk and he carried her to the end of the aisle toward the exit, his bow still strung over his shoulder.

"What took you so long?" she gasped, arms around his neck, drinking him in. He was scarred, his face ravaged by the fire, but she could still see the man he'd been, the man he still was, the strong jaw and clefted chin, the full lips, and the same beautiful dark eyes.

"I came as fast as I could." He looked at her in the light of day as he carried her outside, fully exposed to her now. "Are you okay? Did he hurt you?"

"Yes," she replied, swallowing. "And yes."

"I'm so sorry." He pressed his forehead to hers and then kissed her cheek, looking down at her still zip-tied hands, her fingers bent.

"It's okay." She rested her cheek against his chest as he walked, carrying her easily in his arms, as if she weighed nothing at all. "You can take me home and fix me up and make it all better. You've done it before."

"True enough."

She felt his lips against the top of her head.

"How long were you there waiting to take the shot?" she asked as they walked past Carlos's car, the trunk she'd ridden in still open. She wondered what he'd heard, how much he'd seen.

"Not long." He slowed. "A few minutes."

She lifted her face to look at him, tracing a scar from the corner of his mouth to his jaw. "Did you hear me say it?"

He cleared his throat. "Say what?"

"I love you." She watched his eyes fill with tears.

"I heard." He blinked fast, his gaze drifting away and then back to her. "I just didn't know if you meant it."

"Oh I meant it." She kissed him softly, marveling at the familiarity of his mouth, his arms around her. This was Silas, *her* Silas, unmasked. "I promise you, I meant every word."

"I was coming home to tell you." He smiled, hefting her in his arms. She knew what he meant.

"But I wasn't there."

He shook his head, his eyes grave. "No, you weren't."

"But you found me."

"Yes, I did." He nodded, a smile playing on his lips.

She wrapped her arms more tightly around his neck. "You can tell me now."

"I love you," he said, and she didn't think she'd ever seen a brighter, more beautiful smile in her life.

"Good." She snuggled up in his arms. "Now take me home so you can kiss it and make it all better."

Silas started walking again, carrying her with him. "Yes ma'am."

Epilogue

"Abe came by this morning." Jolee greeted her husband with the news as he came in the door, shaking off the snow. It was a winter reminiscent of their very first in the cabin—three feet of snow outside and still falling. The world was blanketed in white silence.

"How in the hell did he get out here?" Silas yanked off his boots and set them aside. "It's so deep I can barely make it in snowshoes."

She shrugged, watching him dust the snow out of his dark hair. "He said the county finalized the paperwork. The judge's decision is final, no more appeals."

Silas stopped, eyes wide. "Really?"

She nodded, smiling at the joyful look on his face, knowing now why Abe had stayed so long, wanting to tell Silas himself, but the snow and the lateness of the day finally chased him back home. They'd had a good, long talk, as always. Abe, she'd discovered, had been a good friend of her father's. She was only one-quarter Chippewa herself, but her father had been half, and it was Abe, she discovered, who had left the note in her mailbox, her father's friend, who had come out to the cabin to check on her at night when Silas was gone, leaving his footprints in the snow.

After the discovery and identification of Carlos's body, the Chippewa Indians had come forward with the information Silas had given them. Abe, working as a spokesman, had revealed her dead husband's crimes to the world. Then they'd discovered the most shocking news of all. Carlos had never changed his will—Jolee was the sole heir to his money and businesses.

"That's the best news I've heard all day!" Silas exclaimed, coming forward to kneel in front of her chair by the fire. He put his wet head in her lap and she stroked his hair, smiling. They had both agreed, almost simultaneously, when they'd heard the news about the will, and Jolee stepped forward to claim it. Of course Carlos' partners had contested the will, but in the end, the will was upheld. After three years of appeals, the mining and logging businesses had been ordered to be liquidated, the land donated to the Indian Reservation for restoration.

"Well, you might want to hear my other news before you make that call." Jolee smiled.

"Oh?" Silas lifted his head, raising an eyebrow.

"My water broke." She opened her legs to reveal the towel she was sitting on under her t-shirt.

His eyes widened, his jaw dropped and she almost laughed out loud. "What?"

"You ready to have a baby?"

"In a snowstorm?" He gulped. "We can't get to a hospital."

"Who needs a hospital?" She wrapped her arms around his neck. "Would you rather have a baby in the truck stuck in the snow or here in our own nice, warm bed?"

"Home." He smiled, recognizing their "would you rather?" game. "But Jolee, are you sure—?"

She rolled her eyes, feeling the baby stir, knowing another contraction would come soon. They were coming more steadily now. She wasn't worried. It was all going to be okay.

"Would you rather kiss me or keep talking?"

Silas hesitated and then pressed his lips to hers, giving her the only answer that had ever really mattered.

GOLDILOCKS

"Most people go to Brazil to work on their tan." Goldie sighed, watching Campbell use his iPhone to bypass the alarm system. She kicked at a Styrofoam cup in the alleyway, startling a cat—or a really big rat—behind a dumpster. It bolted in the darkness and her heart jumped in her chest in spite of her outward calm. "

"We can do that later." He glanced up at her and then nodded at the door. "It's all yours."

"Promises, promises." She unholstered the drill out of her belt like a six-shooter, making quick work of the bolt. No alarm went off. The cameras on the side of the building had already been disabled, thanks to Campbell. "Is there a night guard?"

"Nope." He swung the door wide and they went into the back entrance of the bank, down a dark hallway lit red by the *emergency exit* light behind them. "Yet another oversight."

"You know, a lot of people go on their honeymoon in Brazil," she suggested hopefully.

Campbell didn't take the bait.

"The safe?" She could feel it, could almost taste it, heavy gauge steel, lever like a roulette wheel waiting to be spun—everyone place your bets, who's going to get lucky tonight? But Goldie didn't need luck.

"Through here." Campbell was playing with his phone again, glancing up at the security cameras. The red lights on them were off.

Goldie drilled through another door, this one with two bolts. She heard the secondary locking mechanism at the bottom and swore under her breath.

"They got a backup," Goldie warned him, already feeling around on her belt. She found what she was looking for, pulling out the hand-held plasma saw.

Campbell raised his eyebrows. "Nifty gadget."

"You know I love my toys." She smirked, grabbing her goggles off her belt and pulling them on. "Step back."

He did as he was told, getting out of her way as she pressed the trigger, waiting for it to spark. She was through the secondary lock in less than ten seconds and Campbell pulled the door open, revealing the vault room behind it.

"Pretty." Goldie pulled her goggles off to get a better look. "Dual combination. I assume it's on a timer?"

"Of course."

She approached the vault with reverence, touching her gloved palm against the surface. Could she do it? She'd had the opportunity to crack a dual combination lock only once before, and that had been in the light of day with the head of banking security breathing down her neck.

"Time me?" She grinned over her shoulder at him, taking her gloves off so she could feel the combination dial in her hand.

"Sure." He fussed around with his iPhone again. "On your mark…get set…go!"

She closed her eyes and started turning the dial, hearing her father's voice in her head—*just line up the gates under the fence. It's easy as one-two-three.* Well, in this case, four. It was a four digit combination lock, and there was a twin right next to it with a different combination waiting to be discovered.

All combination locks were a set of wheels. All you had to do was line up the notches on the wheels with the contact points and you were in. Of course, with a four-digit combination, there were ten thousand possibilities, and this little gadget couldn't be hacked with a computer. Goldie didn't use sound-enhancing equipment or earphones. She used what her father had taught her, along with just her ears and her hands.

"Thirty seconds." Campbell spoke softly, knowing not to break her concentration.

"Got the first one," she muttered. Her fingers just seemed to "know" or "see" where the wheel was. She'd always had an incredibly sensitive sense of touch. Even her father had been surprised when she had started to surpass him in her ability to crack a safe. It was a little like flying once she really got into the zone, working the lock around, back and forth, slowing as she neared the sweet spot, and then—ahhhhh, such a lovely jolt when she found it.

"Got the second." It didn't hurt that her memory was like a steel trap. She could hear Campbell's breath beside her, smell the Altoids on it—curiously strong, cinnamon and sweetness.

"Three minutes." He sounded excited, but he always was when they were on a job. He loved watching her work, even though it always felt like a competition. She didn't know why he worried about it. There was no man alive who could do what he did. He could hack anything, bypass any electronic system ever made, usually just from his modified, jailbroken iPhone, but he couldn't do what she did and he admired her for it. He truly appreciated those things he wasn't good at. She liked that about Campbell.

"Third one." She redoubled her efforts, nearing the end now. For some reason, the first number came easy, but last was always the most difficult. Slowing her motions, she focused, concentrating hard, her tongue sneaking out to touch the corner of her mouth. Her father used to tease her that she was going to bite it off some day.

"Four minutes. Damn. What did you do the last one in?"

Goldie turned the dial, searching for the sweet spot. "Six minutes and eight seconds."

And she found it. "Got it."

He gave a low whistle. "Four minutes and fifty three seconds!"

"Got one more to go." She moved to the second combination lock and started working it. It was all the way at the other end of the door, far out of reach of the first. This safe required two people to open both locks at the same time, an added security measure. She got the first number right away, unmindful of the time. This was just another job, another lock to crack open. The second and third came almost back to back, the notches lining up and falling like dominoes. And again, it was the last one that tripped her up, forcing her to focus her efforts, making that final release an exhilarating thing, leaving her breathless as she turned to Campbell.

"That's it."

"Woo!" His eyes were bright. "You did two of them in six minutes and forty-seven seconds!"

"Write them down." She rattled off the combinations and he punched the numbers into his iPhone. "We have to do it together or it won't work, and we only get one shot."

"I know." He leveled her with a withering look and she grinned, hand still on the dial. Campbell turned the other combination lock to zero it out and she did the same. He glanced at his iPhone, reading off the numbers to double-check the combination.

"Ready?" she prompted, eyeing the silver vault wheel with anticipation.

"Go." He started turning the dial and she did too, both of them focused intently on doing it correctly. They waited anxiously when they'd finished, stepping away from the vault, and saw the light at the top go from red to yellow. There was a green one next to it that hadn't lit up yet.

"We're in!" Campbell crowed, grinning.

"How long do we have to wait before we can open it?" she asked, referring to the timer that was set the moment the light went yellow. The green one would go on after the allotted time.

"It's a quickie," he said "Twenty minutes."

"That's it?" She pouted, already unhooking her tool belt, letting it drop to the floor. "How many times can you make me come in twenty minutes?"

"Let's find out."

He peeled her out of her black catsuit like a banana, leaving it limp at her ankles. She wasn't wearing anything underneath, her body thin and lithe in his hands. He had big hands and she liked that, feeling him pull and grab and tug, gripping her ass as he wasted time kissing her, his tongue probing between her lips.

She discouraged his efforts at romance by dropping to her knees, unbuckling his belt and unzipping his fly. His cock sprang free in her hand when she pulled his jeans and boxers down and she turned her mouth and tongue into a delightful distraction, sucking him deep, feeling him swell between her lips. Her pussy was so wet she could feel her own juices on her thighs. She'd been wet for hours imagining this moment and she knew it was in her eyes when she looked up at him, seeing his excitement feeding off her own.

Her attention to his cock made him moan, his hips beginning to rock, shoving his length to the back of her throat. She gagged a little but didn't stop, wrapping her hand around the base of him and sucking faster still. Campbell's hand moved over her head, shoving the black knit cap she wore off and letting her gold curls spill down over her bare shoulders.

"Easy," he begged as she used her other hand to cup the heavy weight of his balls, rolling them gently, tracing the line between with her thumb. "This was about how many times *I* can make *you* come, remember?"

She took him out of her mouth long enough to murmur, "I know," but resumed her sucking regimen, making him buck and fist his hand in her hair, pulling backward until his cock popped fatly out of her mouth, leaving a thick strand of saliva between the tip of it and her lower lip.

She whimpered but didn't protest when he reached down to grab her, pulling her up against him. The buttons of his shirt dug against her bare skin and she let him kiss her this time, let him taste his precum in her mouth as she sucked at his tongue.

He groaned when she found his cock with her hand, fisting and pumping him, rubbing her thumb over the wet head.

"Damn you," he gasped, stepping out of her grasp and sweeping her up into his arms. She squealed in protest as he laid her out on the cold counter—the one the bank had installed to give them a place to set safe deposit boxes, to sign papers and checks—yanking her catsuit off entirely along with her boots and running his big hands over her naked body. Goldie stretched and purred at his attention like a cat, arching when his hand dipped between her thighs, encouraging him to delve deeper.

"So wet!" he murmured, eyes widening as he began to finger her. She moaned and rocked against his hand, feeling his thumb rubbing against the aching, sensitive bud of her clit. He could make her come in seconds that way and by the look in his eyes, he knew it. Campbell grinned, leaning in to suck one of her nipples into his mouth. Her breasts were small, her nipples normally a puffy pink, hardening into pebbles against his tongue.

"Oh fuck!" She grabbed a fist full of his hair, twisting on the counter, his hand shoved hard and deep between her legs, and let her orgasm come, rolling over her in wet, hot spasms, a deluge of pleasure. She fucked his fingers, her hips rising up off the counter to meet him, quivering with her release.

"One," he announced, lifting his fingers to his smug, grinning mouth and sucking them. She found his cock with her eyes still closed, tugging, and he gasped in response, shaking his head. "You're so impatient."

She didn't open her eyes, asking breathlessly, "How long do we have now?"

"Fifteen minutes." Campbell grabbed her hips, moving her around on the counter, making her lose her grip. "And I'm going for my personal best."

"*Your* personal best? They're *my* orgasms." Goldie snorted, opening her eyes in surprise when his mouth covered her pussy. "Oh! God…" She leaned back on her elbows, her eyes on his. "What's the record again?"

He eased up a little to answer. "Four."

"In twenty minutes?" she squeaked, his tongue slipping down into her slit.

"Yep," he confirmed, his words muffled against the soft blonde curls of her pubic hair. "And I've got you up on the all-you-can-eat buffet."

His tongue was expert against her clit, giving her exactly what she wanted, what she needed, and Goldie gave into it. Her pussy was still spasming lightly from her first orgasm, like butterfly wings, and she longed to have him inside of her but she knew better than to argue. Besides, the wet lap of his tongue was too good to resist and she spread wider for him on the counter, opening her thighs and pulling her knees back.

"Good girl," he murmured approvingly, eyes bright at the sight of her. His tongue moved back and forth at the top of her cleft, teasing her clit, making her shiver, thighs so tense they quivered in his hands. His fingers moved inside her, making her grit her teeth and work toward her climax. She moaned as he crooked his fingers inside of her, rubbing deep. Her pussy felt swollen, hot, his fingers filling her, stretching wide.

Goldie planted her heels on the edge of the counter and lifted her ass to his mouth, eager for more, too greedy for words. Campbell followed her hips, standing to lick her now as her trembling thighs spread wide and she shoved her pussy against his face. She chased her climax from tip to tail, feeling the lash of it first between her legs, rippling outward through the center of her body, curling her toes, her hands clenched in fists at her side.

"Two." Campbell gasped as Goldie collapsed on the counter, her legs dangling off the edge, pussy juices dripping down the crack of her ass to pool on the white surface. She couldn't catch her breath. Her pussy clamped down against his fingers, still inside of her, and she felt a keen longing for his cock.

"Fuck me," she begged, reaching for him. Campbell didn't hesitate this time. The counter was too high, but he used it first, pulling her to the edge and lining her up against the mushroom head of his dick. Then he slid her off onto it, impaling her to the hilt, making her cling, wrapping her arms and legs around him as he carried her like that. He pressed her up against the wall next to the vault, pinning here there and rocking his hips into hers.

"Oh god." She clung to him, burying her face against his neck as he shoved deep into her swollen pussy. She heard him grunt with every thrust, his cock filling her completely, and yet still she wanted more of him. Her fingernails raked his back and she wished for more of his skin, but there wasn't enough time. She bit and sucked at his neck, nibbling at his collarbone, feeling the hard muscles of his ass flexing against her heels as he fucked her.

There was no stopping the next one and she didn't even try. Campbell had her plastered to the wall, his cock driving in, fast and furious, focused on his own pleasure, groaning into her hair, and it was his absolute, abandoned frenzy that pushed her over the edge. Her whole body shuddered as she came with him inside of her, calling out his name and begging him to stop or he was going to tear her apart.

"Three," he growled, holding still, her pussy spasming, dripping down his shaft.

"Please," she pleaded, trying to wriggle out of his arms but he held her fast. "I can't, no more. Let me suck you off."

"No." He let her go, sinking to his knees in front of her, and Goldie cried out as he lifted her thigh over his shoulder, burying his face into her quivering flesh. She looked down, seeing his fist wrapped around his still-wet cock as he ate her, pumping furiously. His eyes were on hers, his mouth fastened to her mound, her clit so sensitive she thought she might faint.

"Campbell, nooooo," she begged, trying to twist away, but he was too strong, insistent. His hands gripped her slender hips, forcing her still against the wall, his tongue focused, relentless. Goldie gripped his arms, feeling the flex of his biceps, her head tipping back, eyes closed, becoming only sensation. There was nothing else in the world except the growing heat between her thighs, the thick lash of Campbell's tongue pushing her to the ends of bliss.

Her pussy began to flutter again, ass clenching, thighs tensed, and Campbell felt her climax coming even though she didn't give him any verbal warning at all. He focused his attention right on her clit, his tongue fluttering fast, a low sound building in his throat. She couldn't hold it back, crying out as she came all over his face, bathing him in her cum.

"Four." Campbell grinned and managed to catch her as she collapsed to her knees in front of him. He held her trembling body in his arms, her breath catching in her throat, soft whimpers lost in the fabric of his shirt, her face buried against his chest.

"I can…" she gasped, barely able to breathe, reaching blindly for his rigid length. "Suck you…"

"No," he insisted again, manipulating her body like hot wax, turning her around and forcing her to her hands and knees in front of him. "I'm going to fuck you until you come again."

She groaned and buried her face in her arms as Campbell buried his cock into her pussy from behind, everything forgotten. She could barely remember her own name let alone the fact that they were in the middle of breaking into a bank in Brazil, that the vault was going to open in less than five minutes. He grabbed her hips and fucked her until she came, just as he'd promised, but he helped things along by reaching underneath to find her throbbing clit, rubbing it into a frenzied heat. And there were little detours along the way.

"Oh fuck," Campbell groaned, slowing the motion of his hips a little and she felt his cock swell inside of her, his first burst of precum a sweet tease. "You feel too good."

Goldie teased him, squeezing the silk walls of her pussy around his cock. He grabbed her thigh with one hand, lifting her leg to expose her to him and she shifted forward with a gasp, her shoulders to the floor. His other hand moved between her legs, manipulating her clit between thumb and forefinger, pulling and tugging at it like a little cock.

"Please," she begged, delirious with lust. She wanted him, all of him, more. "Oh god, baby, please, please!"

"Please what?" Campbell rolled her clit and fucked her into the floor, her body so slick with sweat she slid across the tile with every thrust.

"Make me come," she gasped, pressing her own hand over his between her thighs, rubbing, rubbing.

"Number five?" he asked, rolling his hips in circles, teasing her from the inside out. "Think we can break our record?"

"Yesss!" she hissed, closing her eyes and arching her back. "Do it! Do it, baby! Now!"

He groaned, flicking her clit with his thumb and sending her into the stratosphere, his cock pounding into her from behind and she knew he must be close but she couldn't focus on that. She was coming again—again!—for the fifth time in twenty minutes, her body so spent she was unable to do much more but twitch and moan as the sweet waves rolled through.

"Five," Campbell announced sounding both proud and pained as Goldie collapsed to the floor, her knees giving out completely. He curled himself around her, spreading her thighs with his as he gave one final, deep thrust, bottoming out and filling her with fast, hot, shuddering bursts of his cum. Goldie bit her lip as he spent himself, his cock throbbing thickly between her thighs.

"Time's up." Campbell gasped, looking up as the light above their heads went to green and something deep inside the vault unlocked.

"How long before the cops get here?" Goldie was unsteady on her feet as she pulled her catsuit back on, slipping into her stealth boots—black, flat-soled, they fit like a second skin and allowed her to walk softly anywhere she went.

"Right about…" Campbell consulted his iPhone, running a hand through his disheveled hair. His jeans were already done up, his shirt tucked in. "Now."

"Polícia!" The door burst open down the hall and Goldie's heart jumped in her chest. "Coloc suas armas e saia com suas mãos acima!"

She sighed, looking back over her shoulder at the vault as she picked her knit cap up from the floor, dusting it off. "Don't we even get to open it?"

They both heard another voice, "Batente! Batente!"—the Portugeuse word for "stop." It was the bank manager, the one who had hired them to test the bank's security system, telling the police to stand down.

Campbell leaned against the counter, waiting for them all to rush in. He loved that part. "I'm sure, since we cracked their safe, Mr. Bank Manager will let us see what's inside."

"I should hope so." Goldie buckled her toolbelt, grinning at him. "That's half the fun."

* * * *

The Behr brothers had impossible standards and they liked to test them. That's why they'd hired Richard Campbell in the first place and he knew it. So when they called him into the eldest brother's office—they always used Rolf's office with its oversized leather chairs and sofas, as if the furniture itself might make him, or anyone else they were dressing down, feel diminutive in their presence—Campbell wasn't surprised at all.

"You've been our head of security for three years, Mr. Campbell."

He gave the youngest Behr brother a brief nod of acknowledgment. Wilhelm was the spokesman of the three, always the bearer of bad news, and he did so with a measure of glee Campbell found unsettling.

"In that time, we have had exactly one breach in security." Wilhelm held up a finger, eyes narrowed, glittering even in the low light. Campbell waited. He knew it didn't matter that he'd provided them with one thousand and ninety-four days of invulnerability—it was just one day that mattered, the day their bubble of safety had popped. He'd been selling in this business long enough to know the psychology of it. Safety was an illusion the human ego clung to with voracious tenacity, and people like the Behr brothers were arrogant enough to have faith in it like small children believed in Santa Claus and the Tooth Fairy.

"To be fair, it was a minor breach," Campbell pointed out. "The hacker found a back door in the system. We've isolated and eliminated it."

"That may be." Wilhelm shrugged. "But it certainly does make us concerned about other potential back doors."

"Real ones." Otto, the middle Behr brother, piped up. He was always getting in the middle, the mediator. "Mr. Campbell, you came highly recommended and so far, you have proven to be everything you were purported to be. However, given this latest snafu, we thought it might be good to run a little test."

"A test?" Campbell braced himself.

"You have a competitor." Rolf spoke up, turning away from the window he'd been standing in front of. "I assume you've heard of Saul Lax?"

Campbell's jaw tightened. "You know I have."

"Until he retired, he was the best in the business," Otto interrupted, looking between his older brother and his younger one. They all had strong German jaw lines and Aryan features—blonde with ice blue eyes. "His company served our family for generations."

"I'm aware," Campbell acknowledged.

"You only received this job because of he got out of the business," Wilhelm reminded him and Campbell gave him another brief nod. He'd found it best not to supply the youngest Behr brother with too much feedback or information. He liked to use it as ammunition.

"But we hear his granddaughter has opened Saul's business doors again." Otto sat forward in his over-sized chair.

"Is she any good?" Campbell asked.

Wilhelm looked at him over tented fingers. "We're going to find out."

"What are you proposing?"

"A test." Rolf crossed his arms over his chest. "You have assured us that our most prize possessions are secure. Our systems are impenetrable."

Campbell gritted his teeth. "They are."

"So then you have nothing to lose," Wilhelm piped up.

"Are you proposing a wager?" Campbell walked right into the trap.

"Just so." Rolf nodded. "If Ms. Lax fails in her endeavor, things will go on as they have been."

Wilhelm leaned forward, grinning, hands gripping the arms of his chair. "However, if she succeeds, we will hire her as our new head of security instead."

Campbell considered the proposition, as if he had some sort of decision to make. Clearly, they had already made up their minds. The Behr brothers weren't just wealthy, they were ghastly rich, and their estates spanned the globe. Besides this one, there were two in California, one in Texas, three in Florida, four in New York, thirteen total in Europe, and one in Asia. That didn't count the businesses, which were more numerous still.

"That's quite a wager."

Wilhelm giggled. It was a throaty, gleeful sound, and it made Campbell want to punch him and break his round little glasses. "You've assured us that you're up to the challenge."

"I am," he snapped. "Have you engaged her services? How do you know she even wants the job?"

Otto smiled. "Her family has worked for ours for generations, Mr. Campbell. I'm surprised she hasn't already yet approached us for your job."

"So..." Campbell spread his hands wide, giving in. "Where? When?"

Rolf laughed deeply from his barrel chest, shaking his head. "Ah, Mr. Campbell, we can't tell you that. It wouldn't be a very accurate test of your abilities then, would it?"

"Fair enough." Campbell straightened, looking between the three of them. "Is that all, gentlemen?"

Rolf gave him a nod, dismissing him with a wave of his hand and looking back out the window. Campbell swallowed his rage, turning to go.

"For what it's worth," Otto called as Campbell opened the door. "I hope you win."

Campbell glanced back and smiled grimly. "So do I."

* * * *

"He'll be glad to see you." Jenny, the aide at the front desk, smiled and waved as Goldie passed carrying a bunch of freshly picked lilacs.

"Do you have a vase?" Goldie stopped at the desk, holding up the flowers. "I saw them in a field on the way here and had to stop. I thought, you know, my grandmother loved lilacs so much, and he used to cut some for her every spring. Maybe it will help him remember..."

"I'll find something for you." Jenny was young, just out of high school, and wore far too much makeup, but she was a sweet girl and really seemed to care about the patients. Goldie liked her. "They just finished lunch. He's out on the back porch."

"Thanks." Goldie flashed her a grateful smile and pushed open the double doors. They were locked from the inside, and when her grandfather was lucid, he called himself an inmate, not a patient, and the nurses and health care aides wardens. A life lived picking locks had left him seeing everything as a prison.

She found him, as promised, on a patio they called "the back porch." The ratio was one aide to every three patients, so her grandfather was lined up next to two other people in their wheelchairs, brakes locked, all of them just sitting, as if waiting for something to happen. One of them was a woman, her hair in a long, thin white braid down her back. The other was a man much younger than her grandfather and much less mobile. His multiple sclerosis had left him unable to move his limbs or control his bowels and she could smell him even in the fresh outdoor air.

The aide was reading a magazine and when the doors to the patio opened, she folded her issue of *People* and tucked it under her. "Here to see your grandfather?" the woman asked, shading her eyes against the sun as she looked up at Goldie.

This aide was older, middle-aged, with crow's feet around her eyes and a broad, red lipsticked smile. Goldie couldn't remember her name. She hadn't been around long, and unfortunately the turnover for health care aides was enormous. Goldie didn't like this one much—too negligent, as far as she was concerned—although she was better than some. Even if she didn't know them, all the aides knew her. Goldie came every Sunday to visit for a few hours, usually in the afternoon because her grandfather seemed a little more aware between lunch and dinner.

Goldie wrinkled her nose as she got near her grandfather's chair—the smell of the man sitting in his own elimination beside him was overpowering—and grasped the handles. "I'm going to take him for a walk. Do you mind?"

"Go right ahead." The woman smiled, standing to look busy, tucking a blanket around the old woman's legs. She didn't even look up. "Oh goodness. Mr. Benedict needs some attending to, doesn't he?"

Goldie made a face behind the aide's back as she unlocked Mr. Benedict's chair brake and began to wheel him backward, turning him around to head inside. Who knew how long the poor man would have sat there like that if Goldie hadn't arrived? She didn't want to think about it.

"Hey Poppy." She squatted down in the space left by Mr. Benedict's chair, between the old woman and her grandfather. He was dozing, his chin to his chest, snoring lightly, the breeze blowing wispy strands of the white hair that was left above his ears. She couldn't see any resemblance anymore to her own father, although everyone said and pictures confirmed that the two could have been twins in their youth with their blond hair and blue eyes and imposing height.

"Poppy?" She nudged the old man's knee gently with her forearm, not wanting to jolt him too much. He snorted, snoring momentarily louder, and then lifted his head, staring at her with rheumy blue eyes that looked right through her. For a moment she thought it was going to be a bad one, one of those days when he called her Raisa and mistook her for her grandmother, but then his gaze shifted to the lilacs and his eyes focused and he smiled.

"Spring already?" His voice was hoarse. "How long did I sleep?"

"A hundred years." She returned his smile, putting the lilacs on his lap. He fingered their stems as she stood, taking a step behind him and pushing his chair off the patio and onto the concrete path. It was a nice facility, her father had made sure of that, with an acre of rolling, manicured lawn and private rooms but she still felt the institutionalization of the place, no matter how nicely they trimmed the hedges.

"How's your father?" Poppy inquired, glancing over his shoulder at her.

The pain twanged like a guitar string wound too tightly in her chest. "He's dead, Poppy," she reminded him gently. "Remember? Three years ago—a heart attack."

She didn't envy Poppy. He'd outlived them all. Not just his wife—Goldie's grandmother had died over ten years ago, a few days after Goldie's sixteenth birthday—but his children too. When no parent should ever have to bury a child, he'd buried three. His only daughter he'd buried as an infant, back when SIDS was called crib death. That had been her namesake, Golda Sisel Lax, a family name passed on, that of her great-grandmother. That particular Goldie, Poppy's mother, had been in a concentration camp with him. He'd told her the stories many times, although they all ran together these days, about how his mother had died.

Poppy had asked his son to pass the name down and so she had become Golda Sisel too—Goldie for short—upon her birth. But Poppy had no other grandchildren to pass any other names on to, because he'd buried his other son, dead of an overdose in his twenties. Goldie was his only heir once her father, Saul Lax, Poppy's last remaining son, had died in his kitchen at the ripe old age of fifty-seven. She had been there at the time, helping him recover after knee surgery, and she would probably always wonder if he'd still be alive if he hadn't stubbornly insisted on getting up to fetch a soda from the kitchen himself while she was in the shower.

She remembered the whole thing, although she didn't let herself think about it often—calling 911, doing CPR, willing him to breathe, *breathe*, worried she was hurting him as she locked her elbows and did chest compressions, knowing already that this was one safe she couldn't crack, one lock that wasn't going to be undone. He was gone and she was all alone in the world, except for Poppy.

"How's business?" Poppy inquired as she rolled him along. The day was bright and fine, the air redolent with freshly cut grass.

"It's good," she assured him, not wanting to say much more. Goldie's father had been the only one interested in the family locksmith business, continuing on in his father's footsteps before him. Poppy claimed Saul was better at it than even he had been, although she had worked with the old man in her teens and thought, perhaps, he was being generous to his only son. Saul had been good—very good—but the ability to crack a safe with just the senses had skipped a generation from

Poppy to Goldie herself. "I just came back from a job in Brazil. I'm consulting all over the world."

She parked the wheelchair near a bench and took a seat across from her grandfather, who looked at her fondly, his withered chest puffed with pride. She liked telling him about the work, knowing how much he missed it, at least on the days he was lucid, and there were precious few people she could share the experience with.

"Do you remember the Ursas you told me about, Poppy?" She saw the old man's eyes light up with a fire she rarely saw in him anymore and knew he did. "I'm going to get them back."

"How?" His eyes narrowed and he looked at her shrewdly. His mind was working just fine today, she thought.

She shrugged, unable to conceal a smile. "I have a plan."

"Goldie." He reached a hand out to touch her arm, his skin as thin and soft as tissue paper, the veins on the back of his hand a blue roadmap. "Don't you do anything to get in trouble. You're all I've got left."

"Have you ever been to Brazil?" she asked, changing the subject. "It's like this all the time. Lovely weather. I think you'd like it."

He eyed her, skeptic. "Is that so?"

"Oh, Poppy, I didn't tell you." She patted his hand, still smiling. "I found out about your friend, the one you told me about."

He sat back in his wheelchair, frowning. "Daniel?"

"He's still alive," she assured him, seeing the anxiety on his face. "Still living in Europe. Want to know how he's doing?"

"Probably same as me." Poppy grinned, his teeth yellow and small. "Everything hurts—and if it don't hurt, it don't work."

She laughed. "I talked to him on the phone. He's a very nice man."

"Did you?" He blinked at her.

"He's working as a museum curator," she told him. "At seventy-four. Can you believe it?"

"He's just a young pup." Poppy's gaze went far away and she knew he must be remembering.

"His son, Jakob, mostly runs it for him," Goldie explained. "But Daniel is still very much involved."

"He named his son Jakob?" The sad look in Poppy's eyes made her want to hug him, and it made her miss her father, which she knew he was doing too. "And did he tell you about the Ursas?"

Goldie nodded, her face grim. "He told me the whole story."

"Here you are!" The aid from the front desk had found them and Goldie startled. "I found a vase for those flowers."

The aide held up the vase as proof, smiling.

Poppy looked down at the flowers in his lap. They'd both forgotten them. "Your grandmother loved lilacs."

"I remember." Goldie nodded. Her own mother had walked out on them when she was just a baby, but her grandmother had tried to make up for that and had mostly succeeded.

"He's having a good day," Jenny whispered, nodding at Poppy like he couldn't hear her.

Goldie nodded again, reaching for her pocket as her cell phone rang. When she saw the Caller ID, her heart nearly stopped.

"I have to take this," she said to Jenny. "Can you take Poppy back to his room?" She put her hand on his shoulder, squeezing, and leaned down to tell him, "I'll be there in a minute, Poppy. I have to take this call."

He patted her hand and she stepped back to let the aide push him down the path, watching as they walked away, Jenny already chatting. "Let's go for a walk, Mr. Lax! Those flowers are so pretty. I love lilacs. We're going to have to get them into some water…"

Goldie answered her phone. "Hello?"

"Goldie Lax?"

She blinked up at the sky, her heart in her mouth, not sure she could answer. "Yes."

"My name is Otto Behr. I have a job for you."

She'd been waiting for this call—not just today, or this week—she'd been waiting for this for years, ever since Poppy had told her the story about Jakob and his son, Daniel.

She did very little talking and a great deal of listening to Otto Behr. By the time the call ended and she walked back to Poppy's room, she found him sleeping in his chair by the window. Not wanting to disturb him, she leaned over and kissed his forehead, deciding to tell him all about it later, when she could show him instead. Then, she moved the vase of flowers from the windowsill to his night table so he would see them first thing when he woke, and left.

* * * *

Campbell hated having to find time for her, stolen nights in hotels—sometimes in motels that charged by the hour. What he wanted was all the time in the world, every minute of every day, endless hours with nothing to do but spend time together. He watched her sleeping, her golden hair spilling around her shoulders and over her breasts, the sheet pulled up to her waist. They rarely spent whole nights together, but this was an anniversary and he'd insisted.

He slid into bed behind her, spooning. She wasn't wearing anything at all—most of her clothes were still in a heap by the door, along with his—and he loved the feel of her skin, like silk, against his. She shifted against him in her sleep, half-smiling, and he hoped she was dreaming about the three hours they'd spent in every possible position from the bathroom to the Jacuzzi tub to the bed to, yes, even the little hotel desk. He liked to cover all his bases.

Goldie murmured something, wiggling, and Campbell felt his cock stir. He smiled as he saw her hand working against the sheet. She was actually turning combinations in her sleep, not dreaming about him after all, but about cracking some safe. He chuckled to himself, deciding to give her something else to do with her hands.

"Baby," he whispered, wedging his cock against the crack of her ass. That made it quite stiff. "It's already open. You got your prize."

"Mmm," she murmured, reaching a hand back and clutching his hip. "I did," she agreed. "It was the best prize ever."

"But there's more where that came from."

She groaned, shaking her head and hiding her face in the pillow. "I don't think I have any fluids left in me."

"Don't make me go watch porn," Campbell teased, sliding a hand over her hip.

She laughed. "You have to pay extra for that."

"I think we used your credit card for the room," he mused, moving his hand down her belly, dipping a finger into her navel.

"I saw Poppy today." She wiggled around to face him, putting her arms around his neck, and the shock of her little breasts, nipples pressed into his chest, made his cock dance against her bare thigh.

"Don't try to change the subject," he warned, sliding a leg between hers, feeling the sweet slide of her pussy against his skin. "Besides, I know for a fact, he's got a crush on that Jenny."

"Campbell!" She protested, laughing, as he kissed her neck and shoulders, working his way slowly down to her breasts.

"I don't blame him." God he loved her breasts, so little and pert. Her nipples got hard as he licked and blew on them. He watched the skin around them pucker, delighted. "She's cute."

"Campbell!"

He lifted his head to look at her, seeing her smile. "Hey, did I say happy anniversary?"

"A few hundred times…" She ran a hand through his hair, eyes still sleepy and half-closed. "And if orgasms count, then… six more after that?"

He grinned. "Orgasms definitely count."

"Well then I owe you a few," she murmured, sliding her hand down over his chest, tweaking his nipple. That made his cock throb against her hip and he gasped as she grabbed it, tugging.

"Oh god. I'll never catch up," he protested, letting her roll him to his back.

She looked up from where she settled herself between his thighs, rubbing his cock against her cheek, her lips, teasing. "Remember the first time we did this?"

"Five years and I still can't think about any other woman." He smiled, watching her tongue sneak out, trailing around the head of his cock. That first lick was always pure heaven. He shivered.

"You were thinking about Jenny," she reminded him and then sucked the tip into the hot, wet cavern of her mouth, using her tongue underneath, making his hips move.

"Jenny who?" he gasped.

She grinned. "Right answer."

"Shhh, keep your mouth on it." He pressed her head back down, gently forcing himself deeper, hearing her gag, knowing she loved it—which just made it all the more exciting. He slowly fucked her mouth that way, his eyes never leaving hers. Okay, so occasionally he let himself focus on the way his shaft disappeared between her lips, how red her mouth got when she sucked him, but if he did that too much, he was going to come. And he didn't want to come, not for a long, long time. He wanted to spend all night doing this, until both of them were so dry they had to crawl to the sink to rehydrate.

He couldn't believe he still wanted her this much after five years. Every committed guy he'd talked to, from his friends to his brother, claimed to be looking at other women by year five. Some after just a year. But they'd had two before they had started living this way, separate yet together, not daring to meet at her place or at his, and even then he hadn't been thinking about anyone else. Although sometimes he wondered if it was this sort of having-an-affair-like existence that made things so hot.

"Play with yourself," he whispered, but she already was, her fingers moving wetly between her pussy lips. Just the sound made him hungry. He could still taste her in his mouth from earlier and the memory of her pussy grinding on his face almost sent him over. He grabbed her hair, pulling her slowly off his cock.

"Feel good?" His gaze moved between her thighs, her hand rubbing furiously. She nodded, panting. "Show me."

She knelt up, using two fingers to spread her lips for him and he could see her clit clearly as she pulled the skin back. He couldn't help himself. He grabbed her hips, lifting her easily in his hands—she was slender, with hips like a boy, and he could move her around any which way he liked, tossing her around, which they both loved—and brought her pussy to his face.

"Oh god," she whispered, her hand moving through his hair. "Oh yes…yes…"

"Show me," he said again and she obeyed, using both hands to spread her pussy wide for him. He loved the way she looked, the sounds she made, the way she tasted. His tongue probed between her lips, finding her clit and teasing it with his tongue. She swayed back, arching, her little breasts just buds on her chest, her pink nipples pointing to the wall behind his head. He swallowed the taste of her, tang and musk, and went back in for more, using his tongue like a spoon to lap at her slit.

"Oh baby," she moaned, rocking her hips, grinding, finding his tongue with her clit. "Please, please. Make me come!"

He focused there, lashing back and forth, arms wrapped around her slim hips, feeling the first shudders rocking through her, watching the taut pull of her belly. She was coming, tugging at her own nipples as she rocked her pussy against his face, her moan building to nearly a scream. She would have collapsed if the wall hadn't been there. Instead she leaned her arms against the headboard, breathing hard, her thighs trembling on either side of his ears. He didn't think his cock could get any harder.

"Suck me," he growled and although she groaned in protest, she turned around on him, taking his cock with the wet pull of her mouth, making his toes curl with pleasure. He couldn't get enough of her, wrapping his arms around her hips again and pulling her pussy to his mouth. She squealed and squirmed, but eventually relented, letting him devour her. Her lips were swollen, the nub of her clit sensitive, and he spent time sucking on her labia, his fingers playing around her hole but not fucking her—not yet, not until she begged him. Which came a lot sooner than he expected.

"Please," she moaned around his cock, the sensation of her tongue moving over the head making him grit his teeth. "Oh god, don't tease me, please, put them in me."

"My fingers?" He stroked her slit, wiggling them around her hole.

"Yes!" She gave his cock a long, hard suck and he shuddered, his balls tightening another notch. "You know I love it hard."

"Like this?" Her pussy was like velvet inside, the walls smooth. He stretched her with another finger, feeling her thighs tense. "One more?" He slow gently slid a third in, making her whimper, and then started to fuck her nice and slow.

"Oh, oh, oh," she cried, moving back against his hand. "Noooo, no, hard! Hard! Harder!"

He did as she asked, plunging his fingers in deep, fastened his mouth over her clit and waiting for her climax, all the while fighting his own. Thankfully she'd forgotten about his cock, her fist wrapped tight around it, her face buried in the crook of his thigh as he fingered her to orgasm.

"Now!" She moaned, fucking back hard, threatening to shove his whole hand in as her pussy clamped down around his fingers. He was grateful she had hold of his cock, squeezing hard, because he would have come right then if she hadn't.

"Oh god," she whispered, rolling off him onto the bed. "No more. Oh no more."

"Yes more," he insisted, moving up to his knees and plunging his hand, still wet with her juices, back into her pussy. She shook her head, trying to push him out, but he didn't let her, keeping his fingers deep inside, catching a rhythm.

"Oh! Fuck!" She tried to roll but he pressed his palm flat to her belly, pinning her to the bed. Instead, she grabbed his cock, knowing it would distract him, and it did, oh Christ, the way she pumped him in her hand made him want to shoot all over her little tits.

"Don't make me," she begged, biting her lip. "I can't. No more!"

It just drove him crazy to hear her say that. Maybe she knew it, he wasn't sure, but he fingered her faster, harder, using his thumb against her clit.

"Noooo!" she panted, thrusting up now, following his rhythm, her eyes squeezed shut, pulling her own knees back so he could get deeper access. She was so fucking beautiful he could barely stand it. "Ohhhhhhh! No! No! Yessss!"

He smiled, watching her come again, feeling the wet suck of her pussy around his fingers, her little asshole clenching with every spasm. For a minute he felt like he was going to pass out just seeing that, the hot pucker of her rosebud opening and closing gently with her climax.

"Fuck me," she insisted, her voice throaty, reaching for him.

He gave her what she wanted, but he flipped her onto her belly first. He wanted to see her little asshole while he fucked her. Goldie spread for him, arching her back and lifting her bottom in the air. His cock slid in easily and he groaned at the sensation, so good, *too* good. He let out a slow breath, bottoming out and looking down to see his cock going into her, his gaze moving up to the slight curve at her waist.

He couldn't help it—his wet his finger, licking her juices off his hand, and pressed it against the tight pucker of her ass. She protested, whimpering, as he knew she would, but just feeling her sphincter clench gave his cock a jolt.

"Campbell, please," she begged, looking over her shoulder at him.

"Please what?" He slipped his wet finger in, just up to the first knuckle, feeling her tense. She buried her face in her arms and cried out, shaking her head. "What are you gonna let me crack this, hm?"

She gave a muffled moan as he dared a little more, wiggling his finger in deeper. "Okay!"

Everything in him stopped. He stared at her flushed cheeks, her hair clouded around them, her lips wet and red from biting them, and was sure he'd just heard her wrong.

"Okay?"

"Yes," she breathed, pushing back against his finger. His cock felt electrified inside her pussy and he swallowed hard. "I packed KY. It's in my bag."

He didn't need to be told twice. Besides, he was too worried she might change her mind. He lubed himself up nicely, not spending too long stroking though—he was far too close to coming for that. It would probably be two strokes in her ass before he came as it was.

"Are you ready?" he asked, dribbling KY down the crack of her ass and pressing the head of his cock against her asshole.

"Easy!" She tensed the moment she felt him there. "Oh god, it's so big! Campbell!"

"Sorry," he apologized, although he was grinning. What guy didn't like to hear that? "I'll go slow."

"You better," she panted, closing her eyes and gripping the hotel comforter in her fists.

"Just try to relax," he murmured, biting his lip and watching as the mushroom head of his cock disappeared slowly under the ring of her sphincter. Goldie didn't cry out. She didn't even move. She just breathed, slow and even, nostrils flaring, her lower lip drawn between her teeth.

"Oh god." Campbell felt his cock slip under that ring of muscle, the feeling so good he could barely stand it. His instinct was to fuck her fast and hard, to bury himself into her, but he resisted, adjusting himself between her thighs and easing in a little more.

"Is it in?" she cried, feeling him move.

"Almost," he assured her, judging that he was about a quarter of the way there. Maybe it was like a Band-Aid and if you did it fast, it hurt less? He grabbed her hips and gave into it, shoving his cock deep into her ass.

"Ohhhh!" Goldie reached back with one hand, trying to push him out, but he was in now, buried to the hilt. The heat of her was almost too much and seeing her asshole stretched to accommodate him made him crazy with lust. He closed his eyes, the sight alone enough to send him over.

"Are you okay?" he panted, realizing he was gripping her hips hard enough to leave bruises.

"Yes," she breathed, and he felt her move. His cock came to life as she slid him slowly out and then wiggled back into the saddle of his hips.

Campbell groaned, knowing it was over and he'd barely begun to fuck her ass. "Fuck! Baby!"

"You like that?" she teased, rocking back, that tight ring of muscle massaging his cock with every pass. "You like fucking my asshole?"

"Oh Jesus." He was a goner. Grabbing her hips, he gave it everything he had, pounding into her ass, making her squeal. The cum had reaching a boiling point in his balls and there was no going back now. "Oh yeah! Baby, I'm gonna come in your ass!"

She cried out with him as he came, every hot burst of his cum a new geyser of pleasure filling that humid hole. His whole body shook and it felt like it was never going to end, every burst of cum another jolt of sensation, sending him howling down into her on the bed with all his weight, writhing on top of her in total abandon.

When he remembered where he was, he rolled off her panting body, apologizing, but she was already wrapping herself up in his arms, cooing and purring like Goldie always did after sex, whispering how much she loved him, how much she wanted him. He closed his eyes, smiling, just soaking her in. They didn't have enough time like this, but with a woman like Goldie, there wouldn't be enough time in the day.

"Campbell?"

"Hm?"

"How did you know it would be the Ursas?"

He smiled. "We're not allowed to talk business."

"But you were right. That's what they want me to steal. The Ursa diamonds."

"Of course I'm right." He pulled the edge of the hotel comforter over them, not wanting to think about how many other people had done this very thing on these covers. "I'm always right."

"You're so humble."

He laughed. "I try."

"It's almost over," she whispered, touching her fingertip to his lips. "We're almost there."

He felt the excitement of her words in his belly. She was right. Years of planning, building trust, getting the Behrs to move the Ursa diamonds from their estate in Zurich to this one in Colorado, hours of hacking, creating backdoors in the system that even his own tech guys couldn't find. It was all coming together.

"And then you can marry me," she teased, nibbling gently at his nipple.

"Hey!" He laughed, twisting away. "Who says I'm marrying you?"

"Poppy says if you don't marry me, he's going to come after you with a shotgun."

He snorted. "I'd like to see that—an eighty year old man chasing me down in a wheelchair."

"I love you, Campbell."

He kissed her forehead, stroking her hair, and he knew she was waiting for him to say it, but in five years, he never had. God knew, he certainly felt it, but somehow the words always got stuck in his throat. After a while, he heard the deep, even sound of her breathing and closed his eyes and slept too.

* * * *

It's as easy as one-two-three. Goldie used the application on Campbell's iPhone to disable the security cameras around the Behr estate. They weren't disabled, per se—Campbell had explained the feed would be replaced with a dummy one for fifteen minutes—but by then she'd have what she needed and be gone. The wall around the estate was ten feet high, but she was over it in no time, repelling down the other side and dropping in behind a cluster of trees.

The back part of the estate was well lit, but without outside flood lights it was impossible to illuminate an entire area. Goldie stuck to the shadows and made her way to the side of the house, using Campbell's iPhone again to disable the alarm to the doorwall. He had it figured to allow her time to get in without causing undue attention at the main security station. According to Campbell, there was only one guy on duty at night, but it was always better safe than sorry.

She had studied the floor plan extensively. Most people didn't know that the entire floor plan of their house was usually accessible online—you just had to know where to look. In this case, it was public knowledge, because the Behr estate was also an historical home, registered with the state. She used her glass cutter to create a perfect circle and a suction cup to remove it, setting the glass aside and slithering through the hole onto the tile.

If she'd been a regular burglar, she would have entered through a door, probably into a main room, and started rifling through drawers, hunting for bedrooms. The Behr's were smart, she knew, and left cash accessible in those places, just as she did, on Campbell's advice. Most thieves were looking to score hot and fast—and if they found cash right away, they were less likely to go looking for more, since time was always a factor. The real valuables were usually safe from regular burglars in those instances.

Of course, if she'd been a regular burglar, she would have already been caught.

Even if Campbell hadn't already told her, she would have known where to look for the safe. Most people put them in walls or floors in their bedroom, which was always a good place to start. A safe, especially one that wasn't bolted down, was a thief magnet. Of course, with Goldie's talent, the safe didn't need to be bolted down, it just needed to be accessible. This one wasn't. The safe itself was through the indoor pool room, in the sauna, behind a door that was accessible only with a combination lock hidden behind a panel that looked, for all intents and purposes, like a breaker box. It was also set with an alarm she had to disable through Campbell's iPhone.

Goldie then got to work on the combination, her real talent, lining up the contact points in less than a minute. The lock opened a small door with a keypad inside. She could have played around with that forever but instead she shined a black light on it, revealing the last four digits touched. There were then only sixteen possibilities. She found the correct one after four tries. The keypad electronically opened a door to her right without any handle, almost seamlessly set into the wall.

She pried it open, slipping in, the cool metal inside a relief from the heat of the sauna, the room automatically lit when the door opened. It was a vault, the door behind it 10 gauge steel, two pieces of 5/8 fireboard in between, with a 3/8 inch steel plate door. The vault could be used as a panic room—the red lever on the door inside was a lock and release. There was a remote re-locker on this door, she noted. The hammer would have dropped if she'd tried to drill it. Of course, you would have had to know the door was there in the first place, which most thieves never would have guessed.

Thanks to Campbell, she knew exactly where to go. Almost done now—just a little more work. Behind her on the wall was a row of boxes, similar to safe deposit boxes, except they all had combination locks instead of keys. A smaller combination lock was always harder to crack than the big ones. Their contact points were tiny, the variations in the system small. This was going to be a real challenge.

Goldie found the right box—they were numbered like safe deposit boxes as well, and she noted the number she was looking for with not a little irony: 102398. It was the same as the one on Daniel's arm. He'd shown it to her himself when she went to Europe last May, rolling up his sleeve to reveal the faded blue numbers tattooed into his wrinkled skin. He had survived the concentration camp and for some reason the Behr brothers had used his tattoo number rather than his father, Jakob's. She glanced at the other boxes, noting that they, too, had similar numbers, non-sequential. Did that mean what she thought it did? Were those tattoo numbers?

She didn't want to think about that. It was bad enough imagining her grandfather in one of those concentration camps, how he'd seen his whole family die, either from disease or starvation or, in the case of his mother, a bullet to the head. He'd been a young man then, just twenty-one, strong and virile and, thankfully, useful. Once they had found out he was a locksmith, he'd been employed immediately to crack all of the Jewish safes collected during the war.

"Thousands of them," he'd told her, looking both excited and horrified at once. She knew. She loved cracking a safe, loved the feeling it gave her, no matter what the reason, whether she was there to help a bank fortify its security system, or in this case, to steal something outright. It didn't matter—cracking was cracking.

And then one day he'd told her about Jakob—his friend, his fellow locksmith, the one who had discovered, among those thousands of metal safes, his own family's valuables. There had been three priceless jewels in Jakob's father's collection—

Ursa Major, Ursa Minor and Ursa Median—all blue diamonds of very rare quality. Jakob had found those diamonds and, instead of handing them over with the other contents of the safe—his parent's marriage license, the now useless deed to their house in Sundern, other cash and jewels—he had swallowed those diamonds instead, all three of them. And he had kept swallowing them. For three months Jakob swallowed them until, according to Poppy, one of the guards had discovered his secret.

Goldie found the combination to the box in less than three minutes. She opened it and almost laughed. When she was about eight, she had wanted a little porcelain figurine she saw sitting in the drugstore window, a pretty ballerina. She told her father every time they passed how much she loved it. That year for her birthday, she received a gift in a box so big that she nearly burst into tears—her doll was far too small for a container so large. Her father just stood there and grinned, watching her unwrap the thing with a trembling lower lip, to find another wrapped box inside. And then another. And then another. Until finally she unwrapped a tiny box revealing the doll she'd wanted all along.

Instead of opening the safe door to reveal the jewels—there was another door instead, another combination lock. Campbell hadn't told her about that, but she was sure he probably didn't even know. He could bypass security cameras and alarm systems, figure out digital keypads and get his hands on the blueprints of the house, but a combination lock was always a problem. Drilling a safe like this could easily destroy the contents, or trigger a secondary locking mechanism that would make it impossible to open. The only way in would be to know the combination, and those were kept secret, even from the Behr brother's head of security.

Goldie went to work again, thinking about the jewels inside, about who they really belonged to. Poppy's story about Jakob had touched her deeply. The man had sacrificed everything to keep them in his family and had ultimately failed. The hasty German bullet to Jakob's head had rendered the natural waiting for the diamonds impossible, so they had instead been surgically removed. The German officer who had shot the young locksmith had laid claim to the jewels and had been allowed to keep them.

"Still have them today," Poppy had told her bitterly. "The Behrs own more Jewish wealth than any German family from the war. They stole it all from those safes. Those diamonds belonged to Jakob, something he could pass down to his son."

Jakob's young son, Daniel, was his only remaining heir, and had survived the concentration camps, Goldie had discovered. Her trip to Europe had proved quite informative.

"Wait…" Goldie had interrupted him, making a connection. "The Behr brothers. They're one of dad's clients."

Poppy had nodded, looking at her with that same shameful face she'd seen when he told her about cracking Nazi safes. The Behrs were rich. The Behr brothers, grandsons of the man who had ordered Daniel cut open to get the jewels from his intestines, paid very well.

They're finally going to pay up today, Goldie thought, hearing the satisfying click of the second combination lock, swinging the little door open—only to find another door, yet another combination. She swore, shaking her head in disbelief.

Three jewels, three locks. There was something apropos about it, she supposed, going to work on the third combination. Campbell wouldn't believe it when she told him. He'd gotten hired as their head of security, had earned the Behr brothers' trust, had planned this operation down to every last detail he could manage, but he never would have anticipated three combination locks on the box.

It's a good thing I have magic hands, Goldie thought, focusing on lining up the last gate under the fence, feeling the subtle shift with her fingers when she found it. She pulled the latch and the door opened. She almost expected yet another door and lock, but instead found a blue velvet drawstring bag. Pulling it out, she opened it up and peered inside, seeing a faint glint in the light.

Carefully, she turned her palm face up and gently shook the bag, spilling three diamonds into her hand—Ursa Major, Ursa Minor and Ursa Median. They were beautiful, three round cut gems ready for setting in three graduated sizes. The big one had to be as large as the Hope diamond, forty-five, maybe even fifty carats. Poppy couldn't remember their weights to tell her, but he'd been a locksmith, not a jeweler. She knew from talking with Jakob's son, Daniel, that they were beyond priceless. In fact, they were worth so much money it left her breathless just to touch them.

Glancing at her watch, she saw that only ten minutes had passed since she had climbed the Behr's fence. She slipped the jewels back into their velvet bag and secured it deep into one of her catsuit pockets. Then she closed all three combination lock doors and slipped back through the vault door into the sauna, shutting it quietly behind her. The pool gave a queer aqua glow, lit from inside, and she edged around it, heading for the doorwall she'd entered through. Back out the hole she'd made with the glass cutter, through the grass, over the wall, and she would be home-free.

She made it through the door and was squatting by the side of the house, surveying the lawn, when she heard the voice, distant, but still far too close for comfort.

"Right here at the fence."

Goldie froze, hearing the words and knowing immediately what they meant. She could have pulled her ropes up, probably should have, but fifteen minutes was such a short time and leaving them saved her time on the way out. She slipped behind one of the shrubs next to the house and strained to hear the voices—were they inside or outside the wall?

"I'm Richard Campbell, head of security. Can I help you, officer?"

Goldie breathed a sigh of relief when she heard Campbell's voice and took the opportunity to slip around the side of the house, heading toward the front. There was only one way out now that she didn't have the equipment to climb the wall and she prayed she could get there before the security cameras went back to their real-time feed. She pulled Campbell's phone from her pocket to check and saw the countdown timer gave her four minutes to get to the front gate. She would have made it over the back wall easily, of course, but that's where Campbell and their unexpected police visitor were talking.

She had to hurry. She took off, a black streak in the night, her golden hair covered and tucked under a black cap, hoping no one was watching, that all their focus and attention was now on the back of the house. When she reached the front gate she was breathing hard, a stitch in her side, only to discover that the security here wasn't the keypad she'd hoped, but rather sliding card access—and she didn't have a card.

Thankfully, there was no guard posted, but according to her iPhone timer, she had less than thirty seconds before the security cameras went back to a live feed and she'd be fully visible on them. She looked at the phone, considering placing a call to Campbell, and then at the gate, steel bars rising up in the darkness against a black diamond-studded sky. There was no way over them.

But maybe through *them...*

Goldie turned herself sideways and slipped a leg through the gate. Her thigh cleared it without too much trouble, but she stuck solidly at her hips. She couldn't guess how much width there was between bars, but it was certainly less than a foot. There was no way she could squeeze through something so small, was there?

The rounded curve of her behind held her up and she wiggled her hips back and forth, feeling the steel of the bar digging into her flesh, finding brief relief when it slipped between the crack of her ass. Halfway there! She used all her strength to push against the bars, wielding her weight as leverage, feeling the bar sliding past her other ass cheek. Her slender middle was easy, her ribcage small and light—and she'd never been this grateful to be so flat-chested in her life!

But she'd forgotten one thing. She'd forgotten about her head. And bone didn't give.

Ten seconds, according to the timer. She was going to get caught just like this, with her head on one side of the Behr's gate and her body on the other, the Ursa diamonds in her pocket. Campbell was going to laugh his ass off. Goldie groaned, twisting and turning her head, her hair spilling free. Her knit cap fell to the ground, and she reached for it, her head slipping lower between the bars. She was on her knees on the pavement now, butt up in the air, a very undignified position to say the least. She expected to hear Campbell's smug, "What do we have here?" any minute now.

Three seconds. It was over. The security cameras would be back on. Goldie grabbed both bars on either side of her head and, with a grunt of frustration, pushed as hard as she could with her hands, pulling at her head, and slipped free! She sat dazed on the pavement, ears ringing, realizing the bars must have been just a centimeter or two wider at the bottom than the top, before standing and breaking into a run—the opposite direction from Campbell and the cop, of course. Freedom was just around the corner.

* * * *

Campbell sat in the corner of the library, waiting. Goldie was due to enter the Behr estate, this time through the front door, shown, as he had been, by the Behr's butler—an actual butler—up the wide, winding staircase to the library. His employers talked quietly amongst themselves, standing by a fireplace taller than all three Behr brothers. Campbell sipped his brandy and kept an eye on the door.

"Ah, there she is!" The oldest Behr turned as the door opened, already flashing a smile. He was handsome man, his blonde hair thick and wavy and perfectly styled, his eyes bluer than the blue velvet bag Goldie held in her hand, and Campbell wondered if her reaction—half-amusement, half-infatuation—was real or an act. "I'm Rolf Behr."

His extended hand swallowed hers briefly and he guided her toward the fireplace, his other hand moving to the small of her back. Campbell smiled behind his glass as he saw her move away from Rolf's casual but too-friendly touch as they neared the fireplace.

"My brother, Wilhelm," Rolf said, nodding toward the smaller man holding a brandy snifter. He had lost the genetic lottery his older brother had won, his hair thinning, his face obscured by little round glasses. "And my brother, Otto." The middle brother was a strange average of the other two, and Campbell watched her shake both of their hands as introductions were made.

"And this is our current head of security." Wilhelm waved in Campbell's direction, his voice full of gleeful disdain. That was his cue. Campbell stood, striding toward the fireplace, hand outstretched.

"Richard Campbell. Nice to meet you." He shook Goldie's hand briefly. "I hear you somehow managed to slip through my system." His voice sounded harsh, even to him.

Goldie flushed prettily and shrugged, accepting Otto's offer of a drink, her usual—rum and Coke.

"Very impressive." Rolf smiled and Campbell saw the look of interest in his eyes as he gazed at Goldie. "I can't wait to hear how you did it."

Wilhelm sneered, looking pointedly at Campbell. "She certainly made it look easy."

"I suppose it would have looked easy," Goldie agreed, smiling smugly and sipping her drink, taking full credit for months, hell years, of Campbell's hard work. "If your security cameras had been working that night."

Rolf laughed. "Touché."

"How *did* you do it?" Otto inquired, looking at her quizzically. "I, for one, truly believed Mr. Campbell when he told us our defenses were impenetrable."

Campbell felt heat filling his face. "So did I."

"Well you have to know, if someone wants something badly enough, they're going to come in and take it," Goldie reminded them.

"Over my dead body." Rolf threw his shoulders back, standing to his full, not inconsiderable height.

"Sometimes." Goldie shrugged. "But in this case, I was able to enter the premises, crack the safe and retrieve the items in a space of about fifteen minutes—without detection."

"Indeed." Rolf's eyes gleamed and his gaze swept over her lithe form, her pencil-thin skirt and silk blouse perfectly respectable, but Campbell had to admit, the woman was a knock-out. He couldn't blame Rolf for being interested. He also couldn't help the heated rage filling his chest at the thought of this man getting his hands on her in any way, shape or form.

"Oh, and I'm sorry about your doorwall." Goldie gave Rolf a sweet apologetic smile.

He waved her words away. "We had an agreement. We all understood that there might be damage involved."

"Oh, I know," Goldie agreed. "It was in the contract. Still, I always feel bad when I have to damage something to get in."

"I'm sure you'll be able to tell us how we can improve." Otto looked between his brothers, smiling. "But I'm really curious how you got into the box. Never mind the alarms and finding the safe and opening the vault. The boxes themselves are thrice-protected."

"I noticed." Goldie laughed. "If you know what you're doing, alarms can be bypassed. As for the location of a safe, well, you have to know that the walls have ears. You do have servants, and in this day and age, it's hard to expect loyalty. They'll give you all sorts of information—where safes are located, which jewels are kept in what safe deposit boxes…"

Campbell hid a smile, her irony not lost on him. Oh, but the poor Behr butler—the old gentleman who had shown them to the library was going to get an earful. He imagined the Behr brothers lining them all up for an inquisition.

"As for getting into the box itself, well…" She glanced at Campbell, just a flicker of her eyes.

"That's the part I don't understand." Otto frowned. "If I didn't know better, I'd swear you must have already had the combinations."

Campbell laughed. "They don't even give them to me."

"Combination locks are my particular forte," Goldie explained. "I can open pretty much anything."

Rolf flashed her a smile. "Well, I'm glad you use your powers for good."

"It's true, I could have opened any box in that vault," Goldie assured him, turning the little velvet bag over in her hand. "I'm sure there were many more priceless objects available to steal."

"True enough," Rolf agreed. "But if you had, employing you as our head of security would be out of the question."

Otto chimed in, "Not to mention the fact that we know where you live."

"Of course we do." Wilhelm smiled. Campbell always found his smiles creepy, even when he was pretending to be genuine. "We've been having you followed for weeks."

Goldie straightened. "You…what?"

Rolf clucked at her concern. "If you are going to be in our employ, we have to know everything about you. Consider it our version of a background check."

Campbell saw brief panic flash in Goldie's eyes and knew what she was thinking. Did they know? They'd both been careful, never using the same hotel entrance, changing meeting places. But anything was possible…

"Well, if you're so untrusting, I should give these back to you." Goldie held the velvet bag out to Rolf but he waved her away.

"Oh don't bother. Why don't you keep them as a souvenir?"

Her eyes widened and Rolf chuckled, telling her, "They're cut glass."

"Of course they aren't the real thing," Wilhelm scoffed. "It wouldn't be prudent to let you steal those."

"Let me see." Campbell held out his hand and Goldie reached over to place the bag in it. He dumped the glass stones out into his palm, studying them. "Nice imitations." They really were, quite impressive, although a jeweler would be instantly able to tell the difference, the layman wouldn't know. He tossed the bag onto the desk, looking at Rolf. "I'm sure she'd like to see the real thing."

He knew the man wouldn't be able to resist showing off.

"Of course!" Rolf turned and strode over the a painting on the wall of his father. The resemblance between him and the elder Behr brother was striking and Campbell couldn't help but wonder if his great-grandfather had looked like that in his SS uniform, shooting Jakob in the head because he'd just swallowed the family jewels. If nothing else came of this, he was going to be glad to be through working for this family at the very least. "They're here in our safe."

Goldie followed him, looking amused. "It's in a rather obvious place."

"It's our decoy safe," Rolf explained, his brothers following them as well. Campbell stayed back. "They'll be tucked into their box tonight—with changed locks of course."

Goldie smirked. "It wouldn't keep me out."

"I'm really curious," Otto said, nodding toward the heavy metal safe anchored into the wall. "Would you mind? I'd just like to see if you can crack it?"

"If?" Goldie scoffed, twisting the combination dial. Campbell reached for his iPhone and started his timer, watching her work. It was a thing of beauty, seeing her golden head cocked to one side, her attention like a laser and yet her eyes focused on nothing until she got the first digit. Then she glanced at the dial, noting the number, and started again. When she pulled the safe open, less than two minutes had passed on his timer.

"One minute thirty-nine seconds," Campbell announced, slipping his phone back into his pocket, unable to keep a little bit of awe from his voice.

"You know, half the fun of cracking is finding out what's inside," Goldie remarked, opening the safe door more fully.

"Go ahead." Rolf nudged her. "Take a look."

Campbell watched Goldie take out an exact replica of the blue velvet bag. He also glimpsed a wad of cash and a few other jewelry boxes with several large cubic zirconium in them, quite a haul for any thief looking to score. She closed the safe, swinging the picture back into place as well. *Good girl,* he thought, watching her spill the jewels into her palm. Everything was going so closely to plan it was hard to believe.

"They're beautiful." Goldie held the three Ursa diamonds, looking at them in the firelight. "Just exquisite."

"They were passed on to us from our father," Rolf explained.

"Here." Goldie put the jewels back into the bag, pulling the string and handing it to Rolf. "I was nervous enough carrying those around for twenty-four hours."

"So tell us." Rolf smiled, slipping the bag into his left suit coat pocket. "How did you do it?"

Goldie sipped her drink, following the eldest brother toward the fireplace. "Honestly, your security wasn't that difficult to bypass. You had several backdoors. Any hacker could have found them."

"Is that so?" Wilhelm perked up, shooting bolts of lightning at Campbell with his eyes as he joined his brothers and Goldie by the fireplace.

The anger in Campbell's response was quite real. "Now wait a minute, I just did a thorough sweep of our system."

Goldie offered him a little smile and a helpless shrug. "I'm sorry, Mr. Campbell, but I'm afraid you missed a few. It happens."

He took a step toward her, blazing. "Listen, you smug little…"

"Whoa!" Rolf stepped into his path. "Easy!"

"You expect me to sit here and listen to this?" he snarled.

"It's your system that failed, Mr. Campbell," Wilhelm reminded him, ebullient.

Don't hit him, Campbell reminded himself, fists clenched at his sides.

"So you hired a comb-lock genius to test your system, but how many thieves out there can do what she does? I wish I could alleviate your paranoia, but the reality is there is no such thing as a foolproof security system!" Campbell threw up his hands, rolling his eyes, giving Goldie her cue. "Jesus Christ!"

She went down like a stone, just as they'd rehearsed, eyes going wide and then closing, the glass in her hand shattering against the fireplace, splashing rum and Coke all over the hearth. The three Behr brothers ran to her side, focusing their full attention on Goldie. Campbell palmed the velvet bag on the desk, hearing Goldie murmuring embarrassed apologies for fainting and Campbell took the opportunity to step close, peering over Rolf's shoulder, slipping his hand into the big man's suit coat pocket as he did so.

Easy as taking candy from a baby, he thought as the blue velvet bag with the glass diamonds slid in to replace the bag with the real Ursas. Campbell pocketed the real jewels as Rolf helped Goldie to her feet, the other two brothers fussing around her. He took the opportunity to put the real jewels back onto the desk, although he was loathe to let go of them. *Work the plan,* he reminded himself. *And let the plan work.*

"Are you okay?" Rolf asked and Campbell gritted his teeth, seeing the way he held her steady, far too close.

"Fine." Goldie smiled up at him, practically batting her eyelashes, and Campbell wished she'd lay off the act a little. Goldie brushed at her skirt, feeling the back of her head. She'd gone down on the carpet but he was sure she'd probably have a lump there. It wasn't easy to pretend to faint. The body instinctively wanted to resist injury if it was truly conscious. "I'm fine, really, I'm just pregnant."

"You're what?" The words were out of Campbell's mouth before he could think, his heart stopped dead in his chest. He wondered for a moment if it was going to beat again, but then it took off like a race horse.

"I'm sorry," she apologized, looking at the glass on the floor. "I can clean that up."

"Don't worry about that." Rolf waved his hand, using Goldie's elbow to steer her toward the soft and sitting her on it. Otto had already gone off to find the butler to clean up the mess. "I just want to make sure you're all right."

"I'm really fine." She gave him an embarrassed smile. "I never knew it was true what they said about pregnant women fainting."

"Well I guess double congratulations are in order then," Campbell spat, leaning over and grabbing the blue velvet bag off the desk. "A baby and a new job. Bully for you."

"Now listen here..." Rolf stood to his full height, frowning, but Campbell cut him off.

"Fuck you, Behr." He heard Goldie gasp. *Nice touch,* he thought. "And fuck this job." He turned to Goldie, sneering. "You can have it. Here's your prize."

He tossed the bag in her lap and strode toward the door, not looking back. It took every bit of effort he could muster not to turn back, to walk out of the room and leave her there. He hated this part of the plan, hated that he wasn't in control, able to protect her. But he left, passing Otto on the stairs, the butler following behind.

"I'll show myself out," he said gruffly when Otto inquired, concerned, about where he was going. His brothers would fill him in, he was sure. It took him fifteen minutes after getting into his car and heading down the Behr's long driveway to get the rendezvous point. It took Goldie another fifteen and he couldn't believe his relief when he saw her little black Saturn pull into the parking lot beside his car. His whole body relaxed the moment she opened the driver's side door, seeing him leaning against his Mercury, just standing in the glow of a streetlight, waiting for her to arrive.

"Do you have them?" he asked first thing and she pulled the velvet bag out of her pocket to show him.

"You were right," she admitted, pocketing the jewels again."About everything. They switched the diamonds just like you said they would. How did you know?"

"How did I know they would ask you to steal the Ursas?" He winked. "Come on, I've worked for these guys for three years. Give me a little credit."

Goldie raised her eyebrows and Campbell grinned. "Okay, I might have fed their paranoia a little and made a suggestion here or there, as head of security and all..."

She laughed. "You hatched the perfect plan."

"Speaking of hatching..." Campbell's heart thudded in his chest just thinking about posing the question. "Are you really pregnant?"

Goldie hesitated, then shook her head. "No. I just thought it would lend credibility to the whole fainting thing. Why, did I scare you?"

He shrugged, lying. "No."

"Liar." She grinned, glancing over at the building they'd parked in front of, the sign illuminated with floodlights: *Parkview Nursing Home*. Goldie sighed, patting the bag of jewels in her pocket. "I'll feel better once these are in Daniel's hands and we're on a plane to Brazil. Although I'm sure going to miss Poppy..."

"Speaking of that." Campbell reached into his inside pocket, pulling out an envelope. "I have something for you."

He watched her face as she opened them, seeing her expression turn quizzical as she counted them in the light of a street lamp. "There are *three* plane tickets here."

"Yep," he agreed, waiting for the realization to hit her.

"Poppy's coming with us?" She looked at him, incredulous. "But how? My father's will only provides for him if he stays here."

Campbell smiled. "I've taken care of that."

Goldie stared, eyes wide. "What did you do?"

"Well, you might be the goddess of combination locks—and a great actress, I might add—but I'm awesome at hacking and password retrieval."

She gaped, jaw dropped. "Campbell!"

"Let's just say we now have an offshore account that's going to take care of us for the rest of our lives. And that includes your Poppy. Let's call it…reparations."

He waited for her reaction and she bowled him over with it, throwing her arms around his neck and kissing him fully on the mouth.

"I can't wait to tell him everything," she breathed, tears in her eyes. "I never could have done this without you."

"That's true," he agreed, trying to sound humble, but the adoring look in her eyes melted his heart. Everything about her made him want to sink to his knees and worship her. He kissed the corner of her mouth and hugged her close, whispering, "But I don't know what I'd do without you, so we're pretty even."

Epilogue

Goldie stretched out, cat-like, practically purring in the sun. She'd divested herself of her bathing suit top already and was considering losing the bottoms, too. Her pale skin had already turned a lovely golden brown in the two weeks they'd spent at this villa in Brazil.

"Hey doll." Campbell plopped down in the sand beside her wearing khakis and a loud Hawaiian shirt. He looked ridiculous, and she loved him. "Guess what?"

"If there's a tsunami coming, I don't want to know," she murmured, closing her eyes again. "Is Poppy okay?"

"He's fine," Campbell assured her. "Back at the house, getting his second sponge bath of the day. The old guy's sure taking advantage of having a live-in nurse."

Goldie giggled. "You men never change."

"Sit up. I have something for you."

She sighed, loathe to move, but she did as he asked, turning herself over and facing him. "What?"

"Just a little something." Campbell reached into his pocket and pulled out a small, black velvet box. Seeing it made her stomach drop to her knees.

"Campbell…"

"Actually, more a medium-sized something," he countered as she took it from him with trembling hands.

He didn't, she thought, but he had. Inside was the Ursa Median, now set in a platinum band.

"What…?" She choked, staring at the ring. "How?"

"Daniel said most people only know about Ursa Major and Ursa Minor," Campbell explained. "And he wanted to give us something for donating the diamonds to the Holocaust Museum, so…"

"So it's ours?" She looked from him to the diamond and back again.

"It's yours." He nodded, reaching out to take her hand. "If you'll agree to marry me."

She blinked and then laughed. "Are you really proposing to me naked?"

"Well I'm not naked, you are." He grinned, leering. "And I rather prefer you that way."

"Okay." She couldn't help the tears welling up in her eyes. "But I have to tell you something."

He raised an eyebrow, waiting.

"Remember when I told you I wasn't pregnant?"

Campbell nodded and she swore he turned another shade of pale under his straw hat.

"I lied." She looked down at the ring instead of at him. "I am pregnant," she rushed on. "But don't think you have to marry me because I am. You don't."

Campbell grabbed her to him and kissed her hard, crushing her mouth with his and she gasped for breath when he let her go.

"My god, woman, I've wanted to marry you for three years!" he exclaimed. "If I could have done it without arousing the Behr's suspicions, I would have had you at a Justice of the Peace in a heartbeat!"

She swallowed, wanting to believe him. "That was the only reason?"

"What other reason could there be?" He shook his head, smiling."I love you, silly woman."

She let her tears fall, looking down at the ring and whispering, "I love you too."

"Why are you crying?" he inquired, wiping at her tears with his thumb. "Don't you want to get married? Don't you like the ring? Is it too big? Too small?"

"No it's just right." She looked up at him and felt the truth of it for the first time in her whole life. "Everything is just right."

BRIAR ROSE

Google's my lifesaver.

Rose snorted at the irony, mentally correcting her own error as she slipped naked into the hot water—life-*ender* was more like it. But without Google, she would have just done what she'd seen in all the Hollywood movies and used the razor blade horizontally, and what good would that have done? She would have just ended up in the hospital amidst a whole lot of drama, her aunts clucking and pawing and chiding, while Sam scoffed and said she was just looking for attention.

If he even showed up at all...

She put the box of razor blades on the edge of the tub, the cardboard soaking up the water splashing onto the edge from the running spout. But what did it matter if the entire box rusted? She only needed one. Although she had been careful to buy a box-cutter at Home Depot, along with the blades, so as not to draw any undue attention to herself.

Why would he show up?

Thinking about Sam made her whole body curl into itself, going instinctively fetal, her knees drawn up, eyes closing, as if she could escape her own pain with darkness. Well, that was the point, wasn't it? She had experienced her fair share of heartache in her thirty-three years, but the pain of losing Sam was far too much for her to bear. One person couldn't possibly live through the loss, not to mention the humiliation, of losing her fiancé the night before the wedding.

It's your own fault.

That was the hardest thing of all to accept. If she'd just kept on pretending, if she had let things go on as they always had, she and Sam would be staying the night right now at a sweet little bed and breakfast she'd found on the Florida coast before heading off to St. Barts for the rest of their three-week honeymoon in the morning. Instead, both tickets were tucked into her purse and the engagement ring he'd given her a year ago would never get the addition of its twin wedding band.

She opened her eyes to admire the two-carat diamond. Although she'd protested at the extravagance, Sam had insisted, and secretly she loved the exclamatory reaction she received from everyone from shopkeepers to manicurists. Of course, she'd offered to give it back, but Sam had insisted, "I don't want anything from you!" shaking his hand off her arm as if she was a leper before storming out of her apartment, slamming the door behind him so hard it made Mr. Neiman upstairs pound on the floor for quiet.

Well, Mr. Neiman wouldn't have to pound on the floor anymore when she was playing The Ramones too loud while she was in the shower, or when she and Sam got a little too exuberant during sex, would he? They used to laugh about it, the memory so painful it was like an open sore, imagining the two of them naked and panting and giggling in the dark as Mr. Neiman pounding his cane on the floor.

The truth was, Sam liked it when she was loud, and she saw no reason not to indulge him. She knew just what turned him on. In fact, she'd gotten the sounds and movements down to a science, and had learned to throw in a new sound or moan or some dirty talk on occasion to change it up and give him a little thrill.

Rose opened the box of razor blades, removing one from the package and contemplating its sharp edge as she remembered Sam's question after sex the night before. It was the first time he'd ever brought it up. Maybe she would have offered him the truth in the beginning, if he'd asked. That's what she told herself as the level of the hot water rose around her in a cloud of steam and the thick pulse of blood through her veins pounded in her ears.

I deserve this. Rose traced a finger down her arm from her wrist to her elbow, shivering at the sensation. *I earned it.*

Maybe if she'd been honest with Sam—honest with herself—things would have been different.

Instead, for two years, she had let him believe a lie. Hell, she'd lived that lie for him, with him. It hadn't been difficult, not really. It wasn't as if she'd lied about how she felt about Sam—she loved him, always had and always would. It wasn't as if she'd cheated on him with someone else, or had a scary former life or some big secret buried in her past. There were no skeletons in her closet waiting to pop out and surprise anyone.

It had seemed like such a small thing—an innocent white lie. She had never imagined that her admission would lead to this—to losing Sam forever, to a pain beyond any she'd ever known, to a despair so vast she could do nothing but attempt to escape it, running away from the pain and seeking a distant, shimmering point in the distance that could only be her own end.

"I'm sorry, Sam," she whispered, feeling hot tears on her already wet cheeks, salty on her lips, as she pressed the edge of the blade against the tender skin of her wrist, testing its sharpness and her own vulnerability. A bright spot of blood bloomed immediately from the miniscule cut, assuring her that her skin was permeable, that the line between life and death was very thin. She was glad.

"Hard and fast," she whispered, studying the pale blue roadmap of her veins under the tender, thin covering of her skin. "Straight down from wrist to elbow."

She didn't wonder what Sam would say, or what her mother and father would think. She wasn't thinking of anyone or anything else at all. Her whole being was consumed with an emotional pain so far beyond this realm of existence she was sure she'd already left this world. This final act was just a matter of course, like completing an electrical circuit.

The doorbell startled her, forcing the blade in a little deeper, the red flower of blood on her wrist spreading. Rose looked up at the bathroom door, closed but not locked, shocked by this intrusion. She had given them all plausible excuses about being alone right now—her mother, her father, her aunts, the multitude of family who had flown into town to see her walk down the aisle today—and of course, she had turned off both her home and cell phone.

"Rosie?"

Oh no! She knew that voice. It was her aunt Poppy, knocking and ringing the bell. Her family had obviously conferenced and decided to send Poppy over see if poor little Rosie was all right. *Well no, to tell you the truth, I'm not all right. I'm broken. I've always been broken. No one could every want me or love me or—*

"Rosie!" The voice was closer. Poppy had let herself into the house! Rose cursed herself for not locking the front door. "Rosie? Are you okay?"

If only it was Sam...

That was her last rational thought before she did the inevitable, the blade far sharper than she'd ever imagined. She didn't make it from wrist to elbow—less than halfway, but the cut was a good four inches long and quite deep, slicing between all the tendons and ligaments, finding the artery with lucky precision. That was all she could do—pain like a white hot poker shot through her arm and her hand spasmed uncontrollably, her fingers turning to claws. She couldn't help the scream, although she tried to hold it in—it felt ripped from the raw hollow of her throat, a bright, inhuman sound echoing off the white tiles. Looking down, she saw her own arm as if someone had turned it inside out, blood bright red and pulsing from the wound into the warm water around her.

"Rosie!" The door flew open and she saw her aunt's wide eyes, had just enough time to register her horrified expression. "No! Oh no, Rosie, nooo!"

Her last thought was that she wished it had been Sam who had either burst in to save her—or perhaps witness her death. She really didn't care which. She had just wanted it to be Sam.

* * * *

"I didn't even think they sold transferable airline tickets anymore." Rose's mother handed them back to her daughter, frowning as she scanned the airport. Rose knew she was looking for her ex-husband, Rose's father, who was due to show up to see his daughter off. "Late as usual," her mother whispered under her breath, but Rose heard and winced.

"I think it's a sign!" Poppy slid an arm around her niece's shoulder, patting the girl's head with her other hand. Rose let her do it, even though the gesture made her feel five years old. "You were meant to go to St. Bart's after all."

Rose didn't say anything. Telling Poppy how much pain that statement caused her wouldn't do anyone any good. What did it matter that she should have used those tickets for her honeymoon with Sam? They had come in handy, that much was true. And Sam… She closed her eyes, swallowing and looking away, pretending interest in seeing the planes taking off and landing outside the window. Thinking about Sam was still too painful. That hurt far more than the scar on her wrist—eighty-seven stitches later.

"There's your father." Her mother was readying herself, mouth puckered, arms akimbo, foot already tapping on the airport carpet. Rose ignored her mother's reaction, smiling as the tall, handsome man in a suit strode toward them, a congenial smile spreading over his tanned face, showing more lines than Rose remembered.

"There's my princess!" Her father swept her into his arms and hugged her tight, and this, too, make Rose feel small—but she didn't mind. He set her down and kissed her forehead, asking, "How's my girl?"

"Fine, Daddy." Rose smiled, realizing they'd had the exact same exchange while she'd been lying in a hospital bed two months ago, her arm still heavily bandaged, her head fuzzy from the morphine.

"You'll love St. Barts." He turned, acknowledging Poppy for the first time but clearly avoiding meeting the glaring eyes of his ex-wife. "Won't she, Sis?"

"I think she'll get just what she needs in St. Barts," her aunt agreed.

Rose glanced between her parents, wondering how that much hostility could still exist between two people after twenty years of being divorced. She'd long ago given up trying to reconcile them or even to try to keep the peace. They were adults—she couldn't control the way they behaved, even if that behavior resembled two children.

"Are you sure you packed enough?" Rose's mother eyed her daughter's carry-on. "Isn't this supposed to be for a month?"

"They have laundry facilities," Poppy piped up, intervening quickly. "They're boarding."

"Well I guess this is it." Rose offered a tentative smile to both of her parents, taking one of each of their hands, making some sort of bridge.

Her father said, "You have fun," and kissed the top of Rose's head and her mother squeezed her hand and said, "Get better, okay?" illustrating the vast difference between her parents and her relationship with both of them in one brief moment.

Rose let her parents' hands go and leaned in to give her aunt a hug, whispering, "Thanks for everything."

She had once wished it had been Sam who burst into the bathroom that night, but she didn't wish that now. Poppy had taken charge—twenty years of nursing experience took over, of course, but it wasn't just that. Her aunt had protected her from then until now, staying with her at night after she was released from the hospital, and ultimately finding the unorthodox treatment center she was heading to now.

The truth was, Rose didn't want to die anymore. But she wasn't quite sure she wanted to live either. It was a strange place to be, like walking through life like you didn't belong, as if it was all someone else's dream. Maybe this place really would help. At least, Rose figured, it couldn't hurt.

She waved to her family as the flight attendant took her boarding pass, seeing them gathered into a little trio of worry. Even her father look perplexed and unsure, an expression she hadn't seen on his face since that first day in the hospital when he saw the enormous bandage on her arm.

Rose settled herself into her seat on the plane, stowing her carry-on in a very small overhead compartment and wondering at the safety of the tiny aircraft. The seats were narrow, just two on each side of the aisle, and regardless of who she would be sitting next to, it would be close quarters. *It should be Sam.* But she didn't want to think about that. Instead, she took out her Kindle and enjoyed her window seat, her eyes unfocused on the words on the screen.

"They're going to make you turn that off during takeoff you know."

Rose glanced up, experiencing a horrible, dizzying sense of déjà-vu—except it wasn't an image of something that already happened, but something that *should* have happened. Sam was taking a seat beside her, stowing a briefcase under the seat in front of him, just as he would have if this had been their honeymoon flight.

That's not Sam! She had to remind herself of that fact as she put her Kindle face-down in her lap, attempting to smile at the man who resembled her ex-fiancé so much they could have been brothers, if not twins, as he reached down to get something out of his bag.

"But we can sneak in a little reading time before then, huh?" He winked and showed her a tablet device. "Those Kindles are great for reading at the beach, but I gotta have my *Angry Birds*."

"Angry…birds?" She gave him a quizzical half-smile, shaking her head.

"It's a game," he explained, swiping his finger across the touch screen. "An app, actually." He glanced at her, seeing the quizzical expression growing more confused. "An application." He laughed. "You've got a Kindle, so you're not a Luddite…how is it you have never heard of *Angry Birds*?"

He turned the screen to show her three fat cartoon birds in front of an empty nest with question marks over their heads.

"I kind of outgrew video games when I was a kid." Rose shrugged, watching as the man used a slingshot to fling one of the birds toward a structure with round-faced green animals trapped in it. "I think the last video game I played was Space Invaders on Atari."

He laughed, handing the tablet to her. "Oh well here—you have to try *Angry Birds*."

"Really?" She looked doubtfully at the game.

"Just pull back the slingshot and shoot." He demonstrated by leaning over and using one finger to do so, flinging a fat little bird into the air.

Rose followed his lead, getting a little thrill when the structure tumbled and a little green animal inside was obliterated, leaving a score in its wake. "Why are the birds angry?"

"They're mad at the pigs," he explained.

"Oh, those green things are pigs!" She peered closer, seeing the resemblance now. "Why are they mad at the pigs?"

"The pigs stole their eggs."

She laughed as another structure tumbled to the ground due to her new, amazing sling-shooting ability. With just a swipe of her finger! "Pigs like eggs?"

"They must." He smiled. "But the Freudian in me would say all that pent up rage must have something to do with the birds' mothers."

Rose went to hand the tablet back to him but he waved her away. "Play! But be careful, it's addictive."

"It is," she agreed, starting another level, introducing herself without even looking up. "I'm Rose, by the way."

"Matt," he replied, leaning his seat back with a sigh. "Nice to meet you, Rose. What takes you to St. Bart's all by yourself?"

"Oh I'm…going on vacation, of course," she lied. "How about you?"

"Going home." He winked. "I'm one of the, oh, I don't know, eight-thousand or so permanent residents of the island."

"Lucky you," she commented, moving on to level three. The structures were getting larger and the pigs she had to eliminate by flinging the angry birds at them more numerous.

"I am," he agreed happily, putting his hands behind his head and closing his eyes, stretching his long legs into the aisle. .The gesture reminded her so much of Sam that Rose swallowed the emotion rising in her throat, trying to concentrate on the game in her hands.

"Damnit," she swore softly as she ran out of birds—but the pigs survived, the structure still intact.

Matt opened one eye and grinned. "I told you it was addictive."

"But amusing," she contested, starting the level again.

"An irresistible combination."

"So do you own a hotel on the island or something?" Rose asked, making small talk as she continued playing on her seat mate's tablet.

He didn't open his eyes. "I'm a doctor."

"Oh well that makes sense." She glanced up as someone stepped over Matt's feet in the aisle, making their way to a seat. "They need doctors everywhere. Why not choose a tropical island to practice on?"

"Would you tell that to my mother?" Matt straightened up as more people began to filter onto the plane. "She thinks I should be practicing back in New York."

Rose smiled. "Parents always think they know best."

"What do your parents think you should do for a living?"

"My father wanted me to be a doctor, but I became a first-grade teacher instead," she told him. "My mother? She just wants me to marry a doctor."

"Ha! My mother keeps telling me I'll understand when I have children of my own." He shrugged, folding his arms over his chest and looking over her shoulder as she played the game.

"Pushing for grandkids, is she?"

"Putting the cart before the horse, as usual. I need a wife first." He pointed at the screen. "Try a lower angle for this one. And don't pull back so far."

"Thanks." Rose did as he instructed, killing off a whole building full of evil green pigs and feeling quite proud of herself. "You could always adopt kids if you really wanted them."

"Nah." He shrugged. "I'm an old-fashioned kind of guy."

Rose looked across the aisle, noticing a young couple sitting together, holding hands and smiling. *Honeymoon,* she thought, a twinge of pain tightening her chest.

"You all right?"

She blinked at her seat mate, lying again. "Fine."

"You sure about that?" He glanced over at the happy couple and back at her.

"Oh, well... I guess I'm a little nervous." She gestured around the plane. "About the flight."

He waved her concern away. "I promise you, these little puddle jumpers are safer than the big commercial airplanes. And these pilots could land a plane on the edge of a dime if they had to."

"Well that's good to know." She tried to smile, tried not to notice the couple across the way leaning in to kiss.

"Miss, could you please put that away while we take off?" the flight attendant asked, moving on before Rose could respond.

She handed the tablet back to Matt. "Thanks for letting me play."

"See, I told you they'd make us turn them off," he muttered, taking it from her. "Oh hey, that's a nasty scar."

Rose pulled her hand back quickly, hiding her scar under the edge of her long-sleeved blouse. She wore them all the time now, even in the Florida heat.

"Excuse me." She stood, not looking at him. "I'm going to use the rest room before we take off."

He stood to let her pass, not saying anything. When she'd splashed water on her face and inspected her eyes to make sure it didn't look like she'd been crying, she made her way back to her seat to find him stretched out again, eyes closed. Definitely asleep.

Instead of disturbing him—that's what she told herself, it didn't have to do anything with not wanting to face him again—she asked the flight attendant if she could sit in an empty seat up near the front and thankfully, the woman obliged.

Settled alone by the window, Rose watched the land below her disappear, wondering what she was getting herself into. Poppy had assured and reassured her, had shown her brochures and emailed her testimony from other clients whose lives had been changed at this treatment center.

She hadn't told Poppy or her parents, but this was it. It was her last-ditch effort to figure out what was wrong with her, to see if anyone could fix the thing in her that was broken. If they couldn't… well, she'd already experienced the heartache of losing Sam. She didn't think she could ever risk something like that again in her lifetime.

* * * *

This can't be happening.

Rose had asked to be seen by another physician when she'd seen him through the little check-in window—*oh my god it's the guy from the plane!*—flipping through charts and chatting with the nurses. There was no way she could possibly strip naked in front of him. She'd avoided his gaze after they landed, barely acknowledging his wave and smile from the other end of the plane as everyone filed down the little aisle. Thankfully he'd been forced off first and Rose had gathered her stuff and spent a good ten minutes in the airplane bathroom—long enough for the flight attendant to knock and check on her—before getting off the plane herself. By then he'd been gone, and she'd been so relieved.

She should have known, when he'd said he was a doctor. But how could she have known he was *the* doctor, the one who ran the treatment center? His picture or name hadn't been in any of the brochures, not that she remembered anyway. And she would have remembered.

"He's our only doctor," the confused red-headed, freckled receptionist told her. "Is there a problem?"

"No, no." Rose shook her head, had backed away from the window, thinking of bolting out the glass doors. But where would she go? She'd already checked into her room at the facility, been given the tour, gone through a two-hour orientation and eaten lunch with several of the other clients. The physical examination was part of the process. She couldn't avoid it forever.

And it turned out that he had been quite kind. Of course, he had. He was witty and charming, acknowledging their chance meeting on the plane, trying to put her at ease. It was just impossible to feel comfortable while she was naked except for her little paper gown, answering "Dr. Matt's" intimate questions and trying not to choke on her answers.

"So you've never experienced an orgasm?" Dr. Matt chewed thoughtfully on the top of his pen and Rose distracted herself from her own rising, uncomfortable blush by noting how mangled and twisted the tip was from his constant gnawing. It was a nervous habit she wouldn't have expected from a professional, but somehow it made him seem more human, and for that she was glad.

"I'm not sure." She could feel the roses blooming in her cheeks and looked down at the paper dress she wore. It hardly covered anything, but Dr. Matt didn't seem to notice or care. He was a doctor, after all, even if he'd insisted she use his first name after the title instead of his last, and that meant he might really be able to help her. She had to tell him the truth. "You see, I have these dreams…"

Dr. Matt waited patiently for her to go on, still chewing on his pen. His teeth were very white and very straight, his eyes dark and watchful. He reminded her so much of Sam it hurt. Dr. Matt was decidedly handsome, somewhere around her age, and she found it very difficult to speak about her problem to a man who looked and sounded far too much like her fiancé. *Ex-fiancé.* Finally, she went on, feeling the slow burn spreading down from her cheeks to her neck.

"I think I do… have orgasms…" She swallowed, feeling the heat filling her chest. "In my dreams."

"So you're having nocturnal emissions?" He noted something on his clipboard, glancing up when she didn't respond. "Wet dreams?"

She nodded her assent, not trusting her voice.

"But you've never had an orgasm while you're awake?" he inquired, cocking his head, a sad sort of sympathy in his eyes that made her want to either crawl under the table or smack him—she couldn't decide which. "Either alone or with a partner?"

"No," she finally confessed. "Never."

He nodded, tapping the pen against his straight, white teeth. "And you've tried all the usual methods of stimulation—fingers, vibrators…?"

Rose closed her eyes, shaking her head. "I've tried *everything*." She couldn't even begin to tell him the things she'd tried, the various implements and manipulations that had gone on between her thighs over the years in an attempt to bring her some semblance of pleasure.

"Interesting." He was writing on his clipboard again.

"So do you think you can help me?"

"Don't worry, we'll get to the bottom of this." He stood, putting his clipboard aside and standing. Rose shrank as he came toward her, towered over her, far too close for her comfort. "If that's really what you want. Is it?"

"I—" She hesitated, meeting his gaze. It was straightforward and far too knowing. "Of course I do. Why else would I be here?"

He smiled. "You did read all of the consent forms you signed, didn't you?"

"Of course." Rose squirmed on the table, feeling the paper beneath her naked bottom crinkle. Her answer wasn't exactly true. She'd been tired and the forms were long and involved.

Dr. Matt reached out and took her hand, clasping it between two of his. His touch was shockingly warm and familiar. "Rose, we're not going to get to the bottom of this if you lie to me."

She stared at him, mouth agape. "What—?" She couldn't help flashing back to the look on Sam's face when she admitted that yes, she had lied, she'd been faking her orgasms all along. The pain of the moment took her breath away.

"No lies." Dr. Matt's hands squeezed hers gently. "Let's start there, okay?"

Rose felt tears pricking her eyes and blinked them back. "Okay."

When she complied with his request to recline onto the table for the physical exam, Rose realized her aunt had been right. This place really was different from any other place she had ever been for treatment, and this Dr. Matt was different as well. She just didn't know yet if that was a good thing or a bad thing.

"I've reviewed all your medical records," he said as he snapped on a pair of gloves. "Your last pap smear was about six months ago?"

"Yes."

"No need to do another one then. I'm just going to examine you manually." He stood at the side of the table, smiling down at her so warmly she could almost feel it. "Can I touch you?"

She hesitated only a moment. "Okay."

His hands were warm, even in gloves, sliding under her paper gown from the side and cupping her right breast, his fingers and thumb moving over her flesh just like any other doctor's, doing a typical breast exam. "Any pain in your breasts?"

"No." She met his eyes as he moved to the other breast. "Well sometimes before my period."

"That's normal." He nodded. "Does it feel good to have your nipples touched?"

Rose gasped when he tweaked her nipple, nodding. "Yes."

"Close your eyes," he instructed. She obeyed, although her already high anxiety level rose to even greater heights when she did. "On a scale of one to ten, one being horrible and ten being the best thing ever, tell me how good this feels."

Dr. Matt rolled her nipple slowly between his thumb and forefinger, back and forth, as if turning a dial.

"Three," she managed to squeak out.

"Physically, not emotionally," he chided.

"Oh." She smiled, eyes still closed, feeling herself relax just a little. The sensation increased the moment she did, sending little sparks down her nerve endings. "Six, I guess."

"So you do experience pleasure?"

"Oh, yes." She felt her belly tighten when his other hand began manipulating her left nipple the same way. "It feels nice."

"You can open your eyes." He was smiling when she did. "Do you mind if I touch your vagina?"

She made a face at the clinical word but nodded her head.

"We like to use terms you're comfortable with," he said, interpreting her look. "During sex, what would you call your genitals?"

"I don't have a penis." Rose giggled. She couldn't help it. "I'm not a guy. I didn't *name* it."

He laughed. "Okay, complete this sentence. 'I'd like you to touch my blank.'"

The heat filling her cheeks moved down to her chest, but she managed to take a deep breath and say the words. "I'd like you to touch my…pussy."

"Okay." He nodded, still smiling his approval. "May I touch your pussy?"

Rose winced again. Now it had moved from far too clinical to far too intimate. But what else could she do?

"Yes."

She closed her eyes without being asked this time, feeling his fingers parting her lips, sliding two of them inside. His other hand pressed gently over her belly and he rocked his hands, checking the position of her uterus. She'd had the examination often enough to know just what he was doing, but his next question surprised her.

"Have you ever shaved your pussy?"

"No." Her eyes flew open to see him looking down between her legs, where his hand disappeared under her paper skirt. "Why?"

"It's been known to increase sensation."

She got up on her elbows to peer at him. "Really?"

"I'd like to take a closer look," he said. "Do you mind getting up in the stirrups?"

"Okay."

He helped her put her legs up and scoot down to the end of the table, the most humiliating position in the world. She noticed for the first time that there was a poster on the ceiling, just a little one with a picture of an acorn and a quote by Ralph Waldo Emerson—*what lies behind us and what lies before us are tiny matters compared to what lies within us.*

Rose didn't think whoever had chosen the poster had really thought about the literal interpretations, but she was thinking about them as Dr. Matt slid two fingers into her vagina—pussy—again. It made her want to giggle like she was twelve-years-old.

"See anything wrong?"

"Decidedly not." He chuckled. "Everything appears physically normal. I'd like to try something. Would you mind if we did a stimulation test?"

She sighed. "Okay."

"I know you've been through this before."

She had, numerous times, but she still gasped when a strong buzzing sensation met the sensitive bud of her clit. It was so strange to be in a clinical setting like this and have someone testing your capacity for arousal. It was like walking a tightrope over an unknown drop into nothing. Dr. Matt continued rubbing a vibrator against her clitoris, back and forth, up and down.

"How does that feel?"

"Nice." Rose blinked up at the ceiling.

"I'm going to leave this here on your clitoris for a moment while I do an internal examination. Do you mind?"

She shrugged. "No."

His fingers were feeling around inside, gentle but pressing firmly. "And you've had your g-spot explored?"

"Thoroughly," she assured him. "It's broken too."

He hesitated for a moment and then stood up between her legs, looking down at her. "You're not broken, Rose."

She couldn't help the tears that stung her eyes. "Yes I am."

He shook his head violently. "Do you feel that?"

"What? The vibrator?" she asked, swiping at her eyes with the back of her hand. "Of course."

"No, this." He removed his gloved hand from her pussy and brought it up to her stomach, pressing her hand there along with his. "Feel how tight your muscles are? How little breath is getting down here into your belly?"

She looked at him, incredulous, as he removed the vibrator, snapping his gloves off. He helped her out of the stirrups and took her elbow as she swung her legs around so she could sit on the examination table.

"You might as well be wearing armor," he told her as he went over the sink to wash his hands. "It's no wonder you can't feel anything beyond 'nice' right now. It *is* a kind of armor."

"What do you mean?"

He dried his hands on paper towel as he talked. "You've just built up a lot of walls. The good news about those walls is that they've protected you when you needed protecting. You've walled out all the bad things—and good for you! But the problem is that while you've walled everything out, you've also walled yourself in. And you're going to have to break those down before you can get where you want to go."

Her aunt Poppy had been right. This place—this doctor—was very different from anything she'd ever experienced before. She felt frozen by his words, unable to respond.

"Okay, examination over." He smiled as he walked toward the door. "You can get dressed. I'll see you in the morning."

"In the morning?" she managed, her throat tight.

"Group therapy," he reminded her before he left. "Nine a.m."

* * * *

I so don't belong here.

She knew, of course, that this clinic dealt with all sorts of sexual issues, and maybe she was just being naïve, but she hadn't expected to be in a group session with ex-prostitutes, sex addicts, and one woman (or man?) she still couldn't quite determine the gender of. Rose couldn't believe some of the things she was hearing.

"My father told me I deserved to get Aids."

That was from the woman (man?) with the long, curly dark hair, mouth painted brightly with red lipstick. But he (she?) had a day's worth of stubble. *It has to be a man,* Rose reasoned.

"And how did that make you feel, Kennedy?" The other group therapist—besides Dr. Matt—was a petite blond woman who said on the first day to call her Dr. Kelly and who seemed to think matching her eye shadow to her outfit was a good idea. Today it was a shimmery pink to go with her blouse.

"Fucking fantastic." Kennedy—his (her?) name just served to cause more gender confusion—snorted laughter and pulled a pack of cigarettes out of his t-shirt pocket. They weren't allowed to smoke inside, but Rose, and she supposed the rest of the group as well over the past week, had become familiar with his routine of smacking the edge of the pack against the arm of his chair over and over. It annoyed her but she just watched, knowing that her own habit of tracing the side seam of her jeans during the whole session probably drove someone else nuts. They all had their little quirks, she supposed.

"Bullshit." The girl with the dragon tattoo—just like the book, which so amused Rose she thought of her that way even though she knew her real name was Ann—practically spat the word from her pierced mouth. She had a ring on either side of her bottom lip—"They're called snake bites," Ann had told her while they were eating lunch the other day.

Kennedy glared. "Are you not familiar with sarcasm, you stupid bitch?"

"Fuck you." The girl with the dragon tattoo give him the middle finger and a snarl.

"No name calling, Kennedy," Dr. Kelly reminded him, waving one of the big guys back. There were two of them, both with shaved heads, that were part of their little group, and Rose thought of them both as Mr. Clean 1 and Mr. Clean 2. The one who actually had an earring in his left ear liked to stand up as everyone's protector. Besides those two, their group was rounded out by a skinny young girl about Ann's age with thin, lanky blond hair and dull eyes, and a chubby kid who couldn't have been older that twenty-five with severe acne. He hadn't said more than two words the entire week.

"Sarcasm is just the body's natural defense against stupid." Kennedy smacked his maroon pack of *Pall-Malls* against the chair, flipping it before doing it again.

"You're half right," Dr. Matt interjected. "Sarcasm is a natural defense mechanism."

Rose smiled over at him and then looked at Kennedy. "If my father had said that to me, I would have been devastated."

"Yeah?" Kennedy scoffed, dismissing Rose's comment and sneering at the dragon tattoo girl. "How about you, Ann? Would *you* have been devastated?"

"My father?" Ann flashed him a smile, those snake bites rising with the stretch of her lips. "He started fucking me when I was five. If I had a penny for every time he told me I'd be better off dead, I'd have more money than Warren Buffet." She allowed this shocking news to sink in, letting the silence stretch. Rose didn't know if anyone else heard her mumbling, but she did. She was right next to her. “Funny thing is—he was right.”

“No he wasn’t.” Rose turned and put her hand on the girl’s forearm, over the dragon tattoo. It was a horrible rendition, red faded to pink, more amusing then menacing. “He wasn’t right. You aren’t better off dead.”

“This coming from you?” Across the room, Kennedy scoffed again. “You think we don’t know about your scars?”

Rose shrank into her chair and could almost feel her wrist burning beneath her long sleeved blouse. She’d been so careful… yet someone had seen. They knew. They all knew.

“So what did Daddy do to you, Rosie-girl?” The blond chimed in, her dull eyes brightening for a moment. “Or was it maybe Mummy?”

“Neither,” Rose insisted, looking around at the group. “My parents are good parents. I’m sorry for what happened to you…” She glanced between Kennedy and Ann. “Both of you. But nothing like that has ever happened to me.”

“So why are you here?” The blond leaned forward so far Rose thought she might fall out of her chair.

“That’s a good question.” Rose felt tears coming and didn’t want to show them. Not after hearing that they knew, they all knew about her suicide attempt. She couldn’t stand the humiliation, the shame of it. She knew she would hear about it later in an individual session, but she did it anyway—she bolted.

The group therapy room was around the corner and down the hall from the residence rooms. They all had private quarters with their own bathrooms. There were no roommates at the facility, and after hearing some of the stuff people said in group therapy, she understood why. They really didn’t want fraternizing between clients going on.

She passed one of the women who cleaned their rooms every morning but Rose didn’t stop. Her room opened with a key card and she flung it onto the desk, giving into her tears now, real sobs ripping through her body, making her shake with them.

What am I doing here?

She still didn't know the answer to that question. Because Poppy had made the recommendation? Because her father was paying for it? Because she didn't want to hear her mother complaining about how she'd let "the good one" get away in Sam? Because she felt fundamentally flawed and wanted to find a way to mend the cracks in her veneer?

Whatever the reason, she felt as if it wasn't working. She'd been there a week and so far it hadn't been *that* much different from other places and methods she'd tried. Sure, there was the live-in aspect of this place. And she couldn't complain about the view from her room or anywhere else in the facility. Everywhere you looked, it was an island paradise outside. But how was that helping her with her issues?

Rose flopped face down onto her bed—even those were nice, double-size not twins, better than most hotel mattresses she'd been on—and buried her face in the pillow. *I wonder if you can suffocate yourself?* She hadn't thought about suicide in months, but she thought about it now. Not in a real way, not in the same way she had the night it happened. But the thought of not being here, not experiencing this life, walking around like she was in a dream, was more than a little appealing at the moment.

What are you running away from?

Dr. Matt's voice in her head. They had individual sessions for an hour every day. It was, she had to admit, the most intensive therapy she'd ever had. It was as if he had become part of her consciousness, definitely more than just background noise. Instead, he was a constant presence, and she often heard him in her head like this, asking questions, making comments. She hadn't told him about it though.

"Nothing." She whispered it out loud, closing her eyes, feeling a dull ache behind them. She lied to herself again, hoping she might actually believe it as she let herself drift off. "I'm not running from anything."

She was dreaming something strange but couldn't remember what it was when the knock came on her door. Glancing at the clock, she saw it was nearly noon. Group therapy had been over for almost an hour. She thought about not answering it, but then she heard Dr. Matt's voice on the other side.

"Rose?"

He smiled when she opened the door, holding out a small blue box. "I have something for you."

"A blue box." She took it from his hands, inspecting the name on the top. *Lelo*. What was Lelo? "You know, most women see a blue box and think Tiffanys."

"Not this time." He laughed. "This is to help you do your homework."

Her head came up fast, eyes widening, knowing immediately what it was. "Okay, well, I'll open it later." She set the box on her desk, but she couldn't help the blush spreading on her cheeks.

"Are you okay?" he asked, leaning against the door frame. He was long and lanky but he seemed to fill every available inch of space anyway.

"Fine." She offered him a smile, a shrug. "Just fine."

He raised an eyebrow. "Can we please stop with the lies?"

"I'm not lying," she protested, crossing her arms over her chest. "I am fine. Now that I've had some time away from that...group. I'm fine."

"So you're not enjoying group therapy?"

She smirked. "Am I supposed to enjoy it?"

"Not exactly." He grinned.

"I'm not like those people," she confessed, hugging herself as she looked up at him.

He nodded, but disagreed. "You'd be surprised."

"But...none of them have my problem."

"No," he said. "But that doesn't mean you don't have things in common."

Rose sighed, not knowing if what he said was true or not, but feeling bad anyway. "Well I'm sorry I ran out."

He shrugged. "You can apologize to them tomorrow."

"Great." She rolled her eyes and laughed. "Something to look forward to."

"Well, it's almost lunch time," he told her. "Are you hungry?"

She shook her head. "I think I'll just get back to napping."

"You could always do your homework," he reminded her, turning to go.

"You're not the first therapist who's prescribed daily masturbation you know." She got the reaction she wanted when he turned and looked over his shoulder at her.

"Are you doing it?"

"Yeah, but it does nothing," she countered. "I feel nothing."

"Do it anyway." He started out.

"It just makes me cry," she called.

"Good." He smiled over his shoulder at her. "Crying doesn't sound like nothing."

"It's depressing," she muttered.

"Do it anyway."

"Okay! Okay!" She started to shut the door behind him.

"Don't nap too long," he reminded her. "We're conducting your sleep study tomorrow. You need to be awake for twelve hours beforehand."

"I remember." She leaned against the door as she closed it, contemplating the box on her desk. It felt strange having Dr. Matt give her a vibrator, like it was a personal gift. Of course, it wasn't. It was just another tool, something to help her with her "issues." She'd been instructed by plenty of sex therapists to masturbate daily. She was familiar enough with the idea.

And she'd been a diligent student, just as Dr. Matt had told her to. Ten minutes of masturbation every night, by the clock. She set her cell phone alarm so she was sure it was actually ten minutes. So far, she had barely even felt a tingle. She felt strung too tight here, stretched thin, always too aware that there were people around, even when her door was locked.

"It's not going to work," she told the blue box as she opened it, sliding the lid off to find just what she expected inside—a vibrator. There was a little card that Dr. Matt had written on.

It's rechargeable. Six variable speeds. Very powerful. Experiment all you like!

Rose giggled, pulling out the cord that went with it. It looked awfully small to be powerful. *What the hell,* she thought, checking to make sure the door was completely closed and locked before heading over to the bed. She left her jeans in a ball on the floor but her panties still on, lying back on the bed and turning the *Lelo* on.

It buzzed gently in her hand as she looked at it, running her fingers over the navy blue tip. The texture was soft and hard at the same time, like velvet over steel. So sleek, so tempting. Masturbation was usually an exercise in futility. She could work herself up to a fever pitch, but it was like starving to death, standing outside of a four-star restaurant, watching everyone else eating a gourmet meal—why torture herself like that?

Still, that sweet tingle between her thighs felt so good. If only…

She traced the Lelo vibrator over her fat, pink nipples, around and around. They hardened immediately, pointed toward the ceiling in anticipation. The sensation was delicious, sending sweet waves of pleasure down between her legs. She let the vibrator travel over her ribcage, down her trembling belly, under the elastic of her panties, parting the thick nest of blonde hair at the apex of her thighs.

The Lelo hummed against her clit and she waved it there, back and forth, hoping that Dr. Matt had finally found the perfect magic wand to break the spell, to cure her curse. It felt so good, she almost, for a moment, hoped and believed it was true.

"Mmmm." She closed her eyes, letting herself be carried away by the sensation. The gentle buzzing made her ache, her body flushing with pleasure. She could feel the wetness increasing, her pussy beginning to swell. She focused at the center of the sensation, moving the wand in circles, hearing her own breathing grow ragged.

"Oh Matt," she whispered, flushing with his name filling her mouth, wishing it was his cock. Oh god, what was she thinking? She hadn't fantasized much during her "homework" sessions so far. It was too easy to flash to memories of Sam, and that ended things pretty quickly. And while Matt looked so very much like her ex-fiancé, they were so different she could have told them apart in the dark.

"Oh god, yes, lick my pussy." She couldn't help imagining it, Matt's sweet mouth between her legs. She loved that feeling so much, although she hated asking for it, hated when Sam did it, because he liked her to have multiple-orgasms. Which was easy when you were faking them, of course, but it made it difficult to concentrate on the actual feeling—which was delightful—of a warm, wet tongue between her legs.

And what would his cock look like? Taste like? Feel like? She licked her lips as she fantasized, closing her thighs around the persistent buzz between them, the Lelo caught between her swollen pussy lips, tucked under the edge of her panties. Would he fuck her long and slow? Hard and fast? She wanted the latter but fantasized about the former, hearing his breath in her ear, his sweet urgings, *"That's it. Nice and slow. We'll get you there, I promise."*

Oh to reach that blessed destination. If only she could. Rose sighed, knowing she'd reached that point, her whole body aching for release, belly tight, breathing fast, but like a starving orphan standing at a restaurant window, she would have to go home hungry with that empty, gnawing feeling in her belly.

She realized she hadn't set a timer for this session, but her eyes were closed and she was already drifting off, too lazy to check. Their schedules were so full here, she barely had time to breathe, and a moment to herself in the middle of the day for a quick cat nap couldn't be resisted.

"Feel that," he whispered. "Feel everything."

She was. Every nerve ending in her body was alive at his touch. He was touching her there, between the legs, his fingers moving, probing, manipulating. She moaned in response, shifting her hips.

"Good," he encouraged. "Tell me how it feels. Tell me what you want."

"Oh god, Matt," she whispered, the feeling too full for her to express. "Please don't stop doing that."

"Like this?"

Oh god yes, just like that, she thought, rocking her hips, stretching up like a flower reaching toward the heat of the sun, more more more. She couldn't stand it. She wanted him. Her whole being screamed out for him again and again, like lightning flashing in the dark, followed by rolling waves of thunder.

"Matt!" she cried, thrashing, and he kissed her mouth, his breath hot, just as ragged as her own, his fingers buried between her thighs. "Oh yes, please, make me come! Please make me come."

"I will," he promised, but no, promises were empty, no one ever kept them. She moaned and tensed and tried to escape, but he held her fast, panting in her ear. "Give me what you want. Give me everything. I can take it."

"Noooo," she wailed, but her body gave in, oh god, yes yes yes, this was it, this was pleasure and pain and love and—

"Matt!" Rose woke with a start, her body covered in sweat, the Lelo still buzzing between her sticky thighs, a faint pulse—*What? Is that it? Was that an orgasm?*—the sweetest sensation, so close she could almost grasp it, fading between her legs.

"Not fair," she whispered, grabbing the vibrator and tossing it aside. "So much for magic wands."

She could have all the orgasms in the world—while she was sleeping, apparently. But she couldn't remember them, couldn't really fully experience them. It was like feeling full, but not remembering eating a meal. There was no pleasure in it.

* * * *

"I feel like Frankenstein's monster," Rose complained as Matt attached another sticky circle to her skin and then another lead. The wires snaked out under the hospital gown she'd been asked by a nurse to put on. She hadn't seen the nurse though, since Matt showed up.

He smiled, checking the machine she was attached to. "No lightning bolts, I promise."

"So I'm just supposed to sleep with all this stuff on?" She shrugged helplessly, trying to move with all the wires attached—to her chest, her belly, her thighs, her temples. "How is that possible?"

"I've actually got one more to attach," he said, looking sheepish.

She groaned. "Where? I'm hooked up all over."

He cleared his throat. "Inside."

She looked at him blankly.

"Inside your…pussy."

She gaped at him. "You've got to be kidding me."

"I'm afraid not." He gave her an apologetic smile. "Can you lay back?"

She sighed but did as he asked.

"Let your knees fall open," he said. She felt his gloved hand on her thigh, and even through the latex it felt hot. "That's good. It will only take a second."

"What if I have to pee?" She felt him probing between her legs and flushed, remembering her dream. This was somehow very different from the first exam he'd done. Things had changed between them, had definitely become more…intimate.

"That's why we restricted your fluids," he reminded her. "Okay, all done." He snapped off his gloves and helped her sit.

"Why are we doing this again?"

He busied himself gathering the wires trailing out from under her gown into one bundle. "These leads go to machines that will give us important information about your body."

"Information like…what?" she inquired, watching as he used adhesive bandage tape to secure the leads together.

"Heart rate, breathing, brain waves." His hand brushed her knee and she shivered. "We'll even be able to tell when you're dreaming."

"You will?" The thought of her dream the day before made her face flush with heat.

He seemed to anticipate her concern. "Don't worry, we can't tell what you're dreaming about… not exactly."

"What does that mean?" She looked at the machine across from her, dubious.

Matt cleared his throat as he stood fully. "Well, we can tell if you're experiencing arousal."

"Oh."

"And of course, we'll know if you have an orgasm in your sleep," he added.

Rose shook her head. "No pressure."

"Well that's kind of the point." Matt smiled, gathering the blankets and quilt from the end of the bed. They'd made it as cozy as they could, with a real bed, not a hospital one, and thick blankets and quilts and plenty of pillows. "You're completely vulnerable when you're sleeping."

"Right." Somehow that didn't make her feel any better. "And you'll be watching." She nodded toward the mirrored wall across the way. She knew two-way glass when she saw it.

"Yes," he admitted, helping her get under the covers. It was almost like he was tucking her in, which was both sweet and a little strange. She hadn't been tucked into bed since she was little. "I'll be monitoring the machines all night."

She reclined on the bed, still too aware of all the wires trailing under the covers. "That's not creepy or anything."

"Well, I can give you something to help you sleep, if you want it. It's just better for our results if we record a natural sleep cycle."

"No, no." She waved his offer away. "I'll give it the old college try first."

"Are you tired?"

She rolled her eyes, which were already heavy with sleep now that she was warmly tucked into bed. "I've been up for the past eighteen hours—what do you think?"

Matt grinned. "Sometimes patients can't make it."

"You can thank *Angry Birds* for that." She nodded toward her bag, where Matt's iPad was stored. He'd loaned it to her at dinner, suggesting it might help keep her awake all night.

He laughed. "I hoped that might do it."

"That damned game is far too addictive."

"Isn't it?" Matt adjusted the lights, turning off the overheads and dimming the ones over the sink. "I've got an intern who wants to do a study on why it's so addictive."

Rose felt her eyes closing already. She was so tired. Flinging fat little video game birds all night was exhausting. "He can use me as a test subject."

"Well let's see if we can get to the bottom of this problem first, shall we?" Matt's hand moved over the covers, literally tucking her in now, adjusting the wires.

"Sounds like a plan," she murmured, feeling his hand moving through her hair, stroking gently. She held her breath, his fingertips brushing her cheek, and when she opened her eyes he was looking down at her, gaze soft and a little dreamy.

It made her stomach do flips. She whispered her question, as if it might break the mood. "Will there be anyone else out there or just you?"

"It'll just be me," he assured her, his eyes meeting hers. They were so warm and dark and there was something there, an emotion she hadn't seen before, but maybe she was just imagining things, hallucinating from lack of sleep. That's what she told herself.

That was, until Matt leaned down at kissed her forehead, his mouth soft, breath warm. "Goodnight, Rose. Sweet dreams."

She was so surprised she couldn't reply, and then he was gone. She couldn't help the small smile playing on her lips as her heavy eyelids closed and she finally whispered, "'Night, Matt," knowing he was there, just on the other side of the glass. It made her feel safe enough to sleep.

She was floating in a golden haze, sweet honey on her lips, between her thighs. There were hands touching her but she could see no faces. She drifted on a cloud, the darkness giving her no reason to protest, no shame, no fear, just pure pleasure and sensation.

And then she was in an alleyway, pressed against a wall, a man between her thighs, hard cock seeking entrance to her heat. She was afraid but excited, eager, even greedy, but she thrashed in his arms, saying, "No! No!"

There was no one to hear.

"Open your legs for me." Alone on a table, the voice somewhere far above. She did as she was told, whimpering, crying, begging. "Touch your pussy. Yes. Like that. Rub your swollen cunt."

She flushed in shame, but the wet heat between her legs begged for more and she rubbed and rubbed her swollen flesh. A mouth on her breast, licking her nipples. A cock in her mouth, thick and thrusting deep into her throat. She gagged and choked on the length, but she never stopped touching herself.

Naked, following a white thread in a black maze. How could she possibly find her way? What if the thread broke? Then what? She kept her fingers on that thin line to freedom, feeling her way in the darkness. Someone calling her name. A familiar voice.

"Rose!"

There was no door, no entrance, just a sudden shift and she was in his arms, covered with kisses, his cock pressed against her hip like a brand.

"I want you." It wasn't a question or even a demand. It just was. He sank to his knees and buried his face between her thighs, the sensation almost more than she could bear. She cried out in pleasure, curling her fingers in his hair.

"Fuck me!" she begged. "Please!"

And he covered her with himself, like a blanket, like fire, sweaty, hot, thrusting deep and hard, making her teeth rattle, her pelvis creak in protest, and still it wasn't enough.

"Harder! Faster!"

He grunted and thrust, biting at her neck and shoulder, tongue lashing her nipples. She grabbed his hips and fucked him back, rocking and rolling like a carnival ride. There was no stopping now.

"Come for me," he panted. "Oh fuck, Rosie, come! Come for me! Come for you!"

And in the darkness she knew it was him. She screamed his name as she came.

* * * *

It was the closest thing they'd ever come to an argument during a session.

"But I thought Sam was the one," Rose protested. "He was my everything."

"And he left you." Matt leaned forward in his chair, his eyes dark as he said those devastating words. Rose tried not to show a response, but she couldn't help her sarcastic reply.

"Yeah. Thanks for the reminder."

"I'm just wondering what kind of man would do that?" Matt pressed on. "I'll be honest with you, Rose, if you had been my fiancé, I wouldn't have left."

"But I lied to him," she said, feeling the weight of that fact in her chest.

"There are lies…and then there are *lies*," Matt said, dismissing her excuse. "I'm not saying lying is good or right, but the fact is that everyone lies. You have to decide how hurtful a lie is before you start making judgments. The lie you told hurt his ego, nothing more." He gave her plenty to think about, but he always did. He was very good at his job, and sometimes she hated that. His next words startled her out of her thoughts. "But I can understand why he left."

"You can?" She met his eyes in a slant of sunlight coming across his desk from the open window. It was a gorgeous day and she could even heard the waves crashing on the beach.

Matt smiled grimly. "At worst, he had a very small, easily bruised ego. At best, your confession forced him to face up to the fact that, for two years, you weren't able to fully trust him."

Rose gaped. "But it wasn't his fault."

"No, but Rose, we all pick partners for a reason." Matt sighed, leaning back in his chair. "We just usually don't understand what that reason really is until much later in the relationship—if we ever discover it at all."

She chewed on his words, using the window as a distraction. She could see the water from here, a beautiful expanse of blue. "My mother told me Sam reminded her of my father."

"How so?"

"I don't know." But she did know and Matt gave her that look, the one that said he knew she wasn't giving him everything. Sighing, Rose went on. "I guess I can see it a little. He was kind of larger than life, like my father. He wasn't a bad guy. All he ever wanted to do was take care of me. Sam liked to fix things. I think that's one of the reasons I never told him—because every problem I ever had, he tried to fix. And I knew he couldn't fix this one."

"And your father is like that?"

"In some ways." Rose shrugged. "Like when he found out about my…problem…he sent me to the best medical specialists in the world."

"Right. How did he find out again? Did you tell him?"

"Let's just say my aunt Poppy has a big mouth." She rolled her eyes. "I was only twenty-two. I honestly didn't even know what I was missing until I got drunk with a girlfriend in college and we ended up playing around with her vibrator…"

Matt's eyebrows raised and he leaned forward onto his elbows on the desk. "What happened?"

Rose gave him a long, steady look and then laughed. "What is it with men and lesbian scenarios?"

"I didn't ask for the purpose of arousal," Matt assured her.

"But the thought arouses you, doesn't it?" she countered.

He smiled. "I could tell you the answer to that, but then I'd have to pay you instead of the other way around."

She couldn't help laughing. "Well my father's footing the bill for this place, so however that impacts the metaphor, it's probably just creepy…"

"So how did you figure out what you were missing?" Matt pressed.

"I watched her have an orgasm," Rose admitted. Sometimes she felt like she could tell Matt anything, especially given how many compromising positions he'd seen her in and how much information he already had about every fabric of her being. "I'd never seen anything like it before. I mean, I'd seen porn orgasms, and I knew there were supposed to be lights and fireworks and stuff at the end of sex. And it did feel good for me. I just never got to that 'oh my god' point all the porn actresses were screaming about. I thought it was fake, honestly."

Matt nodded. "But when you saw your friend…?"

"I knew it was real then," she confessed, remembering her college roommate and their experimentation. Lesley had been an athletic girl who played soccer and field hockey and was loud both on and off the field. She'd been very up front about her sexuality and it both shocked and thrilled Rose. "The way she moved, the sounds she made, that look on her face. It was really that look of…of…pure pleasure. She clearly had one final, blissful moment of release that convinced me." Glancing over, she saw Matt was hanging on her every word. "It was nothing like the movies. And it was definitely real. That's what made me want to know what it felt like."

Matt didn't say anything. He did that sometimes, waiting for her to go on, but this time it was different. The air was thick with her words, heavy, as if a spark might ignite them.

Rose felt her mouth curling into a half-smile. "Would it turn you on to know that she tried, I can't count how many times, to give me an orgasm?"

He cleared his throat. "Perhaps."

"She was very persistent," Rose assured him, wondering if he really was turned on by the thought of her with another woman. The realization that his cock might be hard under his desk, that the hand she couldn't see might be pressing it to ease the ache through his trousers, made her wild with lust. "She was very athletic, and she had these long, tanned thighs that could clamp around me like a vice..."

Matt sat up, interrupting her. "You didn't disclose in your entry interview that you're bisexual."

"I'm not." Rose grinned. "It was college—we were experimenting. And I was desperate."

"So you finally went and told your aunt?" He was clearly trying to change the subject.

"No—my nosy aunt read my journal while I was staying at her house for the summer." She remembered it with the same burning humiliation and betrayal she'd first experienced when she discovered the fact. "My father was away that year setting up factories in China and my mother was gone to Brazil."

"Then what happened?"

"We've been over this." She shrugged. "Besides, it's all in that pack of paperwork you guys made me fill out to get in here."

"I'm just wondering how your father fit into the picture."

"I wasn't abused, Matt." She waved his concern away, just as she always did. "No one ever touched me inappropriately. I was a virgin until college, just like I said. I've had a total of five sexual partners in my life. Six if you count my college roommate." She smiled at the way he shifted in his chair when she said that. "My father never beat me or touched me in any way that he shouldn't have touched his daughter."

Matt nodded, but he didn't give up. "Most of our psychological wounds don't have physical causes."

"He didn't emotionally abuse me either," she assured him. " In fact, it was more the opposite. He tried to shelter me as much as possible from the bad things. I was his only child, his only daughter—his little princess."

"Is that what he called you?"

She smiled, remembering. "Yes."

"What about your mother?"

"She didn't abuse me either." She rolled her eyes. "I'm telling you, Matt, my life has been pretty void of trauma."

"Aside from your parent's divorce," he reminded her.

She snorted. "Over half the people in this country have parents who get divorced. I bet most of them can still have orgasms."

Matt just looked her. He always knew when she was deflecting, being defensive. Of course, it was his job to know—but sometimes it was disarming.

Then he changed tactics. "You were having a dream the other night…"

She froze in her chair. "Do we have to talk about this?" She had been worried about it and of course, it had actually happened—she'd dreamed about him, had even called his name.

But Matt was going in a different direction. "You mentioned a woman's name. Cathy. Who's Cathy?"

She stiffened, her breath gone. "I have no idea."

"Are you sure?" That look again. Damn, he was good.

"Did I say anything else?" she asked, discovering she preferred talking about her salacious dream starring Dr. Matt to telling him about Cathy.

He smiled. "Did you know you talk in your sleep?"

"Yeah." She knew, and she hated it. "Sam mentioned it a couple of times. He thought it was funny. I'd wake up and tell him he needed to remember his breathing apparatus for work in the morning. Only I wasn't awake at all. I don't remember any of it."

"Can I show you something?" Matt opened the laptop on his desk, signing in. Rose didn't say anything, she just watched as he turned the screen toward her and she saw a grainy image of her in the bed where she spent the night a week ago, hooked up to wires and machines. She was definitely sleeping, hand curled up by her cheek, mouth hanging open.

"This is it?" She raised an eyebrow at him. "Me, pillow-drooling?"

"Keep watching."

Suddenly she was thrashing on the bed, calling out. Oh god. She thought nothing could be worse than hearing herself call Matt's name.

"Daddy! No!"

Her eyes were silver in the darkness on the video as she sat up, staring into space at nothing, yet seeing something in her mind. And then a scream tore from her throat, so loud even through the laptop speakers that Rose covered her ears as she watched herself screaming hoarsely over and over, the words finally making sense.

"It's not Cathy's fault! It's not her fault!"

Matt hit a button on the laptop and the image disappeared. He closed the lid, looking at her, gauging her reaction.

"So…who's Cathy?" he asked again.

She shrugged, not meeting his gaze. "Obviously someone in my dream."

"Remember what I said to you about no lies?"

Damn him. He knew just what to say. It felt so manipulative—but she knew his motivations were pure. He really did just want to help her.

"She was my nanny." Rose sighed, giving in. "From the time I was a baby until… oh, I guess I was twelve or thirteen."

Matt nodded thoughtfully. "Do you remember this dream?"

"No." That much was true, although she could guess what it had been about.

"Was she a good nanny?"

Rose smiled thinly. "She was my best friend."

"What happened to her?"

"Oh I don't know. I guess she quit." Why she couldn't tell him the whole truth, she didn't know. What did it have to do with anything? But she couldn't, so she lied. "Went off to college or got a boyfriend or something."

"Mm hmm."

“Oh don’t give me that therapist ‘mmm-hmm’ crap,” she snapped, hating the knowing look in his eyes. “I don’t know what you’re getting at.”

He shrugged. “I’m not sure either. Let’s call it a hunch.”

“So much for psychiatry being a science,” she spat, crossing her arms and looking pointedly at the diplomas on his wall.

“It’s a soft science.” He was trying to hide a smile. “That means we fly by the seat of our pants a lot. So let’s see where this goes. Humor me.”

“That’s what I’m here for.” She wrinkled her nose at him. “To humor you.”

“So was this nanny like a second mother to you?”

“More like a big sister,” she corrected. “She was only twenty-something when my parents hired her.”

“And that was her job for ten years?” Matt asked, surprised. “She was exclusively your nanny?”

“My father pays well,” she said, but that wasn’t enough for him. He knew. He knew something. And what was the harm in telling him anyway? It had been a long, long time ago. “Plus there were… fringe benefits.”

“Oh?”

She sighed and gave in fully. “He was fucking her, okay?”

“So…what wasn’t her fault?”

Rose looked out the window, feeling the breeze, wishing she was on the beach, long sleeves and all. “It was my fault my mother found out.” Glancing at Matt, she saw he was listening. He had that leaned-in posture to encourage her to go on. What the hell? He wanted a story—she’d tell him a story. “I had a huge crush on Sting at the time and my new Teen Beat had arrived. You know Teen Beat?”

“Vaguely familiar.” He smiled.

“It had this giant, sexy poster of him in it and I was excited to show her. I ran through the kitchen calling for Cathy, and ran into my mother, drinking a manhattan and reading a book. She asked me what I was so excited about…but I didn’t stop. I wanted to tell Cathy. My mother yelled after me that Cathy wasn’t feeling well, that I shouldn’t bother her. But I ran up to her room anyway.”

"And?"

"The door was locked." Rose paused, remembering. The memory alone made her palms sweat and her limbs tingle. "I didn't knock. I just tried the door. It was locked. Then I tried it again…and it opened."

Matt looked confused. "Someone unlocked it?"

"No. I think someone had slammed that door really hard at some point and the lock didn't always close all the way," she explained. "Anyway, the door opened. And guess what I found?"

"I can imagine." Matt made a face. "He was having sex with the nanny with your mother was right downstairs?"

"It was a big house." She shrugged, trying to make it sound like it wasn't a big deal. It wasn't a big mystery or anything. Matt wanted to hear her tale of woe? Fine. "And here comes my mother, right behind me, scolding me for bothering Cathy... and there's Cathy on her knees with my father's—"

Matt interrupted her tirade. "So what did your mother do?"

That took the wind out of her sails and Rose collapsed into her chair, feeling incredibly small. "She fired Cathy. And she divorced my father. In that order."

"I'm so sorry, Rosie." Matt's voice was soft, gentle, as if his words alone might comfort her. It was the first time he'd used her nickname. "You lost your best friend and your parents split up and your whole world turned upside down—just at a time when you were coming to sexual maturity."

"I guess so." She avoided his gaze, watching a dog run down the beach after a stick someone had thrown. "I haven't thought about *She-Who-Shall-Not-Be-Named* in years."

"Do you miss her?"

"I did, at first," she admitted, remembering. The house had felt so empty after Cathy left, she could barely stand it. She'd stayed in her room a lot after that, listening to her Walkman. "But I didn't understand any of it. I felt betrayed by Cathy, by my father. And—" Rose snorted at the realization. "My poor mother. I blamed her for firing Cathy and breaking up the family."

"You were betrayed," Matt assured her. "And I can understand your feelings of anger at your mother. And your confusion."

She looked at him, speculative. She hadn't expected that response. "Cathy told me she loved my father. And I could understand that. But she also told me...she said that men weren't worth it. That all they could ever offer you was pain. 'It might feel good for a while, Rosie, but in the end, it always ends up like this.'"

The silence was deafening, stretching between them, like a pent-up breath. She felt tears stinging her eyes at the memory, could see Cathy's young face, practically snarling, the words choked out as if she was drowning in them.

"She said... 'No man is worth the pleasure he promises. I wish I'd known that ten years ago.'" Her father had caused this, Rose understood. It wasn't Cathy's fault, not really. It was his fault. He had betrayed her mother, betrayed their marriage, and had hurt them all. Cathy's pain had been too hard for her twelve-year-old self to bear. "'Don't ever give yourself to a man the way I did, Rosie. Don't do it. Don't ever do it. *Promise me.*'"

Oh Cathy, I'm so sorry. She wondered where she was now, that poor woman. Ten years of her life wasted on a man who didn't really care about anyone but himself.

"And then what happened?" Matt asked gently.

"I promised," Rose admitted, meeting his eyes.

"Are you still keeping that promise?"

"I think I am," she whispered softly. The realization left her breathless and she searched for some escape, looking at the clock on his desk. "Our time's up, Matt."

"So it is." It had been up ten minutes ago, but he hadn't said anything, and now she knew why. He tented his fingers on the desk, looking at her thoughtfully. "Rose, I'd like to talk to you about something... unconventional."

She laughed. "This whole place is unconventional."

"Have you ever heard of a sexual surrogate?" he asked. Rose shook her head as he continued. "We have a few on staff. Basically, it's someone who engages in intimate contact with a client—always with a therapeutic goal in mind of course."

She blinked at him. "Intimate contact…you mean…sex?"

"It can include sexual intercourse, yes," he confirmed. "I think you might benefit from some one on one contact. I don't think we're going to have a breakthrough with masturbation alone. You need to learn to trust another person first."

"But…" Rose frowned, trying to absorb just what he was proposing. Therapeutic sex? How did that work, exactly? And…did she really want to know? "But I don't want to have sex with a stranger."

"Well, you still have two weeks left here at the facility," he explained. "That would give you some time to get to know each other, to establish trust…"

"No." Rose shook her head. "Matt, no. It won't work and you know it."

"Why?"

She loved how he so often asked her to explain herself. So few people in her life had ever given her that opportunity. "I was with Sam for two years and I still couldn't trust him enough. Why do you think a few weeks with a stranger is really going to make a difference?"

Matt sat thoughtfully for a moment—his turn to look out the window. Then he sighed and turned to face her. "You've made such good progress, Rose. I really want to see you have a breakthrough."

"Do you?" She leaned onto his desk, searching his eyes, coming to another realization that startled her. It probably should have been obvious, but somehow the thought, the idea—the feeling—had snuck up on her.

"Yes."

She reached across the desk and slid her hand into his. No wedding rings, no attachments, no excuses. She took a deep breath and said, "Then do it yourself."

"…What?" His eyes widened, but he didn't reject her. In fact, his hand enveloped hers and she felt like the heat of their skin together could have burned a hole through the desk.

"I want *you,*" she whispered, watching his face, gauging his reaction—and seeing exactly what she hoped for flicker in his eyes. There was more than a spark between them. "If I'm going to do this, I want *you* to be my sexual surrogate."

"Rose…" He turned her hand over, palm up, and traced the lines there. "I'm not sure that's ethical. Or wise."

"But it's right," she insisted. "And I think you know it."

He lifted her hand to his lips, kissing her palm, eyes closed. "Maybe." Then he let her go.

Rose sat back, breathless. "So that's not a no?"

"It's a maybe." God, she loved the man's smile. "Let me run it by legal. Get some clearance so I don't lose my job in the process."

In her haste, she hadn't even considered that. "I don't want to get you into trouble."

"With you, I think I'm already in trouble." He grinned. "Besides, I think your instincts may be right on."

She stood, picking up her bag and slinging it over her shoulder. "They usually are."

"I'll have an answer for you tomorrow after group," he called as she shut the door behind her.

Leaning against it, she took deep gulps of air, her hands shaking, her belly trembling with excitement—and fear.

What, exactly, had she just signed up for?

* * * *

Rose was tired of waiting.

The moment Matt told her that they'd received the green light for him to be her sexual surrogate, it was like she couldn't wait. She felt like a racehorse at the starting gate, chomping at the bit. Matt, on the other hand, was the opposite. He was taking things so slowly she thought he might actually be part snail.

The first night they'd done nothing but hang around one of the conference rooms talking about communication and relationships and birth control (she had been on the pill since she was a teenager). There wasn't even a bed in there! She knew Matt wanted her to understand that the sexual surrogate relationship was temporary, that after the two weeks was up, their relationship would have to end. But she knew that. She was prepared for it. She told him so.

She thought, with that out of the way, things would really start rolling—and the fact that they met in a different room this time, this one with a big queen size bed, helped bolster that idea—but even their second meeting had involved very little touching. They'd talked a lot more and Matt had given her a slow massage, which felt great, but none of her clothes had come off.

At this rate, she reasoned, they wouldn't get to intercourse and orgasms until Christmas! The third and fourth night had been a little better, she reasoned. At least it involved more touching—and more nudity. He'd brought in a massage table and some scented oils and oh god, his hands on her made her feel as if her whole body was on fire. But the third night they didn't even kiss!

On the fourth, though—last night—things had become much, much more intimate. First, he had stripped her naked, and had even allowed her to take off his shirt. Then he'd given her the all-over relaxing body massage (although it was funny how non-relaxing it could be, since all she could think about was sex!) and had made a suggestion. "I want to shave your pussy."

Of course, she'd agreed. And although Matt had touched her most intimate parts before, this had been very different. He had lovingly—and carefully!—trimmed and shaved her until she was completely smooth. He had asked if she wanted a bit of hair left up top—*"A landing strip? A triangle? Maybe a heart?"*—but she had laughed and said, "Shave it all off!" so he had.

But the thing that really thrilled her was that—finally!—he had kissed her. There hadn't been any discussion or questions, he had just leaned in and captured her mouth with his like he couldn't help himself. He had made some joke and she had laughed, delighted, and he had kissed her, just like that. It had taken her breath away, giving her tingles.

And then it had been over. He was helping her get dressed, talking about their next meeting, and she had gone back to her room to toss and turn on the sheets, looking for a cool place and finding nothing but heat.

"Don't forget your homework," Matt had told her before they parted and in the darkness ,Rose had touched herself, remembering the press of his lips, the way he looked at her completely shaved pussy, his eyes dark with lust. He wanted her as much as she wanted him, she knew it was true, whatever they were calling this strange little therapeutic dance.

"Sexual surrogate, my ass," Rose muttered, her fingers soaked with her own juices, her pussy throbbing for release. But there was none. Instead, sleep finally found her and she didn't even have the benefit of remembering any dreams about Matt.

Now, finally, she was tired of waiting. She couldn't stand it anymore. She knew they were supposed to stay focused on her pleasure, her communication with him, telling him what she liked, what she didn't—but her longing for him went far beyond the physical. She didn't even understand it herself.

"Rose?" Matt gasped when he opened the door. "How did you get in here?"

She didn't answer, didn't tell him that Kennedy—who had done a lot of breaking and entering when he wasn't prostituting himself on the streets—had used his powers for good this time, helping Rose with her nefarious plan. Instead she stayed still, naked in the middle of the bed, her eyes closed, concentrating on keeping her breath slow and even.

"Rose?" He put down his baggage, she could hear it clatter and thud on the floor. She knew he was probably carrying the portable massage table he had brought the other night and a bag she knew was full of scented oils. She felt more than heard him approach, and she knew exactly how she looked, because there was a mirror on the ceiling and she had seen herself, long blonde hair spread out like a golden field of wheat beneath her shoulders, lips red and swollen and aching to be kissed, the pink nubs of her nipples hard with excitement.

"Oh god," he whispered and she felt his weight shifting the bed, his knee pushing down on the mattress. "You're so fucking beautiful."

She couldn't move, couldn't breathe. His hand moved through her hair, his fingers trailing over her cheek. She felt the heat of his breath on her shoulder, felt the press of his lips against her collarbone, her throat. A soft moan caught in her throat, her eyelids fluttering, her stomach tight with anticipation. *Please, oh Matt, please, please…*

And then he was kissing her, his mouth soft and open, exploring hers. This time she did moan, meeting his growing urgency, her limbs tingling with feeling as she wrapped her arms around his neck, pulling him fully onto the bed. She gasped when he pressed the full weight of his clothed body against hers, feeling the bite of his belt buckle against her navel. Thank god, Matt had given up his white coats for these meetings, coming in jeans and a button-down shirt.

"Oh Matt, please," she whispered, giving voice to her pleas. "I want you so much. I can't stand it. Please, please, please…" She punctuated each please with a kiss along his throat, her hands already working the buttons of his shirt.

"How did you get in here?" he asked again as she peeled off his shirt, delighting in the sight and feel of his bare skin.

"Magic," she whispered, giggling, working on his belt—and he let her. *He let her!* Not only that, he helped, unzipping his jeans and sliding them down his slim hips. The feel of his cock against her hip—already so hard for her—was all the reassurance she needed. "I want you, Matt. Every bit of you."

He groaned when her hand reached into the flap of his boxers to caress his growing length, dropping his forehead and resting it against her shoulder, letting her touch him. She was already so wet, so ready. She'd skipped dinner and had been here for hours, waiting, anticipating his arrival.

"I want your hands, your mouth, your cock." She slipped her tongue along the shell of his ear, feeling him shiver.

Matt cleared his throat, looking at her. "Well, I guess the communication lesson was effective."

"Yes," she agreed, slipping her hand lower, cupping his balls. "I know exactly what I want."

"Then tell me." His eyes were bright, his mouth curled into a soft smile.

She hesitated just a moment before asking for her favorite thing, the only thing that had brought her anywhere near a climax before.

"Your mouth." She pressed her fingers to his lips. "Lick me."

He obliged, spending far too long kissing and licking her nipples on the way down until she was writhing and whimpering and truly begging him to lick her pussy. Matt settled himself between her thighs, admiring his handiwork—he hadn't been kidding about the sensation increase, all day she'd felt exposed, her pussy swollen and wet in her panties—before beginning his tonguing exploration.

"How are you feeling?" he asked her, kissing her shaved mound, the soft press of his lips making her shiver.

"Scared," she whispered, her thighs tense, her belly quivering. "Excited. I'm afraid it won't happen. I'm afraid it will."

"It doesn't matter," he murmured, kissing all around her cleft. "Just let yourself feel the pleasure of this moment." He touched her clit with his finger, nudging it back and forth. "And this one…" And then he was kissing her clit, just his lips brushing it. "And this one…"

"One moment at a time." His tongue, oh god, his sweet tongue, flicking at her sensitive clit. Rose whimpered, her hips shifting to give him better access. "Orgasms don't matter," he told her in between soft, slow licks.

She giggled. "Your reverse psychology is showing, Dr. Matt."

"Orgasms don't matter," he repeated and then made his tongue flat, pressing against her clit hard, then soft, then hard again. "Pleasure does. If it stops feeling good, if you start tensing up, getting scared, tell me…"

"Okay," she breathed, closing her eyes. "Right now it feels fucking fantastic."

His only response was to focus on the job at hand, his tongue moving back and forth, around and around, teasing, driving her crazy with pleasure. Rose let her hands wander down, feeling the soft, dark hairs curling at the nape of his neck, guiding his mouth, shifting her hips.

"Like this?" He moved his tongue in long, slow licks against the side of her clit.

"Nooo," she whispered, rolling her hips. "Circles. Oh yes, like that! Faster! Ohhh!"

He stayed right there, doing just what she told him, and the feeling shifted from pleasure to almost pain. She felt on the verge of something delicious, her nerves stretched taut, her breath coming fast and hot, but every time she came near the edge, she'd get scared and back off again, afraid to fly. Then a sort of numbness would set in for a moment until the cycle started all over.

Matt's fingers replaced his tongue so he could ask, "What is it?"

"I'm worried you're going to stop," she admitted, quivering. "I'm afraid it will take too long. I'm afraid you're bored. I'm wondering what you're thinking…"

"I can assure you that I am *not* bored," he replied. "You taste so good, god, Rose, I could do this all night long."

"Don't make promises you can't keep."

"Oh I'll keep it, believe me." He chuckled, flicking her, teasing, with his tongue, but his fingers never stopped rubbing her, keeping her engine fully revved. "As for what I'm thinking… I'm not. My cock is so hard it hurts."

She groaned at the thought, aching for him. This was the point where she always insisted on pleasuring him, not being able to stand her own, but Matt wasn't having it.

"I told you, I can stay here all night." His tongue was making those sweet, hot circles she loved. "What happens when you touch your nipples?"

Rose did, thumbing the hard points on her chest, feeling the sensation between her legs increase tenfold. She moaned softly, closing her eyes, lifting her hips to his eager mouth. The sound of him eating her pussy was heady, the low growls and sweet smack of his lips against her flesh making her flush with heat.

"That's so good," she gasped, feeling his fingers slipping into her, probing gently. The sensation increased again, making her tremble.

"Oh Matt. Oh no. I can't. Please." He didn't stop and his greedy, eager persistence gave her permission to thrash on the bed, as if she was trying to escape something.

"Noooo," she wailed, eyes squeezed shut tight, feeling that slow numbness creeping in, her body tensing.

"Shhhh," Matt murmured, rubbing his cheeks, his lips, over the swollen wet flesh between her thighs. "Easy. It's okay."

"Don't stop," she whispered, meeting his eyes.

"No." And he didn't, staying focused, his whole mouth covering her mound, his tongue circling.

"Yes," she cried, squeezing her breasts, tweaking her nipples, knowing this feeling, nearing the edge of darkness, afraid to jump. "Oh god. Oh god. That's…ohhhh…Matt!"

"Mmmmmfffff," was all he could say. She had both hands buried in his hair now, grinding her pussy up against his face. She wanted it so much, and yet still, it eluded her. There was no making it happen, no willing herself to come. There was nothing to do.

"I give up," she cried, feeling tears stinging her eyes, falling down her temples. "Oh I give up, I give up!"

Matt's tongue slowed a little but he didn't stop, his hands holding her hips as she stopped thrashing, her body growing still. The sensation between her legs had moved off into nothing, nothing. It was never going to happen. Even here, with Matt, sweet Matt, who wanted nothing more than to please her, to help…

"Ohhh," Rose breathed, feeling a little flutter as his tongue flicked at her clit. "Oh Matt…mmm."

Her lungs pulled at the air, deep, gasping full breaths, as if she were her own center of gravity, pulling in the tides like the moon. It came like a whisper, not a bang, like she imagined the universe must have begun—a sweet, lovely surprise, an opening in the whole fabric of the world. Her body trembled, clenched, and then fluttered with release, again, again, again.

"What…was…that?" she gasped, sitting up on her elbows and staring at him with wide-eyed wonder.

"What did it feel like?" He lifted his face, glistening with her juices in the lamplight, and grinned.

"An orgasm?" She blinked. "I think…I think that was an orgasm."

"Well, let's do it again to be sure…" He covered her with his mouth and she squealed and wiggled, rolling away, finding the tender flesh between her legs far too sensitive to be touched so soon.

"Matt…" She sat up fully, staring at him, incredulous. And she burst into tears.

He gathered her into his arms, rocking her on the bed, letting her sob. It felt more like vomiting than crying, as if a huge, uncontrollable force had taken over her body, tossing her about on its whim. And still Matt held her. He didn't quiet her, he didn't tell her to stop, he gave her no platitudes. He just held her until it had ebbed and she had been reduced to a puddle of fluids in his lap, her breath hitching like a five-year-old after a tantrum.

"I didn't know it would be like that," she said finally, accepting the t-shirt he offered so she could wipe her face. She knew she must look awful—red nose and puffy eyes—but Matt gave no indication, his hand stroking her hair, down her back, a soothing, calming motion. "Is it always like that?"

"Kind of." He smiled, his fingers lightly trailing over her shoulder, giving her shivers. "I imagine, considering the blocks you've had, that you won't soon forget this orgasm, even if you have a thousand more."

"A thousand!" She gulped, sitting up to look at him. "What if I can't do it again?"

He laughed. "It's like riding a bike."

"Which means we should practice," she said slyly, sliding her hand along the inside of his thigh. His cock had gone soft but it responded nicely to her touch, swelling in her fist as she squeezed and rubbed it. "A lot."

"Indeed." He kissed her and she could taste herself in his mouth. His face was just covered with her juices and he moaned softly as she used her tongue like a cat to lick along his jaw, over his chin, the taste of her pussy exciting to her. "Rose, you're so sexy, I can't stand it."

"I bet you say that to all your clients." She giggled as he kissed her down onto the bed.

"Actually, you're my first. I was trained as a sexual surrogate, but I've never…practiced…" He groaned when she caught him in her fist, pumping him against her hip.

"Wow, you're my first… and I'm yours." She felt how stiff he was, thick and throbbing in her hand, and she moaned softly at the sensation when she slipped him up and down her shaved cleft. "You ready for some more practice?"

"Definitely." He slid inside of her in one slick, fluid motion, both of them shuddering at the delicious sensation. He paused to kiss her, his tongue delving into the sweet crevices of her mouth as he began to move, nice and easy, his hips barely shifting between her legs.

"Mmm." She wrapped her arms around his neck. "That's nice."

He groaned. "That's an understatement."

She let him just fuck her, slow and lazy, his breath hot in her ear, sending little shockwaves down her spine. The sweet throbbing of her orgasm had long gone, but she wasn't thinking about that. She wasn't really thinking about anything—she was just soaring, wrapped in Matt's arms, rocking to his rhythm, loving the feel of him inside of her.

Matt slowed, panting in her ear, waiting for his breath to slow before he told her, "It can take a long time for some women to experience a climax during intercourse. Some women never do."

"I don't care," she whispered, cuddling him against her breasts, whimpering when he licked first one and then the other. "I just want you."

"You can touch yourself if you want," he reminded her, sliding one of her hands down between her legs. She could feel the place where they were joined and glanced down as he propped himself above her so she had more room to maneuver. "And it's kind of hot to watch."

"Mmmm, it is," she agreed as he started to move. Watching his cock disappear into her pussy was a delicious thrill and she slid her wet fingers through her slit, finding that sweet spot. She'd never masturbated during sex before. She didn't ever have orgasms anyway, so what was the point? "Oh yes… ohhh god… ohhh! That feels really good!"

"Then don't stop." He moved a little deeper, a little faster, giving her more of his cock with every thrust, keeping himself propped over her, his knees on the bed, his thighs pressing her wide, wider.

"It's okay if you come," she murmured, eyes half closed with pleasure. "You don't have to wait for me. I don't mind."

“I’m not sure I could stop if I tried,” he panted, biting his lip, his face almost pained. “You feel so good. God… so… fucking… good!”

“Are you close?” she whispered, watching his face change, feeling his cock swell between her legs.

“Oh fuck,” he said between gritted teeth, driving into her so fast he was moving her on the bed, sliding her up toward the headboard. “Rose! Oh! God! Take it! Fuck! Take it!”

She did, grabbing him in her hand as he pulled out and thrust against the soft flesh of her naked vulva. The first wave of his cum blasted over her fist, flooding her pussy with incredible heat. Rose pumped him hard against her mound, the head of his cock erupting again and again over her flesh, rubbing in rhythm against her clit.

“Matt!” she gasped, wiggling her hips to meet his. “Oh! Oh! Again! Ohhhhhh!”

And it was just as good the second time, oh god, yes it was, her pussy clenching with each shuddering, ecstatic wave. It made her head spin and her ears ring and her body tense and release again and again until she was limp and whimpering beneath him on the bed.

“See, I told you,” he panted, kissing her cheek as he rolled to the side of her, pulling covers over them both. “Just like riding a bike.”

“Only better,” she agreed, looking up at the mirror over the bed—what did they usually use this room for, she wondered?—seeing them cuddled together. She’d never seen either of them look more relaxed or satisfied. Was that disheveled, blissful-looking woman in the reflection really her?

“I think our time’s up,” Matt murmured after a while, checking his watch.

“Don’t say that.” Rose sighed, closing her eyes against his words. “It makes me feel cheap.”

“I’m sorry,” he apologized, squeezing an arm around her shoulder. “You’re not.”

“Matt,” she whispered, looking up and seeing him watching her in the mirror. She met his eyes and felt tears welling. Normally she would have turned away, gotten up to go to the bathroom so he wouldn't see. Instead, she let them fall. "I don't want this to end."

"That's normal," he murmured. "Learning to trust someone isn't easy, and letting go… it's very hard. But I promise, we'll spend time easing into it. We won't end it like turning off a light switch."

"What if…" She took a deep breath, turning to face him. "What if I don't want to turn it off at all?"

He lifted her hand in his and kissed her palm. "We don't have a choice, Rose."

She buried her face in his neck, hating his answer, but knowing he was right. This was temporary. He wasn't doing this because he loved her—he was doing this because it was his job. She had to keep reminding herself of that fact.

"We'll meet again tomorrow?" she asked.

"Yes," he assured her. "In fact, I've got something special planned for tomorrow."

She smiled, cuddling as close as she could. "Today was pretty special."

"Yes it was," he breathed, holding her so tightly she could barely breathe. Not that she cared.

* * * *

"We shouldn't be doing this." Matt said it like he was reminding himself, rather than talking to her, but Rose didn't answer him as he unlocked the front door of his bungalow and invited her inside.

"Oh Matt, what a gorgeous view." A door wall in the living room opened up to a beach view in back. The sun was just setting over the horizon, giving everything a warm glow.

"You should see it from the bedroom."

"Okay," she agreed, turning to see him grinning at her.

"Race you."

And they were off, Matt in the lead of course—he was faster and he was the only one who actually knew where he was going. But she was right behind him, giggling all the way up the stairs and around the corner. They'd had the best day, not just the best day she'd had at the treatment center, but maybe the best day she'd had in her life. Ever.

Instead of meeting in the evening after dinner as they usually did, Matt had applied for an all-day pass and had taken her snorkeling in the morning—which of course meant that she had to buy and wear a swimsuit, something that had required a great deal of effort on her part. Matt had seen and acknowledged her scar, kissing it gently, but hadn't made a big deal out of it and no one else on the boat had noticed—or if they had, they didn't say anything.

Then it was shopping and walking around Lorient, where they discovered a gorgeous old Catholic church. They, strangely, both shared a love for old cemeteries and had explored the local island graveyard for hours. Matt had brought a picnic lunch and they ate it in a local garden park. But dinner had been on a tour boat just before sunset—she was still full of shrimp and lobster and crab.

They were scheduled to go back to the treatment center for their evening appointment, but Matt had suggested stopping by his place instead, and...well, here they were, standing on his balcony wrapped in each other's arms, watching the sun set over the horizon.

"I don't ever want this day to end," she murmured, tucking her head under Matt's chin.

He breathed deep, breathing her in. "Me neither."

And then they were kissing themselves back into Matt's bedroom, all the way over to his huge king sized bed—*"What do you need a bed this big for?"*—*"I'm a restless sleeper!"*—where they rolled and wrestled and tore at each other's clothes until they were sweaty and naked and desperate for each other.

"Fuck me, baby," she begged him, but he wasn't having it. Instead he rolled onto his back and pulled her in until she was straddling his face, his tongue already practiced at sending her quickly into orbit. She moaned and rocked and let him lick her, lost in the sensation, pinching her own nipples, twisting them to send white hot sparks between her legs.

Matt gasped in surprise when Rose repositioned herself so she could suck his cock, her mouth covering the fat, mushroom head, focusing her tongue there, around and around while he teased her clit. He wasn't so much licking her pussy as devouring her flesh, burying his whole face between her legs, arms wrapped tightly around her hips to keep her from wiggling away.

"Matt!" she cried, trying to give him a warning, maybe just preparing herself for the imminent. His fingers slipped deep inside and he fingered her hard as he licked her, the jarring of her pelvis exploding through her hips, making her pussy clench. "Ohhhh yes! Baby yes! Gonna come so hard for you!"

And she did, pumping his cock in her fist with the same rhythm, matching the intensity of the orgasm rolling through her, every spasm pushing her further toward heaven. She covered the head of his cock with her mouth, whimpering with her climax, tasting his pre-cum, hungry for more.

"No," he protested, grabbing her hips and pushing her to the bed. "I want you."

And then she was on her knees and he was fucking her like a dog, his thighs driving her forward on the bed with every thrust. There was nothing therapeutic about this, she thought happily as she rubbed her still-throbbing clit, the sound of their fucking filling the room.

She didn't think she could come again so soon, but Matt was an animal, taking just what he wanted, using her pussy for his pleasure. The sounds he made, the low grunts and growls, the way he grabbed her hair and pulled her back so he could kiss her, shoving his tongue deep into her mouth, made her crazy with longing.

"I'm going to come inside you," he panted, giving her a warning.

"Yessss!" she hissed, welcoming him with the arch of her back. "Oh baby, please, come inside me! Come in my pussy!"

That's all it took, for both of them. Matt grabbed her hips and pumped his cock in short, hard bursts deep into her pussy, moaning long and loud, and she felt the first hot blast of his cum rushing up the underside of his cock to explode against her cervix. The sensation was surreal, completely out of this plane of existence, and Rose felt herself flying right along with him, the velvet walls of her pussy contracting around his rigid, pulsing length with an intensity she hadn't known was even in the realm of human experience.

"Oh Rose," he murmured, wrapping her in his arms as they collapsed on the bed, him spooning her. "Oh god."

"Thank you, Matt." She smiled, eyes still closed, as he took her hand in his, lifting her arm and feathering kisses along the length of the angry, red scar. That horrible, desperate day seemed very far away. "I don't know what I would have done without you."

"You're welcome," he said softly.

"And here I wondered if I could do it again…" She giggled lightly, wiggling her bottom back against his, and in a sing-song voice, she said, "I can climax on a train and I can climax in the rain and…"

Matt laughed, hugging her tight. "Girl, I'm in so much trouble."

"Why?" she inquired, glancing back at him. He was smiling, but his eyes were serious.

"Because I don't want to let you go."

She frowned, turning in his arms, her fingers tracing the sweet curve of his lips. "But you said…we have to."

"I know what I said." He sighed. "And I know what I feel."

She pressed her forehead to his, knowing exactly what he meant. "What are we going to do?"

"I don't know." He hid his face against her neck and whispered, "I just don't know."

* * * *

"Hey girl, you got a visitor!" Kennedy poked his head into her open door, his wide eyes thick with make-up. He was going for the school girl look today, a blue and white plaid skirt, complete with white blouse, navy vest and tie. Although he had neglected to shave his legs or put on tights, and the pink flip-flops he had on didn't exactly match. "And he is cuuuu-ute!"

"Are you sure he's here for me?" Rose paused her game of *Angry Birds*—poor Matt never got to use his iPad anymore—and started following Kennedy down the hall. None of them except the chubby, adolescent looking Alex, had received any visitors in the past month—and his parents had only stayed for a few hours. There were heads popping out of the residence doors all the way down the hall at the excitement.

"He said he *had* to see you," Kennedy informed her, pushing through the double doors.

"Oh my god." Rose stopped, staring at the man standing in front of the welcome station. "Sam."

"Hi." He came toward her as Kennedy slipped back through the double doors behind her and she couldn't do anything else but let him embrace her, feeling the familiar shift of his body, smelling the heady scent of his cologne. Polo, an old standby. "God, it's so good to see you. How are you doing?"

"Sam…" It was like she couldn't say anything else—couldn't think of anything else to say. "I…Sam, what are you *doing* here?"

He smiled at her, so warm and sweet. "I came to see you, of course."

"How did you know I was here?" She shook her head, incredulous—but then she knew.

They both said "Poppy" at the same time and laughed.

"Come on, let's get out of here," she said, glancing at the receptionist. "Go for a walk."

It was a short distance down to the beach. Sam's hand found hers as they walked toward the water. The shoreline was deserted here this time of day. This stretch of sand belonged to the facility and, since it was nearly lunch time, everyone was inside.

"God it's gorgeous here." He took a deep breath, glancing down at her. "Are you loving it?"

"It is beautiful," she agreed, adding softly, "It would have made a great honeymoon spot."

He stopped, taking her other hand and looking down at her. "It still could."

"…What?" His words wouldn't register. The surprise of him being there in the first place was enough of a shock, but this? She'd thought, maybe, he'd come to apologize—but to propose? that just wasn't possible.

"Why do you think I'm here?" He smiled at her stunned expression, putting his arms around her waist. She registered the fact that he was going to kiss her just before it happened, turning her head aside just in time, so his lips landed on her cheek.

"I can't even begin to guess," she told him, slowly extracting herself from his embrace. They stood there, face to face, in the sand.

"Are you kidding me?" Sam's brow wrinkled, his eyes darkening. She knew the look well enough. He was getting angry. *He* was getting angry?

"Actually I'm not," she replied, trying to keep her voice calm, even. "Sam, maybe you remember things differently than I do, but you practically left me at the altar." She saw him wince and thought, maybe, she might be getting through to him. "I was so devastated I tried to commit suicide."

She'd never done anything like it before, but she reached down, unbuttoning the sleeve of her blouse, so she could pull back the material and show him her scar. He stared at it, aghast.

"And for what?" she asked, feeling the weight of her lies somehow being lifted off her chest as she spoke. "Because I faked a few orgasms?"

"A few? Try all of them!" he protested, nostrils flaring.

"So what?" she fumed. "It wasn't about your sexual prowess or the size of your dick. It was about me. It wasn't about you. Not everything is all about you!"

Then he said the words she'd been longing to hear for months, although now, somehow, they didn't mean what she thought they would. "I'm so sorry, Rose. I overreacted. What was I supposed to do?"

"Over…reacted." She stared at him, dumbfounded.

"I wasn't thinking. I just…

"What were you supposed to do?" Her hands were shaking and she hugged herself to still them. "You were supposed to love me. You could have loved me enough to stay instead of leaving."

He just looked at her, but she saw the pain in his eyes, knew she'd somehow gotten through to him. It was little consolation.

"Look, Sam, I'm sorry you came all this way for nothing."

He frowned, shaking his head. "You really don't want me here?"

"No," she said softly. "I really don't."

"I do love you, Rose." He took a step toward her, but she backed away.

"And I love you, Sam," she told him. "I'll always love you. But sometimes love just isn't enough."

He turned to look out at the water, hands shoved into his jeans pockets, looking morose. "Well… this is awkward." He looked over at her and half-smiled, trying to make the best of it. "Can I least take you to dinner?"

"Actually, we're having a special farewell dinner tonight," she told him. "Tomorrow is our last day."

"Okay then…" He shrugged, turning and starting to walk back. She followed. "I guess I'll just go see if I can get a standby flight."

"Listen, thanks for coming all this way, Sam," she said as they neared the doors. "Thanks for thinking of me."

He stopped, looking down at her. "I pictured this happening differently."

"Yeah, well, life is never picture perfect, is it?" She offered him a small smile.

"Have a good life, Rose."

She let him hug her, but again turned her head when he attempted a kiss. "You too, Sam."

He drove away in a little rental car, giving her a brief wave, and she marveled at her own lightness. She was sure, with a good running start, she could actually fly. Never in a million years would she have believed that could have happened. Confronting Sam? Rejecting him?

He'd been the only thing she ever wanted—but he just wasn't enough anymore.

Kennedy poked his head out the door. "Well!?"

"Well what?" She snorted, letting him drag her back inside. "Hey, I've got some wax—do you want to borrow some for your legs?"

He raised his eyebrows. "Is that a hint?"

"Just a suggestion, sweetie," she told him, but he wasn't having the distraction.

"Was that your boyfriend?"

Why not be honest? "Ex-fiancé, actually." And then she saw Matt, standing by the welcome desk, watching her. The look on his face made her heart stop. He knew Sam had been here, that much was obvious. Had he seen them together?

She approached cautiously. "Hey."

"Hi," he said, handing something over to the receptionist, not looking at her.

"Awkward," Kennedy whispered under his breath, turning to Rose. "Okay, well, stop by my room. We'll talk. Besides, I want to borrow that wax."

"Okay." She smiled as he disappeared down the residence hallway.

Matt crossed his arms, looking at her. "So…that was Sam?"

"You just missed him," she said. "He's flying back to the states."

"Good."

She hid a smile. "Are you jealous?"

"No." His jaw tightened. "Yes." Glancing at the receptionist—she was on the phone but they both knew she was listening to every word—he took Rose's elbow and steered her away from the desk. "Can we take a walk?"

"Sure." She felt a sense of déjà-vu as Matt led her down toward the beach. Same beautiful setting, but with an entirely different man. Everything she had felt walking down to the shoreline with Sam was reversed with Matt.

"So you're going home tomorrow," he remarked.

"I know."

"And I shouldn't say this," he admitted, turning to take her into his arms, something she'd been hoping, waiting for. "But I don't want you to go."

"Me either," she breathed against his neck, feeling the long, lean heat of his body against hers. She slipped her arms around his waist, resting her cheek on his shoulder, and smiled. "But I'm afraid my father isn't going to pay for another month."

He kissed the top of her head. "You know what I mean."

"Yes…I know."

"I know what I said, when we started," he said, taking a deep breath. "And ethically, I'm bound by that contract."

"Right."

"But Rose…" He pulled her in tight, his gaze sharp and desperate as their eyes met. "I can't stop thinking about you. I can't stop wanting you. Every time I imagine you getting on a plane and leaving, everything in me goes cold at the thought."

"Oh Matt…" She kissed him. She didn't care if they weren't in a session, that anyone who glanced out of one of the windows in the facility could see them. She kissed him with all the force and emotion she had, feeling him acquiesce, his body giving her all the answer she could ever want.

They broke apart, gasping, and she smiled. "Why do you think I sent Sam away?"

"Because all of the work we've done has given you enough self-worth to realize he's nowhere near good enough for you?"

She laughed. "Besides that…"

"Tell me why."

"Because I love *you*," she confessed, knowing it was the truth. "I don't want *Sam*. I want *you*."

He kissed her again, this time softly, sweetly, his lips accepting her admission and giving it back without a single word. She had once thought that she couldn't live without Sam, but she now knew that wasn't true. Now she had a man in her life who, although she knew she *could* live without him—she didn't *want* to. It was a vast difference.

"Matt, please tell me we can be together," she whispered, kissing his cheek, the hard line of his jaw. "I don't know how it's going to be possible. I don't want to jeopardize what you have here, your work, your whole career…"

"Maybe my mother's right." He was only half-joking, she could tell. "Maybe I should apply for jobs in New York."

"I just told Sam that sometimes love just isn't enough." She felt tears welling. "Maybe that's the truth for us too."

"Rose, listen to me." He held her by her upper arms, urgent, almost pleading. "My contract says that we have to end our therapeutic relationship for at least six months before we can… you know…"

She grinned. "Date?"

"Yeah." He laughed. "Date."

"So…maybe we should make a date for six months from now?" she suggested.

"Can you wait for me?"

"Forever," she assured him, sealing the promise with a kiss.

RAPUNZEL

"Are those extensions?"

Nina Malden noticed everything and Rachel's new hair was no exception. None of her other clients had said a word—they talked about vacations in Cabo and how difficult it was to get dinner reservations at *Tru* while Rachel mixed color and folded foil for highlights and the sharp snip of her scissors accompanied the endless chatter—but no one had mentioned her hair.

"It's—" Rachel glanced in the mirror over Nina's perfectly coiffed head. She'd never understood the phenomenon—who went into a salon for a cut with their hair already styled? But every client at *Rapunzel's* showed up made-up, even dolled-up, for their appointment. As a stylist, she had to un-do before she could re-do, and sometimes up-do, the hair in question.

Rachel fingered the hair on her head, thick and long, as close as she could get to natural, a trifecta of color, brownish-red with bright golden highlights that no one could ever define. It fell past her shoulders to the middle of her back in luxurious, beautiful waves. She couldn't admit the truth, not even to herself, let alone to Nina Malden. Telling her it was a wig would open a door she preferred to keep firmly closed.

She was thankfully saved from responding by a crisis up front. The raised voice of one of the stylists—she was sure it was Joshie—caught her attention immediately. She made sure Nina was seated and comfortable before she excused herself to go handle the drama, which involved two appointments—one cut, one perm—scheduled at once for the same stylist. Her new receptionist, just twenty-six and a graduate of NYU, had proven to be a disaster so far. Rachel was usually such a great judge of character, but she'd been distracted when she hired Carly. Unfortunately, Carly didn't work Saturdays, so Rachel couldn't scold her. Instead they were taking turns between appointments manning the phone.

"I can't do them both at once!" Joshie's big brown eyes, rimmed with silver eyeliner, actually filled with tears. He was wringing his delicate, ring-adorned hands as if he'd dipped them in something very unagreeable and couldn't get it off. "It's impossible!"

Rachel glanced at the lobby where the first client, a model in need of a spiral perm, checked her perfect profile in a compact. The other patron was just a young girl, maybe fifteen, bright and freshly pretty. Rachel envied her. The man beside her had to be her father—*better be*, she thought, taking in his age and demeanor, or else he was in danger of serious prosecution under pedophile laws, the way he was holding her hand and whispering into her ear.

"Oh I think you've done two at once before, Joshie," Rachel murmured, shocking her stylist into a choked laugh and letting him know his salon gossip hadn't escaped her ears. "You take the perm. I'll take the cut."

"But you've got the dragon-lady," Joshie mock-whispered, glancing over her shoulder toward Nina Malden who was flipping through a *Cosmopolitan*, her lips set in a grim line. She wasn't going to be happy.

"Well, this might be news to you, but I can do two at once too." Rachel winked and Joshie's cackle followed her into the lobby.

"Just a cut today, sweetie?" Rachel saw the girl's nervous glance, first at her, then at the man beside her. He squeezed her hand encouragingly but the girl just blushed and didn't speak. Rachel laughed lightly. "Not your first, I hope?"

The girl's hair was very long, to her waist, a thick black curtain. Her father—Rachel was sure of it now, they had the same dark, wide eyes, and his hair was just as thick and black, although much shorter and curlier—cleared his throat and gave Rachel an apologetic smile.

"I think she's in shock." He shrugged one shoulder in Rachel's direction. "But it was all her idea!"

"Something drastic?" Rachel guessed, glancing over as Joshie brought a cappuccino out for the model and took her back into the salon. She turned to check the appointment book and saw the girl's name—Emma Malden—and then saw the note written beside it, just as the girl's father offered the information.

"She wants to get her hair cut for *Locks of Love*," he told her, looking a little sheepish at his next admission. "Her mother doesn't want her to, so I brought her."

The two facts hit her simultaneously. This was Nina Malden's daughter—the name and dark tresses were far too much to be coincidence—and she wanted to get her hair cut off for charity. As a hairdresser, Rachel was familiar with *Locks of Love* and had collected a great deal of hair for the organization over the years so they could make it into wigs for disadvantaged kids whose medical diagnosis left them humiliatingly without any, either temporarily or permanently. She'd done it with a vague sort of sensitivity in the past, but never with any real empathy. Not until now.

"How much do you want taken off?" Rachel inquired, glancing toward the back and catching a glimpse of Nina Malden in the mirrors. She was swinging one very expensive Jimmy Choo pump at the end of her silk stocking foot, a black stylist cape draped around her neck, obscuring her Vera Wang suit. She was thankfully still perusing a magazine, still distracted. Good.

"All of it." The girl finally spoke up and Rachel heard the steel in her voice. Must get that from her mother, she surmised, seeing the dark flash of Emma Malden's eyes, the hard set of her jaw.

"Well, I don't think we have to shave you bald." Rachel smiled and went over to where they were sitting, touching the girl's hair. It was beautiful, healthy, and she'd been growing it out a long time. "You have a good eighteen inches here at least, even if we just give you a cute little pageboy cut." Rachel used her hands to indicate the line at the girl's jaw.

Emma frowned, looking over at her dad. "Are you sure that's enough?"

"Ten inches is the minimum," Rachel explained, this time looking at Emma's father. She wondered what kind of hot water he was going to be in when his wife found out he'd taken their daughter to cut off most of her hair. Well, that was his business, right? Besides, it was for a good cause. "You've got plenty to spare."

"That's almost double, Em," Emma's father offered, nudging her. "That's a lot of hair."

"Okay, let's do it." Emma stood, swinging the dark curtain of hair over her shoulder, possibly for the last time.

"Come on back." Rachel put them at a station up front but around the corner, out of the way. Somewhere they were unlikely to run into Nina, unless they had the unfortunate synchronicity to pass on the way out. Of course, having them all there together was a bit of coincidence to begin with. Joshie was two stations down with the supermodel and he waved at her and winked.

"So your mom doesn't want you to get a haircut, huh?" Rachel opened the bottom drawer and took out a packet. Inside was a certificate from the *Locks of Love* organization and a long red ribbon they used to tie the hair.

Emma's father had followed them back and he stood leaning against the wall behind her, arms crossed, just watching. Rachel nodded to the empty chair at the station beside her. "You can have a seat, Mr. Malden."

"Jake." He took her up on her offer, sitting down and swiveling the chair in a circle so he was facing his daughter. "And you are…wait, let me guess. You're Rapunzel."

"For all intents and purposes," she agreed, combing Emma's thick tresses into her hand and then tying the length of it off with the ribbon. Glancing up at Jake, she saw his teasing smile. His words and expression seemed genuine, but the man had a sharp, rich look about him that most of her clients—and her client's husbands—exuded. She wasn't surprised he was Nina Malden's husband.

"My name is Rachel," she disclosed, picking up her scissors. She met Emma's eyes in the mirror. They were big and dark and huge. The poor girl was terrified. "Are you sure you're ready for this?"

Emma nodded, swallowing. "Do it."

"Okay." Rachel held the thick length of ponytail in her hand, glancing over at the girl's father for one last indication of permission. It was no small thing, cutting off this much hair. There was a great deal of power in it, both in the length of the hair and the act of cutting it.

"She's getting it cut off for her friend, Liv." Jake's gaze went to his daughter and his expression softened.

"Liv has leukemia." Emma's eyes filled with tears and she blinked them back. "Oh damnit. I said I wasn't going to cry."

"It's a very kind and generous gesture." Rachel swallowed tears of her own. She hadn't even considered how difficult this was going to be. The *Locks of Love* program had, strangely, not even crossed her mind since her own diagnosis and the universe had given her a two-month reprieve from doing this. But here she was.

"Just do it." Emma closed her eyes and Rachel cut, the sound of the scissors bright and keen, even over the noise of the salon. When Rachel put the thick, dark ribbon of hair on the counter, the red tie trailing down the white countertop, bright as a trickle of blood, Emma opened her eyes and stared at it with surprise, as if it was a finger or a limb instead of a length of her hair.

"I'm so proud of you, sweetie." Jake reached over and touched his daughter's hand and the girl burst into tears. He stood and opened his arms and she went to him, sobbing. He stroked what was left of her hair, cut above her shoulders, and looked helplessly over her head at Rachel. "Oh, Em, it's okay, you're beautiful—even more beautiful now."

Rachel felt a lump growing in her own throat. She spoke before it threatened to cut off her voice entirely. "Can you excuse me for a moment? I'll be right back."

She took the opportunity to give them some privacy and left them hugging each other, a few of the patrons watching, curious, but most still chatting and combing and cutting, oblivious. Rounding the corner, Rachel stopped near the lobby, blinking fast and tilting her head back, willing tears not to fall. Not here, not now. Nina Malden was waiting.

"There you are!" Nina slid her phone closed and tucked it back into her purse as Rachel returned. "I was thinking about calling out a search party."

"I'm sorry," she apologized, glancing at herself in the mirror. Her eyes were a little bright, but that was all. No other signs of grief. "We had a little scheduling snafu up front. The new girl isn't working out so well."

"Ugh, the help." Nina shook her head and smiled at Rachel as if they shared something in common. "I know how it is."

"Well, let's get you shampooed, shall we?" She'd been in the business so long she never questioned using words like 'shampoo' or 'condition' as a verb. Nina's hair was just as lovely as her daughter's and Rachel washed it, trying to hurry, knowing Jake and Emma were waiting, but it wasn't easy getting the sticky mass of mousse and hairspray and various other styling products out.

"I'm glad you could get me in today," Nina remarked as Rachel squeezed the water out of her clean hair with a thick, fluffy white towel. "I've got a date tonight."

"A date?" Rachel's towel stopped abruptly. "Where are you and your husband going?"

"Didn't I tell you?" Nina raised her eyebrows and lifted her left hand, waggling her fingers. "We're divorced."

Well, this was news. Rachel was stunned into silence.

"Has it been that long since I've been in? It's been three months since it was final." Nina followed her over to the styling station, taking a seat, smoothing her skirt. "We're both dating again."

"I didn't know," Rachel murmured, squirting thick white lotion into her hands and kneading it through Nina's hair. It was shorter than her daughter's, only shoulder-length, more appropriate for a woman her age, but still long and thick. She required a lot of the conditioner.

"Well, we didn't tell anyone until it was final." Nina cleared her throat and Rachel saw her looking at her left hand as if there was still a ring there to admire. She remembered the thing—three carats, platinum, so shiny it could have blinded any magpie coming to steal it.

"You have a daughter, don't you?" Rachel gathered Nina's hair up with clips and covered it with a plastic cap.

"Emma?" Nina smiled, relaxing a little. "She's with her father this weekend."

Well that explained it. Rachel listened to Nina talk about her date—an Illinois congressman. That was a step up from a corporate lawyer, wasn't it? Nina's eyes seemed to ask. Rachel didn't say anything, she just led her client over to the dryer and handed her a stack of magazines.

"Okay, I'll be back in ten minutes. You stay here and get conditioned." Rachel smiled and turned the blower on, raising her voice so Nina could hear her. "Your hair will look ten years younger when the heat treatment's done."

"Ten years?" Nina touched the plastic cap tentatively. "Can we do twenty? Then Emma and I could be twins."

Rachel laughed, setting a timer for ten minutes and putting it on the counter behind Nina. "If I could do twenty, I'd be a magician, not a hairdresser."

"I'm sentimental about hair, I admit." Nina flipped through the magazines, choosing a *People* with a smiling Brad and Angelina on the cover. "I haven't let Emma cut her hair since she was ten."

"It must be very long." Rachel swallowed, remembering that a decidedly less hirsute Emma and her father were waiting for her to return.

"It's gorgeous." Nina flipped the magazine open, situating herself in the chair. "She wanted to get it cut for some charity. I told her I'd write them a ten-thousand dollar check before I let her cut her hair."

"I'll be back in ten minutes," Rachel said faintly, really realizing for the first time just how big of a deal it was going to be when this woman found out what she'd done to her daughter's hair. Maybe she won't have to know it was me personally, Rachel thought as she swept past the stations and rounded the corner. Then she saw Emma, sitting back in the chair, laughing at something her father had said.

You're a coward, Rachel Lange.

She was. Here was this young girl who had given up her mane of beauty as a sacrifice for a friend, who was going to have to face Nina Malden at the breakfast table every day with that fact, and Rachel was worried about one little confrontation with the woman?

She touched her wig, checking the adhesive—she did this obsessively all day long—and put on a professional smile. "Are you ready to get your style on?"

Emma's returning smile was radiant, making her even more beautiful, and Rachel got to work, spraying her hair down to wet it and picking up her scissors. The girl's hair was a joy to cut, thick and healthy and truly, as her mother had remarked, just gorgeous.

"I bet you feel lighter," Rachel remarked.

"Loads. For so many reasons," Emma agreed, glancing over at her father. He sat back in the stylist chair, arms crossed, just smiling. Rachel wondered if he was gloating, if this was some sort of payback to his wife. Ex-wife, she reminded herself.

"Your mother is going to kill me," Jake said, crossing one very expensive Prada shoe over the other as he watched more of his daughter's hair fall to the floor. "But I'm pretty sure my life insurance is all paid up, so you're set, Em."

"Very funny." Emma rolled her eyes. "I'm almost seventeen. It's my hair. It's my life."

"In theory, that is correct." Jake grinned and looked at Rachel. "Hey, I bet you know my wife. She comes in here to get her hair done."

"Really?" Rachel's scissors only stopped for a moment before she decided to continue to play dumb. "What's her name?"

"Nina," Emma piped up, holding her head straighter when Rachel gently tilted her chin.

"Same last name?" If she was going to play dumb, she might as well play really dumb, Rachel decided.

"Yes. Malden," Emma offered again before her dad could speak.

But Jake was quick to point out, "We're divorced." He glanced at his watch and then back at his daughter. "How much longer, do you think?"

"A few more minutes, not long," Rachel remarked. She was cutting Emma's bangs.

"Dad, you're not missing anything." Emma rolled her eyes again. She was quite good at it, but most teenagers Rachel knew had perfected the gesture. "The game will be on DVR when we get home."

"But it's the finals, Em!" Jake looked at his watch again.

Rachel perked up. "Hockey?"

"Yeah." Jake looked at her speculatively.

"Game one." Rachel positioned herself in front of Emma, checking the sides of her hair, pulling them forward to see if they were even. "Blackhawks and the Wings."

"You like hockey?" His voice had changed entirely, Rachel noticed. It had gone from that formal chit-chat tone she heard all day to something more rich and warm, like chocolate.

"Love it," she agreed, picking up the blow dryer.

"Me too." Jake looked a little blindsided, like he'd rarely come across a woman who loved hockey before.

Well, she supposed that might have been the case, but she'd grown up with it. Her father had been a huge hockey fan and she'd gone to all the games with him. It was his one indulgence. He had been Rachel's whole world, but he'd been gone two years now. Cancer. Ah, life's little ironies.

Jake's words brought her out over her reverie. "I've got season tickets."

"Don't tell me that." Rachel sighed. "I tried to get tickets to game two. I even went to the scalpers on Craigslist, but no luck."

"I'm not surprised." Jake shook his head sadly. "They've been sold out for a month."

"I know—the Blackhawks and the Wings—such a big rivalry." Rachel turned on the blow dryer and talked over it, using a rounded brush to style Emma's hair. "They're two of the original six."

Jake sat up, looking incredulous. "I know."

"I think my dad has a death wish," Emma remarked, a little non sequitur. Rachel gave her a puzzled smile. "He's a Red Wings fan living in Chicago," the girl explained. "And, you know, then he takes me to get my hair cut…" She shrugged in that awkward way teenagers had, so caught somewhere between adult and child, knowing it but not quite sure what to do about it.

"Well, if that's the case, then you *are* brave, Mr. Malden," Rachel teased.

"Jake," he insisted, shrugging. "And I'm not all that brave."

"Oh, I don't know." Rachel turned off the blow dryer, combing out the girl's hair. "I've met your wife."

Jake laughed. "You have a point."

Rachel grabbed the hand mirror off the counter and turned Emma around in a circle in the chair. "But I have to admit, I'm secretly rooting for the Red Wings myself."

"Do you have a death wish too?" Emma asked, looking at the back of her hair in the reflection of the hand mirror.

"Hardly." Rachel swallowed the irony of her response and changed the subject. "How do you like it?"

"It's so short!" Emma ran a hand through her hair, fluffing it and cocking her head to the side. Her bright eyes met Rachel's. "I love it!"

"Truly lovely, Em." Jake stood, pulling out his wallet. "What do we owe you, Rapunzel?"

Rachel raised an eyebrow at the platinum Visa in his hand. "Come on up front. You can pay there."

This was the dangerous part. Nina was still under the dryers in the back, facing the front of the salon, and she could probably see the lobby from where she was sitting. If Rachel didn't want a big scene, she was going to have to get them out of there—fast. She wrote the ticket up quickly and gave him the total.

Jake gave a low whistle, handing over his Visa. "And that was just a haircut. No wonder Nina spent a mint here every month."

"The price of beauty can be very high." Rachel smiled and ran his card, glancing over her shoulder. Nina was still reading, that was good. But ten minutes was almost up and the timer she'd set would be going off. She didn't want the woman to come hunt her down, that was for sure.

"Well it must be some sort of sign, both of us being Red Wings fans in Blackhawks country." Jake leaned on the counter as Rachel waited for the authorization. Emma wandered through the lobby, picking up a bottle of styling product and reading the back.

"A sign of what?" She glanced over her shoulder again, trying not to be too obvious. This time Nina saw her. Damnit. She moved a little left, hoping to block her view of Jake. "The apocalypse?"

"Could be." He laughed. "Hey, I have an extra ticket to game two…if you're interested."

Rachel handed his card back as the authorization came through on the machine. "How much?"

"Free. You'd just have to put up with my company the whole time, if you could stand it." He took his card back, slow, his fingers brushing hers and Rachel looked up in surprise. His eyes were smiling but he had a nervous sort of look, an expression she didn't expect to see on his confident face.

She stared at him, forgetting everything, including the receipt in her hand and the fact that this man's ex-wife had been sitting in the back of her salon while Rachel had just willy-nilly lopped off a foot-and-a-half of her daughter's precious hair. "But that would be like…a date."

"Yeah, that was kind of what I was thinking." His whole body posture spoke anxiety. If he'd been a teenage boy, Rachel swore he would have been hopping from one foot to the other like a two year old who had to pee. His nervousness appeared more subtle—a shift of his weight, the way his card missed the slot when he was trying to slide it back into his wallet—but to her, it might as well have been a neon sign.

"Oh." Rachel swallowed, considering the offer. She hadn't been out on a date in…god, she couldn't remember when. Two years? It wasn't that she hadn't had opportunities. And she couldn't be considered on the rebound anymore, since she and Stephen had been broken up for five. He'd married a woman ten years younger than they were and had moved to Georgia to be near the girl's family, last she heard. And it wasn't that she didn't like men, because god knows, she did.

It was mostly work at *Rapunzel's* that had her so busy, keeping her from starting or, god forbid, maintaining a relationship. At least, that's what it had been before she got sick. Now she had even more reasons for her self-imposed exile.

But what harm was there, really? And this was game two of the Stanley Cup Finals! The Chicago Blackhawks and the Detroit Red Wings! Could she really turn that down? All these thoughts ran through her head in an instant—but it was long enough for her to hear Nina Malden calling out her name from behind and Jake's head to snap up in surprise.

"You've got a deal." Rachel handed over his receipt with a business card stapled to it. She'd quickly scrawled her name and cell phone number on the back. "Call me."

Jake took the paper and folded it, putting it into his wallet. He opened his mouth to say something but Rachel cut him off, speaking in a harsh whisper. "Your ex-wife is here. I suggest you take Emma home. Now."

Jake's eyes widened and they both heard Nina this time. "Rachel! My timer went off!"

"I'll call you." Jake grabbed Emma's hand and he practically dragged her out the door. She protested but they were gone before Nina made it to the front of the store, looking very put-out.

"My time's up!" Nina announced.

Mine too, Rachel thought, watching Jake's retreating back. He was still holding Emma's hand but they were walking at a more normal pace through the mall, heading home. *Rapunzel's* was located on the lower level of a high-rise apartment complex in downtown Chicago, just one shop in the midst of many. The residents didn't have to go anywhere if they didn't want to. They had all the amenities located on the bottom floor.

"Okay, let's get you rinsed." Rachel touched Nina's shoulder and turned her away from the store front, nudging her down the aisle. "Sorry I missed the timer, I had to ring up a customer."

"Do you do everything around here?" Nina inquired as she settled herself into a chair at a sink.

"Pretty much." Rachel turned the water on and began to rinse Nina's hair. The woman started talking and Rachel just listened—this time it was Hollywood gossip, something about Charlie Sheen and a meltdown. That was easy to say "uh-huh" and "oh really" to without too much effort, and that was a good thing, because it took Rachel an hour to finish Nina's hair to the woman's satisfaction and the entire time, she was thinking about Jake.

That, and wondering what was going to happen when Nina found out her daughter's hair had been cut off—and that Rachel had been the one to do it. While Nina herself had been sitting at the back of the salon drinking cappuccino and reading *Cosmo*. Of course, that was probably nothing compared to what the dragon-lady would do or say if Nina had known her hairdresser was going to go on a date with her ex-husband.

It would be the most sensible thing, and probably best for business, Rachel decided, if she just politely told Jake when he called that she'd changed her mind. She was going to be in enough trouble already for the hair incident.

Which is why, when the phone rang that night in her apartment at the top of the high rise, with *Rapunzel's* lights dark far below her, she closed her eyes and said, "Six? That sounds great, see you then."

So much for being sensible.

* * * *

She knew she was in trouble when Jake pulled up in a limo. At least he didn't bring a dozen roses, she thought, blushing as a driver opened the door for her and she stepped in. Jake was drinking something amber colored from a fat glass.

"Hey there, Rapunzel." He smiled when she got in and slid into the seat across from him. "Ready for game two?"

"Let's hope it's better than game one." Rachel made a face. The Red Wings had lost game one in overtime three-to-two.

"I'll drink to that." Jake lifted his glass. "Do you want anything? Wine? Champagne?" He nodded toward the bar and she glanced over to see it was fully stocked. He'd really gone all out.

"Is that brandy?" she asked, looked at his glass. He nodded. "Got any scotch?"

He raised an eyebrow but reached over to the bar without comment. The car began to move as he poured her a shot and handed it over. Rachel took it with trembling hands. She'd spent an hour and a half getting ready for this non-date. That's what she kept calling it in her head—a non-date. How a woman could spend so much time on beauty when she didn't even have any hair was a paradox, she was sure, but that's how long it had taken her. She didn't even want to know how long she might have spent if she'd considered it a real date.

But this was a non-date, just a ride and a ticket to the playoffs. She reminded herself of that fact when she chose to wear her Red Wings jersey, but then forgot it when the short white mini-skirt made it into the mix. She reminded herself that it was a non-date when she decided not to put her hair up, but then forget it again when she found four-inch black strappy heels on her feet. And she tried to remind herself of their non-date status as she sat across from Jake in the limo, but totally forgot it when his hand brushed hers as he handed over her glass and little tingles went up her arm like electrical current.

"Nice limo." She looked around the car. It wasn't a stretch, but it was still a limo with a bar and a little flat screen and leather seats. Big time luxury, at least to her.

"I just thought it would be easier." Jake shrugged. "Parking sucks at the arena." He sat forward to take her glass and she relinquished it, ignoring that damned buzzy feeling in her limbs whenever he got close. She shook her head when he asked if she wanted another drink or anything to eat. There was also a little fridge. They'd already agreed on the phone not to do dinner. She'd been in a non-date mood at the time she insisted upon that. They'd also talked about Emma's hair and Nina's reaction—which hadn't been good. Not good at all.

"Well, I haven't heard from your ex-wife." Rachel glanced out at the city flying by. They really didn't have far to go, just a few miles. "I guess that means she's not going to sue me?"

"If she was going to sue you, you wouldn't hear from her at all." Jake finished his brandy and set the glass on the bar. "You'd just hear from her lawyer."

"Eek." The thought of being slapped with a lawsuit wasn't a happy one. She needed less stress in her life, not more. "Well I haven't heard from her lawyer either."

"Actually you have." He grinned, sitting back against the seat, his arm stretched casually over the back. He was dressed for the game, jeans and his own Wings jersey—white on red instead of red on white like her own. Another guy might have looked sloppy or casual but Jake looked…well, good. There was no other word for it.

"I have?"

"I'm her lawyer." He looked out the tinted window as the car began to slow. They were in traffic now. "At least, I was."

"Didn't that present a conflict of interest?"

He snorted. "Justice lets you represent yourself, remember?"

"So you're a lawyer."

He nodded. "And you're a hair stylist. I guess we've got the basics out of the way."

"Yes, the important things," she agreed with a smile. "Career, marital status, children or lack thereof, and favorite sports team. What else is there?"

"Um…" He seemed to consider this. "Dog person or cat person?"

She laughed. "Dog."

"Me too. Chinese or Sushi?"

"Sushi, definitely."

"You obviously prefer scotch to brandy. Pepsi or Coke?"

"Coke Zero. With lemon."

"Ugh, how can you drink that stuff?" He made a face. "Okay let's see…modern or classical?"

"Both. Although I have a soft spot for the classics."

He nodded. “Jazz or blues?”

"Definitely blues. It makes me want to take my clothes off.” The confession just slipped out.

"Good to know." The look he gave her made her blush all the way to her toes. "I'll have to beef up my collection of B.B. King. Rock or country?”

Now it was Rachel’s turn to make a face. "Rock. But I like some Garth Brooks on occasion."

"So you could tolerate a little Johnny Cash?"

She smiled. "Tolerate being the optimum word there."

"Here's a tough one. Love or money?”

"Love of course."

"Do you think rich people and poor people answer that question differently?" he asked.

"You're rich, you tell me."

He laughed. "I'm not rich."

"Compared to me you are."

"I'll give you that,” he conceded. “Okay, how about freedom or security?"

She hesitated. “Security.”

"I would have chosen freedom."

“I think rich and poor people would answer that one differently."

“Probably. The red pill or the blue pill?”

She shrugged. “Blue.”

“Give or take?”

"Give of course."

“Of course." He looked out the window again. They had stopped, and the arena was just up the block. "Half-empty or half full?”

She paused, considering the question and then just said, "Yes."

He wagged a finger at her, shaking his head. "That's cheating. Has to be one or the other."

"Then...half-empty."

He looked at her speculatively. "A pessimist then."

"Just lately, yes." She shrugged.

“On or off?”

She glanced at him, at the light in his eyes, and wondered what he was thinking. “Off.”

"On." He disagreed, grinning.

“Wait…was that lights or clothes?”

He laughed and asked, “Top or bottom?”

She flushed and was glad the lighting in the limo was so dim. "Top."

"Looks like we'll have to pick this game up later."

The driver was opening the door and Rachel was glad. The seats were just a little to the left of the blue-line—section 101. And they were only a few rows from the glass.

“I can see them sweating," Rachel exclaimed, turning to Jake with wide eyes. They were right behind the Red Wings' bench.

“Is that sexy or gross?”

She laughed. “A little of both.”

“I thought so."

He bought her cotton candy from a vendor even though she said she didn’t want any.

He told her, “I want to watch you eat it.”

The pink stuff was sticky and melted on her fingers and tongue and he really did seem to enjoy watching her. And she enjoyed him enjoying it.

He bought himself a water and her a Coke Zero—with lemon.

“Where did you get the lemon?”

He shrugged. “I raided the Long John Silver’s stand.”

The little gesture almost made her cry and she chided herself and drank her lemony Coke through a straw, giving herself another mental lecture about their non-date status.

When the Red Wings scored the first goal, Rachel stood up and danced in the aisle and the cameraman found her and put her on the big screen in her Red Wings jersey. By the second period, she had screamed herself hoarse and the score was tied three-to-three. When the Wings scored the winning goal—in overtime—Rachel jumped up and hugged Jake, who was pumping his fist in the air and yelling as loudly as she was. Then he pointed up, grinning. They were on the big screen again—probably the only two Red Wings fans in the whole place. The rest of the crowd was grumbling, if not outright booing the Blackhawks' loss.

"Bet me we're on the news tonight. Emma's gonna be psyched." Jake had called their driver and had him meet them up front. It was a madhouse trying to get out of there, people pressed together like cattle being herded to slaughter, and Jake held fast to her hand so they wouldn't get separated. She liked feeling him against her, solid as a wall, when they stopped.

"You mean…we'll be on TV?" The idea might have thrilled Jake's sixteen-year-old daughter, but the thought made Rachel go cold.

"Sure, the game was televised."

She paled. "I hope your wife doesn't watch hockey."

"Nina watches the home shopping network and the Lifetime channel."

"But does she watch the news?"

He gave her a steady look. "Who cares if she does?"

He was braver than she was, Rachel thought.

They found the limo parked half a block away and Jake held her hand as he helped her into the car. He slid in after, not across this time, but next to her. They couldn't stop talking about the game, reliving every goal. Jake poured more liquor and they drank it as the limo idled in traffic. The fifteen minute ride in to the arena was going to take them an hour to get out but neither of them noticed the time.

What Rachel did notice was the lightheaded feeling the alcohol was giving her, although she wasn't sure it was just the scotch. It might have been the way Jake's jean-clad thigh flexed against hers every time he reached for the bottle, or the way his hand brushed hers when he took her glass. She felt too warm, confined.

"You have really lovely hair."

The comment made her breath catch and Rachel touched her wig, suddenly self-conscious. "Thank you."

She felt his hand moving, brushing the hair over her shoulder, and glanced at him. He wasn't looking at her face. His gaze followed the line of her jaw, her throat. She knew it was an opening—she could have said something, told him about her illness, but she didn't. What she really wanted to do was to erase the thought entirely from her mind and she could only think of one way to do it.

"Hey there…" He accepted the weight of her, surprised, when she turned and put her arms around his neck.

"Do you want to kiss me?" She could smell her own breath, thick with alcohol, her mouth so close to his. The liquor had given her courage, a boldness she didn't normally possess, but it had opened up something else too, an empty space inside of her, a fierce hunger, a need demanding to be filled.

"Desperately," he admitted. "Haven't thought about anything else all night."

She pressed her mouth to his, trying to recall…was this how you did it? It didn't take long for her body to remember and Jake helped her along, his tongue parting her lips, exploring the soft recesses of her mouth, the taste of scotch and brandy together making her heady.

"I take that back," Jake breathed as they parted, breathless. "A few other things have crossed my mind tonight."

"Like what?" As if she didn't know. She was turned toward him, stretched across the seat, half in his lap, and his cock was a hard bulge against her hip through his jeans. Her intended distraction had turned from boldness to lust in an instant.

"I'd rather show you." His hand moved up under her shirt, touching bare skin at her waist. She felt like a teenager in the backseat of her date's car.

"I think you should." Was she really doing this? Oh god, yes, yes she was.

He groaned at her assent, his mouth capturing hers again, hand moving up higher to cup her breast through her bra. She had forgotten about their non-date status when she'd chosen her underwear—black silk bra and panties and lace-topped sheer black thigh highs. Now she'd forgotten any agreement or non-agreement between them altogether, letting him feel her up and returning the attention, her hand moving against the swollen crotch of his jeans, making him shift and press up against her effort.

"Oh Rachel," he whispered her name, his hand moving through her hair, and she cringed, aware of how long it was, how it spread out over them like a curtain, too much of it, as if it had a life of its own, eager to give away her secret.

She moved away from his hands, finding herself sliding to the floor of the limo between his thighs. His eyes lit up as she knelt and peeled her jersey off, revealing the black bra underneath.

"And I didn't even pull out my harmonica," he remarked, referring to her comment about blues music earlier in the night and she laughed, blushing. He had an incredible memory. And incredible hands, she noted, when they suddenly found more interesting things to do as he fondled her breasts, thumbing her nipples through the material. The sensation made her shiver and they kissed again, tongues entwined.

Jake let one hand wander around to the zipper on her skirt, easing it down. She helped him wiggle her out of it, feeling exposed. She glanced over her shoulder at the tinted glass where the driver sat. They could see him, but he couldn't see them. At least, she hoped. Jake turned her attention back to him when his hand slipped down between her legs, cupping her mound. She rocked, moaning softly against his mouth as they kissed.

"Come here." Jake pulled her quickly into his lap again and she straddled him, his hands exploring her body, up and down her sides, over her hips, pressing her against his crotch. They danced that way, rocking together, Jake's mouth covering the tops of her breasts with wet kisses, the heat of his cock through denim rubbing against her panties, creating a horrible friction, making her want him with an urgent, keening ache. What had started out as a temporary distraction was quickly turning into a force of nature she couldn't control and couldn't stop—and she didn't want to.

"We have to be quiet," Jake murmured, cupping her face in his hands and kissing her again. "Can you do that?"

She gasped when his fingers nudged her panties aside, tracing the puffy swell of her lips. They were as smooth as her scalp—she didn't have to shave at all anymore. As much as she hated the treatments that made the hair on her head fall out, it was a benefit when it came to other parts of her body.

"I'll try to be quiet," she whispered, whimpering as Jake slipped a finger inside and found her wet—embarrassingly wet.

"Oh god." His finger moved in and out, eliciting little noises from her throat. "When you say that, I want to make you scream."

"I'll be quiet," she promised, shivering and biting her lip as his thumb found the sensitive nub of her clit. He rubbed there as he fingered her, her nipples hardening under her bra. "Just please don't stop."

He gave a low growl, pulling the material of her bra down with his other hand, letting her breasts spill free against his face. She arched so he could reach them with his mouth and he teased them back and forth, round and round, matching the motion of his tongue with the fingers between her legs.

"Don't stop," she whispered, reaching back to feel him. His cock strained against his zipper. She undid it, sliding her hand in and finding the tent of his boxers underneath. Jake helped her, slipping his cock free and groaning softly, her nipple between his lips, when she took him in her hand.

"Quiet," she reminded him, smiling at his soft moan into her breasts as she stroked him against her behind, his precum wetting the silk of her panties.

"I'll try," he breathed, his fingers pumping in and out of her wetness, matching the tug of her hand between his legs. "But oh my god, I don't think I've ever felt anything so good…"

"I know." She swallowed, rolling her hips, wanting more. It had been so long, too long, and he was right, it felt far too good to stop. "Wait."

She shifted her hips, rubbing the tip of his dick against her clit, circling it there, and then sliding it down her slit, nudging the fingers away with what she really wanted—his cock—pulling her panties further aside for him. Jake grabbed her hips as she positioned herself, easing down slowly, taking his length. They both sighed when she bottomed out, rocking her pelvis up against his.

"I was wrong," he gasped, looking up at her. "This feels even better."

"Mmmm hmm," she agreed.

"And look at that," he teased, shifting his weight, making her gasp at the pressure of him inside. "You're on top, just how you like it."

"So I am." Rachel laughed softly, her fingers gripping his shoulders for balance. His hands were moving again, up over her sides, her breasts, cupping her face so he could bring her to him and kiss her. She sucked at his tongue, feeling his cock throb in response, but when his hands moved through her hair again, she distracted him by putting them somewhere else, this time her ass.

He grabbed her behind and thrust, making her moan. She remembered her promise to be quiet and bit her lip.

"So where did our little game leave off?" he inquired, moving his hips to meet her.

"Game?" she gasped. She couldn't think. She could barely speak.

"Hard or soft?" he asked, demonstrating, first with a few hard strokes, followed by a slower, easier pace.

"Oh god." She dug her fingers into his shoulders. "Hard. Please."

"Deep or short?" Another demonstration—long, deep strokes, followed by short, fast ones.

"Ohhh! Deep! Deep and hard!" Rachel begged, her thighs trembling as they clenched his.

Jake gave her just what she wanted, keeping his hands on her ass and fucking up to meet her. Rachel couldn't take much more. Her clit was throbbing, her whole body aching for release.

"Up or down?" Jake whispered.

"Yes!" Rachel cried.

He smiled, eyes half-closed. "In or out?"

"Yes!" Rachel panted, grinding her pussy down on him. "Oh god yes, more, all of it, everything, please!"

"Oh god." Jake's grip tightened and she felt his thighs flex under hers. "Rachel, baby. Oh…wait…"

"I can't," she breathed against his ear. "I'm going to come all over your cock."

"Yes!" He forgot all about being quiet, shoving deep and hard and fast into her pussy, driving her up toward the ceiling of the limo with his hips, groaning loudly with every thrust. She knew he was coming, could feel the heated throb of his cock deep inside, and she was just seconds away from coming too.

"Oh please," she begged, reaching down and rubbing her clit in fast, hard circles, sending herself flying over the edge into a blissful freefall, trembling and writhing in his arms as her orgasm rolled through her. Her pussy seized his cock with such force he howled and buried his face against her breasts in an effort to muffle the sound. She milked him with her climax until he shuddered and begged her to stop, stop, please, god, I can't take it anymore…

Rachel came to earth slowly. The sound of their breath came to her first, still harsh and panting. Then the movement of the limo—they were on the road again, going fast, probably on the highway. Then the realization that they were naked—well, she was, mostly. He had just undone his jeans.

Rachel reached for her jersey, pulling it back on over her head and then adjusting her bra underneath. Jake zipped and straightened, and soon they were both dressed again, tucking and smoothing things over.

"So much for being quiet," Jake teased as she picked up her purse—it had fallen to the floor in the middle of things.

Rachel felt her cheeks grow hot and she glanced toward the tinted glass. "You think he heard us?"

He chuckled. "I think they probably heard us down in Texas."

The car slowed to a stop and she leaned over, looking out to see her apartment building towering above them.

"Looks like we're here." Rachel met his gaze for a moment but she was too overwhelmed to do it for long. "I had a great time, Jake. Thank you."

He didn't say anything for a moment and the silence stretched. She knew he was waiting for her to ask him up—and she should have, considering. But she couldn't do it. Her apartment was her sanctuary, the place where she could let her hair down—quite literally—and she didn't know if she could trust anyone there, even him.

When the limo driver knocked on the car door instead of just swinging the door wide, Rachel knew he must have heard them.

"Open up," Jake called and she flushed at his words. The driver opened the door and waited. Jake grabbed her hand as she started to slide across the seat, stopping her. He slid close enough to kiss her softly and she melted at the touch of his lips, the draw of his tongue, but when his hand moved in her hair, she shrank away.

"Goodnight, Jake," she murmured.

"Goodnight, Rapunzel," he whispered. She gave him a little smile, hearing him say, "I'll call you!"

She slipped past the driver and pushed the door open to her building and escaped, afraid to look back to see if Jake was following her with his eyes.

* * * *

"Rach, he's on the phone again," Josh hissed, holding his hand over the receiver.

It was a Tuesday—almost two weeks since she'd gone on a non-date with Jake and had non-sex with him in the limo—and Carly should have been answering the phone but Rachel had finally had to fire her after she'd double booked two more appointments and then failed to show up to work without calling last week.

Rachel sighed and shook her head. "Tell him I'm not here."

"Like you're ever not here." He snorted, uncovering the receiver and putting on his phone voice. "I'm sorry, Mr. Malden, she's unavailable."

Rachel cringed and continued sweeping the floor. Joshie had just finished a cut, but it was a touch-up for one of the other stylists who had gone home early. It was now the two of them now and the place was pretty much dead, which wasn't surprising for near closing on a Tuesday night. Well, *Rapunzel's* might have been empty, but she had to find something to do to keep herself busy.

"I will..." Joshie nodded against the phone, rolling his eyes. It reminded Rachel of Emma and she wondered how the girl was doing, how her friend had fared with her cancer treatments. She could have asked Jake of course, if she'd taken any of the three hundred phone calls she'd received from him since that night in the limo, but she was too ashamed to answer. Thank god for voice mail and Joshie.

"You really need to talk to that man." Joshie put down the phone and gave her a long, steady look. Rachel shrugged, using the dust pan to sweep up wisps of hair. "So you had sex on the first date—lots of people do, you know. It doesn't have to be the end of everything. It can be a great beginning!"

"It's not that." Rachel hid her blush as she dumped the hair in the bin and hung the broom and dust pan. Okay, so it was that. She was embarrassed by how she'd acted, how much she'd let happen that night, but it wasn't *just* that. Life was too complicated right now. She couldn't afford a relationship, and she certainly couldn't do crazy things like having sex with practical strangers.

"Pul-eeeeeeeze!" Joshie rolled his eyes so far back in his head he looked like he was going to pass out. "You are so transparent. I'm gonna nickname you 'Casper,' girl!"

She turned to face him, crossing her arms over her chest. "I am not."

"You like him." Joshie smiled, a slow, knowing sort of smile that made Rachel want to strangle him. "You like him so much it scares you."

"I do not." She turned and stalked to her station, straightening, putting scissors away, the blow dryer back in its place.

Joshie came over to stand beside her. He was short and stocky and his chin was the perfect height to rest on her shoulder as he looked into the mirror.

"Look at that." He pointed to her reflection, meeting her eyes. "You're a beautiful woman. He was attracted to you. Believe it."

"Without this?" She tugged on her wig, feeling the adhesive underneath starting to give. It was a strong sort of glue, but as the day wore on, it became less and less effective.

He put his arms around her waist and gave her a strong squeeze. "He's not going to like you any less because you're sick."

"How do you know?" She let herself relax a little against him.

"Because he's a good guy," he insisted. "And if he leaves when he finds out, well then hell, we both know he wasn't worth it."

Rachel sighed and moved out of Joshie's arms, sitting down in the salon chair and giving herself a long, hard look. The wig was a good one—she'd paid a mint for it—and didn't look too obvious. But she knew what was underneath it—the few golden-auburn wisps that were left. And what was underneath that—her insecurity, her self-pity, her fear of rejection, her self-doubt and how it had all made her question her own basic femininity.

Josh peeled up the edge of the wig, peering at her hairline. "How's it going under there\ anyway?"

"Awful." She made a face. "It's almost all gone."

"It's a barbaric treatment…almost worse than the damned disease." Joshie petted her wig. It was real human hair, a big luxury in wigs, especially one so long. Someone like Emma had donated her hair for a wig like this, Rachel thought, leaning her head back against Joshie as he smoothed the hair over her shoulders. "Sometimes I think they might as well just use leeches."

"Don't say that." She reached back and squeezed his hand. "I'm hoping it works."

"I hope so too." His smile was bright—too bright, and she knew it was for her benefit, a sort of fake optimism. But she didn't blame him. It was hard to be truly hopeful in the face of mortality, your own or anyone else's. "How many more treatments?"

"I'm done for this round." Rachel sounded relieved, and she was. "Now it's just wait and see."

"Want me to give you a scalp treatment?" Joshie brightened, for real this time. "Come on, no one's here and our appointments are done for the night. It will do you some good. And you've got to be suffering under that thing."

"I hate it." Yet her wig was gorgeous, the envy of everyone who came into the salon. They all thought it was her real hair. Her deception was a good one.

"Then let's get it off you."

It took a lot for her to let him, but in the end, she trusted him enough to say yes. Joshie applied adhesive remover under the edges of her wig and sat her down like a client in a chair with a magazine and brought her a cappuccino to wait for it to start to work while he mixed some sort of concoction in a tray.

"What is that?" she asked, sipping her coffee, glad she splurged for the good stuff for her clients.

"Lots of stuff that's good for your skin." Joshie looked like a mad scientist with bottles lined up on the counter. "My last boyfriend shaved his head and I used to do this for him once a week. Made his head soft as a baby's bottom."

"You must have enjoyed that."

Joshie grinned. "You have no idea."

"You said we didn't have any more appointments." Rachel put down her coffee and stood as the bell to the front door rang.

"We don't." Joshie looked up. "Must be a walk-in…"

"Oh no." Rachel recognized him immediately—that dark curly mane of hair and mischievous smile—but she put on a professional face, walking past a stunned and rooted-to-the-floor Joshie, already greeting them as she reached the lobby, "Hi Mr. Malden. Emma! Good to see you. Who's your friend?"

There were three of them this time, Jake standing just behind the two young girls.

Emma introduced her friend, although Rachel would have guessed, just from the colorful scarf tied around her head. "This is Liv."

"You can't be here for a haircut," Rachel remarked. She heard Joshie coming up behind her, recovered from his shock. "You just had one."

"Actually, we are." Emma reached over and grabbed Liv's hand. "I want to get my head shaved."

"Ummmm…" Rachel glanced at Jake, incredulous. He shrugged. Just looking at him made her knees feel weak and she chided herself, focusing her attention back on Emma. "Are you sure about that?"

"Liv wants to get her head shaved too," Emma explained.

"We're gonna go all Britney Spears together." Liv spoke up for the first time, doing something so brave it took Rachel's breath away. She pulled the scarf off her head to reveal the typical cancer-treatment hairdo with little tufts of fine blond hair sticking up on her scalp.

"Completely bald?" Rachel managed to ask, finding breath left somewhere in her lungs.

"Completely." Emma's face was resolute.

Rachel looked over at Jake. "How do you feel about that?"

"I'm fine with it." Jake ruffled Emma's hair. It was short, yes—but it wasn't *gone.* That was something Rachel wasn't sure Emma was prepared for. It was one thing to donate a length of your hair to charity. It was another thing altogether to shave your head completely bald.

Rachel took a different tact. "How did your mom react to you getting your hair cut for *Locks of Love*?"

"She went crackers." Emma grinned. "I got grounded for a month."

Rachel sighed and said gently, "I'm not sure this is such a good idea."

"I can do it with a parent's permission, right?" Emma's jaw tightened as she nodded toward Jake. "Well this parent says I can do it."

Rachel tried to let her down gently. "Cutting your hair was one thing, sweetie, but shaving your head…"

"I'll do it," Joshie chimed in. Rachel glared at him and he grinned. "Go ahead, fire me."

"Joshie…"

He was already putting an arm around their shoulders, ushering them into the back. "Come on, girls, let's get out the clippers and go wild."

Rachel stared after them, sure she should stop him, but not saying anything. Instead, she turned to Jake and asked, "Are *you* sure about this?"

"I'm sure it's what Emma wants, and she's a little like her mother in that regard. If she wants it, she's going to get it." Jake shrugged and then looked at her with eyes so hungry the man might have been starving. "Besides, it gave me a good excuse to come see you."

Rachel felt heat filling her face. The way he looked at her, everything was out in the open, so raw and naked.

"Listen, Jake…"

He moved closer, not close enough to touch but close enough she could feel his heat and hear his whispered words, "I really want to kiss you right now."

"Don't…" she breathed, glancing over her shoulder. The girls were back at Joshie's station around the corner and couldn't see them, but she could hear them giggling.

"Oh, I won't…but I want to." He grinned. "My sixteen-year-old daughter would just tell us to go get a room. Which I am very tempted to do."

"Might be more comfortable than a limo." Now she was really blushing. She could feel it.

"Oh I don't know." He moved closer enough she could feel him, long and lean and solid. "I didn't have too many complaints."

"Me either." She felt herself giving in and tried to fight it.

His breath was sweet and smelled wintergreen. "I was hoping you'd say that."

She tried again to distance herself, but only verbally. She didn't step back. "It's not you, Jake…"

His hands moved to her upper arms, squeezing gently. "Oh, you mean the reason you haven't answered any of my phone calls?"

She nodded helplessly.

"Well it can't be you," he insisted, searching her eyes with his. "Because you, Ms. Rapunzel, are pure perfection."

She knew he was going to kiss her and she didn't stop him. His lips were warm and soft and just as sweet as she remembered.

She gasped when they parted, pleading for mercy. "Jake…"

"And if it's not me…" He kissed the corner of her mouth. "And it's not you…" Another kiss, this one at her jaw line. "Then what could it possibly be?" Fiery kisses rained down over her throat and she moaned softly, her lust for him already igniting in her core. Joshie had been right. This was the reason she hadn't answered his phone calls, she admitted to herself, feeling his thigh sliding between hers, his hands moving at the small of her back. She couldn't help herself. She wanted him.

"Hey Rachel, where's our body paint?" Joshie called from around the corner.

They broke apart and Rachel straightened her skirt and checked her wig reflexively, realizing the adhesive remover was working. It was very loose.

"Our…what?" She gave Joshie a startled response as he came around the corner. Jake took a guilty step back but she could still feel his heat and it made her breath come too fast.

Joshie rifled through the drawers under the cash register. "They left some here last month, for the model shoot they did for *Vogue* remember?"

"It's…" Rachel slipped in beside him, opening the bottom drawer, the catch-all, the salon's version of a junk drawer. "Here it is." It was a little kit, including brushes. She handed it over, frowning. "What are you going to do with body paint?"

Joshie grinned. "Come see."

Jake and Rachel found the two girls sitting in chairs next to each other, both of them shaved completely, shockingly bald, as promised. The sight paralyzed Rachel with emotion—fear, sadness, pride. Her eyes brimmed with tears and she willed them not to fall.

"Oh Em…" Jake took a step toward his daughter and then stopped. He seemed paralyzed too.

Emma perked up when she saw her father. "Isn't it awesome?"

"Totally awesome," Jake said finally, his voice a little hoarse.

"Time to unleash my inner artist." Joshie opened the body art kit and was doing something with one of the brushes. "Are you girls ready?"

"He's going to paint our heads for the party, Daddy," Emma explained as Joshie's brush began to move over the girl's scalp. She had a lovely-shaped head, round and smooth.

"What a great idea." Jake gave Joshie an approving smile.

"You two are going to be the belles of the ball." Joshie returned the smile and then focused his efforts back on his work.

"There's a class party tonight," Liv chimed in, watching her friend get her scalp painted. "I was too scared, but Emma decided we were both going to shave our heads and make a big entrance."

"I think that's a great idea." Rachel sat down in the chair beside Liv, blinking back her tears. She wanted to touch the girl's smooth scalp and restrained herself. Liv was smiling, probably more happy than she'd been in a long time, and Rachel was glad she had a friend like Emma. Nina Malden's determination had clearly been harnessed in her daughter for a good purpose. She'd never seen anyone do something so selfless, so courageous, so kind.

"You know what, Joshie?" Rachel reached up, feeling her wig slip as she touched it. The adhesive had worn completely off. She glanced over at Jake, feeling her stomach clench. She had tried to tell him, but maybe it would be easier this way. She could just show him instead. She slipped the wig off her head and let it fall into her lap, revealing her own chemo-hairdo. "Let's paint the town red."

The girls gaped. Rachel didn't have the courage to look over at Jake to see his reaction. Liv seemed to know right away, making the connection faster than Emma did.

"What kind?" Liv asked, her eyes soft and wet.

"Same as yours," Rachel replied softly. "Leukemia. We can be twins."

"I'm so sorry." Emma's eyes filled with tears and then all three of them were crying—and then laughing, and then hugging in a big circle.

Joshie tsked and cooed and ushered them back into their seats so he could finish his work. He painted all three to perfection—purple paisley for Emma and blue bird's wings for Liv and orange and black tiger stripes for Rachel. In the end, they all had so much fun Rachel hadn't realized Jake slipped out until his daughter called for him.

"Daddy! Come see!"

Rachel touched her head self-consciously, glancing into the mirror. She looked strange, foreign, her eyes bigger and rounder in her face. The tiger stripes made her look wild, feral. What was Jake going to say? And then, as Emma called for him, wandering toward the lobby, Rachel realized he was gone.

He had found out she was sick and had left, unable to handle the news.

"Hey." Joshie read her mind. "Stop it."

"It's okay." Rachel put on a smile, sliding an arm around Liv's shoulder. "Ready for your party, beautiful?"

Liv's smile was so bright, it could have powered a small third-world country. That alone made it worth it. They walked toward the lobby, where Emma was peering out the front glass door, frowning.

"I don't understand where he could have gone." Emma turned to Rachel. "Did he say anything to you?"

Rachel shook her head, not trusting her voice.

"There he is." Liv pointed toward the door and they all looked as Jake walked toward the salon, holding the handles of a small bag swinging at his hip.

"Where did you go?" Emma protested as he opened the door, his eyes widening. They must have been quite a sight, Rachel realized, the three of them standing there with their bald, painted heads.

"I thought the three of you could use a little bling." Jake put the bag down on a chair, reaching in and pulling out a blue box Rachel recognized immediately. There was a *Tiffany's* right around the corner on North Michigan Avenue. He handed the first one to Liv. Her jaw dropped when she opened the little box to find a pair of heart-shaped diamond earrings inside.

"Mr. Malden…" Her voice shook

"Shh." He leaned over and kissed the top of her head. "You're like my own daughter. You know I love you."

Emma squealed when she opened her tear-drop diamond earrings, hugging her father and quickly grabbing Liv's arm and dragging her over to one of the salon mirrors so the girls could try on their jewelry. Joshie went with them, exclaiming over the sparkly treasures, and Jake pulled out another blue box from the bag, this one long and thin.

"Jake…" Rachel took a step back, swallowing hard as he held the box out in front of him. "No…"

"Yes." He pressed the box into her hand. "It's yours. Open it."

"I can't." Her hands were trembling too much. "You do it." She handed it back to him and he obliged, taking the necklace out and tenting it in his fingers.

"Do you like it?"

"It's lovely," she whispered, looking at the bird-shaped diamond pendant. "A dove?"

He shrugged, undoing the clasp. "They didn't have any hockey sticks."

She laughed. "I really shouldn't accept this."

"Yes you should." He lifted the chain over her head as she turned, doing the clasp up behind her neck. "Beautiful."

There was no hair to lift out the way as he kissed the nape of her neck, his breath warm, and murmured, "Hope is a thing with feathers…"

"I'm sorry I didn't tell you," she whispered, her back still to him.

"I'm sorry you had to." His hands rested on her shoulders, squeezing gently. "But you don't need to hide anything from me."

"I just thought you wouldn't…" She swallowed her words, unable to finish her thought.

"What? Like you? Want you?"

"Stay."

"I think I used all my rollover minutes just talking to your answering machine in the past two weeks." He grinned as she turned to face him. "I'm not going anywhere."

"Thank you, Daddy!" Emma kissed his cheek. "We're gonna go. Can I have the keys?"

"And just how am I going to get home?" But Jake was already digging into his pocket and producing the desired object.

Emma rolled her eyes. "Can't you get a taxi?"

Rachel took a subtle step closer to Jake, giving him a quick, heated, side-long glance. "You can come up to my place and call one."

"Here." Jake quickly handed the keys over to his daughter. "Call my cell if you need me."

Emma gave them both a knowing look. "Don't wait up."

"You either." Jake grinned.

"Dad!" The teenager made a face, pulling her friend toward the door, as if he'd crossed some invisible line with his words.

"Bye!" Liv waved as Emma dragged her out.

"Have fun!" Rachel smiled and waved back as the girls practically ran down the corridor, heading for the parking garage. She glanced over at Jake. "Think they're going to be okay?"

"I think they're already more than okay." He took her hand.

"She's a really special girl, your Emma." Rachel squeezed his hand. "You should be proud."

Jake nodded, sounding a little choked up. "I am."

"You two go on," Joshie interrupted, waving them out.

"I need my wig," Rachel protested. "I can't go out like this."

Joshie and Jake exchanged glances but Rachel ignored them. She found her wig at the station next to Joshie's. She didn't have any adhesive left in the salon so she just slipped it on over her newly painted head, straightening and fluffing. It would do until they got upstairs.

"Go already!" Joshie insisted. He had Rachel's purse and he slung it over her shoulder, practically pushing them out the door. "I'll close up shop."

Jake was quiet on the way to the elevator. Most shops were closing for the night, although there were still a few people coming out of the all-night grocery. Rachel fiddled with her wig as they got into the elevator and she pressed the button for her floor. There was a mirror on the back wall and she checked it again. It had moved a little.

Jake slipped between her and her mirror image and she looked up, meeting his gaze, although tilting her chin made her wig slide and she grabbed onto it self-consciously with one hand before it could fall to the floor.

"Come on, Rapunzel." He put a hand over hers on her head, slowly moving her wig back. "Let down your hair."

"Jake…" She swallowed, feeling it slip further. She knew he'd seen her without it already and yet she was still too afraid to let go when they were here alone together.

He dipped his head down and kissed her, mouth insistent, the hand holding her wig moving to her lower back. The cool air against her neck made her shiver—and so did the way he turned and pressed her back against the mirror, his body a wall of heat as the kiss grew deeper, his tongue drawing hers.

She left her hair puddled on the floor, her scalp bald and naked. It was a strange, backwards equation, but somehow the more exposed she was to him, the better she felt. His thigh slipped between hers and she opened her legs, skirt riding up high as he pressed against her. One of his hands reached around to grab her ass, lifting her more fully to him, the other twisted in front, grabbing her breast and squeezing through her blouse.

Then she remembered they were still in the elevator and it could stop at any time, letting on one of her neighbors, maybe even a client. She broke the kiss, breathless, meeting his own half-lidded gaze.

"Wait," she pleaded, whimpering as his thigh flexed delightfully between hers. "At least until we get to my apartment."

"I can't wait anymore," he murmured against her neck, licking and sucking at her skin. "I want you. I want you so fucking bad I can't breathe. I can't think. I spend all day thinking about you. My clients are beginning to wonder if I'm on drugs or something, I space out so often, daydreaming about you."

She twined her arms around his neck, hanging on tight, as if she could get closer to him somehow, crawl inside his skin.

"And the nights..." He gave a long, frustrated groan, sliding both hands under her ass and grinding his pelvis against hers. She gave in, wrapping her legs around his waist, feeling the hard press of his cock bent and straining through his trousers. "I feel like a damned teenager. I can't stop jerking off and thinking about you."

She flushed with pleasure at his words.

"And just when I think it's over, when I make myself come remembering your hot little pussy or your sweet, gorgeous tits..." He kissed her again, quickly, his breath hot, his words mumbled against her mouth. "You've got me under some sort of spell. I swear, I can come like I was fifteen again, over and over. All I have to do is remember the feel of you riding my cock and I'm hard again in an instant." His admission made them both fill with heat. He met her eyes, his expression pained, hungry, desperate. "And this just goes on and on and on…" He pressed his lips to hers again and again. "All. Fucking. Night. Long." He punctuated each word with a hard thrust of his hips, driving her against the back wall of the elevator.

"I know how you feel," she breathed when the elevator slid to a stop and the bell went off letting them know they'd arrived at her floor.

"Do you?" He gripped her in his arms as if he couldn't let her go and she wondered if he was going to, but he finally did as the doors started to slide open. Rachel retrieved her wig and went to put it back on but Jake took it from her hands.

"What—?" she protested.

"I like seeing all of you." He hid both hands behind his back when she went to grab her wig. She was afraid she might run into a neighbor in the hallway. "And I'm gonna see a lot more of you in a minute. Which one is yours?"

"At the end of the hall." She nodded in that direction and they made it without incident. Rachel's hand trembled as she slipped her key into the lock, but they'd barely burst into the apartment before Jake was kissing her again and she found herself pressed against the door they'd closed behind them.

"Jake—" She tried to protest, to keep up some semblance of appearance or decorum, although she wasn't even sure why, until he thrust her half the way up the door with his hips, using both hands to tear her blouse open. The buttons popped and scattered like marbles all over the floor and she had time to wonder if she was dreaming this before her bra was pulled down too and he buried his face against the flesh of her breasts like he was coming home.

"Oh god!" She ran her hands through the dark curls on his head, her hips moving on their own, grinding back against his. Her skirt was long, but he had it pushed far up her legs, the soaked crotch of her panties wetting the zipper of his trousers with every thrust. "Jake, please, please…"

"Please what?" His tongue bathed her nipples, back and forth, sending exquisite shocks of pleasure down between her thighs.

"I want you," she begged, reaching down between them to touch herself, something she had done thinking about him a hundred times since the limo, getting herself off again and again just from the memory. But he was here now, real flesh and pounding blood and she had to have him. Had to. Now.

"You want me to fuck you?" He was already fumbling with his zipper, freeing his cock.

"Yes!" She moaned when she felt the length of him spring free between her thighs, the only thing separating them now the thin fabric of her panties. They were plain white cotton—nothing special today—but they nudged aside just as easily as her silk ones had. "Do it! Oh please don't tease me, put it in! Put it in!"

He groaned and thrust, finding her center with delicious accuracy and pounding deep. There were no words then, just the hot pant of their breath as they kissed and he fucked her hard against the door, the whole thing rattling with every thrust, alerting every neighbor in the place to just what they were doing.

Rachel had a brief flash of fear that someone might call the cops but the hot pounding of Jake's cock inside her pussy grew so intense so fast, like a flash fire between her thighs, the thought burned away, leaving her shaking in its wake. She was going to come like this, with him buried inside of her, fucking her so hard her teeth jarred, her head banging against the trembling door.

She clutched him, arms and legs wrapped tight, and tried to warn him, but it was no use. Her orgasm burst forth like a dam breaking, her juices flooding them both.

Jake moaned as her pussy enveloped his cock in climax, squeezing his length, the head buried so deep she thought she could taste it in her throat. Rachel screamed in release, her nails digging into his shoulders, hips bucking, but he managed to hold onto her and even come himself, following her by just moments, shoving into her so hard she thought the door might just splinter in half and spill them into the hallway.

"Oh god," she whispered, still hanging onto him tightly as their bodies started to relax. "It was really real? I thought I dreamed it..."

"It was real." Jake's kisses found her neck, her jaw, her ear. "And this time you're not going anywhere."

"Mmm," she agreed, whimpering as he grew soft and slipped out of her pussy. She wanted him still, more of him, always. He groaned when she reached a hand down to find him, slack and wet with their cum.

"Hungry little kitten," he chuckled.

"Meow." She scratched lightly at his balls with her fingernails and he jumped, gasping. "Do you like my tiger stripes?"

He studied her head in the dim light—Rachel had one lamp on a timer in the living room and the light barely reached the foyer.

"I'd like to see your whole body painted like that." He grinned. "We could do a new animal every night. Tigers, zebras, giraffes..."

"Giraffes?" She laughed. "What do giraffes say?"

"Umm...I think giraffes say...'gnork.' The 'g' is silent."

"Gnork! Gnork!" she called, both of them laughing as he followed her directions to the bathroom, not letting her down, keeping her legs wrapped around his waist the whole time until he could sit her on the bathroom counter and run the shower. He slowly stripped her down, inspecting every inch of her with his eyes, until she was sitting naked on the edge of the sink.

"Now you," she insisted, watching as he hung his suit coat on a hook on the back of the door and undid his tie. He peeled his shirt off quickly, his trousers and boxers dropping to the floor, and Rachel noticed he wasn't kidding—his cock was half-hard again already. He left his shoes and socks in the pile and stepped into the shower.

"Come on," he called, peeking out of the shower curtain.

She glanced at herself in the mirror. Joshie had done an amazing job painting her scalp. He was quite the artist. It seemed a shame to wash it all away without even taking a picture, but she knew she was hesitating for more reasons than just that.

Jake raised an eyebrow at her and she bit her lip, meeting his gaze.

"But then I'll be totally naked," she murmured, touching her tiger stripes.

Jake grinned. "That's the idea." He held a hand out to her and she took it, letting him pull her in. They spent a long time soaping each other up and rinsing off. The body paint came off easily enough and Rachel touched the smooth expanse of her scalp with trepidation. There weren't even any wispy hairs left. She was completely bald.

"You're beautiful," Jake whispered into her ear, his fingers moving between the wet, swollen lips of her pussy as he pressed her against the tiles. She remembered how he'd taken her, fucked her, and her clit throbbed in response.

"No, I'm not," she protested softly, whimpering as his fingers parted her, finding her aching clit and circling it with his thumb.

"Yes," he insisted, bending to capture a nipple between his lips. She moaned and spread wider for his attention. "You're so fucking beautiful I can't stand it."

"Jake…" she whispered as he sank to his knees in the shower and spread her lips with his fingers, his tongue taking up where his thumb had left off. "Oh god. Oh my god. That's so good…"

His mouth covered her pussy and he drank her in like nectar, sucking and licking and driving her wild. Before long her knees began to give way, but Jake didn't give up—instead he just threw her legs over his shoulders and delved in deeper, sucking insistently at her little clit. His fingers probed her hole, sliding into her wetness and mimicking the motion of his cock, in and out of her pussy, and that sent her shuddering over the edge into ecstasy.

"Oh fuck!" she gasped, her heels digging into his back, mashing her flesh against his lapping tongue. "Make me come! Make me come all over your face!"

Jake just mumbled something affirmative, his fingers thrusting in deep as she spasmed around them, the walls of her pussy contracting with pleasure. She moaned and felt her whole body collapsing, melting like jelly, and Jake took her weight in his arms, sliding his body up hers, keeping her pressed to the tiles as he kissed her. She could taste herself in his mouth, feel the heat of his erection against her hip.

"I want you again," he whispered, reaching over and turning off the water.

"So I feel," she teased, gripping his length, making him growl.

"I told you, it's like I'm fifteen again." He grabbed a towel and started rubbing her down as they stepped out. She let him dry them both off, even laughed when he shook his head like a dog, spraying them both with water.

"I can't do that anymore," she said a little sadly, running a hand over her bare scalp. She was afraid to look in the mirror.

"True," he agreed, stepping close and pulling her into his arms to kiss the top of her head. "But you give a whole new meaning to the term 'wash and go.'"

She laughed again, letting him kiss her, his hands roaming all over her body. She felt like a teenager again too, eager but self-conscious, excited and a little afraid. He followed her directions again, this time to her bedroom, and they rolled around, kissing and petting on her down comforter until they were breathless with lust.

"I can't get enough of you," he groaned, kissing his way down between her thighs. She couldn't let him focus on her pussy again like that, giving her so much attention without any distraction, so she turned herself around and rolled on top of him, playing with his cock. It was leaking precum and she licked it off, enjoying the taste, the silky feel of his skin against her lips and tongue. She hadn't had a cock in her mouth in a long time.

"Oh Rachel," he moaned as she took his length, as far as she could, deep into her throat. "Oh Jesus, sweetie, go slow…fuck!"

She smiled as she came up on his cock, rubbing the head over her lips, smearing more precum there. His mouth was still busy between her legs, licking and sucking at her pussy, greedy with lust.

"Are you close?" she teased, smacking his cock lightly against her mouth and tongue.

"You have no idea," he gasped, his voice strained. She could actually feel his thighs trembling beneath her with the effort to hold back. "Your mouth is so good."

"Think if I made you come now, you could get hard again?" She gripped him in her hand, stroking fast, making him thrust up into her fist.

"For you?" He gave a strangled cry, a half-laugh. "I have no doubt."

"Good." She ran her tongue around the head, still tugging on his cock. "Because I want you to come in my mouth before you fuck me again."

"Oh god," he whispered against her pussy as she started to suck him in earnest, working her mouth and tongue up and down his length. He seemed to forget about her altogether for a moment, just resting his cheek against the smooth expanse of her thigh as she took him again and again into her eager mouth.

"Rachel," he warned, his arms wrapping tightly around her hips, squeezing. "Oh god, baby, you're gonna make me come!"

Her only response was to suck him harder, faster, cupping his balls in her hand and feeling their weight, the skin there tightening in anticipation. He was very, very close, and she wanted it, she wanted to feel him explode against her tongue, wanted to swallow every drop of his cum.

"Ohhhhh!" He finally gave in, driving his cock so deeply into the back of her throat she had no choice but to take his cum. It flooded her in hot, sticky waves and she gulped madly, trying to catch it all and not spill a drop. His cock pulsed between her lips as he emptied himself completely into her waiting mouth.

"Yum." She turned around on him, kissing the corner of his mouth. He was still shaking with the force of his orgasm. "Now…how long do you think we have to wait?" Her hand was already grasping the softening length of his cock.

Jake groaned, barely opening his eyes to focus on her. "Suck all you want—we'll make more."

"I want to fuck you," she murmured, sliding a thigh over his to straddle him, rubbing the wet flesh of her pussy into his crotch. "Just like this. Remember the limo ride?"

He held onto her hips. “Not likely to forget that ride for the rest of my life.”

“Me either.” She rocked on top of him, using the still half-hard length of his cock, rubbing it against her clit. “I come so hard when I think about it.”

“You too?”

She nodded, biting her lip. “I have a little vibrator in that drawer. I use that.”

Without another word, Jake reached over and opened the night table drawer, fumbling around inside until he found it. It was small and sleek, and it hummed nicely when he turned it on.

“Here.” He handed it to her, still buzzing.

She slid it down between her pussy lips, rubbing her clit with the tip, letting out a soft moan. Jake jumped when the vibrator touched the head of his cock.

“You like that?” she asked, using the vibrator to tease them both.

Jake just moaned, his fingers digging into her hips. She could feel him getting hard again as she slipped the humming tip of the toy back and forth, around and around. Her pussy was on fire. She’d lost count of how many times she had come already but she wanted more, and she desperately wanted his cock inside of her when she came again.

“Ready for my pussy?” She grasped his length, squeezing, tugging, testing his hardness, but there was no need. He was thick and stiff and ready for her again. He just nodded, gasping when she slid down onto his length, settling herself into the saddle of his hips.

“Oh god.” Jake’s head went back, eyes closed. “I’m gonna come too fast.”

“Wanna race?” She smiled as she slipped the vibrator between her pussy lips, focusing on her clit, the sensation almost too good to bear.

“On your mark…” Jake muttered as she started to ride him, grinding her pussy down into his crotch. “Oh fuck…”

“Get set…” She squeezed her muscles hard around him, her pussy already contracting in anticipation of her orgasm. Her vibrator always made her come fast. Very fast.

"Ohhh!" He began to thrust up into her, unable to resist the sweet pulse of her pussy.

"Go," she whispered, rolling her hips, feeling his swollen cock growing even bigger inside of her as she rode him. There was no stopping now, either of them. She moved in easy circles, making the same motion with the vibrator on her clit. Jake closed his eyes and drove up into her, the look on his face alone enough to send her over, but the anticipation was so delicious she tried to hold out, waiting, not wanting to cross the finish line yet.

"Rachel!" His eyes flew open when she slid the vibrator down to touch his shaft as well as her pussy, sliding up on him so the whole thing rubbed against them both as they fucked. "Oh god! What are you doing?"

"Winning." She couldn't hold back anymore. Her orgasm shook them both and she cried out with her release, her clit throbbing rapidly under the hum of the vibrator. Jake groaned and give up too, giving her a few more long, delicious, shuddering strokes before burying himself to the hilt and coming up inside her. She felt every pulse of his swollen cock as he drove up into her, pushing her toward the ceiling and making her drop the vibrator and clutch him, trying to hang on.

When they were both spent, Jake pulled her close, wrapping them up in the comforter, their bodies sheened with sweat, breath still coming fast with their effort. Rachel waited for her heart to slow, listening to Jake's racing too under the hard muscles of his chest.

"My god, you're so beautiful," he whispered, kissing the top of her head and she remembered her hair was on the floor somewhere in the foyer.

"You better stop saying that," she whispered, tracing a finger down to his navel. "I'm starting to believe you."

"Good." He chuckled. "My evil plan is working."

"Don't fall asleep," she reminded him. "You have to get home for Emma."

"Don't worry." He glanced at his watch, blinking his eyes, trying to focus. "We have hours to go before I sleep. And I'm going to make you come at least three more times."

"Aiming low, are we?"

"Gimme that thing." He grabbed for the still buzzing vibrator and Rachel squealed and tried to roll away, but he caught her and she gave up, knowing she was going to let him do whatever he wanted, for however long he wanted.

Even if her mind wasn't ready to accept it yet, her body knew, had known since the first time he touched her—she was his.

* * * *

Rachel could barely hold the phone. It trembled in her hand as she dialed Jake's number and she had to sit down before he answered, only on the second ring.

"Rachel?" He must have known from the caller ID because she hadn't said a word. "Did Nina call you?"

So he knew.

"She came into the salon." Her voice didn't even sound like her own, too faint and far away to be real. "She said she was going to sue me. She said…she said…"

"I know, I know." Jake swore softly. "Rachel, turn on the news."

"Joshie." She put her hand over the receiver and called him over. He was gathered with the other stylists, all of them buzzing like bees about the drama Nina had caused when she'd burst in and made her little scene. Thankfully they'd only had three clients in chairs at the time and the damage to *Rapunzel's* had been minimal. "Turn on the TV."

It was a flat screen on the far wall. It was hardly ever on, but occasionally they'd get busy and a client would want to watch something. Joshie did as she asked, grabbing the remote and pushing the power button.

"What channel?" Rachel asked.

"Any local news channel."

Her heart dropped at his words and it sank again when Joshie flipped to a local station. Nina was there, perfectly dressed, coiffed and composed, speaking into the microphone. "I'm sorry she has cancer, but that doesn't mean she has the right to shave my daughter's head."

Rachel put her head on the table, whispering, "I'm going to need a lawyer."

"I am a lawyer," Jake reminded her.

"The salon." She closed her eyes, feeling tears burning. "It's over. No one will ever come here again."

"You're wrong." Jake sounded angry, resolute. "I have an idea. Leave it to me. Will you leave it to me?"

"Yes." She was remembering the night before, the way they'd been together, how she'd felt falling asleep in his arms. She hadn't felt that calm and safe in a long time. Besides, what other choice did she have?

"Then let me rescue you."

She gave a short, sharp laugh. "I'm not a damsel in a tower."

"Sure you are," he protested. "And I'm a white knight. Didn't you see my horse parked around back?"

"I must have missed it," she said faintly, but she was smiling. "Was it behind the BMW?"

He laughed. "Okay, hand the phone over to Joshie."

"What?"

"Trust me," Jake insisted.

"I do." It was the truth. She called Joshie over and handed him the phone.

* * * *

Rapunzel's was all over the news. There wasn't a local news station that hadn't picked up on it, and now even CNN and the other major news networks had sniffed out the story and started to run with it. Rachel stood in the salon, Joshie by her side, staring at the screen, incredulous.

They flashed a picture of Rachel and the two young girls, three goddesses with their bald, painted heads put together, their smiles stretched wide. Joshie had done a beautiful job, taking hours on each of them this time and adorning them with sparkles and glitter. All three looked radiant and beautiful. Even me, Rachel thought, looking at the picture in wonder.

Then it was gone, and Jake was there on the screen. "Speaking as a lawyer, I can tell you that this is a frivolous lawsuit and I'd be surprised if a judge will even hear it. Speaking as a human being, I think this whole thing is just heartless and cruel. Speaking as a father, I fully support my daughter's decision and I'm very proud of her."

The whole salon cheered at that.

"Rachel, this is Mandy." Emma presented another of her classmates, this one a cheerleader with long blond hair. Rachel knew she was a cheerleader because the teen was actually wearing a cheerleading outfit. Probably for the cameras outside, Rachel realized. "She wants to get her hair cut for *Locks of Love*, too."

"Hi Mandy." Rachel smiled at the girl. "Come sign in."

The list on the wall was growing. So was the line out the door with the professionally printed sign Jake had put up with that same picture on it, the one the news kept using—Emma and Rachel and Liv smiling, their bald painted heads pressed together. Locks of Love *Drive - We're Too Sexy For Our Hair!*

It matched the billboard Jake had put up on the freeway.

"This is crazy," Joshie called on his way by as he directed another *Locks of Love* donation client back to his stylist's chair. "I think your boyfriend may have saved the salon."

"That's not all he saved." She smiled, seeing Jake pushing his way through the crowd toward her.

"Did I hear something about rescuing damsels in distress?" Jake slipped an arm around her waist and kissed her cheek. She wanted more, and from the look in his eyes, she knew he did too, but there were too many people around.

"Listen, Mr. Cocky, there's still the lawsuit to deal with," she reminded him, but she couldn't help smiling up at him.

"I told you to trust me," he reminded her.

"I do."

He nuzzled her neck, no hair in the way. "I like hearing you say those two little words."

She gave him a sharp, surprised look. "No blue *Tiffany* boxes."

"Not today." He chuckled. "But maybe someday."

"Maybe someday," she conceded, whispering her response into his ear and daring, for the first time in a long time, to hope about the future.

Epilogue

"We feel very vindicated." Jake spoke into the microphone, Rachel at his side. On his other side stood Emma and Liv, holding hands. Both girls had hair now, cute little pixies just like Rachel's. "I've said since the beginning that this was a frivolous lawsuit that should have been dismissed months ago. I'm glad the judge finally saw reason."

Rachel felt Jake's hand slip into hers and she smiled up at him. She barely heard the questions being peppered at them.

"No, the judge didn't award *Rapunzel's* any damages," Jake countered to one of the reporters. "We didn't countersue for any. But the judge did say that if we had, he would have awarded them to us."

Rachel glanced out into the crowd. Nina wasn't there. She'd been in the courtroom but had left almost immediately after the verdict. Emma had tried to talk to her mother but she'd disappeared too quickly. Emma saw her only on the weekends. Jake's daughter now lived full-time with her father, a request she'd had to make before yet another judge.

"That's correct, Olivia Riley is in complete remission." Jake smiled down at the girl and she smiled shyly back. The news had come just a few weeks ago and they'd taken the girls to Disney for the weekend to celebrate, their choice. "So I guess everyone gets a happy ending after all."

"What about Ms. Lange?" one of the reporters inquired. Rachel's head came up at the mention of her name.

Jake's smile faltered as he glanced down at her. "Well, we're still waiting for test results, but we're hopeful…"

Rachel leaned in to the microphone, her heart thudding in her chest. She hadn't planned this. She'd wanted to wait until after this whole court thing was over to sit both Emma and Jake down to tell them the news. But somehow this just seemed right.

"Actually, I heard from the doctor yesterday." Rachel cleared her throat and spoke into the microphone, wincing a little at the sudden feedback. Jake's hand tightened in hers and she glanced up at him, seeing the blindsided look on his face. Her eyes filled with tears. "It seems this happy ending thing must be catching because he told me my cancer is in remission too."

The crowd around them exploded with cheers and applause—it was even louder than the first wave, when they'd just come out of the courtroom. Jake pulled her into his arms and kissed her so hard she could barely breathe.

"Why didn't you tell me?" he whispered harshly against her ear, hugging her tight.

"I just did," she gasped as he held her at arm's length, his eyes drinking her in, looking at her as if she might disappear at any moment. Emma and Liv were around them, jumping up and down and hugging them both at turns. "Surprise."

"Daddy's got a surprise for you too," Emma whispered as her arms went around Rachel's neck, but the teen spoke too loudly. Jake heard and shot her a warning glance. "Oops."

"Surprise? What surprise?" Rachel asked, not realizing they were so close to the microphone.

The reporters heard the word and started asking the same question. Soon the crowd caught on and started chanting, "Sur-prise! Sur-prise! Sur-prise!" Jake flushed and stammered into the microphone, but it was hard to resist pressure like that.

"Okay, okay!" he relented, turning to Rachel in front of the crowd. "Rachel, I have to ask you something."

"What?" she asked, puzzled. She didn't fully understand, although she had hoped, had held fast to that hope for months. They both had. "Jake? What are you doing?"

"Loving you," he replied simply.

Then she did understand, and the hope that had settled in her heart, right under the dove pendant Jake had given her months ago, took flight in her chest as he reached into his suit pocket and pulled out a blue *Tiffany's* box.

Then, like a magician, he got down on one knee and turned hope into something with wings.

RED

It was one of those weeks that tease you, pretending spring was really here. Back in Nebraska, the tender shoots of flowers might even be fooled into popping their buds up through the soil, seeking warmth. They would be disappointed and wither a week later, unable to turn back and now unable to go forward, frozen in place, stunted. It made Mae think of home with a painful twist in her belly, and she almost wished again for the cold and damp.

But her body yearned for sun, betraying her heart, and the warmth brightened her mood, in spite of herself. Mae found herself humming as she spread the homemade rye bread with a thick layer of mayonnaise and followed that with splotches of mustard, upon which she stacked ham, bologna and salami so high Dagwood himself would have been envious. Her one window was open wide, and although the sound of the city eighteen stories below was nothing like the soft bray of the horses or the bleating of the young lambs at home, the air was a cool reminder of the real warmth soon to come. Spring came, even here, in the concrete jungle of New York City.

Sandwiches made, wrapped them in waxed paper and slipped them into the basket at her feet. A glass-lined thermos filled with lemonade, two ripe tomatoes for her, and a bag of those yummy new Lay's potato chips. She was practically addicted to them. There were also two moist, chocolate cupcakes for dessert spread with fluffy white cream, and two cloth napkins—white with an embroidered monogram and delicate lace edges in which she'd carried home pastries from her grandmother's house.

She took a dizzying glance down at the street before she reluctantly shut the window above the sofa. The apartment was an L-shape with living room, dinette and kitchen, and a small bedroom she barely fit a twin bed and dresser into. It had a window, but she had discovered it painted shut. No amount of complaint had motivated the landlord to action, however, and her strength was no match for the stuck window.

The breeze as she slid the living room window closed reminded her that while the air might promise spring, winter was still around the corner, and instead of going out in just her skirt and a sweater, Mae plucked her coat off the chair and slid her arms into the sleeves. For quite some time, she had nothing but her old patchwork coat to wear against the elements. It only took once of getting caught in a cold downpour though, dragging into Grandmother's like a drowned cat after running the last few breathless blocks, before her grandmother had presented her with a solution at their next weekly meeting—a brand new, slick, red umbrella.

Of course, Mae just never remembered the umbrella, but her grandmother had anticipated her granddaughter's absent-minded nature and accompanied her gift with a matching thick, wool, hooded coat. She wore it with secret pride and a great deal of satisfaction, the hood hiding her face from the crowds on the street. And if it hadn't been for her concealing red hood, she never would have bumped into Griff in the first place—literally.

Smiling at the memory, she buttoned her coat and cinched the red, wool belt before slinging her basket over her arm. She was almost to the door when she remembered the real reason she was taking this trip in the first place, still sitting in a white bag on the table.

"Stupid girl," she murmured, doubling back to pack the crinkly white bag into her basket. There was a mirror at the entryway and she paused to check herself over. Her long dark hair had been one of the first things to go, now cut short and fashionably, little curls pasted to the sides of her cheeks. She had spent hours in her bathroom learning how to use the make-up her grandmother insisted on, painting her lips a bright, luscious red, as if she'd been picking raspberries all afternoon and eating half of what she'd gathered. Grandmother didn't like untidiness and she was careful to groom herself appropriately before she left.

There was just enough room left on top for the white bag, but the lid didn't want to latch and she had to force it, glancing at the clock, anxious to be gone now. There was no spoken time between them, no said arrangement, but the assumption was noon. He was always there at noon, looking surprised to see her every single time, and yet she knew he really wasn't.

He couldn't be.

Could he?

* * * *

He was waiting for her, watching. Following someone in the crowded streets of New York was easier than anywhere else in the world. He was a magician, fading into the crowd, ducking under an awning if she happened to look his way. If she saw him too soon, it wouldn't be the end of the world, but he was a careful predator, his tracking sense honed and sharp. There was no sense alerting the prey before you were ready to pounce.

So he sat where he had every day, waiting with an open paper in front of him, the news more crushing today in 1933 than it had been years ago, when the depression had officially started and investors had reportedly taken nosedives from the high windows of New York skyscrapers.

He glanced up, wondering what it had been like. He almost wished he'd been here then, but the grift hadn't brought him this far, not yet. Back then, he'd been running small-time in podunk towns in the Midwest, little mom and pop cons that left him with some food in his belly and some money in his pocket, but not much else.

Now he was in the big time, and the girl he'd followed was his ticket to milk and honey. His mouth watered at the thought, his nostrils flaring almost as if he'd caught her scent, although the only thing he could smell was the overripe apple cart and the oppressing weight of exhaust fumes. There were far too many autos in the city, although the mayor claimed they would have better public transit than the elevated train lines they had now, promising Roosevelt's New Deal would help them finish the underground subway, making it the largest mass transit system in the world.

I'll believe it when I see it. He wasn't cynical—just realistic. The world didn't hand things to you, after all. You had to go and out and take them. By force, if necessary. And unfortunately, he'd found it necessary far too often in his life. But a man had to eat, didn't he? He didn't necessarily believe in Roosevelt's New Deal—but he damned well knew he could make his own new deal, and that's just what he intended to do.

He caught a flash of red out of the corner of his eye, his heart thudding in his chest, although he showed no outward sign of excitement. Instead, he folded his paper slowly and neatly, tucking it into his pocket as the girl swept out of the tenement looking as fresh as a ripe strawberry, ready for plucking. He couldn't believe his luck when she'd started to wear the red cape, making it ridiculously easy to spot her, but while sometimes there were little hiccups in his plans, just stumbling blocks or speed bumps in the road, most of the time the world seemed to conspire to give him just what he needed or wanted. Almost as if it had been meant to be.

He let himself smile, trying the expression on, his muscles flexed and ready. The time was now.

* * * *

Mae felt her stomach drop when she got to the corner and didn't see Griff. It was a little after noon, but not by much. Where could he be? She stood there, watching the cars go by, wondering what to do.

She knew, of course, what she *should* do—go on to her grandmother's, as she had planned, and drop off the medicine she'd picked up at the pharmacy. She'd taken the phone call from the pharmacist that morning, knowing it meant a trip across town, and had been secretly thrilled. The telephone in her apartment was one of the things her grandmother had insisted on and had even paid for, renting the model from the phone company, and while it was a luxury Mae wouldn't have even considered if she'd been on her own entirely, it had served to be quite an amazing convenience.

Of course, there was no way to call Griff. He was just here every day, waiting for her—somehow she was sure he was waiting just for her, even if he looked busy every time she arrived. She didn't even know where the man might reside. Did he live anywhere? Maybe in one of the shanty towns by the river? She shuddered at the thought.

No, Griff was clean, respectable, if a little rough around the edges sometimes. He had a job—had made one for himself right there on the New York street corner, selling apples out of his cart. He was a survivor with an entrepreneurial spirit she admired. He reminded her a little of her father.

But your father wasn't the man you thought he was, now was he?

That thought made her swallow hard and blink fast and look for something to distract herself. The cars had stopped now—the traffic officer high up in his tower had changed the light—and she could go, but she didn't. She didn't trust herself to make it across, even following amidst the crowd, with the sudden rise of tears stinging her eyes. Instead, the horde parted around her, jostling to get to the other side of the busy street before the light changed again.

Mae backed away from the intersection clutching her basket, letting the people pass her by. She probably would have just run home and called her grandmother to tell her she wasn't feeling well, that she'd come by tomorrow instead, if he hadn't run into her like a brick wall coming around the corner, making her drop her basket, the already-straining latch popping open and spilling the contents onto the concrete.

"Excuse me!" she exclaimed, trying to catch her breath, wondering if the glass in the thermos was broken as she stopped its roll with a swipe of her hand, kneeling gracefully on the sidewalk to try and replace the basket's contents.

She didn't realize it was him until he was squatting down beside her, helping her put things back, and she saw the deft movements of his hands. She knew those hands.

"Griff!'"

"Hey, Red." He grinned, giving her a wink. "We really have to stop meeting like this." He sounded breathless, like he'd been running when he'd literally run into her—again.

She giggled, remembering the first time she'd met him, on her way to grandmother's, a farm girl in a big city hurrying through the streets in her new red wool cape, her hood so low she could barely see anything at all. She certainly hadn't seen him, stepping out from behind his apple cart, and he hadn't been looking her way—instead he'd been focused on the four apples he'd been juggling to the delight of a small crowd. She had hit him square in his very solid chest with her pert little nose, surprising them both. He'd done the very same thing that day, she remembered, as apples rained down onto the concrete—that sly smile and the greeting he now used every time they met, "Hey, Red!"

She smiled and held up one of the sandwiches. "I made your favorite."

"You are an angel." He snatched at it, already unwrapping the waxed paper to get to the bread and meat before he'd even fully stood, holding his other hand out to help her up. "I'm starving."

"Where were you?" She knew her voice sounded accusatory, and she didn't want him to know how worried she'd been. "I thought you'd been kidnapped."

He shrugged. "I thought I saw someone I knew." He talked with his mouth half-full of sandwich, nodding toward the corner he'd come sailing around and swallowing. "But I never caught up."

She pursed her lips, eyes narrowing. "Oh. I see."

"It wasn't a dame," he assured her, giving a lopsided smile.

"No?"

"No, Red." He took her by the elbow, steering her toward his apple cart. "Besides, with a doll like you around, what man could look at anything else?"

"You're crackers," she protested, but she was smiling.

"That's a fact."

But now he had her curious. "So who was it?"

"Just some Joe I used to know." He pulled her behind his cart, as familiar to her as home now. "Come on, Red, let's take a load off."

They sat on wooden folding chairs behind Griff's apple cart, eating food out of the basket and watching the city walk by, dabbing their mouths with the embroidered cloth napkins Mae had packed as if they were eating in the finest restaurant in town. She couldn't have been any happier if they had been, she figured, when Griff dotted a bit of frosting from his chocolate cupcake onto her nose.

"Hey!" she protested, making a face and wiping at the sticky stuff with her napkin. "Didn't your mother ever tell you not to play with your food?"

"Where's the fun in that?" he asked, his mouth mostly full of cupcake as he licked his sticky fingers. Grabbing three of his apples, he tossed them casually into the air, juggling them easily. He always sold more apples than anyone because he did all sorts of tricks with them. He could juggle and make them disappear and had even once turned an apple into the fat, juicy orange she'd packed in her basket for him, although she still wasn't quite sure how he'd done it.

"So what's eating you, Red?"

She sighed, shrugged, and looked out at the people passing them on the street. Most just walked by and didn't see them at all. Griff was good at getting people's attention when he needed to, though. She glanced at him leaning back in his chair, hands behind his head. He looked casual, but she knew he was waiting for her answer. She wondered how old he was. Older than she was, certainly—she hadn't even decided what college to go to when her parents had died—but not old.

No, not old. His face was unlined, but tanned from the sun, his eyes a bright, mischievous blue. His hair was cut nicely, his face shaved, his clothes clean, although his shoes were rather shabby looking and his hat, a fat little black cap, had seen better days. He was quite handsome, really, although she didn't think he knew it, and he wasn't a small man. His shoulders were broad and full under his button-down shirt and suspenders.

"It's my grandmother," Mae finally confessed, contemplating her tomato. She ate them like most people ate apples, and Griff still teased her about it, saying he should start selling tomatoes for her on his cart. "She wants us to move away."

The legs of Griff's chair came down slowly. "Away? Where?"

"She's not well." Mae decided against the tomato, tucking it back into the basket, seeing the white paper bag inside. "It's her heart. The doctor says she's got too much stress here in the city. Says she needs to get away."

"I'm sorry," he said, frowning. "I'm sure you'll miss her."

Mae glanced at him again, meeting his eyes only briefly. "Well that's the thing. She wants me to go with her."

"Oh." The word was barely a breath.

"I'm really doing okay by myself," she assured him, as if he'd given some protest. "I have the insurance settlement from my parents' accident. It's more than enough for me to live on. But my grandmother…" Mae glanced down, smoothing her skirt over her knees. "She can't stop talking about finding me a husband."

Griff nodded. "Pretty girl like you should probably have one," he agreed.

She smiled shyly, picking lint off her skirt. "I suppose I wouldn't mind. If it was the right one."

He raised an eyebrow in her direction. "Did you have someone in mind?"

She felt herself blushing and looked away.

"Hey, Mae…" He knew her real name, but he hardly ever used it. The sound of it thrilled her. "I was wondering… would you like to go to a picture with me?"

"Which one?" She held her breath as if the answer really mattered.

"King Kong," he replied and she smiled. Of course. It was all anyone could talk about. "It opens tonight."

She wondered if he could see the stars in her eyes. "I'd love to."

"Really?" He sounded almost as surprised by her assent as she'd been by his question.

She knew she was breathless, but she couldn't help it. "When?"

"Tonight? I'll pick you up at seven."

"Here." She pulled a pencil and a receipt out of the little purse hidden at the bottom of the basket, writing down her address and apartment number. Now he knew where she lived and the thought made her feel a little lightheaded. "I should go. My grandmother will be waiting."

She pressed the piece of paper into his hand and it closed around hers. His touch was like fire.

"Tonight."

She smiled, closing her basket and slinging it over her arm. "I can't wait." Which was the truth. Seven o'clock was only four hours away, and she wanted to get home so she could torture herself over what to wear.

"See ya, Red," he called as she walked away.

She couldn't remember how she got to her grandmother's. She thought maybe she flew. The walk was blocks and blocks but she didn't see any of the usual scenery, didn't stop at the other street vendors or delight in the performers. She didn't see or hear anything but Griff and that bright light in his eyes when she'd said, "Yes," didn't feel anything but his hand swallowing hers.

That's probably why she didn't see Lionel until he grabbed her arm, catching her up short, causing her to gasp and look up in alarm. She was in a much better neighborhood now, nearing Central Park West where her grandmother's apartment overlooked the city, but she was always worried about "getting snatched," as her grandmother phrased it. In her new clothes, with her hair styled, she practically made herself a target. Which was, of course, why her grandmother kept telling her she needed to move in, and another reason she insisted they move away from the city altogether. "It's too dangerous a place for wealthy people to reside," her grandmother had decided.

"Lionel!" She recognized him immediately, feeling a connection to home she hadn't even realized she'd been missing. She could suddenly see her father's office from her usual vantage point under the desk, smell the sharp, dark ink he used to sign his contracts and the pipe he smoked when he was deep in thought. Her father was a rancher, but he also singlehandedly ran eight of the biggest slaughterhouses in the Midwest. He'd made his own fortune, although she'd never been spoiled like most children with rich parents. Granted, she hadn't really wanted for anything, but her life with her parents on their ranch didn't speak of great wealth.

She'd spent lots of time playing and reading in the kneehole of her father's desk—until she got too big to fit, and then she would loll around in the fat, black leather armchair, wearing dungarees with hay in her hair and her nose in a book, while her father talked on the telephone about cows and pigs and chickens or railed about the unions. Occasionally people would come into the office to talk to him. One of those people had been Lionel Tryst.

"Well, Maeve Eileen Verges!" he exclaimed, sweeping his hat off his head and bowing low. The gesture wasn't as foreign to her as it once had been, but it still made her want to giggle. That, along with hearing her full name, made the moment even more surreal. She'd been named after her grandmother, a family name passed on, but no one ever said it out loud. "What a pleasure to find you in New York!"

"How are you?" she inquired, slowly extracting herself from the man as they walked—he was still holding her arm, a little too familiarly for her liking. "I haven't seen you since…"

He nodded sympathetically. "I'm so sorry about your loss, Mae. Your parents were wonderful people."

She swallowed the lump in her throat that always rose whenever anyone mentioned them. "Thank you."

"So what are you doing here in the big city?"

"My grandmother." She nodded at the building they were now standing in front of. "She lives in the penthouse."

"In the Century building?" Lionel gave a low whistle, squinting as he looked upward. "That's an expensive piece of real estate."

Mae laughed. "I thought you were in the insurance business?"

"I'm a jack of all trades." He grinned. "I just sold an apartment in the Majestic for five thousand a year."

Mae gasped. "It's amazing anyone can afford that nowadays!"

"With great collapse comes great opportunity." He winked. "You let me know if your grandmother is looking to sell. I'd be happy to find her a buyer. In fact, I talked to someone just last week who was asking me about the penthouse in the Century."

"Really?" She hesitated. Her grandmother had been so ill, and part of that, she knew, was living in the city. Fresh air would do her good. But the truth was, as much as Mae missed the country herself, there was now an even bigger reason for her to want to stay. Griff had just asked her for a date! But as much as she wanted to just bid Lionel a quick goodbye, in spite of his connections to home, she knew she had to do the right thing. "Actually, she's been trying to sell it for a few months now, but in this market…"

"Is that so?" Lionel's eyes widened in surprise. "Well, muffin, what say you and me go pay your grandmother a little visit?"

The doorman at the Century knew Mae and he let her up with Lionel without question. They chatted in the elevator about Nebraska, and Mae inquired about mutual acquaintances. She'd left her best friend, Irene, just as the girls were planning to find a college to attend together. Lionel said Irene had gone on to some art school in California, but Mae couldn't even imagine it.

"Grandmother?" Mae knocked and then slipped the key into the lock when no one answered, opening the door at the end of the hall. The entire top floor was hers, but it was sectioned off, and her grandmother only lived in part of it. She opened up the other wings only when she had guests or entertained. The foyer was open and there was a large living area with a fireplace almost as tall as she was and hardwood floors her grandmother had covered with ornate rugs. The dining room to the left showcased a gorgeous oak table underneath a chandelier so heavy Mae often wondered how it stayed secured to the ceiling.

"I'm in the kitchen, dearest!"

Mae smiled at the sound of her grandmother's voice, motioning Lionel to follow. In spite of the fact that Mae hadn't even known the woman existed before a few months ago, she'd grown quite fond of her in the time they'd spent together, and it seemed the reverse was also true.

Mae found the old woman stirring a cup of tea and she wondered at that, frowning. Usually her grandmother had plenty of help—two maids to clean and a butler to answer the door, as well as a nurse who came in once a day just to check. Her grandmother rarely lifted a finger to do anything for herself. She didn't have to, and she seemed to like it that way.

"Where's John?" Mae inquired after the butler, kissing her grandmother's cheek, catching the scent of lavender and rose water. The old woman's skin was as soft and thin as the Kleenex Mae used to take cold cream off her face at night.

"I gave everyone the night off." Her grandmother smiled as she turned to face her granddaughter, her eyes still bright, although her face was heavily lined. She was always impeccably dressed, still wearing heels, even at her age. "I have a surprise for you." The woman's eyes widened as she saw the stranger standing in her doorway. "And who's this?"

"Oh, this is Lionel." Mae smiled at him as he swept his hat off and bowed low. "Lionel Tryst. He worked for my father back home. Lionel, this is my grandmother, the first Maeve Eileen Verges."

"So pleased to make your acquaintance, Mrs. Verges."

Mae noticed that Lionel's manners had already won her grandmother over, which was probably a good thing. If he had a buyer for the penthouse, that would go a long way toward getting it sold more quickly. Although she wasn't sure anymore if that was a good thing. But she couldn't deny that meeting Lionel right out front of her grandmother's building had to be some sort of sign. It was too much of a strange coincidence not to mean *something*.

"He thinks he may have a buyer for your apartment," Mae explained, taking the old woman's elbow as she started toward the doorway.

"Oh that would be wonderful!" The old woman glanced up at Lionel as he flanked her on the other side, also taking her elbow as they made their way to the living room. "How did you know my son, Mr. Tryst?"

"He was a business associate," Lionel explained as they settled themselves. "A finer man I've never met."

Her grandmother beamed at his praise of her son and Mae couldn't help smiling. The old woman got teary eyed every time his name was mentioned. She'd missed so many years of his life, and all of Mae's up until now, just because she couldn't stand the woman he'd married. Mae's mother had been, as her grandmother politely put it, "Not of the same social stature" as Mae's father. She'd never known her father had come from old money, or that her mother had been born poor and was just a young tennis instructor he met at summer camp his senior year.

There had been a great deal about her parents she didn't know, she realized now. It didn't make her love them any less, but it did make her sad, for all of them, at the time they'd missed. Her grandmother had changed her mind and had tried, many times she'd said, over the years, to reconcile, but Mae's father was a stubborn man. He refused to return her calls and wouldn't let her see her own granddaughter.

Of course, after the accident, her father hadn't had a say in Mae's life anymore, and when her grandmother had contacted her, asking her to come to New York, she'd gone in a haze of grief, looking for any connection she could find to her dead parents.

Now she couldn't have been more glad she'd made that decision.

"Where are my manners?" her grandmother exclaimed. "Lionel, would you like something to drink? Something a little stronger than tea, perhaps?" The old woman's eyes brightened as she looked at the younger man.

Lionel raised his eyebrows. "Now, Mrs. Verges, you have heard about prohibition, haven't you?"

"Oh indeed, but there are ways around it, Mr. Tryst, if the price is right." She winked and Mae swore she actually giggled before taking a sip of her tea.

"I'm sure that's true." He chuckled. "But thanks all the same."

"You have alcohol, Grandma?" Mae looked at her in mock disapproval.

The older Maeve primly sipped her tea. "It's medicinal."

Mae met Lionel's eyes and they both hid a smile.

"Speaking of medicine..." Mae opened her basket and removed the white bag. "The pharmacist said to tell you hello."

"Oh good!" Her grandmother plucked the bag up, peering inside. "I'm sure I'm going to need these tonight."

Mae laughed. "Why? What are you planning?" The pills were nitroglycerin for her grandmother's angina, and she only used them when she was having an episode, which was usually when she got really excited—or angry.

"Your surprise!" The old woman glanced between the two of them, her gaze speculative. "And of course, you're welcome to join us, Mr. Tryst."

"How kind of you." Lionel smiled, leaning back in the chair and glancing at Mae. She blinked, looking between the man and her grandmother.

"I normally hate crowds, but I'm making an exception." The older Maeve smiled at her granddaughter. "We're going to the movie premiere of King Kong!"

Lionel sat up, eyes widening. "*The* movie premiere?"

"Radio City?" Mae gulped, already knowing, with a sick, sinking feeling in her belly, that she was trapped.

And there proved to be no way to get around it. She tried, several different ways, to find an excuse to have to go back home, but her grandmother wasn't having it. She had a new outfit for Mae to wear, so she couldn't say she had to go home to change. And while begging off as ill crossed her mind, she knew how disappointed her grandmother would be.

So she changed into her new dress—Lionel's eyebrows went up when she made her entrance and she flushed, thanking him for his compliments—and continued to make small talk until it was time to go, all the while thinking that there was no way to let Griff know she wouldn't be at her apartment when he came to pick her up. She could imagine his reaction, but she didn't want to think about him knocking and knocking…

The driver held open the door to the Roll's-Royce limousine for her, but Mae barely saw him. She couldn't think about anything but Griff. Would they pass his corner on the way to Radio City? She didn't think she could bear it. She turned her face way from the window and responded to something Lionel said with just a smile.

"You're so distracted." Her grandmother patted her knee and Mae tried to fight the tears threatening. She wanted to tell her about Griff, just come clean and tell her the truth—but how could she? Her grandmother had disowned her own son for less. How could she possibly ever accept a man who not only didn't have any money or a pedigree, but one who peddled apples on the street corner?

"Just excited," she assured her, covering the old woman's hand with hers. Lionel sat across from the two of them, chatting away, something about the new subway system, and it was easy to tune him out.

"Oh goodness, look at that line!" The old woman gasped. "I can't possibly wait in that!"

Mae looked out the window and saw it stretching down the side of the building. So many people!

"Leave it to me." Lionel told the driver to stop at the entrance and let him off. Mae and her grandmother stayed in the car, watching as he went into the building, pushing past the rest of the crowd.

"What is he up to?" her grandmother murmured, but it wasn't long before they found out. Lionel returned, waving three tickets as he helped Mae's grandmother out of the car.

"How did you do that?" Mae asked as he led them in front of the crowd, guiding each of them by an elbow.

"You just have to know the right people." He shrugged. "These are box seats, by the way. We're up here." He showed the tickets to a man in a red suit, who escorted them up a flight of stairs.

"My goodness!" Mae's grandmother exclaimed as Lionel helped her into a seat. The box overlooked the entire theater as it filled with people. From this angle, Mae thought they might just be right on eye-level with the giant ape!

"This is quite a surprise!" Her grandmother sounded like a young girl and Mae couldn't help smiling.

"So a surprise for your granddaughter turns out to be a surprise for you too," Lionel said as he slipped in beside Mae. He leaned over to whisper in her ear. "You look lovely enough to eat."

His words made her flush, and she murmured something that resembled a thank you, although she wasn't quite sure that either his comment or her answer were appropriate. But her grandmother was sitting beside her and she couldn't protest without drawing attention to herself. What she wanted to do was melt into the seat and disappear. Well, that wasn't entirely true—what she really wanted was to be here with Griff, down there on the floor amidst the rest of the crowd, pressed far too close together and warm.

Instead she was sitting next to Lionel Tryst, who kept whispering compliments that made her blush, his knee coming far too close to hers as the lights in the theater went down. There was a stage show prior to the picture—something about jungles. She wasn't paying too much attention, because Lionel's hand had moved from his knee to hers.

By the time the movie started, Lionel's hand had moved to her thigh. Mae shifted in her seat and crossed her legs, hoping to give him a strong enough hint. She leaned away from him toward her grandmother to ask if she was cold—up here the theater did seem a little chilly—and stayed as far from him as she could in her seat.

Thankfully, he didn't touch her again, but while that situation had improved, now she had time to think about Griff. He was supposed to be here beside her, whispering and joking and making her giggle. And when the giant ape appeared and killed the snake, she wanted it to be Griff's hand she grabbed, not Lionel's—she couldn't help herself, the scene made her hide her face against his suit coat in terror—and when the poor creature tumbled from the top of the Empire State Building, she wanted it to be Griff's handkerchief she used to wipe her tears, not Lionel's.

"What a picture!" Mae's grandmother dabbed her eyes with her own handkerchief as the lights came up, the crowd below buzzing with excitement. Mae handed Lionel's handkerchief back to him as they walked down the stairs, making their way toward the car. The driver had been waiting down the street for them to appear and he swung the door wide, sweeping them all in.

"What did you think of the movie?" Lionel inquired, looking at Mae from his seat across from her. He was still too close, his knees touching hers.

She blinked at him, wishing it was Griff asking that question. With him, she could be honest, and she knew he would be too. So instead of tackling the racism inherent in the film, or even the implied eroticism, which was an even more dangerous topic, she just murmured, "Fay Wray is very beautiful."

"Not nearly as lovely as you, my dear," he responded.

Mae's grandmother smiled approvingly, glancing between the two of them, and Mae inwardly groaned. She knew that look. It was her grandmother's, "I have to find this girl a husband" look and more specifically her, "I think I've just found a prospect!" gaze. Lionel was a kind man, and while he did remind her of home, if she'd been interested in him, she would have responded to his advances back on the ranch when her parents were alive.

Of course, her grandmother didn't know that, and she began to question him in earnest about his parents, his employment, his general status and character. At least it kept Mae from having to talk. She watched the city lights go by and thought about Griff. She hope she could repair her jilting him tonight, make it up to him somehow. Maybe they could have a picnic in the park?

"You two run off and play." Her grandmother patted her hand and winked over at Lionel as the car pulled up in front of the Century building. "This old lady needs her rest. But my driver will take you anywhere you want to go."

Mae's heart sank.

"That's very generous of you." Lionel opened the door, helping her grandmother out of the car before the driver could, and Mae took the opportunity, grabbing her red wool coat off the seat and slipping out the door behind them.

"Grandmother, I'm going to walk home." She leaned over and kissed the old woman's cheek. "I need some fresh air."

"You can't walk home alone this late at night!" her grandmother protested, but Mae waved her response away, already walking.

"Don't worry, Mrs. Verges," Mae heard Lionel respond. "I'll see she gets home safely."

He caught up with her in just a few strides and she didn't protest when he fell into step beside her. It really wasn't safe to walk at night, she knew, but she couldn't bear the thought of being cooped up in a car with Lionel and spending the night fending off his advances.

The air was cool and she shivered, stopping to put her coat on, and Lionel helped her. She let him. They walked in silence for a while, until Mae couldn't stand it anymore.

"So do you really think you'll find a buyer for my grandmother's apartment?" she inquired politely as they rounded the corner. The city looked very different at night. The terrain changed, becoming hazy, as if seen through a veil.

"I believe so." His response was short and she had a feeling he was angry with her—probably for rebuffing him in the theater. That made her relent a little and she glanced up at him as they walked.

"What did you think of the movie?" she asked.

"*Beauty and the Bea*st in the jungle?" He snorted. "Except in this version, beauty kills the beast, which is really a little ridiculous when you think about it."

"It wasn't the girl who killed him," she countered. "But I admit, it was a rather doomed relationship. They had nothing in common."

He flashed her a smile and a sidelong glance as they walked. "Oh, I think they had at least one thing in common."

They were coming up on Mae's building and she slowed, stopping in front of it, to look up at him. "What's that?"

He took a step toward her, so close she could feel the heat from his body, even through her thick, red wool coat. He leaned in to whisper against the shell of her ear, "Their primal natures."

Mae took a step back, smiling. "So you subscribe to Darwin's theory?" she asked, started up her tenement steps.

He looked up at her quizzically. "Who?"

"Thanks for walking me home."

He frowned. "Don't you want me to see you up?"

"Good night," she said gently, waving from the top of the stairs. "Thanks again for walking me home."

He didn't look happy, but she left him anyway, watching her from the bottom of the stairs as the door closed and locked behind her. The lift in her building was old and she waited a long time for it to decide to start rising toward the eighteenth floor, making her stomach lurch.

Her thoughts were fully back on Griff again and her belly filled with regret. If only she had found a way to contact him. She had left her basket at her grandmother's, but she would pack something up tomorrow anyway and go over to the apple cart to apologize. Make him a double-decker sandwich. Maybe even bake a pie. She had lots of apples, thanks to Griff, and she made a pastry crust that melted in your mouth.

Decided, and feeling just a little better for it, she stepped off the elevator, glancing down the hall as she looked through her purse for her key, when she saw him out of the corner of her eye. He was sitting beside her door, head leaned back against the wall, eyes closed. *Oh my god, he waited for me. He's* still *waiting for me!*

He was snoring softly as she approached and she could look at him freely. He was wearing a suit, a nice one, and there was a top hat resting on the carpet beside him. His face was clean-shaven and she followed the line of his jaw with her gaze, strong and solid, her eyes drawn down to the tie at his throat. He looked so handsome she could have cried.

"Griff." She cleared her throat, nudging him gently with her knee.

His eyes opened slowly and the look in them when he recognized her made her stomach do little flips. He should have been angry—furious in fact—but he was actually happy to see her. She could tell by the sleepy smile beginning at the corners of his mouth.

"There she is." His smile broadened. "I think we missed the picture."

Mae flushed "I'm so sorry. My grandmother made plans, and I couldn't—"

"I was worried," he admitted, interrupting as he got to his feet. "I'm just glad you're all right."

"I'm fine." She fit the key in the lock of her door, turning and pushing it open. "Come inside at least. Have some tea."

"Are you sure?" He peered into the apartment, hesitating at the threshold.

Mae smiled, reaching out and catching the edge of his sleeve. "Come on. Please."

"Well, since you said please." He shut the door behind him, watching as she turned lights on, taking off her coat and hanging it over a chair.

"Make yourself at home." She put the kettle on, knowing tea would keep her awake, but now that Griff was here she didn't care.

"You look like a goddess." His words stopped her at the stove and she glanced over her shoulder to see him staring at her in the dress her grandmother had bought. It was white with a high neckline but a ruched bust and no sleeves, leaving her arms bare. It was actually quite reminiscent of the dress Fay Wray wore in the movie, and it had probably been intentional on her grandmother's part, she realized.

"Thank you." She joined him at the table, still admiring him in his suit. They were in different territory now and she felt a shift in things. They were both trying to gain their footing in this new place.

"So do you want to try again?" Griff suggested. She had the feeling he was trying not to sound hopeful, which just made him sound even more so. "King Kong isn't going anywhere for a while."

Mae smiled and thought about lying, but that seemed like a bad way to start things off, so she told him the truth, that her grandmother had planned for them to go to the premiere as a surprise and she'd already seen the picture.

"But I kept wishing you were there," she said, hearing the kettle and rising to get it. "Lionel was a poor substitute, I'm afraid."

"Lionel?" he inquired, watching her pour water into cups, plopping in tea bags and bringing them on saucers to the table.

"Do you want milk and sugar?" Mae stalled, kicking herself for mentioning Lionel at all.

"No." He stirred his tea, still looking at her. "Who's Lionel?"

"He's a former business associate of my father," she explained, reaching for the sugar and adding two lumps. "He thinks he has a buyer for my grandmother's apartment. It's not easy to find a buyer for the penthouse in the Century, given the market," she explained quickly.

"Oh." Griff's spoon slowed. "Well that's good news."

"Is it?" She grimaced, putting the tea bag on her saucer.

"No." His answer was gruff and she looked up, seeing his jaw working.

Sighing, Mae sat back in her seat, folding her arms. "I'll be honest, I don't mind leaving the city, but…"

"But what?" Griff leaned in, elbows on her little table, closing the space between them.

"Not what, exactly…" She met his eyes, those deep, blue familiar eyes, and told him the truth. "Who."

"Who?" he asked.

That was the question, wasn't it? She answered that one honestly, too.

"You."

Griff got down on his knees. Mae stared at him, aghast as he knelt beside her chair. He was looking up at her from this position, so strange. This wasn't just new territory, it was the entrance to a whole new world.

"I'm going to do something right now that I really shouldn't," he informed her, taking both of her hands in his.

"Please." She didn't know where she found her voice.

"Please what?" He frowned. He was so close she could smell him, clean and fresh, like apples. "Please don't?"

"No…" She couldn't finish her sentence or even her thought. He was too close; she was too full of him.

“No?”

Mae tried again, leaning in a little, giving him hope with her body language. “No, please…do. Do.”

“I have to,” he murmured, sliding his arms around her and pressing his mouth to hers.

Maybe it was knowing that this was all they could have, that she would be leaving with her grandmother, moving far from the city, and there would be no more stolen picnic lunches—but Mae thought, when thought returned hours later, that it went deeper than that. She gave herself to him because, at the core of her being, she knew she belonged to this man.

He whispered her name, kissing the slender curve of her neck, licking the indented hollow of her throat, his breath so hot it burned her skin. She clung to him, his shoulders wide and broad under her hands. His mouth captured hers again, his tongue slipping between her lips, and she welcomed the deep, gentle exploration, lost in sensation

The press of his body between her thighs parted them, hiking her dress up far too high for modesty, and when she felt the thick heat of his cock through his trousers she remembered to at least attempt to protect her virtue.

“Griff,” she gasped, pushing at his chest, breaking their kiss. “We can’t. It’s not that I don’t want to…” She swallowed, seeing the hunger in his eyes, feeling his urgency. Flushing, she stammered over the words, “But if I get pregnant…”

“I have something.” He pulled his wallet out of his pocket, flipping it open and pulling out a square she recognized, although she’d only ever seen one other one.

Her eyes widened at the sight of the condom. “Those are illegal.”

“So’s alcohol, but you can get it in the speakeasies without too much trouble.” He grinned, putting it back into his wallet and shoving his wallet back into his pocket. “You just have to know where to go and have the money to pay.”

“And it works?”

He shrugged. “It’s better than Lysol.”

Mae made a face. She’d seen the advertisements and had heard that douching with the stuff after relations would prevent an unwanted pregnancy, but just the smell of the stuff made her dizzy and sick. She couldn't imagine putting it inside of her! Of course, there were a lot of things she couldn't imagine putting inside of her, and the cock rising thick and insistent between her thighs was one of them.

It wasn't that she didn't know what sex was or how it all worked—her girlfriends had talked extensively about it, and her best friend, Irene, had lost her virginity the year before with a boy at summer camp and had given her all the gory details—but she was more than a little afraid. Still, she'd never felt this way about any of the boys she'd been with, the ones she had fumbled around in the dark with, their hands groping, mouths open with sloppy kisses, like over-eager puppies looking for a treat.

Griff was different.

Mae stood, holding out her hand, and he took it, rising to meet her and take her into his arms. She felt instantly connected to him, even before he kissed her, his mouth practiced, sure, controlled. This wasn't a boy, but a man. He could restrain himself if he needed to—even if he just wanted to. He wouldn't do anything she didn't want him to do, and that made it safer somehow.

"Come to bed," she whispered, closing her eyes and letting him caress her neck and shoulder with his mouth.

She felt him stiffen, hesitating, his teeth nibbling at her ear. "Are you sure?"

"Yes," she breathed, putting her arms around his neck and pressing her breasts fully against his chest, hearing him gasp at the sensation. That filled her with an incredible sense of power and she wiggled in his arms, wanting more.

"Oh god, Mae," he murmured, and she squeaked in surprise when he swept her up into his arms, carrying her around the corner and shoving open her bedroom door. He pulled the shade and switched on the little lamp on her dresser, pulling her between his thighs and turning her around so he could unzip her dress.

His hands moved over her shoulders, sliding the silk of the dress down her arms and letting the expensive material pool on the floor at her feet. She stepped out of her heels, feeling him lifting her slip, pulling it off over her head. Now she was undressed for him, down to just a bra, panties and stockings, and she turned to face him, seeing the lust in his eyes as his gaze swept over her.

Griff was still almost fully dressed—he'd taken his shoes and suit coat off—when he kissed her down onto the bed and they rolled together, hands and mouths exploring. The twin bed was small and they barely fit together, but neither of them seemed to notice. She found herself impatient with his clothing, wanting to feel more of him, all of him, and she worked the buttons on his shirt as they kissed, rewarded with the heat of his chest under her hands as she slid it over his broad shoulders.

They rocked together, her pelvis into his, separated by his trousers and her panties. She couldn't concentrate on anything but the growing friction and heat between her thighs, but Griff's focus was further up, raining kisses over her cleavage as he worked the hooks on her bra. He groaned when her breasts spilled free into his waiting hands, his tongue making delicious circles around the dark coins of her nipples.

Mae gasped and squirmed, arching toward him for more. She'd never felt anything so good and she couldn't get enough, burying her hands in the thick waves of his hair. When he kissed his way down further, his tongue dipping briefly into her navel, she sighed in disappointment, wanting more of his mouth on her breasts, but then he settled himself between her thighs and, to her surprise, buried his face between them.

"Griff!" she gasped, flushing with embarrassment, but there was no stopping him. He groaned as he pulled her panties aside, spreading her thighs wide with his big hands, leaving her totally exposed. She threw an arm over her eyes, hiding from her own shame, as his tongue delved deep into her cleft.

It took just moments for her to melt into liquid pleasure all over the bed, giving into the pressing flutter of his tongue. The feeling was incredible, beyond anything she could have hoped for even on the nights she'd rolled restlessly around in her bed dreaming of him, twisting the sheets between her thighs and rocking into the sensation. She couldn't have imagined anything like this, so soft and wet and sweet, a dizzying thrill with every pass of his tongue.

"Oh!" she cried, her thighs trembling under his hands. "Oh! Oh! What—?"

Something was happening. The world was tilting, coming to an ecstatic end right there between her legs, and there was nothing she could do to stop it. Not only that, but she didn't want to, she admitted shamefully, grabbing a handful of Griff's hair and crying out with her pleasure as she shoved him hard against her flesh, grinding her hips up to meet the velvety lash of his tongue.

"Oh my god!" she gasped as he kissed his way up her belly, pulling her quivering body to his, holding her close. "What was that?"

He chuckled, kissing the top of her head. "What did it feel like?"

"An earthquake," she panted, feeling the hot steel of his cock pressed against her hip. Curious, she slid her hand down to rub it and heard his sharp intake of breath.

"I would move heaven and earth for you if I could," he whispered, rocking against the press of her hand.

"You did," she breathed, daring to unzip him. "You do."

"Oh Mae." He pressed his forehead to hers, eyes closed, when she found him, stiff and engorged, far larger than she had imagined. She touched him tentatively, her fingers brushing the tip appearing over the V of his zipper. "Here." He took her hand in his, wrapping it around the length and guiding her movement up and down.

"Like that?" she inquired, breathless, watching the look on his face, pleasure almost to the point of pain, as she stroked him.

"Oh yes," he agreed, leaning back on the bed and lifting his hips to give her better access. "Just like that."

She leaned on her elbow, moving him in her fist, watching the head of his cock play peek-a-boo with his foreskin as she began to pump a little faster. He bit his lip and thrust into her hand, matching her rhythm.

"Does it feel good?" she asked, thrilled at the way he groaned in response, arching up to meet her. She hoped she was making him feel half as good as he'd made her feel with his tongue, and then a very naughty thought occurred to her.

Irene had told her about petting with her boyfriend at summer camp, about all the things they'd done before she lost her virginity, and one of those things had been to put his cock into her mouth.

Mae remembered being appalled and a little horrified at the time, but also more than a little curious, too. What did it feel like? She noticed the head of his cock getting wet as she stroked him, leaking at the tip. What did it taste like?

"Mae!" Griff cried out in surprise when she leaned over and kissed the head of his cock, licking her lips and tasting the tangy, peppery liquid.

"Is it okay?" she asked, lightly licking around the head, exploring the ridges with her tongue. He threw his head back with a low growl as she sucked just the tip.

"Mae, wait," he gasped, tilting up her chin and rubbing her mouth with his thumb. "It feels too good. I can't stand it."

"Too good?" she smiled. "Is there such a thing?"

He chuckled. "No. But I want to be inside of you, remember?"

"Yes." She felt a shiver of fear at the thought. "But…"

"It's all right." He slid out his wallet, finding the packet and ripping it open. "We'll be safe."

She helped him slide his trousers all the way down, undoing her garters and rolling her stockings down her thighs as she watched him slip the condom on. Wiggling her panties off, she spread herself like a sacrifice, squeezing her eyes shut and waiting.

Griff moved between her thighs and she winced, gripping his upper arms as he poised himself above her. She expected him to do it quick, but he took his time, kissing her neck, nibbling at her ear, distracting her from her own fear. When his mouth reached her nipples, she whimpered, unable to concentrate on anything but the sweet sensation of wet tongue tracing hot circles around and around.

A fire was burning again between her legs and she begged him to quench it somehow, calling his name as she bucked under his weight, wrapping her legs around him tight. She felt the hard length of him against her thigh and she stiffened for a moment, gasping.

"Easy," he urged, kissing her softly, his tongue exploring as he pressed her thighs open further with his own. She cried out against his mouth when he entered her, a brief, searing moment of pain paralyzing her in his arms. He kissed her cheek, her throat, whispering her name over and over, not moving inside of her.

"Was that it?" she whispered, turning her face up to his, unable to really believe that she'd done it, she had given herself to him.

"That was the worst part." He kissed her forehead. "Now comes the best part."

Mae shivered as he began to move inside of her, his hips circling gently. The sensation was strange at first—she felt full to bursting with him—but the more they rocked together, the easier it became to open up and accept him. His cock throbbed between her legs, his breath coming in hard, hot pants against her ear, and she clung to him with all her might.

"Mae," he whispered, his voice catching. "Oh god sweetheart, you feel so good. I can't hold back."

"Yes," she urged, closing her eyes and lifting her hips to meet his, grinding her pelvis, feeling him move deep inside her. "Yes! Yes!"

He groaned and gave into it, shoving himself in deep and shuddering with pleasure on top of her. She held him close, cradling his head against her breasts as he cried out and buried his face there, his whole body tense with his climax.

"You're so beautiful," he murmured, collapsing onto her. She took his weight with a happy sigh, wrapping herself around him. She knew she should have felt ashamed at giving him her virtue, remorseful, even contrite, but she wasn't. In fact, she didn't remember ever being happier. "Are you all right?"

"I'm perfect." She smiled and brushed his hair tenderly out of his eyes.

"Stay with me." He sighed and closed his eyes, nestled between her breasts. "Don't leave me, Mae."

"I'm not going anywhere." She lifted his palm and kissed it, giggling. "You know, when you got down on your knees in my living room, I thought…" She laughed again, shaking her head.

"What?" He lifted his head to look at her. "What did you think?"

She flushed, admitting, "I thought you were going to propose."

"And what if I had?"

She couldn't tell if he was serious, but she shrugged and smiled. "I don't even know your last name."

"It's Griffon." He pressed his cheek to her breast again. "My first name is George."

"Mrs. Mae Griffon," she murmured.

He was quiet for a moment, and then he said, "It has a ring to it."

Mae felt a little thrill up her spine at his words, closing her eyes and stroking his damp hair. "Yes, it does," she whispered, but he was already asleep.

* * * *

He liked watching her. Like most country girls who found themselves in city confines, she didn't quite understand the new terrain. She lived as if she was still back home, surrounded by miles of farmland, the nearest house a fifteen minute drive away. He enjoyed her freedom, and with the help of a very fine and quite expensive pair of binoculars, because Mae never pulled down her shades.

And she was a beauty. A little unrefined for his tastes, although her grandmother had clearly been trying to shine her up a bit. Of course, without her clothes who could tell? He was stunned by her freshness, the creamy white flesh of her belly exposed as she pulled her full slip off over her head, leaving just panties and one of those newfangled bras to cover her exquisite flesh. She didn't wear a corset, and god knows she didn't need to. Her figure was the perfect hourglass, ripe and full and so lush he swore he could feel the heat of her from a street away.

She often stayed this way a long time, sitting at a little vanity, brushing her short, dark hair, removing her make-up, but eventually she would stand and unhook her bra, letting her breasts free, the nipples dark coins against her pale skin. He would focus his binoculars in as close as he could get to see how the flesh puckered in response to the sudden shift in temperature.

And then came the panties. It didn't matter which direction she was she was facing, both were delicious. If she bent over, he could see the generous swell of her behind, so full it made him feral with lust. If she slipped them off while she was facing the window, he got to view the vast dark triangle of her pubic hair, an arrow pointing to heaven. His cock throbbed in his hand as he stroked it, watching her disrobe herself bare, wanting nothing more than to go over there and take her. And of course, he could do that.

But there were other considerations. The trap had to be set, and hurrying things would just chase the rabbit away from the snare. For now he could be patient. Besides, too much of a good thing was still too much. And waiting was a pleasure. The anticipation built to a dizzying frenzy. Like his cock, the head purple from the pressure of his fist, aching for release but denied over and over, waiting for just the right moment.

Usually that moment came when she squirted a white cream onto her hands and began to rub it all over her skin, spreading the stuff over her breasts, her belly, sliding down into the crevices between her thighs. Then he couldn't hold it anymore, letting loose his own stream of white cream, imagining it splashing all over her breasts, or better yet, coating those ripe, full lips of hers, red even after she'd removed all traces of her lipstick.

He sat, panting, watching, until she turned out the light, biding his time. He wanted her, but if that was all it was, he could easily have her. It was far more than that. He was going to make her completely his. He was going to own her. He just needed to be patient. Soon she would fall willingly into his arms and be his wife, and he would have everything he'd ever wanted. He just had to wait.

* * * *

"Your granny sure is a funny old bird," Lionel murmured in Mae's ear as he watched the old woman go over the paperwork.

"She's stubborn." Mae pulled her coat on, collecting her things into her basket. Although she had it back now, things had still felt so different on her way to her grandmother's this afternoon when she'd stopped by Griff's apple cart. Seeing him always brightened her day, but after the other night, it was like standing directly next to the sun.

They did the things they usually did, eating lunch sitting in folding wooden chairs, talking and joking, but the whole thing felt like cardboard compared to how they had been together in her apartment. She knew she should regret it, should be ashamed and horrified by her own behavior, and maybe part of her was, but a larger part shamelessly longed for more.

"I just don't understand," her grandmother said, shaking her head. "They're offering me *more* than I'm asking?"

"That's right, Mrs. Verges," Lionel agreed. "The penthouse of the Century is a very desirable property, you know."

"Of course it is." She sniffed. "But why would they offer me *more?"*

"Because they want to make sure you accept their offer," he soothed. "It's just a show of good faith. They want you to know they're serious and want the property very much."

"Well I guess I can't argue with that." The old woman glanced up at her granddaughter, frowning. "Mae, are you going so soon?"

"I'm not feeling well," she lied. The truth was she'd planned on eating dinner with her grandmother, but finding Lionel there when she'd arrived had spoiled her appetite. "Maybe we can do it tomorrow?"

"All right, dear." She signed the final paper, folding the stack and handing it over the Lionel. "Would you make sure she gets home for me?"

He nodded, sliding the papers into his suit coat pocket. "Of course."

"That's really not necessary," Mae protested. "I can walk home by myself."

"I have my car," Lionel offered.

"Perfect!" Her grandmother beamed and Mae relented with a sigh.

She kissed her grandmother's cheek. "I'll see you tomorrow."

Lionel's auto wasn't as nice as she thought it would be, but he helped her into the passenger's side and she rode quietly beside him through the city streets.

"Why don't you like me?" His question jolted her.

"I do like you, Lionel," she countered. "You remind me of home."

"I liked you then too." He gave her a little smile, glancing sideways at her as he drove. "I know you miss your parents and you feel all alone in the world."

Not anymore, she thought, but she didn't say anything. She did miss them, it was true, but for the first time since their accident, she felt alive, really alive. Even her grandmother had noticed, although she seemed to think it had something to do with Lionel.

He went on. "But you can't spend all your time looking backward. At some point, you have to start living your own life."

"I know," she agreed softly, thinking of Griff. She frowned as Lionel turned right down a street she didn't know. The buildings stopped and the street opened up into the a clearing, and she understood that this was the other side of Central Park. "Where are we?"

"Hooverville." Lionel smiled grimly. "Pretty, isn't it?"

"Why are we stopping?" She stared at the garden of tin and garbage piled in front of her. Lean-tos had been constructed out of sheet metal and scrap wood every ten feet or so, the structures crowded together, as if for warmth.

Lionel surveyed the scene. "I don't want to ever live here."

"I don't blame you," she murmured, seeing a man in a ragged blue coat shuffling toward one of the shacks.

"I want more in life than this." He turned to her, reaching for her hand, and she let him take it without thinking. "Mae, I want you."

"What?" she asked faintly, too surprised to withdraw.

He smiled, lifting her hand to his lips, kissing the back softly. "I've loved you since the first time I saw you sitting in your father's chair in your overalls."

"Lionel…" Her protest got stuck in her throat.

"We're the same, you and I," he insisted, sliding closer across the seat. "And I know I can make you happy."

She shrank toward the door, feeling the heat of him. "This is all really fast…"

"I asked you once before..." he reminded her, leaning in even closer. She could smell some sort of aftershave, thick and cloying, remembering the last time he had made this bid. It was just a moment, really, a fumbling in the dark after he'd been invited by her father to dinner at their home. She recalled her embarrassed refusal, his sudden flare-up of anger. It had been just a few weeks before the accident and her memory of that time was hazy.

"Lionel, I can't…" She tried to refuse him but his mouth captured hers, his tongue shoving its way in past lips and teeth, his hands already moving over her body, impatient with her thick, red wool coat. She tried to twist away but he palmed her breast through the fabric and pressed deeper, his tongue making her gag.

"Stop!" she cried, turning her head to the side and breaking their kiss with a breathless gasp, trying in vain to push him off her.

"Think about it," he panted, his hungry gaze moving over her as he complied with her request, sliding slowly across to sit behind the wheel again. "At least tell me you'll think about it."

"Okay, I will," she lied, afraid of that look in his eyes. "But you need to take me home now."

Lionel turned and squeezed the wheel for a moment, his knuckles turning white with the force of his grip. Then he did as she asked and drove her home. They made the trip in silence and Mae tried to keep the tremble from her hands as she picked her basket up off the floor.

"Can I come up?" he asked hopefully as she opened the passenger side door, almost before he'd even come to a complete stop.

"Thank you for the ride," she said politely, shutting the door and practically running up the stairs.

Somehow she wasn't surprised to find Griff waiting by her apartment door. He smiled when he saw her, standing to greet her, but as she drew closer, his mouth turned down in a frown.

"Are you all right?" he asked as she fumbled with her key in the lock.

She didn't want to tell him about Lionel. An explanation would just make her cry and that would spoil everything. Instead, she dropped her basket to the floor and threw her arms around his neck, her mouth slanting across his.

"Easy," he laughed, nudging her basket into the apartment with his foot and shutting the door behind them. "Keep doing that, and you're going to get us arrested."

"They can't arrest us in here." Mae sank to her knees in front of him, giggling at the shocked look on his face as she unzipped his trousers and slid her hand in. She marveled at how different he was when he was soft, but with just a little manipulation, he started to grow hard in her fist.

"Jesus, Mae," he whispered, knocking her stylish little hat to the floor and sliding a hand through her hair as she stroked him.

"Can I kiss it?" She did anyway, her lips caressing the head, her tongue sneaking out to lick around the spongy tip. Griff moaned softly, thrusting his hips forward when she covered the whole of him with her mouth, making him wet with her tongue as she went. She could only swallow half of him before gagging and pulling back, her eyes watering.

"Such a good, eager girl." Griff smiled. "You're getting your knees dirty."

She stood, backing away from him while unbuttoning the front of her dress. Griff watched, wrapping his hand around his cock, as she slipped it off her shoulders and stepped out of it. Then she turned and headed for the bedroom, undressing as she went, so she was down to nothing by the time she made it to the bed.

"Don't want to give a show to your neighbors," he remarked, pulling down the shade before turning on the light. He looked over at her reclining naked on the bed and groaned at the sight. "Although I don't mind if you give me one."

"What would you like to see?" She spread her thighs a little further, seeing his gaze dip between them, his hand moving up and down his shaft. He'd lost his own clothes somewhere along the way, she noticed.

"Touch yourself," he urged, kneeling next to the bed as if he was at an altar.

Mae closed her eyes and ran her hands over her body like she had when she was alone in her bed the night before, remembering Griff and how he touched her, how he felt buried inside of her. She had found that little spot at the top of her crevice, a tiny nub of sensation which, when rubbed, drove her to the brink of insanity and back.

"Oh yes," Griff breathed as Mae spread her lips, revealing the deep pink inside, so she could nudge her own tender flesh to life. She dared to open her eyes a little to watch him, his breath hot against her thighs as she rubbed her little clit. "Oh my god, you're so beautiful."

She whimpered, pulling her knees back and lifting her hips. He smiled, taking her not-so-subtle hint, and covered her pussy with his mouth. Mae moaned and let her knees fall open wide for him, her own hands cupping her breasts, thumbing her nipples.

"That's it," he encouraged. "Tug on them. Twist them. Doesn't it feel good?"

"Oh yes," she agreed breathlessly, doing just as he instructed, bucking her hips in rhythm with the hot press of his tongue. "Oh god it's so good I can't stand it!"

Griff crawled up onto the bed, wrapping his arms around her hips and burying his face deep, making her quiver with her own lust. She couldn't control her body or the way it responded to him so she just gave into it, letting herself go completely in his arms. His tongue lapped and licked and lashed at her flesh, the wet sound of his mouth against her pussy both exciting and embarrassing at the same time.

"Oh!" she cried, twisting her nipples as her orgasm hit like a wave of heat, shaking her limbs and undulating her torso with its force. She quivered and spread her thighs even wider, her head thrown back in pleasure, straining to capture every last bit of the climax rocking her hips.

"Mmm." Griff didn't stop, his tongue probing deeper still, sliding down to taste her. Mae squealed and squirmed in protest, but he wasn't having any of it, rolling with her on the bed, keeping her just where he wanted her, his mouth fastened over her mound. She tried to scramble away, but he held her fast, arms wrapped around her hips, and soon she was rocking on top of him, grinding her pussy against his tongue.

"Oh please," she begged."Your mouth feels so good!"

He mumbled something she couldn't hear, working her hips in fast little circles, using his tongue purely for her pleasure. Then he slid he fingers inside of her, sending her flying, her second orgasm chasing the first, her body trembling with the force of it.

"That's a good girl," he praised, sliding his hands up her belly to cup her breasts.

"I can't get enough of that," she admitted, rolling off of him and burying her face in the pillow at her admission.

"That works out well." His hands moved over behind, spreading her thighs with his palms. She flushed. "I could do that all day."

"Nooo!" she protested anyway when he buried his face against her from behind and he chuckled, nudging her legs further apart.

"I thought you couldn't get enough," he teased. "Come here."

He rolled to his back, encouraging her to climb on top of him. Mae couldn't face him so she turned around instead, letting him put his mouth on her yet again, already being carried away by the intensity of the feeling, but found herself face to face with the throbbing pulse of his cock.

"Kiss it, Mae," he urged, shifting his hips, pressing his cock closer to her mouth.

She bit her lip, taking it in her hand, eager to please him but remembering how she'd gagged on the length of it in the hallway. There was clear liquid gathering at the tip and she licked it off, encouraged by his soft, muffled moan. His tongue was magic between her legs, nudging the sensitive nub of her clit again and again.

"Like this?" she asked, sliding her mouth down slowly around the head. Griff's gasp of pleasure thrilled her and she tried to take even more of him, gagging again.

"You don't have to swallow it whole," he teased and she flushed. "Just the tip. That feels…oh, god, yes, Mae… just like that…"

She caught an easy rhythm, her fist wrapped around the base, her mouth going down about halfway on him every time. What she lacked in expertise she made up for in enthusiasm. He moaned and thrust, but he didn't neglect her, his tongue working back and forth, round and round, sending electric shocks through her with every pass.

"Griff!" she warned, pumping him fast against her open mouth. "Oh yes! Yes! Now!"

She sank her mouth back down over his cock, swallowing as much of him as she could, wanting to feel him filling her that way when her climax came. Griff growled and bucked up hard, suddenly flooding her mouth with white hot liquid. She gagged and swallowed the peppery heat, flooding him too with all her wetness, her pussy spasming in yet another blissful release.

"I'm sorry," he apologized as she rolled off him onto the bed, cooling her cheeks against the sheet.

She smiled. "What for?"

"You didn't…mind?"

"No," she assured him, shivering as she remembered the first, sudden blast of the stuff over her tongue, associating it with her own delicious orgasm. "I liked it."

She felt his hand caressing her hip, her behind, his fingers exploring again between her legs. She didn't protest, although she barely had the energy to spread her thighs a little more for him. When she reached over, she found his cock soft and still wet from her mouth.

"I want more," she insisted, squeezing him in her fist. "I want to feel you inside of me."

"Whoa, girl." Griff let out a low moan, shaking his head. "You fillies are a lot better equipped for saddling up for another ride faster than us studs."

"What can I do?" she murmured, leaning up on her elbow to inspect his cock. It had responded a little to her touch in spite of his protest. Griff cried out when she leaned in and took him back into her mouth. It was so different when he wasn't hard, the flesh soft and spongy in her mouth. He panted and groaned as she continued to work her tongue along the length, encouraged by the way he began to fill with a heated pulse.

"Damn, girl," he murmured, watching as she sucked him back to life. "You're something else."

It wasn't long before he rose fully to the occasion and Mae sighed happily as he rolled her to her belly, nestling her into the saddle of his hips. She felt the hard press of his cock and moaned in anticipation.

"Don't forget—" she reminded him, glancing back, but he was already putting the condom on. She was so wet, he slid in without much resistance, and Mae buried her face and moaned into the pillow as he began to thrust. He was so hard, so *deep* inside of her!

"Oh god, so tight," he whispered, gripping her hips, making her yelp in surprise as he shoved in as deep as he could go. He stopped, holding her tight. "Are you all right?"

"I'm sorry," she apologized. "It's just… big."

"Don't apologize for that." He chuckled, slowly pulling out of her and rolling onto his back. "Come here."

She let him guide her so she was straddling his hips, his cock pulsing between them. She could feel how hard he was against her pussy and she rocked against him without thinking.

"That's good," he murmured, lifting her hips, aiming himself. "Keep doing that."

She moaned as she sank down onto him, feeling the head of his cock probing deep inside of her, her hips still moving forward and back, grinding into his. That hot tickle between her legs grew into an impossible itch as they rocked, Griff watching her through half-closed eyes.

"Oh fuck," he groaned, his fingers gripping her ass. "Oh Mae!"

She whimpered, rolling her hips in faster circles, trying to chase that delicious feeling to its conclusion but continuing to fall short. Griff cupped her breasts, tweaking her nipples, hard and pursed, sending shockwaves down between her legs. She moaned and put her hands over his, rubbing them hard against her breasts.

"That's it," he insisted. "Feel good?"

She swallowed and nodded, panting and breathless with the sensation. Then he slid a hand down between her thighs, using his index finger to rub her swollen clit in circles. Mae's eyes flew open and she looked down at him in wide-eyed surprise.

"Oh yes!" she cried, rocking faster. "Do that! More!"

He moved his finger faster as Mae twisted and tugged at her hard nipples, rolling on top of him like the tide coming in, again and again. The wet sound and tangy smell of their sex filled the little room and she found herself heady with it.

"Mae!" Griff warned as she shifted her hips forward and back, eyes closed, biting her lip with concentration. "Oh god, sweetheart…"

"Yes!" She opened her eyes to look at him, feeling the final wave break, washing heat all through her body. She cried out and collapsed into his arms as he thrust deep up into her pussy, grabbing her ass to give him more leverage as he bucked and shuddered beneath her. She felt every hot pulse of his cock, every sweet wave of his climax, matching her own.

They rested, quiet and breathless, their hearts thudding together, until finally Griff asked, "Now are you going to tell me what's wrong?"

She didn't open her eyes. "Nothing's wrong."

"You're lying." He kissed the top of her head.

"Someone proposed to me tonight." She just blurted it out and regretting it almost immediately.

"What?"

"I told you about that business associate of my father's? The one who has a buyer for my grandmother's apartment?"

Griff's voice was stiff with anger. "He proposed to you?"

"Practically."

"And what did you say?"

She laughed. "What do you think I said?"

"So what are you going to do?"

Mae sighed. "I don't know."

She felt him stiffen, and not in a good way. “Are you going to move in with your grandmother? Or maybe you’ll marry the guy and live happily ever after, just like your grandmother wants?”

Mae winced. “She’s the only family I have left, Griff. What can I do?”

He sat up, grabbing for his clothes. “You’ve got enough money to do what you want. Why don’t you?”

“It’s not that simple.” She sat up, watching him getting dressed. “Where are you going?”

“I don’t know.” He tucked in his shirt, grabbing his coat off the floor. “It’s all an illusion, Mae. The whole thing is one giant magic trick.” He waved his hand toward the window. “It can collapse at any minute. It already has.”

He sighed, just standing there in the middle of her bedroom, quiet for a moment. She wanted to go to him, but she wasn’t quite sure how.

“Did you know I used to be a stockbroker?” He turned to look at her, smiling at her wide-eyed look. Of course she didn’t know—she realized she hadn’t even known his first name until a few days ago. She only knew what he was willing to tell her. “Now I do magic tricks and sell apples. And it’s really no different at all.”

“Griff!” she called after him as he started to go.

He hesitated in the doorway, not turning to look at her as he spoke. “I don’t have anything left to give you, Mae.”

“I didn’t ask you for anything,” she protested.

He shook his head. “I know,” he said, and then he was gone.

* * * *

He couldn’t wait anymore. If she wasn’t going to come to him willingly, then he had no qualms about taking what he wanted by force. He’d proven that time and again over the years and this was no exception. Still, he would give her one more chance, he decided. He was a patient man, and he was confident in both his abilities of persuasion and the power of his will. He still believed she would come around. She just needed a little…incentive.

He slid the last document onto the table, watching the old woman sign it. It wasn't the first time he'd run this scam—but it was the first time he'd done so on such a grand scale. It was a simple cash-back-at-closing deal, perfectly legal. Except that he'd had the property appraised at an inflated price, allowing the buyer to make an offer far above its actual value while putting very little in the way of a down payment on the property. The bank had no idea the appraisal was rigged, nor did they know that his buyer was a straw-man, being paid off with the proceeds.

Of course, all of his fake-buyer's income and asset documentation was also fraudulent. He was just a guy from the Hooverville downtown, but he cleaned up well enough and, more importantly, could play the part. Lionel had worked with a lot of grifters over the years, some better than others, but there was always someone new around to play the roles he needed filled.

As the broker of the deal, he would pocket the difference between the actual value of the home and the appraised value—giving his Hooverville friend enough to make him happy—and they'd both be long gone before the bank realized the buyer was a dummy and the deal was bust. The property would go into foreclosure and the seller would be moved already.

So he wasn't really hurting anyone after all, he reasoned. In theory, Mae's grandmother would never know what had happened. She'd be living happily somewhere in the countryside with her granddaughter, none the wiser, and Lionel would be quite a bit richer.

"Goodness, I think I'm getting a cramp!" The old woman shook her writing hand, smiling up at him. "So much paperwork."

"They like to make it complicated, don't they?" Lionel slid all of the documentation into a large envelope. "But now you can walk away free and clear."

And so can I, he thought.

"Mae will be so happy." She gave a little sigh, picking up the tea he'd made for her. The servants had the day off, at

Lionel's suggestion. The woman liked him and didn't question his requests. "She hates the city."

And that was the wrench in the works, wasn't it? He knew he should just take the money and run, but Mae had caught his attention from the beginning, back when he'd been selling insurance in Nebraska. It was mostly on the up-and-up, although he occasionally ran a profitable scam or two. He hadn't been planning to scam the Verges, but the more he found out about the family—and especially after he'd discovered Mae's father's connections to old New York money—the more difficult it became for him to resist.

How was he supposed to know that the old woman had disowned her only son and had written him out of her will? Even he had to admit that his blackmail scheme had backfired disastrously—but lucky for him, his backup plan had still been in play. Mae's parents had purchased a great deal of life insurance from him. All he'd had to do was marry the girl after their untimely death—brake lines failed all the time in these new autos—and he was golden.

"So Mae will be moving in with you?" Lionel asked.

Mae's grandmother laughed brightly, giving him a sly wink. "Well, unless I can find her a husband before we move out."

He smiled and winked back at her, but Lionel's chest burned at her words. If the old woman hadn't swooped in and hurried her granddaughter off to New York City in the first place, he would have married Mae and inherited her father's money, all according to plan. Damned old bat had put the kibosh on that so fast Lionel hadn't even seen Mae to say goodbye before she was gone.

Of course, now the stakes were even higher, he reasoned, looking around the penthouse apartment at the high-end furniture, the priceless works of art the old woman had hanging on her walls. Not only did he stand to gain Mae's father's money when he married her—but her grandmother's as well.

He wanted what he was entitled to—everything he'd worked for. That only seemed fair. He put the envelope down on the table, dropping the medication into her tea while she was looking the other way. He slipped into the chair opposite her, picking up his own cup and sipping it.

She did the same, smiling at him over the rim. He watched and waited, listening to her chatter on about her granddaughter and the estate they'd be moving to in Nantucket. When she glanced up at him, eyes widening a little, he knew the medication was starting to take effect.

Her mouth drew into a comic little "o" before she collapsed in her chair, slipping to the floor with a fat thud. He sighed, hefting her back into place, using the rope he had packed into his briefcase to secure her to the chair. He had more rope in his case, along with various other tools and implements he might need later, if he had to resort to such measures to persuade his bride-to-be that he really was her intended. He just hoped it didn't have to come to that. He hated doing things the hard way.

He checked the old woman's pulse—faint but there. Good. He added a thick piece of rope as a gag, just in case. The penthouse was isolated and all the servants were gone, but you could never be too careful. Now it was time to go collect the rest of his debt. He really was going to try it the easy way. If that failed, well…then, and only then, he would resort to doing it the hard way—if he had to.

* * * *

"I'm sorry, Griff." She didn't find it hard to say at all.

He didn't apologize, but he pulled her behind his apple cart and put his arms around her right there on the street, wrapping her up in safety and warmth, and she melted against him in spite of the public nature of their embrace.

"I just don't want to lose you." His hoarse, whispered words brought tears to her eyes. The truth was she didn't want to go. She loved her grandmother, and she missed living in the country, but this man had somehow become the most important thing on earth to her and if that meant staying in New York City, she was prepared to stand up and say so.

"You're not losing me." She nestled her head under his chin, breathing in the scent of him, always mixed with the sweet smell of apples. "I'm going to be wherever you are."

"Do you mean that?" He lifted her face to search her eyes and saw the tears glistening there. He kissed her then, his mouth hot and insistent, branding her, claiming her, right there on the street.

"Mae!" The sound of her name brought her out of her daze and she broke the kiss to see Lionel pulled up at the curb, shoving the passenger door of his car open. "I've been looking for you everywhere! Your grandmother needs you!"

"I have to go." She looked guiltily up at Griff, seeing the growing anger on his face as he caught a glimpse of Lionel leaning across the front seat of the car.

She didn't want a huge confrontation in the middle of the street. The police had been cracking down on apple vendors lately and she didn't want Griff calling attention to himself or, god forbid, doing something stupid enough to get arrested for. She knew, after what she'd just said, that leaving this way didn't exactly look as if she was choosing Griff over her grandmother—but what if she was ill? If her grandmother had been looking for her, had even sent Lionel searching, there had to be a good reason.

"Don't worry, I'll be back. Please, just trust me."

"Mae!" Griff called after her but she was already sliding in beside Lionel, shutting the door behind her. "Mae, get out of the car!"

"He's got moxie, doesn't he?" Lionel remarked, staring as Griff pounded on the window, screaming at her to get out

"Go!" Mae insisted, sinking lower in her seat, seeing the anger rising on Griff's face. "Please, just go!"

Lionel floored it but Griff chased them, pounding on the trunk, until Lionel swerved around a pedestrian and turned the corner. Mae twisted in her seat but she couldn't see Griff in the crowd on the street.

"Guess he likes you, huh?" Lionel shifted, giving the car even more gas, putting more distance between them and Griff.

Mae blushed, turning back to face him, but ignored his question. She knew he'd seen them kissing, but she decided she'd deal with that later. "How's my grandmother?"

Lionel was quiet, taking another fast corner, and Mae grabbed the edge of the seat to keep from sliding. She frowned, looking over at him, seeing his jaw working.

"Lionel?"

He gave her a long, veiled look and it made her stomach clench. "Are you playing with me, Mae?"

"I don't know…"

He turned another sharp corner. "I think I've make my affections and intentions clear to you."

"Oh…" She saw the Century building on the right, glad they were almost there. Maybe she could avoid letting him down too hard—again. "Lionel, I'm sorry. I told you before, I'm not…we can't…"

He braked hard, the tires actually squealing to a stop in front of her grandmother's building. "Well I guess I know now just why you've been turning me down."

"You're a nice man, Lionel," she said, reaching out to touch his forearm. He looked down at her hand and then met her eyes. The look in them scared her a little in its intensity. "But I just…I don't feel that way about you."

"Well someone's feeling something." He sneered. "No wonder you've been drawing your shades."

Mae stared at him, confused. "My…what?"

"Your grandmother's waiting." He got out of the car and Mae followed, trying to make sense of what he'd said.

"You and I were meant to be together, Mae." Lionel was addressing her as they rode up in the elevator, but it was also, strangely, almost as if she wasn't even there. "I knew it from the first moment I saw you. God, what a hot little dish you were. And you didn't even know it."

"Lionel, I don't think you understand…" Mae struggled with her words as they approached the door to her grandmother's apartment.

"Don't worry, I got the message." He opened the door and Mae frowned as it swung open—unlocked. That was odd… "Now it's your turn to listen to me."

The door shut behind them and Mae froze, seeing her grandmother slumped in a chair. She heard the lock turn, the newest and latest in security, a thick deadbolt, but she was already rushing to her grandmother's aid, sure she was ill. It wasn't until she reached the chair that she saw the ropes she was tied with.

"Grandmother!" Mae shook the old woman gently, but she didn't give any sign she heard. She pulled the rope out of her grandmother's mouth. "Lionel, what is this? What's happened to her? Why—?"

The blow came from behind, knocking her three feet from her grandmother's chair onto the hardwood floor. Mae sprawled, her ears ringing, the hip she'd fallen on aching, her basket spilling open, tumbling the remains of her lunch onto the floor. It wasn't until that moment she realized just how much trouble she was really in.

"No!" She cried out as Lionel grabbed the back of her coat, yanking her to her feet. "Oh god, please, no…"

She tried to scramble away but her heels scraped helplessly along the hardwood as Lionel ripped off her coat and slammed her down into a chair.

"Don't fucking move!"

If his words didn't make her freeze, the knife he'd taken from his pocket and flicked open did the trick. She stared at it, glancing behind him toward the door, wondering if she could make it before he caught her. But even if she did…then what? Her grandmother was tied to a chair, helpless. Was she even alive?

"Help!" She screamed, but knew already it was useless, and all it did was elicit another blow, this time across the other side of her head, making her right ear sting.

"Shut up!" He went behind her, grabbing her arms and twisting them so her hands met behind the chair. It was unbelievably painful and she whimpered as he worked, tying her hands together and then her feet to the legs of the chair. "That's better. A big improvement."

She glanced over at her grandmother, relieved to see her chest slowly rising and falling. At least she was alive. Mae strained to listen, searching the apartment for any other sounds. Where were the servants?

"You know, I wanted to do this the easy way." Lionel shook his head sadly, picking up the briefcase he'd pulled the rope out of and putting it on the dining room table. "All you had to do was say yes. Is that so hard?"

He turned his back to her and she wiggled her hands in the rope, twisting and turning. It was tight, but maybe if she worked it long enough, she could loosen it.

"It's time for you to say yes." Lionel began pulling things out of the briefcase one by one.

"Please don't do this," she whispered, hearing the sound of him putting things on the table, but she didn't know what—his body blocked her view.

"All you have to do is marry me, Mae." He turned to face her. "It's very simple."

She blinked at him, her chest filling with rage. "I can't marry you."

"My knife begs to differ with you." He smiled, hefting it in his hand and putting it back on the table. "And so do my pliers." He lifted the largest, sharpest pair of needle-nosed pliers she'd ever seen off the table and showed them to her. "What's the matter?" he inquired when her eyes went wide at the sight of them.

"They're so…big…" she whispered.

"The better to torture you with, my dear." He snapped them open and closed. "And then there's my gun." He set the pliers down and picked up a pistol. "Also…big. Wouldn't you say?" He leaned forward, caressing her cheek with the barrel, and Mae shivered.

"Please don't do this," she whispered.

Lionel put his mouth against her ear and murmured, "And that's not all that's big, I promise you."

"Please!"

He chuckled. "Begging already?"

"What do you want?" There had to be something to dissuade him from this course, and there was only one thing she could imagine he wanted. "Money? I can give you money."

"I want what belongs to me." He put the gun back down on the table, picking up a tool Mae didn't recognize, but it looked sharp and wicked. "I want everything I've worked for. I just want what I've earned."

"Worked for?" She gulped, blinded by the silver implement in his hand.

"Do you have any idea what's involved in setting up a scheme like this?" He sighed, tilting up her chin. She couldn't take her eyes off the thing in his hand, staring at it in dazed horror. "You really are that naïve, aren't you?" His hand moved down her throat, squeezing gently. "Do you really think your parents buying an enormous life insurance policy from me and then getting into a horrible car accident was just a coincidence?"

Mae gasped, the realization too much for her to fully take in. "…no…"

Lionel sneered over at Mae's grandmother, her chin resting on her chest. "If this old bird hadn't interfered, you and me'd be married right now, living happily ever after with all that lovely insurance money you've been living on."

Mae found her voice, her whole body trembling with rage. "How many times do I have to tell you no, you bastard?"

"Bitch!" He hit her so hard the chair slid sideways and almost tipped with the force of it. "You're going to start telling me yes!"

Mae's face burned, and she closed her left eye against the blood stinging it. He'd hit her with the hand holding the tool and it had cut her, she was sure of it. The pain was blinding, but she glared at him, seething, and screamed, "No!"

Lionel turned and hit her grandmother. The old woman made a noise but didn't actually awaken. A bruise bloomed immediately on her cheek and Mae screamed in protest, struggling against the ropes binding her to the chair.

"Stop!" she cried, tears filling her eyes and then falling, tracking blood down her cheeks. "I'll do whatever you want!"

Lionel's smile spread slowly. "I know you will."

"Please…" Mae begged. "Is she all right?"

He snorted, rolling his eyes. "She's a tough old broad."

"Please, just untie us. Let me help her. That's all I'm asking." Mae knew they were beyond trouble. She knew, if she was actually forced to marry him, that it wouldn't be over. What would prevent him from killing them both then? There had to be another way out of this. She found herself sweating with fear and she continued to work on the rope behind her back, using it.

Lionel leaned in close enough she could smell what he'd had for lunch—something with onions. "Not before we have a little fun first."

"But I said I'd marry you!" she protested, twisting in the chair as his hand moved over the front of her dress, cupping her breast through the material.

"I'm afraid we won't have time for much of a honeymoon afterward," he said sadly, thumbing her nipple and then pinching it, hard.

"No…" she whispered, closing her eyes, expecting him to hit her again, but the knock on the door surprised them both.

"Shhh!" He clamped his hand over her mouth, staring at the door. The knock came again, more insistent this time. "They'll go away," he whispered, shaking his head. That's when she bit him and he let her go in surprise, just long enough for her to let out a short, sharp scream.

"Goddamnit," he hissed, clamping his hand down over her mouth again, using his thumb and finger to squeeze her nose shut, cutting off her air entirely. Mae's eyes widened, and she tried to turn her head, but he had tossed the tool in his hand aside and used that hand to grab the back of her neck, keeping her immobile.

She couldn't breathe. Her lungs burned.

"Mrs. Verges? Are you all right in there?" a voice called from the other side of the door. It was a strange voice with a thick Italian accent, but it was somehow familiar to Mae, even in her panic.

"Fuck." Lionel swore softly, looking into her eyes and whispering urgent instructions. "I'm going to let go. If you scream, I will kill your grandmother. Do you understand me?"

She nodded as best she could, gasping for air as he dropped his hand, her lungs pulling in the cool relief of oxygen. Her vision had begun to blacken at the edges and was just starting to come back.

"Who is it?" Lionel called, grabbing a length of rope and fitting it between Mae's protesting lips. He tied it tight behind her head, shaking a finger at her, whispering, “Not a fucking word.”

She nodded, but she continued to work her hands in the rope. If she could just get free…

“It’s the milkman,” came the response.

“I’m sorry, but Mrs. Verges isn’t feeling well,” Lionel said. “Just leave it outside the door.”

“Sir, I’m afraid I can’t do that—there’s ice cream in here!” The man with the thick Italian accent protested. “I’ll get fired for sure if I just leave it.”

“Oh for chrissake,” Lionel muttered, grabbing the gun off the table and heading over to the door.

Mae cried out around her rope gag as the door burst open, hitting Lionel in the chest, and she understood then why the voice had sounded so familiar as Griff threw a quick left hook, catching Lionel in the jaw and knocking him backward. The door swung shut behind them as Lionel lifted his gun, aiming at Griff’s head, and Mae screamed, the sound just a muffled squeak under the rope.

Griff deflected the shot, kicking Lionel’s hand aside, and a bullet buried itself in the sofa, a thick puff of stuffing rising from the hole. Mae twisted in her bindings, trying to call out to Griff, working the rope in her mouth, loosening it. The men were both on the floor now, fighting over the gun, and Mae realized she hadn’t heard a loud report when it went off—Lionel must have put a silencer on it.

“Jesus, Griff!” Lionel wheezed. “Let go! We can share the damned girl if that’s what you want!”

“We’re not sharing anything.” Griff slammed Lionel’s arm against the floor. The gun went off again. It still made a noise, a loud sort of popping sound, like a cork exiting a bottleneck. “The girl is mine.”

“Listen old buddy.” Lionel wasn’t quite strong enough to throw Griff’s weight off of him as they tussled and even in her panic, Mae realized the men somehow knew each other. “I’m sorry I took the money and ran. Well, not sorry exactly. And the girl? Well she was a hot little ticket, at least the first few times. Then I got bored…”

Griff shoved his elbow into Lionel's throat and Mae heard him squawk with pain. She saw Lionel's knee come up then, and heard Griff groan. His grip loosened on Lionel's gun hand and she watched as they rolled again and again. The gun went off a third time and Mae screamed, seeing both of them lying still on the hardwood floor. She cried out Griff's name behind her gag, turning her head from side to side, lifting her chin and finally working the rope out of her mouth.

"Griff!" she gasped, straining to see any movement.

And then Lionel rolled to the side with a disgusted groan, wiping at the blood on his shirt. Griff's body was inert, sprawled on the hardwood floor, and she could see blood pooling beneath him.

"No," she whispered, watching as Lionel stood and made his way toward her. "Oh no. No, no, no."

"Well, that ties up that loose end." He sighed, making a face at the red stains on his white shirt. "Ugh! What a mess!"

"You killed him." Mae still couldn't believe it was true, staring at Griff, face down on the floor. She looked at Lionel, her body twisted in pain, and screamed, "You killed him! You killed him!"

"I told you to shut the fuck up!" Lionel took a step toward her, clamping his hand over her mouth once again, smearing her face with the salty, copper taste of the blood on his palm—*Griff's blood*—making Mae gag and try to scream. She couldn't breathe, she couldn't think, she just reacted, sinking her teeth deep into the side of Lionel's palm, biting him so hard her own vision went black and she saw stars. From a distance, she heard him screaming in pain, struggling to free himself from her rabid grip, but she didn't let go even after the first blow against the side of her head. It took two more before he knocked her head backward and he snatched his hand free.

"Fucking bitch!" he howled, cradling his hand. He was bleeding badly, she noticed with great satisfaction, his own blood mixing with Griff's. She waited for him to hit her again, to kill her this time—it didn't matter anymore—and he looked for a moment like that's just what he was going to do, but instead he turned and went into the kitchen, turning on the water and sticking his hand under the tap.

"I am so going to enjoy taking your virginity," he growled through clenched teeth. She could see him from this angle, through the doorway.

"Too late," she called hoarsely, the pain of her lover lying dead on the floor so overwhelming she thought she might faint.

"You fucking slut!" He continued washing his hand in the sink, swearing to himself, and Mae closed her eyes, waiting for her fate. She knew it was over, that there was no way out of this mess. Griff was dead, and she and her grandmother might as well be. She could hear her grandmother breathing beside her, deep and even, and she hoped it would end quickly for them, that she wouldn't wake up after all.

"I'm gonna need stitches!" Lionel groaned and she opened her eyes to see him wrapping his hand in a dish towel. She saw blood blooming on the white fabric and smiled. That's when she caught movement out of the corner of her eye.

Griff! She saw him crawling across the floor, leaving a trail of blood behind him. He met her eyes, shaking his head, and she saw the gun in his hand.

"Mae?" Of course her grandmother chose that exact moment to lift her groggy head and look around with bleary eyes. "What happened? Are you all right? Where—?"

"Shhh!" Mae cringed, seeing Lionel stiffen at the sound of their voices. He knew. But her heart soared at the sight of Griff kneeling up, his shirt red with blood, leveling the weapon and aiming as Lionel turned, coming through the doorway into the dining room.

"Oh fuck." That was all Lionel had a chance to say before Griff shot him in the head. He crumpled to the floor in a heap and Mae sobbed with relief.

"Oh Griff," she gasped, watching him go back down to his hands and knees, his head hanging low. "Are you all right? You've been shot!"

"I noticed." His voice was slightly slurred, as if he'd been drinking, while he crawled toward her, far too slowly. "It's a belly wound. Nothing vital. Maybe my spleen. I'll be fine if I don't lose too much blood…"

"Hurry!" she begged, twisting her hands over and over. The rope was getting looser, wet with her sweat.

"Who is this man?" her grandmother asked, glancing between the two of them, confused. "And what is he doing in my house?"

"I'm an apple peddler," Griff slurred.

"An apple peddler who just saved your life!" Mae reminded all of them.

"Mae." He put his head in her lap and she saw him smile. "I love you."

"Oh no, you don't." She nudged him with her knee, watching his eyes flutter closed. "This isn't over. Untie me! Right now! You've got a lot of explaining to do. How did you know Lionel?"

"It's a long story." Griff sighed, not opening his eyes. She didn't like that at all. "He needed a magician. I didn't know it was a scam…"

"I get the picture." Mae nudged him again. "Griff! Wake up!"

"Is he all right?" her grandmother asked, blinking at the young man resting his head in her granddaughter's lap.

"He's been shot," Mae said, swallowing hard. "Are you all right, grandmother?"

"Woozy. And my heart's racing. I need my nitro." The old woman sighed. "But I'm all right. Better now that *he's* dead." She shuddered at the sight of Lionel collapsed on the kitchen tile.

"We're all better off now." Mae set her mouth in a firm line. "Except Griff. Griff!"

He lifted his head, his eyes glazed. "Remember the last time we were like this? You thought I was going to propose."

"Griff!" she pleaded. "Focus!"

"I am." He met her eyes. "Will you marry me?"

"Oh for pete's sake." She gave a short, hysterical laugh.

"Marry the man, Mae."

They both turned to look at her grandmother, open-mouthed.

"What?" The old woman blinked, looking between them. "He's just saved our lives. He's obviously in love with you, and you clearly have feelings for him. And if you say yes, I just might have a better chance of getting out of this position at some point before morning. It's quite uncomfortable."

"Grandmother…" Mae looked at her with tears in her eyes, trying to speak.

"I lost my son," the old woman said, giving her granddaughter a tired smile. "I'm not going to lose you too. You do what your heart tells you."

Mae smiled down at the man in her lap. "If we all live through this, I'll marry you twice."

He smiled. "Just once. Forever."

"Whatever you want," she agreed. "Just untie me!"

"So demanding," Griff grumbled, reaching around to loosen the knots, but he was too late—Mae had just freed her own hands.

"Like grandmother, like granddaughter," the old woman laughed.

"Ha! "Mae held her palms up in triumph. "I just saved myself!"

She was just in time to catch Griff as he passed out.

Epilogue

"Hey Red." He greeted her like he always had, with a sly smile and a wink, as if he hadn't been gone for weeks.

"You're feeling better then?" she asked coldly. She had been to see him in the hospital several times, but then he had just disappeared.

"Much." He patted the wooden chair beside him. "Come on, sit down. I'm sorry. I had to wrap up some loose ends."

"You could have told me." She had to admit, her heart lifted the moment she saw him.

"I had to see a man about a horse," he joked. "Forgive me?"

She slipped into the chair beside him. "As long as you promise, no more disappearing acts."

"I got all the magic I need right here." He held up a little velvet box and she gasped, her eyes widening as she took it from him. He couldn't have… how?

"It's empty."

He grinned. "Look on your finger."

"How did you do that?" There was a diamond on her ring finger sparkling in the sunlight that was going to make her grandmother very proud.

"Magic." Griff laughed as she threw her arms around him in the middle of the street.

And it was.

ALICE

"You're not listening!" Maddie's voice jolted Alice out of her daze.

Her head snapped up and she clutched her iPhone, pressing it closer to her ear and mumbling, "I am, I'm listening. Something about neuropeptides being responsible for pair-bonding in humans…"

"That was two paragraphs ago." Mattie's mouth sounded like it was barely moving. Alice knew that meant her sister was really mad.

Alice snuggled deeper under her mountainous down comforter and decided to try to lighten the subject a little. "So you're telling me Wade and I are together just based on brain chemistry?"

Maddie sighed. "I'm trying to finish my dissertation and you want to talk about your boyfriend? Where are your priorities?"

She grinned. "What priorities?"

"Grow up, Alice!"

"I'm sorry," she apologized, although now she *was* thinking about Wade—about his big smile and big eyes and big hands that turned her this way and that way, and his big…

"Can I just finish this chapter?" Maddie interrupted her thoughts again.

"Go on." Alice assured her, "I'm listening."

And she tried, she really did, but distraction came easily to Alice, always had. Once when she was young and Maddie was babysitting, Alice had wandered off at the beach chasing a lizard across the sand, panicking her older sister to tears and, when she finally found Alice on her belly staring at the rock the lizard had disappeared under, to a sub-zero sort of anger as well. They hadn't spoken for the rest of the day. Alice hated when Maddie was angry and tried to do everything she could to avoid it. If that included listening to the latest chapter in Maddie's dissertation, well, certain sacrifices had to be made.

But Alice couldn't help it—her eyes were already closing, her mind drifting. A faint mew from somewhere way down there on the floor made her smile. Then Dinah jumped up onto the bed, her motor running, rubbing her white head against the hand Alice was using to hold the phone. Alice petted her with the other hand, scratching behind the cat's ears, tracing the line of her spine, making her tail rise. *Wade says I do that when he pets me.* The thought made her shiver.

Dinah mewed indignantly at Alice's distraction, nudging her phone hand again. Maddie was still reading, something about oxytocin and g-protein coupled receptors. Gah! How was she supposed to even feign interest? Dinah gave up on being petted and curled into a white ball of fluff on the covers, tucking her pink nose under a paw to sleep, and Alice gave up on trying to listen, settling down and drifting naturally into thoughts of Wade.

She had eight months of memories to flip through in her head, but the reality of Wade made him so much more of an immediate experience. Memory didn't do the man justice. No matter how much time she had with him, she craved more. They'd spent plenty of time together—movie dates, the theater, a heavenly weekend trip to Bermuda, and whenever he stayed over, he would make her waffles or French toast while Dinah did figure-eights between his feet in the kitchen—but that wasn't the best thing about Wade for Alice. She kept the best thing locked like a smooth, secret heart tucked inside of her beating one.

She hadn't even told Maddie. Not that Maddie would understand with her belief that love was nothing more than biological instinct and brain chemistry. Alice knew better. Love went deeper than those things. It burned like a laser beam through to her core and broke her heart wide open. Love made her do things she never would have considered before. Love was silk and softness, but love was also leather and the bite of a riding crop and Wade's commands. She hadn't told anyone about the ropes and bindings, the endless cycle of pain and pleasure that forced her to her knees at Wade's feet again and again.

Not that she had anyone to tell, besides Dinah and Maddie. Dinah didn't care, and Maddie would reduce it all to hormones and endorphins before declaring her sister insane and having her committed. Or calling the police. Or insisting Alice move back in with the responsible Maddie and stop her work as a freelance writer, a profession that barely kept Dinah in *Meow Mix* and Alice in *Lean Cuisines*, but one that Alice couldn't give up. For her, imagination was everything. To Maddie, it was practically the root of all evil. Even Maddie had wondered aloud how two such different souls had managed to come from the same DNA. For Alice, it proved that the world was bigger than scientific explanation.

"So what do you think?"

Was she finally done? Alice stifled a yawn, searching for a truth to tell her sister. "I think you're awesome, Maddie." She couldn't tell if the silence on the other end of the phone was pleased-Maddie or mad-Maddie, but then her other line rang and when she saw Wade's name on the Caller ID and heard the "Closer to God" *Nine-Inch-Nails* ringtone she'd assigned to him, all thoughts of her sister fled her brain.

"My other line," Alice said, already breathless. It was almost midnight. If Wade was calling this late, it could only mean one thing. "I have to go."

She didn't even wait for Maddie to protest before switching over. "Hello?"

"Are you ready?" His voice was smooth, like butter, and it melted her immediately.

She played coy. "I'm always ready for you."

"The blue one, backless. No panties." He wasn't playing around tonight. She was fully awake and squirming already.

"No stockings. No bra."

"But—" The dress was impossible to keep on, just a wisp of fabric really, and without anything underneath…

"No buts. Fifteen minutes. Out front."

"Okay." She didn't hesitate, not really. She was a good girl and rarely disobeyed—except when she had to. Or she forgot.

"Pardon me?" The smoothness in his voice turned gruff and Alice straightened up even further.

"I meant yes. Sir," she corrected herself. "Yes, sir."

"Fifteen minutes," he said again and the line went dead.

"Fifteen minutes, Dinah," she exclaimed, dumping the cat to the floor along with the comforter as she tumbled out of bed. "Goodness! Can we make ourselves presentable in fifteen minutes?"

Dinah sat back on her haunches and began to wash herself with the pink rasp of her tongue, safe in the knowledge she was always ready for anything. Alice wasn't so fortunate, but she managed to get herself together, just barely, with a five minute wash-down, scrubbed and shaved in the shower. Not her hair though, that was clean already and she brushed it out and left it long and straight over her shoulders like spun gold. There weren't many clothes to put on, just the midnight-blue dress, more gauze than material, and her slip-on heels. She considered leaving the light wrap she'd chosen. He hadn't mentioned her wearing one, but while it was spring, the air outside was chilly and she would be standing on the porch for as long as it took.

"Don't wait up for me, Dinah!" Alice called, checking to make sure the cat had plenty of food and water before shutting and locking the door behind her.

The day had been a lovely, bright blue thing and the night that had followed was crisp and clean, no hint of moisture in it.

She breathed deeply, fending off the lightheaded dizzy feeling that came with Wade's late night calls and gazed at the stars, wondering just what he had in store for her tonight. His basement—he called it 'The Sanctuary' and for Alice, it most definitely was—was crammed full of various implements of pleasure and pain, not the least important of which was Wade himself. Without him, the rest would have been a little absurd.

It could be anything, of course. Or none of those. Some nights they spent upstairs in his big bed making plain old vanilla love and that was good too for variety. But she had a feeling tonight wasn't a vanilla sort of night. He'd mentioned a surprise last week, just a casual comment, and she hadn't pressed him. She'd learned to wait patiently for Wade to reveal what he wanted, when he wanted. It was always better that way, less punishment involved. Besides, the anticipation was delicious.

In the scheme of things, she never had to wait too long. The black car pulling up in front of her little bungalow was proof enough of that. But strangely, it wasn't Wade's car—and Wade wasn't in it. Instead, a driver appeared, a tall man in a dark suit and hat with pristine white gloves, to open the door in the back for her.

"Ms. Lydel?" he called, motioning her forward. "Mr. Knight sent me."

She rushed off the porch, jolted out of her surprise by his words, her mind buzzing with possibilities. Her body was already flushed and ready for whatever Wade might have in store. She thanked the driver as she got into the car. It wasn't a limo, but it was a long, sleek black thing that prowled through the streets with a low rumble and a secret sort of power in its haunches, as if it might launch them into outer space or another dimension with the slightest tap of the gas pedal.

She didn't ask the driver where they were going, she just sat back and waited, watching the world pass breathlessly by. It seemed as if they drove forever, through city streets, then onto a highway and off, the scenery changing to black nothingness after a while, with only faint lights painted on the darkness in the distance. And he drove very fast, making her clutch her little purse in one hand and the edge of the seat in the other.

"Are we in a hurry?" Alice gasped when he took a sharp curve fast enough to tilt her torso nearly parallel to the seat.

"Late," he replied shortly, the car hurtling through the darkness.

She didn't know how they could possibly be late. Wade had told her fifteen minutes and she'd been out there in ten. When they finally stopped, Alice took the driver's white-gloved hand and let him help her out, feeling disoriented. The driver was mumbling to himself about their tardiness as he shut the door behind her.

"She won't be pleased," he remarked, shutting the car door with a thump that made Alice jump. She looked around, trying to see if Wade was waiting for her somewhere, but there was nothing, nothing at all, just a long gravel drive leading up to a building of some sort she couldn't even really see. The night was complete darkness, no streetlights, not even a moon to light the way.

"Excuse me?" Alice called to the driver but he was already striding toward the building, not much of him visible except for the flash of his gloves. "Can you help me?"

"No time," he called back and then he disappeared.

She stood there shivering for a moment, from anxiety or cold she wasn't sure, wondering what to do next. She half-expected Wade to appear out of thin air, but when he didn't, she decided to call him. Her iPhone had no signal though, no matter which way she turned.

There wasn't anything else to do but follow the driver before he got too far ahead. She used the "flashlight" function on her iPhone and with that little bit of light made it to the side of the building where the driver had gone. It was solid black brick as far as she could tell, no windows or doors. So how had he disappeared?

Alice swept the light from her phone this way and that. She walked down the wall, frowning, perplexed, her heels unsteady on the gravel. Sighing, she ran her hand along the wall like she had when she was a kid as she paced and was about to turn and go the other way when the wall ended. Startled, she used the light on that part of the wall and realized it had depth. There was a section missing here, but the brick was so black, so seamless, it all ran together.

She slipped through the opening and found herself on a stairwell leading down. There was nothing else to do but descend. And descend. And descend. There was a handrail on her right, and the steps were wide stone, cold radiating from them the deeper she went. She took her shoes off after a while and carried them because her feet began to hurt, and because she could travel faster that way. Thanks to her phone, she could at least see where she was going, but the end still came so abruptly she nearly ran into the door at the bottom.

She contemplated the door. It had no handle or window and appeared nearly seamless. Remembering how she'd run her hand along the wall, she reached out to touch the door. It was metal, smooth, and when she pushed, it gave.

"Curiouser and curiouser." She pushed harder and it swung inward, letting out a bit of light and the scent of something musky and a little wild, like an animal's lair. She didn't have time to contemplate that though, because there was a hallway, and Alice saw the driver in the dim light hurrying down it, his white gloves flashing at his sides.

"Wait!" she called, hurrying after him. He was her only connection to the outside, to Wade, to anything familiar, so she followed him as fast as she could manage. The floors and walls were stone down here too, the way lit with bare bulbs strung far apart across the ceiling.

The driver took so many twists and turns she knew she would be hopelessly lost if she stopped and tried to go back. Her only hope was to catch up. She walked quickly and then started to run, calling after the driver, but no matter how fast she went, she couldn't seem to catch him.

"Please!" She sounded desperate, and she felt that way too, she realized. The driver seemed to have slowed and that made her hurry even faster in spite of the stitch in her side. She was closing the distance. "Please just tell me where we are!"

He stopped and turned, the white outline of his hand pushing open a door. She was only ten feet from him now and the light coming from the room he'd opened was inviting.

Panting, she made it another five feet, calling out, "Please! Where is Mr. Knight? Where are we?"

"Why, don't you know?" The driver flashed a distracted smile as she neared, pushing the door fully open and waving her through. "This is Wonderland."

She stepped through the doorway and found herself in an oddly shaped room. The floors were black and white parquet and the ceilings sloped upward to a point in the middle. They were draped with fabric, red and white, like a circus tent. There appeared to be no doors or windows, and when the driver stepped into the room, the door behind them disappeared into the obsidian wall.

Alice stood, stunned to silence, perplexed, watching the driver cross the room. He pushed against the wall and another door appeared.

"Wait!" she called, rushing after him, determined not to be left behind again. "Can you take me to Mr. Knight?"

He stopped, turning only briefly, a distracted look of pity crossing his face. "You should take heed of the instructions on the table. Don't worry, Miss. I'm sure he'll join you shortly."

"What table—?" She turned to look at the room and he was gone, the door disappearing as if it had never been there. Alice growled in frustration, pushing at the wall in the same spot, but it didn't give. She dropped her shoes and put her phone back into her purse, leaving that on the floor as well and went all around the room, finding it had eight sides, like an octagon, pushing and pushing, looking for a way out.

She didn't find one, but she did find the little table with the instructions the driver mentioned. She hadn't noticed it at all when they arrived but there it was, a little glass bistro table set with a plate and a wine glass. The glass was full of a red liquid she could only assume was wine. The plate held an hors d'œuvre of some sort. She couldn't identify it, but when she got close, it smelled sweet, like honey.

She'd been hoping for a long list of instructions, or perhaps just the words, "Wait, I'm coming for you." She would have waited for him forever. Instead, there were two small notes, scrawled in someone's handwriting, not Wade's she was sure. The one by the glass said, "Drink me." The one by the plate said, "Eat me."

Which first? She picked up the little hors d'œuvre and contemplated it. She could almost hear Maddie screaming in her head. *Don't do it! What are you thinking? It could be anything! Poison! A date rape drug! Allliiiiiiiccce!*

She defiantly popped it into her mouth and chewed. Honey, she'd been right about that much. Honey and pecans and cream cheese on a tasty little cracker. Yum. She licked her lips and cleaned her teeth off with her tongue, looking at the other note. The honey was still so sweet and bright in her mouth she hated to wash it away with wine. She'd never been much of a drinker.

Of course, she would drink it anyway, if that's what Wade wanted her to do. She smiled and took a slow turn around the room, looking up at the red and white stripes of the fabric hung from the ceiling. It didn't really look anything like it, but it made her think of Wade's 'Sanctuary.' It had the same feel, the same vibe. The thought made her flush with warmth. The anticipation she'd been feeling upon getting Wade's phone call returned as her fingers brushed the smooth, dark walls, her bare feet cold on the stone floor, wondering what came next. She probably should have been afraid—she knew Maddie would have been terrified—but she wasn't. She trusted Wade, and he had brought her here.

Did he, Alice? Are you sure? Maddie's imagined voice made her stop and cock her head like a dog listening for its master. *Wade has always come for you himself in his own car. He takes you to his place, or maybe out to a club. But he's never sent a driver, and he didn't tell you about this place, whatever it is. And by the way, what* is *it exactly?*

All of that was true, but it didn't mean anything. Besides, strange drivers didn't just show up unannounced on people's doorsteps to take them to unfamiliar places in the middle of the night for no reason. She was sure someone had paid him. That Wade had hired him. What other explanation was there?

She didn't have any more time to ponder the question because a door burst open behind her out of nowhere. Alice's heart leapt, but when she saw her visitor wasn't Wade, her belly clenched with fear. The man who entered was a mountain, dressed in a red velvet robe from head to toe, all trimmed in silver. He also wore a silver crown that sat cockeyed on his head. He smiled at her though—that was encouraging. Perhaps he was here to take her to Wade.

"Alice in Wonderland." The man laughed, delighted, and took her hand. She watched, bemused, as he lifted it to his lips and gently kissed her knuckles. He had a mustache that tickled her. She was so involved she missed the other figure standing behind him until she spoke.

The woman was similarly dressed, all in red with silver trimmings and a crown, but she wore far less material. Her corset was red with silver lacings, but it ended below her heavy breasts, pushing them upward. The bottom of the thing was open as well, showing the shaved swell of her mound. The outfit was covered by a red lace peignoir that hung open to reveal her lush body.

Alice saw the woman's sharp look and slowly withdrew the hand the man was still holding. She didn't know who they were, but they were clearly together, and the older woman didn't seem to like the attention the man was paying young Alice.

"You curtsy before the Red King, my dear, or you'll lose your head." The woman's lips were as red as her outfit as they stretched into a slow, sly smile.

"I didn't know," Alice said by way of apology, awkwardly approximating a curtsey before the king. An idea struck her and she turned to the woman, curtsying even lower before her. "Then you must be the Red Queen."

It was simple deduction but the queen seemed pleased as Alice rose again, looking between them both. Clearly this was some sort of game, a scene being played out. She'd been to enough BDSM clubs with Wade to know what they looked like, how it all worked. But where was Wade?

"Come child, it's time to play our game." The Red King moved so quickly Alice wondered at his speed, given the man's bulk. He was more executioner than king, at least in size, but he moved as swiftly as a cat, and before she knew what was happening, her dress and wrap had been slipped from her shoulders to a puddle on the floor and leather manacles were attached to each wrist and ankle. They were secured to the floor with a silver length of cord as thin as thread, but when Alice pulled on them, they held fast.

Then the floor began to rise.

Panicked, Alice tried to jump off the dias but the restraints tightened and kept her in place. The Red King jumped up onto the platform beside her as it rose, but the Red Queen stayed below. Alice let him hold onto her, afraid of heights as she was. They were four feet in the air now, on a round raised section of floor.

"Don't be afraid." The king breathed his words, warm against her neck, and it made her shiver. "This is only a test."

Alice relaxed almost immediately. Of course. Wade had created this scenario to test her. But why? How? And what should her response be? Already she could feel the king's strong hands squeezing her upper arms, the way he held her naked body back against his robed one. He had intentions. But were those Wade's intentions?

"Transmission!" The queen called out from below and Alice gasped when something flickered across the room against the black wall, a faint glow growing in the dimness. She stared as a picture began to take shape and when she recognized it, she whimpered in response.

"Alice, you have been chosen." Wade's words were spoken with a smile. "If you pass this test, you and I will be together. Forever."

The words made her belly clench, her heart race. She knew very well how phobic Wade was about commitment. At the beginning, Alice had talked about marriage and children and houses in the suburbs, but Wade's silence on the subject had quieted her too. She'd learned to let him go at his own pace. You couldn't push a man like Wade. So she had waited and hoped. There had been times, especially with Maddie's voice in her head, that she'd considered breaking it off. But Wade had a way of keeping her coming back for more, yet always leaving her wanting, just a little.

"Kitten…" His pet name for her. She melted at the word, at the almost shy look on his handsome face. "All you have to do is say yes."

If this was it—well, it was a hell of a marriage proposal. Strange and distant and yet sweet and exciting, just like Wade. Alice felt tears stinging her eyes.

"Yes," she whispered. "Yes."

Behind her, the Red King chuckled.

Then the picture went back to black, and the Red Queen cried out, "Consent! We have consent!"

"Wait—" Alice struggled. She'd almost forgotten her restraints, that the king was still holding her in the bulk of his arms.

"No time for that now." The king stomped hard on the floor with one foot and Alice felt things began to change beneath her. The floor itself was moving. No, it was softening, melting, turning into some other substance. She expected to look down and see herself covered in some sort of goo, but the stuff was solid and it cushioned her feet. It was strange, impossible, but true.

The king let her go and she stood, still manacled, in the middle of the dias. He walked around the edge of it, studying her naked body. Alice flushed and went to cover herself, but the instant she even thought about it, the leads on her restraints tightened and prevented the motion.

"I need to go home." Alice saw the Red King flash by out of the corner of her eye. He was behind her now but not touching her. "Have you seen my driver?"

"What driver?" His voice, behind her. "What do you want your safe word to be, Alice?"

"He had white gloves on. And a hat. He was very tall," she explained. His hand moved over her shoulder, his touch light, but his palm huge. "My safe word?"

"The white rabbit?" the king inquired. She gasped when he cupped her breast, kneading the firm flesh in his fingers. "Yes, dear, your safe word. You do know what one is, don't you?"

"White rabbit?" Alice asked, confused, trying to ignore the tingling sensation from her nipple to her crotch as he manipulated it between thumb and finger.

"Well, it's strange, but it will do," the king said with a laugh. "White rabbit it is."

"Wait—" Alice said again, but it was too late, far too late. Behind her, the king had disrobed. She felt the heat from his body and the press of his cock, thick and huge, against her hip. "What are you doing?"

"From now on, the Red Queen asks the questions." The king reached down between her legs and cupped her mound from behind. Alice had shaved smooth for Wade and her vulva was soft as velvet in his hand. "And I do all the dirty work."

"I like the dirty work," he confessed, his fingers parting her lips, dipping in, testing the waters. Then he lifted her like that, in one hand, tilting her hips with the flick of his wrist, and she found herself suspended spread-eagle by silver thread, attached from her restraints to the ceiling. She had time to wonder how things had turned upside down—the string had gone from manacle to floor just moments before—but the strain on her arms and legs, carrying the fullness of her weight, grew painful almost immediately.

"I'll be as gentle as I can." He whispered the words into her ear, which was at mouth-level as he stood beside her. "But she is watching."

"It hurts," Alice gasped, trying to turn away from or into the pain in her limbs.

"It's supposed to!" The Red Queen sang from somewhere below them. How could she possible see? Alice wondered. They were far off the ground and she was down there. She turned her head from side to side and then she saw it, a glimmer of light below—another transmission, this one showing the scene above displayed on the wall. Out of the corner of her eye, Alice saw herself suspended, nude, helpless.

The king made some motion and Alice sighed in relief as the strings holding her up drew closer together on the ceiling. She couldn't see where they were attached, no pulleys or levers. They seemed to disappear in to the red and white material above with no fastening at all. The affect was both good and bad. Her limbs were still holding her own weight, but they were drawn together now, arms parallel with her legs and perpendicular to the floor. It left her body jackknifed and her unable to see, except peripherally, what was going on around her.

"Such sweet skin." The king had something to pet her with. She couldn't tell at first what it was, the touch was so light over the backs of her thighs, behind her knees. "Like peaches and cream."

But when the first blow fell near her hip, she recognized the implement immediately. A riding crop. It was one of Wade's favorite toys.

Alice howled when the crop bit her behind a second and third time, leaving a burning sting. Below her, the queen mimicked her response, howling back, the sound making an echo. It was painfully humiliating, knowing she was not only being punished, but that someone was watching—and enjoying it.

But this is a test, she reminded herself, thinking of Wade. He'd asked her to say yes to this, yes to him. This was part of it, and so she would submit. She would have done anything for him. Maddie would call her crazy, or maybe she would come up for a name for the hormone in her brain responsible for the way she felt, but Alice knew the truth. She wanted Wade, and she wanted what he wanted for her.

"Oh Alice, that's lovely." The riding crop came down again, but this time she didn't cry out. Her body relaxed and the moment she let go, she realized how tense she had been, how much she had been fighting against her restraints.

The king knew just what he was doing. She didn't want to admit it, even to herself, but he was almost better than Wade in his technique. He knew just when to deliver a sting, followed by the soft pet of the leather, and then two more, quick, on one side, then three on the other. He kept her guessing, anticipating, soothing her at turns and then going back at her with great force.

He was warming her up. And it was working. She could feel herself giving into it, floating away on the sensation. The king seemed to sense the shift in her because he slid the riding crop's leather end between her pussy lips, making her gasp and twist and moan. There was nothing she could do to stop him.

Her legs were pressed together, but her pussy was completely exposed to him between her thighs, plump and ripe as a peach.

The flat edge of the leather crop snapped against the top of her cleft and Alice whimpered, twisting, not knowing if she wanted him to stop or if she wanted more. The sensation was something between pain and pleasure, a feeling she knew all too well. Then the other end of the riding crop, the hard handle, found its way between her swollen lips, the tip trailing up and down, teasing her clit and then her hole, back and forth.

"She likes that." The king's voice sounded distant to her, but Alice knew she was far away, transported somewhere else, giving into her own need. Her body was on fire with it. She clutched her ankles as the riding crop slipped inside of her, slow and easy, her breath hot and panting against the flesh of her knees. Moaning, she tried to rock to meet the object fucking her but had no leverage, no range of motion. She was powerless.

"Please," she whispered, knowing better, but she wanted it more than she could say. The crop was removed almost immediately and the business end came down against her bottom, hard, the sound echoing in the room.

SMACK

Alice whimpered and then wailed when another blow fell and then another, teaching her the lesson swiftly, in staccato beats. SMACK SMACK SMACK. They rained down like stinging leather kisses, leaving her bottom in a hot, fiery mess.

She heard the Red Queen laughing somewhere. "Can you do addition, Alice?" she called, still giggling. "What's one and one and one and one and one and..."

"I don't know, I lost count!" Alice moaned, sinking her teeth into her own flesh, biting her knees to send sensation somewhere else besides her sore behind. And as suddenly as the storm began, it was over. The crop was gone, but so was the Red King. She was left alone, hanging, aching, waiting. Alice rested, panting, wanting to cry but holding back her tears. Is this what Wade had wanted? Was he watching her from somewhere? No other man had ever touched her this way. She had never given herself to anyone like this before. Was this her test?

Alice gasped when the threads attached to her restraints began to move. They spread her legs apart and when Alice peered between them she saw the Red King standing there, larger than life, hands on hips, completely nude. His cock was enormous and already covered with a strange lime-green colored condom. At least she hoped it was a condom.

Part of her wanted to beg, plead, tell him no, the same part of her that wanted to save herself for Wade and only him, but she remembered him telling her to say "yes," on the video. And if she was honest with herself, just seeing the length and breadth and thrust of the king as he stroked himself while he looked at her, Alice wanted to be fucked. She had wanted to be tied and punished. She wanted nothing more than to surrender to this giant man's will, his insistent need for her.

So when he lifted her behind with both hands, bringing her pussy to his mouth, she quivered under his attention and gave into whatever he wanted to do. His tongue made delicious circles over her aching clit, drawing it out like a bee taking honey. She almost sobbed with relief, feeling her orgasm building in the tremble of her thighs and belly. When his big fingers slid into her, she gave him her juices in a torrential flood, coming so hard she bucked against her restraints, feeling her connective tissue straining as she arched and spread for him.

"You threaten to drown us all." He chuckled, replacing his tongue with his thumb as he stood between her thighs. His face was covered with her slick wetness. She whimpered as he continued to rub her throbbing clit, eliciting shuddering aftershocks for his cock's delight. The head of it was pressed against her hole, poised at the entrance, aimed and ready, but waiting.

"Do you want me to fuck you, Alice?"

She looked at him through a blurry haze of lust, her body singing with it like a tuning fork. She couldn't tell him no. Even if she'd wanted to—and she decidedly did not—the word "no" wouldn't come from her throat.

She groaned and gave in to it. "Yes. Oh yes, please."

"What do you want?" he asked again. Snapping his fingers, something appeared, another string or thread, and there was a silver thing attached to it. Alice watched as he slipped something over the nub of her hard, pink nipple.

She squealed when she felt it tighten.

"What do you want?" He snapped his fingers again and this time she knew what would appear, where it would go, how she would writhe and moan and grit her teeth.

"I want you to fuck me," she whispered, eyes half-closed, feeling the throbbing promise of his cock between her thighs.

"No." He chuckled, tweaking her nipple, and the thing tightened again. She squeaked in surprise, biting her lip to draw sensation away from the spot. "Tell me what you really want."

What did she really want? She wanted Wade. She wanted a forever life with him, doing whatever he wanted to do, as long as she could follow him. She wanted to love and be loved, to give herself completely, to empty herself, body, mind and soul, and then to be filled up again with him.

Alice moaned when he tweaked both nipples, as if tuning a radio dial, tightening the fasteners and sending hot waves of pain and pleasure down between her thighs.

"I want…" she whispered, feeling his hips shifting, just barely, teasing her with the mushroom head of his cock. *Wade, I love you, this is all for you, everything for you.* She closed her eyes and let herself go limp. "To surrender."

He gave a low, triumphant growl and thrust deep, taking her pussy to the hilt and then digging in a little more. Alice cried out in surprise. She'd anticipated the size of him, but not quite enough. He began to fuck her, using long, teasing strokes, his big hands gripping her hips so hard she knew she would have bruises on the soft flesh of her behind.

Her nipples were tingling, going nearly numb from the pressure of the silver clamps there. Her arms ached from being suspended, but at least he had her hips, relieving some of the pressure at the juncture between her thighs. He began to thrust harder, faster, and Alice thought it would be over soon—far too soon. But that wasn't up to her. He could take his pleasure as he liked it. Her pleasure or pain was his choice.

Alice felt the world slipping and opened her eyes in alarm. The silver threads were moving again and she moved with them, like a puppet on strings. They lowered her head toward the floor until her shoulders rested on the strange, softly gelatinous stuff that had materialized on the dias. She sighed in relief as her arms fell free to her sides. Her body was now at a forty-five degree angle, half-suspended from the ceiling, and the king's gaze swept over her as he plunged between her thighs.

She watched him fuck her, the hot pounding of his cock shaking the whole dias beneath them. She wanted more, *needed* more, but couldn't speak. She didn't want to be punished again. There was nothing to do but give in, no matter what happened.

"Sweet Alice." The Red King was on top of her now, all of the strings gone slack, even the ones around her nipples. The sensation burned there, quicksilver, sending shockwaves between her legs. He used fast, hard thrusts, and she couldn't help it, she wrapped herself around him and began to rock herself toward climax.

It was like taking the weight of a boulder, a mountain, he was so thick and solid under her hands. She couldn't even get her legs all the way around his thrusting hips, so she just dug her heels in and arched. He groaned against her ear and began to grind his hips, not so much thrusting now as rutting.

"Please sir." She dared too much, always, but she couldn't help her need. She whispered the words, barely moving her lips to speak. "Please make me come."

He slowed just slightly and swallowed. She heard it. Fully expecting to be suspended and spanked again, she tensed and waited for the inevitable. Instead, he rocked her back with his powerful thighs, shifting her weight and lifting her legs in the air as he knelt between them.

"Touch yourself," he commanded.

Alice sighed happily, her fingers playing in her own wetness. He watched her, eyes dancing, as she rubbed her clit in circles, panting, eyes closing in blessed relief. From somewhere below them, Alice thought she heard a growl, something animal-like, but she was too distracted to really care.

"Don't come until I tell you." He was watching her and enjoying it, she could tell. She'd expected that command—

Wade asked it of her often enough. She was practiced at keeping herself hovering at the edge of orgasm, sometimes for hours. She'd found the anticipation sweet, and the longer it went on, the better the reward.

She groaned when he slid out of her pussy but she waited expectantly for his next move. Her fingers never stopped rubbing her little clit though. He moved to straddle her chest, rubbing the wet head of his cock against her swollen red nipples. That made her gasp. Then he shifted further up, sliding off that lime-green covering. It didn't snap off like a condom and she wondered at the soft mass it made next to them when he tossed it aside and pressed his cock to her lips.

"Suck it, Alice."

So she did, using tongue and lips and the soft insides of her mouth to caress every glorious inch of him. It was a lovely time. She so enjoyed giving pleasure to a man this way, feeling the involuntary thrust of his hips, the low growl building in his throat. Her pussy was so wet she was dripping juices down the crack of her ass. She had to stop rubbing so fast and instead just used her fingernail to graze her clit, back and forth, keeping herself at the edge of bliss.

"Oh god." His hand buried itself in her hair as he began to thrust in earnest, fucking her mouth, using it like a tight little cunt for his pleasure. She trembled beneath him, wanting nothing more than to taste the fruits of her effort. "Oh fuck, fuck. Alice!" His eyes flew wide and he buried himself into her mouth. "Come! Come for me!"

She cried out, but it was muffled by the enormous cock being driven into her throat, and did just as he asked, quite a feat considering she had to swallow his cum at the same time. All she had to do was press her finger once against her little clit and it went off like someone had lit fireworks between her legs, *pop, pop, pop*, growing bigger, coming faster, and then slowly fading to black. The Red King emptied himself completely into her eager, waiting mouth, and Alice swallowed every last drop, wondering at the taste. His seed was as sweet as honey.

"Oh your majesty." A saccharine sweet voice came from beneath the dias and Alice knew it was the Red Queen.

"Coming," he called, slowly extracting himself from Alice's still suckling mouth.

"Not anymore," Alice whispered and then giggled, wiping her lips with the back of her hand. She noticed with wonder that the restraints she had formerly worn were gone.

The Red King grinned and stood, towering over her for a moment before he stepped over the edge. She screamed at his sudden departure but when she looked over the side of the dias she could see nothing, no king or queen. The room was empty.

Alice rested on the platform, her body slick with sweat, now unrestrained, and stared up at the red and white big-top ceiling. Wade was here, somewhere, she was sure of it. This strange and wonderful night was his doing and there was probably more to come. She just hoped the rest of it included him.

She should have been cold but the room seemed to adjust to the perfect temperature and she drifted easily off to sleep thinking about her man. When she woke, the dias had descended, becoming part of the floor again, and she was resting on the original black and white parquet tiles. She lifted her head and looked around the room, which had been changed again in the time she'd been asleep. The bistro table was still there in a corner, but now there was another, a long thin one, kind of like a doctor's table.

Alice sat up, curious, and looked around. The room was still empty except for her, but she was sure someone was watching. She stood and made her way over to the new piece of furniture, running her hand over the padded surface. It was rather like a massage table. She'd been on a few of them, the kind with the hole at the end. It had seemed strange to her, but putting her face there during the massage had made the experience so much more enjoyable because her body could rest completely flat. Although this hole seemed to be in a strange place, much further down on the table than it should have been.

The other table still held the empty plate with the note, "eat me," which she already had, and the glass full of wine marked, "drink me." She hadn't had a chance before the Red King and Queen had come in and she found herself very dehydrated after that interlude. She lifted the glass, contemplating it for a moment. Maddie's voice threatened to surface and she smiled at the warning. Too late now.

"Bottom's up." She lifted the glass in a toast to some unseen observer and tilted it back. The stuff made her shudder, although a wine connoisseur might have enjoyed it. Alice finished the entire glass, putting it back on the table with a sigh. It was one of those things Wade had attempted to educate her about, and while she now knew various wines and could talk about them, she still couldn't fully appreciate them.

She smiled when the door opened behind her. Somehow she had known the moment the wine was gone, something would happen. She turned, fully expecting and ready to welcome Wade, only to find two large male guards pushing a man into the room between them. He had a red hood over his face and was wearing a ridiculous stretch-spandex suit, white with a red stripe down the side. The thing was crotchless and Alice swallowed when she saw the cock sticking straight out from a dark patch of pubic hair. He was outfitted with a cock ring that clearly kept him hard—and probably also kept him from coming.

"He's all yours, Mistress Alice." The guard on the left gave her a brief bow and the one on the right mimicked the gesture.

"Wait—" How many times had she said that during this strange night so far? "What do you mean?"

"He's your slave," the guard on the right explained. "Do with him what you will."

They started to go and the guard on the left looked back and remarked, "He's a mute."

Alice stared at the door that disappeared into the wall as they departed, aghast. The man stayed on his knees, waiting her instruction. *This isn't happening.* Alice glanced around the room, sure someone was watching her. This was part of the test. She was supposed to...what? Dominate this man? That was laughable. He wasn't quite as big as the Red King, but close. More Wade's size, which was at least double her own. Besides, she was submissive. She wasn't always the best bottom, but she had no desire to be on top.

She cleared her throat, blinking at her predicament. What to do? She moved over to the table to look as if she was doing something. There were drawers on one end and she opened them, stunned by the paraphernalia inside—sex toys, rubber gloves, lube. There were also strange objects she'd never seen before, and lots of packages of those lime-green condom-like things.

I can do this, she told herself, shutting the drawer and trying to imagine what Wade might say or do if he was in her place. By the time she turned around to face the masked man, she almost believed herself. Besides, the wine was making her warm, giving her a bit of liquid courage.

"Come here." She tried to make her voice, normally soft and light and sweet, into some semblance of a commanding tone. It sounded forced, even to her, but the man began to move. First, he tried standing, but then thought better of it and made his way over on his knees. Alice realized her mistake—incomplete instructions—and corrected it.

"Stand up and walk toward my voice."

The man stood, walking slowly in her direction, hesitating. She frowned and then smacked her forehead, realizing she needed to keep talking, "Keep coming. Closer. That's it. Almost there. Good. Stop."

He was quite a fine specimen of masculine flesh, she had to admit, even through the spandex. She thought about asking him to remove it—and the hood—but didn't know if she should. Maybe it would be better to keep this all anonymous, especially if she had to cause him any pain. Did she have to? She wondered, looking back at the table. She didn't know if she could. Maybe there was a way around it…

She turned toward the table, contemplating it, and then it dawned on her.

"Up on the table, big boy." She patted it and he felt his way to the edge, sliding up to sit there. His cock hadn't waned at all. It was still delightfully hard, probably in anticipation of what she was going to do, even though he had to be a little apprehensive with a new mistress.

Mistress. Me! Alice suppressed a smile at the thought. But she had to take this seriously, and she did. When she gave herself over to Wade, it was simply because she trusted him. She'd submitted to this night's strange events only because she trusted him. That was the first and most important thing.

"Safe word," she breathed, nodding. But how, if he was mute? Then she remembered what Wade did when he gagged her and she couldn't speak. "Your safe word will be three taps. Do you understand?"

The hood bobbed up and down.

"Show me," she instructed. He slapped his hand on the table three times, hard. The power behind it made her body flush with pleasure. He was a strong guy. "Good."

Okay, so they could get started. But now what?

"On your belly on the table." She watched him turn, negotiating without being able to see. "There's a hole in the middle of the table. Make sure your cock goes through it." He felt around and found it, positioning himself as she instructed.

She walked around the table, looking at him, at the fine shape of his muscles under the suit. She noticed for the first time that the same gelatinous stuff that had been on the dias was under the table—it was open underneath, resting on four legs, with the drawers at one end. She had an idea.

She was tuned into his breath almost immediately. He was excited, but waiting. She was familiar with that feeling. She raided the drawers for treasure, taking the toys with her and positioning herself under the table. His cock was full of blood, red and throbbing. The cock ring was silver and clutched both his cock and balls together.

"You have a very nice cock." It was dark under the table, but she could see that much. He moaned in pleasure when she took him in her hand, squeezing and pulling and generally testing his tolerance. Fluid gathered at the tip as she manipulated him and she rubbed it into the head. She wanted to lick it off but restrained herself.

"We're going to play a game." Alice reached over for a bottle of lube. "When I ask you a question, you're going to tap once for yes and twice for no. Do you understand?"

One tap.

"Have you ever been to the eye doctor?" she asked, grinning when he hesitated before tapping once. "Good. You know the part of the exam where they flip the little lenses back and forth and ask you, 'Better or worse?'"

One tap.

"This game is a little like that." She rubbed the oily stuff into her hands. "I'm going to do something and ask you, 'Better or worse?' And you're going to tap once for better, twice for worse. Do you understand?"

One tap. Good. "There's only one rule. You're not allowed to come until I say."

He let out a little noise when she wrapped her slick hand around his shaft. He clearly could make sounds but didn't speak. She stroked his length nice and slow, matching her motion with the sound of his breath. As it grew faster, louder, she increased her speed.

"Okay." She took a deep breath and let her fist slide down toward his pelvis, squeezing his shaft, her hand completely still. "Better or worse?"

Two taps.

She started moving it again, slow and easy, up to the head and back down.

"Better or worse?"

One tap. Of course. She smiled and reached over for a toy. It was a small vibrating egg. She pressed it to the head of his cock, right at the frenulum, and turned it on.

"Better or worse?"

He groaned. One tap. She began to rub it up and down the underside of his shaft, following the swollen, pulsing vein there.

"Better or worse?"

He hesitated and she heard his breath catch. Then two taps.

"Tough choice?" she asked, smiling. One tap. "Let's do an easier one."

She picked something else from the pile and used the soft silver thread—where did they get this stuff? She wondered—to tie the weight onto the cock ring. It hung heavily down, putting more pressure on both cock and balls. He gasped.

"Better or worse?" Two taps. Alice saw more precum at the tip of his cock and smiled. "I'm not sure I believe you. I think you might like it a little bit."

One hesitant tap. Indeed.

She hadn't realized how quickly she would take to this, how exciting it would be to hold someone else's pleasure or pain in your hands. Her pussy was on fire and she realized she could touch it any time she wanted. She could get up on the table, turn him over and fuck him, just use that big, gorgeous cock for her own pleasure. Or sit on his face and use his tongue. Oh god. The thought made her knees weak and she was glad she was lying down.

Instead, she took the egg, still vibrating, and tucked it between her swollen lips, right over her clit. Then she closed her thighs. It hummed gently, sending a sweet buzz of pleasure through her pelvis.

"You have a pretty cock," she murmured, scratching her nails over the tight sac of his balls. "But I think it's been bad. You really want to come, don't you?"

One tap.

"I think this cock needs to learn a lesson." Alice slapped it with the flat of her hand and the guy on the table let out a yelp of surprise. Then she slapped it again, this time toward the table. He jumped, jolted by the sensation, so she pressed it there, up against the underside of the table, and spanked the head with her other hand, changing direction, smacking it back and forth.

She stopped as quickly as she had started. His breath was coming fast and the weight on the cock ring was forcing long, sticky streams of precum to dribble from the end of his dick. The egg between her own thighs hummed relentlessly. Just seeing the way his cock bobbed with his pulse made her want to come and she fought the sensation. Not yet. Not quite yet.

She reached for one more toy, a vagina simulator, soft and rubbery in her hand. She made it slick with lube—not that he needed it, he was wet enough with precum and the oil from her hand—and grabbed hold of him again.

He groaned when she slid the sheath over the head of his cock and down onto his shaft.

"Better or worse?"

One very loud tap.

"It's not as good as my pussy," she revealed with a squeeze. "But you can't have that." She twisted the sheath and started to fuck him with it. "Better or worse?"

He grunted and tapped once, trying to thrust, but the table stopped his pelvis. His cock swelled—she could feel it, even through the sheath. He was close. Struggling. She didn't stop.

"Makes you want to come, doesn't it?" One short tap. "So tight and wet and hot…." Her movement increased, faster, faster. His breath matched her motion, panting. The sheath had a hole in both ends and she pressed it all the way down, slipping the head of his cock through the other end to see the red, bulbous head seeping precum.

He groaned and his whole body jerked on the table when her mouth covered the tip of him, sucking hard, swirling her tongue around and around. The egg on her clit was about to send her over the edge and she wanted to taste him, had to. Besides, the lube was tasty—strawberry.

She took her mouth off him long enough to say, "I want you to come in my mouth! Now!"

He let out a strangled cry of relief as she sucked him back in, the toy still bunched around his shaft, the weight hanging from the cock ring, and he did exactly as she'd asked, flooding her tongue with the peppery taste of his cum. Alice moaned and choked on it and swallowed, her own orgasm rolling through her in that instant, making her quiver with pleasure, her clit kissing the humming egg between her pussy lips again and again.

"Oh Alice." The man on the table barely whispered the words but her eyes widened and she knew—maybe she'd always known. In an instant she was standing and pulling off his hood to find a sweaty, half-smiling Wade beneath. "Alice," he murmured, his eyes still glazed, his look dazed. "I taught you so well."

"No." She backed away, holding her hands out in front of her as if she could push him away. Behind her there was commotion, someone coming into the room, but she didn't care.

Alice ran blindly. She didn't know how she got a door to open for her, but she did. The hallways twisted and turned and she could hear the Red Queen somewhere behind her calling, "Catch her! Quickly fools!"

She felt humiliated, unreal. The whole world felt upside down. She didn't understand how any of it had happened, no matter what she'd eaten or drank. People didn't go against their most basic natures, even under hypnotism. She knew that much from Maddie. So what did that mean?

It means you enjoyed it.

But I didn't. I couldn't have. Things were so different here, backwards, wrong. She wished she was home, that she had never come here. But she couldn't go so far as to wish she had never met Wade, had never bent her will to his. That much she knew.

"There she is!"

Alice took a fast left, hearing them behind her, pushing hard against the wall and finally finding what she was a looking for—a hidden black door. She fell inside and it closed quickly behind her, sealing. They rushed by, calling to one another, still chasing after her. She breathed a sigh of relief to hear their voices fading down the corridor. It was only then that she glanced around to see where she might be now.

Her jaw dropped and she flushed at the sight before her. The room was small and filled with a giant four-poster bed. It was draped like the ceiling of the other room had been, with red and white gauze. On the bed was a scene so strange Alice had to blink and rub her eyes like a cartoon to make sure she wasn't dreaming.

A man wearing a tall top hat was standing in the middle of the bed, his arms stretched toward the ceiling, bound somewhere above his head. Three women knelt between his thighs, all of them taking turns sucking the not insignificant length of his cock.

Beside him on the left another man was handcuffed to the headboard. He was watching the display of fellatio with great interest, his own cock thick and full and looking in need of attention. He writhed on the bed making whimpering noises, sounding as if he was in great agony to be just watching instead of participating. This man was so covered in dark body hair it seemed as if he was more animal than man. That fact, coupled with the desperate undulations he made trying to get near the women, made him look, to Alice, like a fuzzy caterpillar.

The man handcuffed to the bedpost to the right of the top hat one wasn't so ambiguously anthropomorphic—his whole body was painted like a cat, a red and white striped one, with whiskers and dark charcoaled eyes. Even his cock had been painted with stripes. He gave out a plaintive wail as he watched the three women giving so much attention to the top hat man in the middle.

The three girls were on their knees, dressed in red corsets that pushed their breasts up high, the crotch splitting to reveal shaved pubes beneath. It wasn't much material, but Alice recognized it at once—it was the same corset the Red Queen wore under her peignoir. All three women were very different—a petite blonde like Alice, a busty redhead and a tall brunette—every man's wet dream trio.

The top hat man had long dark, curly hair and a wicked smile. He thrust his pelvis in her direction, making the redhead gag on his dick. Then he called out to Alice, "Twinkle twinkle little bat, how I wonder what you're at?"

She stood and took in the scene in stunned, embarrassed silence, realizing that she, too, was humiliatingly naked. He was looking at her with bright, hungry eyes. They all were.

"What is this place?" Alice whispered, feeling the words burning in her throat.

But she knew the answer, even as the caterpillar man lifted his head and asked, "Who are you?"

All three women spoke in unison, "This is Wonderland!"

"You're mad." Alice choked on her words, trying to cover herself with her hands. It only seemed to draw their attention to her body even more.

"We're all mad here." The cat man laughed and it sounded like a scream. The three women were already off the bed, heading toward her. Alice backed up against the wall, the cool stone chilling her behind, but the door didn't open.

"Come play," the blonde whispered, sliding an arm around Alice's waist.

She found herself on the bed, stretched out at the end in front of the man with the top hat, while the three women crawled over her like cats, stretching out, licking with their pink tongues, rolling against her softness. She couldn't keep track of all of them, hands and limbs and hair. She knew only sensation—the soft press of a mouth between her thighs, the sweet suckle against her breast, the honey taste of a pussy poised over her tongue.

Alice moaned and came, and came, and came again. She had strange visions of the man in the top hat watching, his cock weeping at the sight of them, his eyes mad with lust. The man beside him howled like a tomcat who'd found a female in heat on the other side of an impenetrable fence. They were all three raging mad, trying to get to the mass of women soaking in one another's pleasure at their feet.

"Check in here!" The door swung wide and Alice lifted her dazed head to see the Red Queen stalking toward the bed. Her wild eyes widened at the sight of Alice spread-eagle on the bed, the three women still working hands and tongues and fingers in her orifices. The queen's guard burst in behind her. "Here! She's here!" The Red Queen pointed at Alice and screeched, "And she's stolen my tarts!"

"I didn't steal anything," Alice insisted indignantly, trying to sit up in the midst of the soft, supple flesh pile they made together. But the women whimpered and looked around with worried eyes and sat up to clutch each other as the Red Queen raved. It took Alice a few moments to understand.

"You stole my tarts!" The Red Queen insisted, waving her finger at the women until, one by one, they climbed off the bed and went to kneel at her feet, head down. "Off with her head! Off with it, now!"

"Off with my…what?" Alice felt as if her blood had turned to ice.

The guards grabbed Alice without another word, one at each arm. She tried to walk but they were too tall and dragged her to the door. The Red Queen followed, the three tarts falling in line behind her.

"I say!" called the Mad Hat Man. "Don't forget us here!"

But the door was closed behind them and the guards were dragging her down the hall before she could hear him say anymore. Poor Caterpillar, poor Cat, poor Mad Hat Man. She wondered who might come along to release them. Certainly someone, and soon. This place had to have rules. They had safe words, after all. That proved something. It had to. They might get kicked out, of course, after being with the queen's tarts, she surmised. That was apparently against the rules.

And she'd been with the queen's tarts, hadn't she?

Oh yes, she most definitely had.

"Tweedledee." The sound in front of them drew Alice's attention. There were two men coming toward them, filling all the available space in the hallway.

"Tweedledum." As they got closer, Alice could see they were both naked, their bellies so rotund and pendulous they obscured their privates. They were twins, had to be, with the same moon faces and wide smiles. They were also holding hands as they came down the hall, making an impenetrable wall of flesh blocking the way.

"Tweedledee." The one on the right would say this, and the one on the left would echo it with, "Tweedledum."

The guards stopped. An impasse.

"Out of our way!" The Red Queen waved from behind them. "Get!"

The two brothers looked at each other, behind them, then back at the queen, incredulous. There was no way they could turn around. Even if the two of them went single file, they wouldn't all squeeze past. The twins grew very distraught, mumbling, *tweedledumtweedledee tweedledumtweedledee tweedledumtweedledee* over and over, their hands flapping at their sides like trapped birds.

"Oh for heaven's sake!" The Red Queen threw up her hands and pushed against the wall to her left. A door opened and Alice watched in wonder as another hallway appeared. How did anyone keep track of where anything was in this place? She wondered. But she didn't have long to ponder the question because the hallway led around into another, and that one let them into a great hall where food and sex and games had all melded into one great orgy of excess.

Alice winced as the guards dragged her to the front of the room, depositing her without ceremony on the floor in front of two large thrones. They were silver, not gold, high backed and upholstered in red. The Red Queen huffed past Alice, sitting in one of them and reaching for a long cord beside her chair. She pulled it, but nothing happened.

"Please." Alice spoke, still trying to cover herself, everything about her trembling. "Let me explain."

"Verdict now, explanations later," the queen snapped. "Did you or did you not steal my tarts?"

"I didn't steal them," Alice protested, glancing over at the women. "They rather stole me."

"What say you?" The queen turned to the trio but they just shook their heads, quivering together.

"This is just a formality." The queen waved Alice's protests away. "I saw you with my own eyes. Collar her."

Alice didn't know what it meant until one of the guards fit a red collar around her throat and snapped it closed. She clawed at it, but it seemed to close seamlessly, like everything else in this strange place.

"Now!" The Red Queen pointed at Alice and one of the guards pressed her down to her knees. "Off with her head!"

This isn't happening, Alice thought, but the flash of a blade behind her made it very immediate. One of the guards was holding an old-time executioner's ax and it looked very real.

"Wait!" There was that word again, but this time Alice didn't speak it. Wade burst into the room wearing a white robe trimmed in red and silver, something similar to what the Red King had been wearing when she met him. And where was the king anyway? She wondered, glancing around the hall. The place was full with bodies, writhing, moaning, piled on top of one another, but she didn't see him.

"I call for mediation." Wade stepped between the guard and Alice, grabbing her upper arms and bringing her to standing. She had never felt so safe and leaned back gratefully against him. "Where's the Red King?"

"Mediation?" The Red Queen snorted and waved her hand. "What do we need that for?"

"For fun of course." The Red King appeared, seemingly out of nowhere, his robe only half-closed, although he was trying to fix that. He grinned and winked at Alice and she instantly relaxed. "The girl has to solve a riddle. How's that, my pet?" He raised an eyebrow in the queen's direction.

"Oh fiddlesticks." The Red Queen turned her nose in the air, waving the idea away.

"Wait." Wade took a step toward the Red King. "If she solves it, we crown a new king and queen."

Both of the king's eyebrows rose. "That's quite a wager."

"I believe in her." Wade looked over at Alice and gave her the smile that made her melt into little puddles.

But she couldn't do this. Solve riddles? It was insane. "Wade…"

"So be it!" The Red Queen's eyes brightened as she looked at Alice. "Solve the riddle and you will be the new queen."

Alice gulped. "I'll do my best."

"Tell me…" The queen leaned forward on her throne, her lips curling into a wicked smile. "Why is a raven like a writing desk?"

Alice blinked, frowned, and looked over to Wade for help. If she failed, what did it mean? Were they really going to chop off her head? And if she solved it, well what did *that* mean? Is this what Wade had meant about being together, forever? Or was this part of the test?

She tried to think of any way the two things could be related but couldn't come up with anything. A crowd had gathered around them, distracted from their own distractions by the queen's proclamation. Finally, Alice had to admit defeat. Ravens and writing desks had nothing in common. They were going to cut off her head and she was never going to see Wade again.

She swallowed hard and met his eyes, blinking back her tears. She didn't regret dying for him, not really. She just hated to disappoint him. More than anything, she wished she could be back home snuggled under her down comforter with Dinah while Wade made pancakes in her little kitchen. Thinking of home made her remember Maddie, and how she'd never see her again either. Her poor sister would always wonder what had happened to her.

And that's when it came to her. Maddie and her solid belief in science was going to save her life in this strange, surreal place.

"A raven is like a writing desk…" Alice swallowed and turned to meet the Red Queen's eyes, feeling rather triumphant. "Because a raven and a writing desk are, without a doubt, scientifically proven to be both made of atoms."

The whole crowd was quiet and then a deafening cheer went up around her. The queen stood, sputtering her protest, but the king, looking proud and amused, stepped in.

"That's as good an answer as I've ever heard," he exclaimed, reaching out and grabbing Alice's hand. He kissed it gently as he had the first time and the way he looked at her made her flush.

"That's not the answer!" the queen screeched. "There is no answer to that riddle!"

But no one heard her. They were all starting to chant: "Long live the White King! Long live the White Queen!" and a white robe trimmed with red and silver was being draped around Alice's shoulders. She smiled over at Wade and he winked at her. The Red King was shaking his hand and passing over his crown and didn't look too upset to be giving it up either.

"Look out!" The cry came from behind her and Alice whirled toward the sound, a woman's voice. One of the tarts pointed at the queen's throne, where the Red Queen had tussled for and won the executioner's ax from the guard. She wielded the heavy, ungainly thing with no grace or skill, but it didn't seem to matter. The queen swung and the ax was headed straight for the red collar around Alice's neck as if it were a magnet.

The last thing she heard was the Red Queen screaming, "Off with her head!"

* * * *

"Alice." The sound of her name was far away, in another world. "Alice! Wake up!"

She jolted awake at his command, gasping and clutching Wade to her. He wrapped his big arms around her and held her close, rocking her in the darkness.

"Was I dreaming?" she whispered incredulously. "Was it only a dream?"

"It must have been something." Wade chuckled and kissed her forehead. "You were screaming 'Off with her head!'"

Alice's hand went to her throat, which was thankfully still attached to her head. And then she felt it—a collar. It was fastened seamlessly to her neck and she was sure, if she turned on a light and looked into a mirror, that it would be red.

"Wade…" she whispered, fingering the band at her neck. "Was it really a dream?"

He was quiet for a moment and then he asked, "Do you want it to be?"

In an instant, she relived every moment in the strange land she'd visited and knew, no matter what her sister said about Alice's imagination, it was as real as she was, as real as Wade or ravens or writing desks.

"No," she admitted.

His lips moved over her neck, kissing her new collar. "Then let's go back to Wonderland."

She surrendered.

Her only regret was that she would have to leave Maddie behind. But maybe, some day, she could convince her sister to come over to the other side.

GRETEL

Gretel loved her big brother and he had to admit—he took advantage of that fact on occasion. It wasn't that Hans didn't care about her. He did. But to him she was just his sometimes-annoying little sister, the one who used to tag along and make his life miserable at pick-up baseball games when she wanted to run around all the bases with him.

He'd finally gotten her to stay on the sidelines, watching him with worship-filled eyes, but he could never get her to stay home, and his stepmother was no help in that regard—the old bat didn't want to be bothered with either of them, especially in the summer when the two of them had an extra eight hours a day, five days a week to spend in her hair.

But Gretel didn't just love her brother—Gretel worshipped him, always had, although he hadn't done anything to deserve the attention. And Hans figured, if you couldn't beat them, why not join them? So he didn't feel too awfully bad about taking advantage of her willingness to do something—anything—for him. She seemed to want to, and who was he to argue?

Although occasionally he felt guilty, like now when his sister presented him with a gift on the occasion of her eighteenth birthday instead of the other way around. He had something for her, of course, but the surprise party wasn't until that night and he didn't want to spoil it for her.

"Gret, it's *your* birthday, not mine."

"I know." She just smiled and held the pretty wrapped package out for him, practically vibrating with excitement. What could he do but take it?

"I shouldn't let you do this," he grumbled, snatching the package from her hands, feeling the heavy weight of it, already wondering, in spite of himself, what could be inside. No one knew him and what he liked and secretly wanted like Gretel did.

"Open it!" she insisted, shifting from foot to foot as she stood in the doorway to his room. There was no dampening Gretel's enthusiasm—she was 220 volts running on a 110 line.

"Did you spend your own money?" He put the gift on his desk where he'd been studying for his organic chemistry final, deciding to torture her a little and increase his own anticipation.

"What other money is there to spend?" She rolled her eyes, glancing over her shoulder as if their penny-pinching stepmother might be lurking in the hallway. "Now open it!" She picked the package back up off the desk, shoving it into his lap. "Before she comes home and asks where I got the money to buy it."

Hans raised his eyebrows, hefting the box again. "Where *did* you get the money?"

"Open! Open! Open!" she chanted, ignoring his question.

He finally did, finding a large obstruction in his throat in the way of a "thank you." Gretel just beamed, exclaiming about the gift, telling him where she'd purchased it and how much she knew it would help his research.

"It's not as expensive as you think," she assured him, seeing the look on his face as he gazed from her to the microscope in his hands. "I got a good deal. At least the Attack Jack taught me how to bargain hunt!"

Hans laughed at her use of that old, secret name for their stepmother—Jack, after the cheapskate Jack Benny, and the "attack" part, well, the woman was known for her malicious, manipulative and underhanded tactics. Even against her stepchildren. Especially against her stepchildren.

"You are the best sister ever." Hans stood and gave her a one-armed hug, still holding the microscope in the other. "What am I going to do without you?"

"Why, what have you heard?" Her eyes widened as Hans sat back down, putting the microscope on his desk, gazing at it fondly. "Are they sending me to military school?"

"Worse." He sighed, meeting her wary eyes. "Finishing school."

"Oh god." Gretel's face drained of blood, her normally rosy cheeks turning to marble. "I'd really prefer the Marines!" She blinked at him in disbelief and then exploded in her usual, spontaneous way. "*You* got to go to college! Why not me?"

Hans winced at the whine in her voice. "I heard her telling Dad that you wouldn't be able to find a suitable husband in college."

"Suitable meaning *rich.*" Gretel snorted, rolling her eyes toward the ceiling.

"Of course." He smirked. "How else are we supposed to pay off all the debt Dad's in?"

"You mean the debt *she* racked up since she married him!" his sister hissed, glancing toward the open door.

Hans shrugged. "As soon as I have a degree, I promise, I'll get a job and we'll find a place together and get out of here."

"You'll probably get married and forget all about me by then." She pouted, crossing her arms and looking unhappily at her own reflection in the mirror over his dresser.

"I won't forget about you, sis. I promise." Hans smiled indulgently, standing to give her another hug, this time with two arms. "Now, you better go get dressed up."

"How come?" She pulled away, giving him that wary look again.

"That's all I'm saying." He made a turning motion with his hand in front of his lips—locked up tight. But she already knew, he could tell by the look in her eyes, and he wasn't sorry he'd slipped. He liked seeing that ridiculously happy look on her face, in spite of her annoying habits, like buying him gifts on her own danged birthday.

"Really?" Gretel squealed, shoving him away and clapping her hands, starting to preen in his mirror. "Oh, I wish I had a new dress."

Hans sighed at the downturn at the corners of her mouth, already giving in. Okay, so his stepmother had picked it out and wrapped it for him—and paid for it too. She insisted on doing all the household purchasing, down to their underwear and socks. But it would make Gretel happy, and that's all that mattered. "Look in my closet. There's a gift for you in there."

His sister squealed again in delight when she opened his birthday present, giving him a quick thank-you kiss on the cheek before running down the hall and around the corner like she used to run around bases, off to try it on.

* * * *

"I still can't get over at this dress!" Gretel nudged her brother again at the punch bowl, her voice dropped to a stage-whisper. Hans handed over a glass of red punch—a disaster waiting to happen with the cream-colored satin backless gown she was wearing, but she took it anyway—and he gave her another once-over with his eyes.

"She picked it out, you know," he admitted, the punch in his own glass gone in one swig.

"I know." Gretel smirked. "But that's what I mean. Why would she get me something so…so…*nice!* So *expensive!*"

"Good question." He shrugged, dismissing her as their father approached, holding his own glass of punch. He smiled at them both fondly, and Gretel sighed at the look on his face. That expression hadn't changed since they were little. It was love mixed, with a deeper sorrow and an even deeper guilt he never spoke and probably didn't even know was there.

"How are you liking your party, little miss?" Her father kissed her cheek, his breath hazy with alcohol. He'd obviously been sneaking it by their stepmother, probably pouring it from a flask into his punch. "Eighteen! I can't believe it! Where did the time go?"

"It's a lovely party, Daddy." Gretel looked around at the room full of adults—all of her stepmother's friends and acquaintances mingling with her father's business associates.

There wasn't one of Gretel's own friends in the bunch. "Thank you."

"Thank your mother!"

Stepmother. Gretel corrected him bitterly in her head, but she let her smile widen as the woman approached, towering over their father, throwing him completely in shadow. If she had been asked to pick an antithesis, someone so different, so frozenly polar opposite from the warm, feminine being that their real mother had been, Gretel would have chosen Vivian without a second thought.

"This is all Viv's doing." Their father looked up at the woman with such a grateful expression it made Gretel want to vomit.

"Thank you for the party." Gretel said what she knew her father wanted her to say, even managing to do it without gritting her teeth, and he smiled approvingly.

"Nothing is too good for our cherubs." Viv flashed them a smile—her smiles were full of straight, white teeth, almost blinding. She was a beautiful woman even at her age, her long dark hair pulled up and back in complicated coils and loops, the material of her dress hugging her curves like blue waves. Gretel knew the tag was likely still attached to it, tucked up somewhere, hidden, just as hers was. Hans smiled, taking his cue and complimenting their stepmother on her appearance. She beamed, but Gretel saw her brother roll his eyes and sneer as Vivian leaned in to whisper something in their father's ear.

"Hey Sis, whatcha think are in all those boxes up there?" Hans nodded toward the gift table piled high with presents.

"Nothing could be better than the dress Hans got me." Gretel winked, knowing who had picked it out, playing the game, appeasing their stepmother. It didn't matter what was in the boxes up on the table and they all knew it—if they contained something her stepmother liked and wanted to keep, she would do so— the rest would be returned for cash.

Vivian brightened at Gretel's comment, stage-whispering, "I picked it out for him."

"Really?" Gretel acted surprised. "Well I love it!" That was the first true thing she'd spoken to the woman all night. The dress really was something, and she was thrilled to be wearing it, even though she knew it would be going back to the dress shop tomorrow. She still couldn't figure out why her stepmother had chosen something so stylish, so adult. She was usually stuck in pink little-girl dresses. *Maybe it's preparation for finishing school.* Gretel blanched at that thought.

"It will make a wonderful first impression." Vivian nodded her approval, taking their father by the elbow. "Come along, Ralph, I have someone I want you to meet."

Gretel watched them go, making a face behind their backs that made Hans laugh. She turned to her brother and asked, "First impression?"

Hans shrugged. "I have no idea."

"Here." Gretel handed him her untouched cup of punch. "After that, I need some air."

He gulped down the drink before calling after her, "Don't go far. Jack Attack said she had an announcement to make around nine and she wants us both here."

"Oh joy," she mumbled under her breath, waving her brother's reminder away as she made her way through the crowd. It was her own birthday and she didn't even want to be here. No one stopped her or said "happy birthday" or even "hello" as she made her way toward the exit. Vivian had rented a hall and had it all catered—on credit, of course. Everything she bought was on credit.

The hallway was five degrees cooler than inside and she took a deep breath, but it wasn't quite enough. She found her way down the hall and around the corner, following the corridors. The rooms back here were dark, unused. They were the only party going on in the place. She came across a metal door with a steel opening bar under a red "exit" sign. It was February and bitter cold outside, but she didn't care, hitting the bar with both hands and flinging the door wide.

She inhaled deeply, standing in her heels on a lighted pathway—someone had shoveled the snow—closing her eyes in relief. It was cold, the wind stinging her bare back, but it felt strangely good, at least for a moment.

"Hey! Wait! The door!"

She heard it swing shut behind her but it was too late. The man who bolted past her to reach for the handle swore, yanking hard, but it was no use. It had closed and locked.

"Oops." Gretel turned to face both the man and the now-locked door, the cold suddenly far more biting than it had just a moment before. "Sorry."

"Me too." He sighed, slipping a cell phone into his suit coat pocket and gazing longingly at the door. "Locked out twice. What are the odds?"

"You came out to make a phone call?" she asked, although that was obvious.

He nodded, giving her the once-over. "You?"

"Just to get some air." Although now she thoroughly regretted the decision, even if the guy she'd ended up stranded with was rather attractive. She turned and pounded her fists on the door. "Hello! Help!"

She waited a moment for a response and started pounding again, yelling louder. Then she waited again—still nothing. She stood there, panting, realizing that even if she wasn't getting an answer, at least the motion had made her feel a little warmer.

"I tried that." The guy leaned against the door, crossing his arms and looking at her. "Until you came along, no luck."

"Still no luck, apparently." She snorted. "Well where are we? There have to be other doors."

He nodded, gesturing to the enclosed space they were in, a patio area they obviously used for gatherings in warmer weather. There were a few doors with that red "exit" sign illuminated from the inside. "Yep. And they're all locked."

"You have a cell phone." Gretel sighed in frustration, her teeth beginning to chatter. She didn't have one of course—neither of them were allowed. Too expensive. "Can't you call someone?"

"It's a great idea," he agreed, patting his jacket pocket. "But unfortunately, I can't get a signal. That's why I came out here in the first place—I was hoping I could get a signal outside. Still no luck."

She didn't doubt it. They were in a sort of cell phone dead-zone. Her father complained about it all the time. "Maybe a window?" She hugged herself, really shivering now.

"That was my next plan." The man frowned, slipping his jacket off and draping it around her shoulders. "Here. Better?"

"Th-th-thanks."

"I'm Drew. Andrew Hess." He was still standing close, his arm around her shoulders, but he was warm and blocking the wind, so she didn't protest.

"Gretel Anderson"

"I know." He smiled at her look of surprise. "Happy birthday."

"Thanks." Of course. It was her party, and everyone knew her—but she knew no one. She wondered who Andrew Hess was. Some business associate of her father's maybe? He had that smart, professor look about the face, but he was a big man—far bigger than her father or her brother.

He guided her down the shoveled, stone path. "Come on. I can't be responsible for the birthday girl turning into a Popsicle."

Gretel watched, acting the part of the damsel in distress, as Andrew tried the first window and found it locked. He systematically went around the patio, trying every window, while her hopes dropped with every failure. Aside from being cold, she was imagining what Vivian's reaction would be when she wasn't there for the grand "announcement." Probably just something about finishing school. She didn't really care if she missed it, but she did care about the repercussions afterward. Vivian would find some way to make her life miserable—*more miserable.*

"Success!" Andrew called over his shoulder. "Come on, princess, let's get you back to the ball!"

Thank God. She hated living her life worried about how Vivian would react to everything she said and did, but it was the path of least resistance. At least she and Hans were in it together.

"Ladies first." Andrew smiled and bowed, waving toward the now open window. The lights were off inside but in the moonlight she could see the reflection of a surface that looked as if it might be a desk.

"Um..." Gretel eyed the window as she approached, frowning down at her dress. "This isn't gonna be easy."

"Want a boost?" He locked his hands together and bent low.

"Um..." She looked from him to the window, debating. "Oh fuck it."

He laughed as she slipped off her shoes and tossed them through the window, hiking her dress high up on her thighs and slipping a leg over the edge. She found herself straddling the window ledge, wincing as she felt a run starting in her pantyhose as she scraped her flesh over the edge of the metal, giving Andrew far more of a view than she'd intended.

"You okay?" he called as she slid to the floor with a muffled "oof," her dress pooled around her in a satin puddle.

"Fine," she assured him, getting quickly to her feet and looking around the dim room. Definitely someone's office, she could tell that even in the dark.

"Good." Andrew swung both legs gracefully through the window and slipped inside. "I wouldn't want to be accused of breaking the birthday girl." He slid the window closed, shutting out the cold, and turned to face her. "Is there a light in here?"

"On the desk maybe?" Gretel felt her way across the surface, trying to see in the silvery moonlight, and found what she was looking for, flicking the lamp's switch and illuminating the room.

"That's better." Andrew bent to pick up her heels. "Yours?"

"Thanks." Gretel took them, using the desk to lean against to slip them back on. "Well, that was quite an adventure."

"Every girl should have an adventure on her birthday." He smiled and she couldn't help notice the dimple that appeared in his left cheek, like a sly wink. She wondered how old he was. Older than her brother, certainly older than she was. An older man, but not old. No, not very old.

"I must be a mess." Gretel touched her hair, a mass of red curls on the top of her head, feeling several stray strands falling around her face. Her gorgeous dress was damp on the bottom from the snow and it stuck to her legs. Probably dirty too, she reasoned, not looking down to check but thinking of the tag tucked into the bodice, realizing she wasn't going to be able to return it. Her stepmother was going to be angry, and although she wasn't looking forward to the lecture, she was rather glad she would get to keep the dress. Especially the way Andrew was admiring her in it in the lamp light, in spite of her disheveled appearance.

"Actually, you look...great." There was that dimple again, just a brief appearance, a flash of a smile. The pause that followed was a little awkward and full of so much heat that Gretel thought she might actually faint. From far away, she heard the faint strains of music, but the look in Andrew's eyes had captured her attention almost completely. He straightened suddenly, taking her by the elbow. "Whoops, I think that's your cue."

"It is?" She looked up at him quizzically as he steered her toward the door and opened it, letting the still-faint sound of "Happy Birthday" seep into the room.

"They're playing your song." He grinned and that dimple deepened. "Come on, don't want you turning into a pumpkin or something."

They followed the sound of the music back to the hall, arriving breathless at the doors just as an enormous cake with a large silver wax "18" candle lit on top was being wheeled up to the front of the room. Drew steered her by her elbow behind the cake as the whole crowd began to sing "Happy Birthday" on cue from the DJ.

Gretel couldn't help the flush creeping into her cheeks as she used the stairs to join her brother and father on stage. Her stepmother was there, furious under her plastered-on smile, as the cake cart came up the ramp to the middle of the platform.

"There's our birthday girl!" The DJ—a master of ceremony of sorts—announced as the birthday song ended. "Make a wish, Gretel!"

She felt Hans slip his hand into hers, giving it a big squeeze. She knew what he was thinking—that she would wish for freedom, for opportunity, not just for herself, but for them both. Glancing over at her father, his tired eyes and faint smile, she would have given that wish away for him in a heartbeat if she thought it might do him any good.

"Psst." The sound was soft but she heard anyway, seeing Andrew standing down in front, just part of the crowd now. She met his eyes as he mouthed the word 'adventure,' waggling his eyebrows, and she nearly laughed out loud.

Closing her eyes, she made her wish—*please let me have an adventure*—and blew out the candles, leaving whiffs of blue smoke hovering above the pink and white cake. The crowd clapped and the cake was wheeled away again, guests already lining up to taste the three-foot high concoction.

"The family has one more announcement before Gretel opens her gifts." The DJ was a short, balding man and Gretel saw the faint look of fear in the man's eyes as he handed the microphone over to Vivian in her heels. She made him look even more diminutive as she snatched it from him, and Gretel almost wanted to apologize and tell him, *it's not you she's mad at, it's me.*

"We have a very special guest here tonight." Vivian was so mad she was practically purring as she handed the microphone over to a woman Gretel had hardly noticed standing behind her brother and her father. The two of them parted so the old woman could come forward and take the microphone, and although Gretel had never seen her before, she looked oddly familiar.

"Thank you so much." The old woman's voice was clear and steady, and so were her eyes. "I'd like to introduce myself to you—and to my lovely granddaughter."

Gretel straightened, looking wide-eyed at her family, seeing her father mouthing the words, "Your mother's mother." As if she wouldn't know. His parents had died before both she and Hans were born. This was the grandmother she had never met, the one her mother had insisted they never have anything to do with.

Gretel stepped a little closer to her brother, whispering, "What is this?"

"An ambush." He shrugged, watching as their grandmother spoke.

"I have been estranged from my grandchildren for many years, but thanks to the reunification efforts of their stepmother..." The old woman nodded at Vivian, smiling warmly, and Gretel felt her stomach clench at the way the two women looked at each other. "Now that both of them are of-age, I am being given the opportunity to be in their lives once more."

She and Hans exchanged glances, his eyebrows rising in surprise. To their knowledge, it had been their grandmother who had disinherited their mother for marrying their father. It has been their grandmother who had told her daughter to get out and never come back. Although their father had assured his wife before she died that he would never allow their grandmother into their lives. *He promised*, Gretel remembered. She'd been young when her mother died—barely in kindergarten—but she remembered that conversation very vividly. Their mother hadn't wanted them to have anything to do with the woman who had given birth to her—although neither she nor Hans had ever found out why. Their father wouldn't talk about it.

The old woman smiled at her and Gretel feigned a smile back, her whole body tensing at her grandmother's words. "My gift to this beautiful young lady—and her handsome brother—is a two-week cruise on my private yacht in Australia so we can all get acquainted."

The crowd gave a collective gasp and began applauding and of course Gretel didn't have to act surprised—she was. She looked over at her brother and saw he had stars in his eyes, probably already planning what he was going to do on this sudden, luxurious vacation. Both she and Hans had a two week mid-winter break starting on Monday. Clearly this had been planned. The smug, greedy look on her stepmother's face told her that much. Something was up, she just knew it. Her grandmother and stepmother had hatched some sort of plan, although she couldn't fathom would it might be.

"What do you say, Gretel?" Vivian nudged her a little too sharply and Gretel smiled, leaning over so her voice would be heard through the microphone.

"Thank you."

What else could she say? Looking down at the crowd, she saw the man who had rescued her from the cold—he saw her too and smiled, showing her that dimple again—and she found herself thinking it might have been better if she'd stayed locked outside. Although, glancing between her grandmother and stepmother, two clearly very powerful women, Gretel knew she was outmatched.

And she had wished for an adventure, hadn't she?

* * * *

Hans felt his jaw clenching as Andrew stepped in front of him, holding out a hand to Gretel to help her off the ladder. Water sheeted off her body, clad in only a black bikini, onto the deck as she pulled her mask and snorkel off, her red hair sticking in dark curls to the sides of her face. Hans stepped back, taking off his own mask and snorkel as his sister looked up at Andrew with big eyes.

"Oh my god you should have seen it!" Gretel exclaimed, shaking her wet head like a dog, spraying a fully-dressed Andrew with water, but he didn't seem to mind. Normally, Hans would have liked Andrew—his grandmother's personal assistant and bodyguard seemed like an all around great guy—but he didn't like the way the man hung around his sister, the way he looked at her.

"Did you see the stingray?" Gretel turned those familiar, worshipful eyes toward him and Hans smiled, about to respond, when her attention shifted back to Andrew again. "There were jellyfish, Drew! And stingrays and turtles! And the coral was magical! And these gorgeous blue and yellow fish—"

"Sweetlips." Andrew nodded, smiling indulgently, that fat dimple on his cheek deepening as he handed Gretel a towel.

"What did you call me?" His sister flushed prettily, using the towel to dry off. He wished she would cover up with it.

"That's the name of the fish." Andrew laughed. "But it would be the perfect nickname for you."

"Oh you! Stop!" Gretel sounded very much like she didn't want Andrew to stop at all.

Hans ignored them and grabbed his own towel from a stack, using it to dry his wet, salty hair. He never in his life would have imagined he would be snorkeling in the Coral Sea—at least not while he was still under his stepmother's thumb. The woman had made their lives hell for years, keeping up the appearance of wealth on credit while denying her stepchildren every possibly convenience. He had blamed his father when he was an adolescent, but the older he got, the more he realized how much his father was just trying to escape the grief of losing his first wife any way he could.

And in some weird way, he knew Vivian had been his father's answer to taking care of two children he had no idea how to raise on his own. His father, like him, was a scientist, a professor, a man of logic and reason who got lost when the world upending in emotional upheaval. Vivian had been the perfect, logical answer—a woman who claimed to love and want him, who would care for his two young children while he did research on one of the world's most important discoveries—the Genome project.

Of course, that was back before the university had lost its funding, back when his father was on track to becoming one of the most well-renowned—and well-paid—scientists in the country. Vivian had hitched herself to his father's rising star, only to see it plummet to earth like a stone. He supposed he couldn't blame the woman for feeling a little bitter, but he knew in his heart, had his mother been alive, she would have been proud of her husband regardless.

Hans draped the towel around his shoulders and walked to the railing of the yacht, looking down at the impossibly clear, deep blue water below, thinking about his mother. Gretel had been so little when she died, she didn't remember too much, but he remembered everything—his mother's pain, the cancer spreading from the tumor on her arm to her bones and finally to her liver and her brain. Redheads were so susceptible to skin cancer, and his mother had been such an outdoor lover, the combination had proved deadly.

He couldn't believe how much of a hole it had left in his life, a gaping wound that even a kind, motherly stepmother would have had a hard time filling. But adding Vivian to his life had been less like putting a band-aid on a bleeding artery, and more like taking a chainsaw to a limb or two. He hadn't realized how much he had longed for someone who would be gentle with him, someone who would attempt to fill that horrible gap.

Until he met his maternal grandmother.

"You'll have to go diving with me instead of just snorkeling." Andrew took a seat next to Gretel on a chaise chair, handing her some sort of drink with an umbrella in it.

"I don't know how to dive." She sipped the fruity concoction, settling herself in her own chaise, soaking up the sun. Her creamy skin was already turning pink.

"Gretel, you should put on more sunscreen," Hans warned, inwardly groaning at the situation he had created when Andrew offered to spread the creamy lotion on his sister's pale skin. She accepted his help willingly enough—too willingly, as far as he was concerned. He didn't know why it bothered him so much. There had been plenty of boyfriends in Gretel's life, and Hans had been part of many a plot to get Gretel out of the house on a date their stepmother didn't know about. So why did Andrew bother him so much?

"Oh, I can teach you how to dive," Andrew assured her, his big hands smoothing lotion down Gretel's slender back and waist. She was leaning forward, looking back at him through a curtain of long, red hair. "You can see so much more wildlife—minke whales, sea turtles, unicorn fish, thresher sharks—"

"Sharks!" Gretel exclaimed, her spine straightening.

Andrew chuckled. "You'd be safe with me."

"The water is so warm." Gretel began lathering sunscreen over her long legs and Hans watched Andrew's hungry gaze follow his sister's massaging hands. "It's like bath water. So amazing."

"Wait until tonight," Hans interrupted, going over to his sister's chaise and sitting down at the end by her feet. "We'll have a light show."

Gretel frowned at him. "What do you mean?"

"Noctiluca Scintillans," he replied, grinning at the way her nose wrinkled in confusion.

"The whatsis?" Andrew inquired, looking none too happy about Hans's intrusion.

"Noctiluca Scintillans," he said again. "They're a bioluminescent species of dinoflagellate."

Gretel sighed. "Can you speak English?"

"It's also called sea sparkle," Hans explained. "They're little organisms in the water that light up whenever they sense a threat or a predator coming near. I saw them last night—couldn't sleep. A boat this size moving through the water leaves a trail of light for miles."

"Really?" Gretel perked up.

"Oh, sea sparkle." Andrew rolled his eyes at Hans's technical explanation. "Yeah, you'll like it, Gret."

"Isn't my grandson brilliant?" The sound of his grandmother's voice made Hans look up in her direction as she came out onto the deck. She was an old woman, probably in her late-seventies, but she moved with a grace he had recognized almost immediately as his mother's. She had the same warm smile and hands and he couldn't help softening toward her, in spite of his initial wariness. She smiled down at him, ruffling his wet hair. "You're going to be a brilliant scientist."

"He *is* a brilliant scientist," Gretel insisted, and Hans noticed that wary, speculative look in his sister's eyes. She hadn't taken to their grandmother the way he had, but he knew she would come around in time. How could resist the woman's sweet smiles and kindness?

"Aw, girls, don't fight over me." Hans grinned, moving to pull a chair over for their grandmother before her bodyguard could do it. She had two of them—Andrew was just one. The other was an even bigger, broader fellow named, of all things, Double, a nickname used in lieu of a real name everyone, including Double, had probably forgotten. When Gretel had asked him, "Why Double?" he'd rubbed a big hand over the top of his dark crew cut thoughtfully before answering, "Probably because it rhymes with trouble."

Double stepped back and let Hans help his grandmother into her chair, making sure she got settled before taking one of his own.

"You kids look like you're having fun," his grandmother noted, accepting the bottled water that Double brought for her.

Andrew seemed to have other duties, including more of the day to day runnings of the big yacht, but Double stayed by his grandmother's side, always a step behind her, waiting, a lurking shadow.

"It's okay I guess." Gretel leaned back in her chaise, putting on a pair of sunglasses to hide her eyes. "But I'm a little homesick."

Hans gave her a pointed look, knowing better, and Gretel backpedaled some, explaining, "I mean, I miss my father."

"But Andrew has been showing you around the yacht, hasn't he?" Their grandmother smiled, her gaze falling onto her young assistant. "He's a very entertaining gentleman."

"Everyone's been very sweet." Gretel shrugged, closing her eyes and leaning back, a way to excuse herself from the conversation. Hans felt angry and a little embarrassed at her attitude. Why was she being so ungrateful? That wasn't the sister he knew.

Hans tried to make up for it. "So grandmother, Drew was telling us that you're the largest candy heiress in the world."

The old woman nodded, sipping her water and smoothing the seam on her dark slacks. "It's true. There are a few other candy conglomerates that have merged over the years and threatened to surpass us, but it's hard to compete with our numbers. If Willy Wonka really existed, we'd crush him."

Hans laughed at her vernacular, at the thought of this sweet, old woman crushing anyone.

"We started mostly as a good, dark chocolate company based here in Australia actually," their grandmother went on, shading her eyes and then accepting the small umbrella that Double opened up and placed in her hands. "My father expanded the market into Europe and even Asia, before taking on the biggest prize of all—America."

She leaned toward him, lowering her voice conspiratorially. "Americans are candy whores, you know. It's true—much more gourmand than gourmet. They like it sweet and simple. The sweeter the better. They turned their noses up at the true delicacies we produced. We didn't hit it big in America until we started really selling sugar."

"What do you mean?" Hans asked.

"Americans drown their sorrows in sweetness. They numb their pain with it. They dissolve their sorrows in it. People believe the world's worst addictive substances are illegal, but it isn't true. The cigarette companies were sued for putting a known addictive substance into their product, but no one touches us." She laughed, her eyes bright. "Sugar is the true white powder of the masses."

"And you're profiting from it?" Gretel frowned at her grandmother, inserting herself into the conversation.

"Someone has to." Their grandmother shrugged. "We still make our delicacies, of course, but our largest demand is for Big Sugar. Still, even as large as our empire is now, I believe my father couldn't have foreseen our biggest seller. In the end, most of our profits will probably come from our actual sugar cane crops."

Hans looked at her, surprised. "You actually grow the sugar cane you use?"

"Of course. We've genetically modified it over the years to grow bigger—and, of course, sweeter." She laughed. "But now…well, we're on the verge of something that will make sugar cane so high in demand it will push our profits into the stratosphere."

Gretel lowered her sunglasses so their grandmother could see the disapproval in her eyes. "This isn't enough for you?"

Their grandmother looked at her fondly. "I just want to have something to leave my heirs, so they can pass the family business on to their children, the way my father did to me."

"Too bad you couldn't pass it on to our mother first." Gretel stood, grabbing her towel. "Drew, would you like to get some lunch?"

"Sure." He took her by the elbow and they sailed by, Gretel ignoring the look Hans was giving her as she passed.

"She'll come around." Their grandmother sighed, looking hopefully after her granddaughter. "Hans, I have something I'd like to show you. Would you come with me?"

He followed her, and Double followed both of them. The main deck of the yacht, actually the middle deck, contained all of their sleeping suites, a dining room where they ate dinner together, a huge room with a bar and a dance floor that Hans assumed was for parties, as well as the captain's suite, just behind the wheelhouse. His grandmother had invited him to the upper deck where her private suite was planked in deep mahogany, the floors a thick, white Italian marble. The whole suite looked out onto the ocean with large bay windows, and it contained an office, Jacuzzi and sauna, home-gym and even a private kitchen.

But Hans had yet to be below-deck, which is where they were headed now. His grandmother was agile for her age, her walk brisk down the narrow hallways. Down here was the main kitchen and pantry, the crews' quarters, the laundry room, the main workings of the big boat. Hans was curious, looking around as they passed and his grandmother pointed out the lower deck's features.

"I had this made especially for you, Hans." She stopped at a door with a small square window at the top, but he couldn't see anything through it, pulling out a key from her slacks. Glancing over her shoulder at Double as she unlocked it, she murmured to him, "Wait outside for us please."

Hans followed her, surprised by her order, because Double followed her everywhere, even sleeping in a small cabin at the front of her private quarters. Andrew had his own suite somewhere on the main deck down the hall from his own.

"What…is this?" Hans asked as his grandmother flipped on a light overhead. The room was small but adequate and outfitted with more scientific equipment than he could have wished for in his wildest dreams.

"It's your laboratory." His grandmother smiled at his jaw-dropping, eye-popping response. "Of course, it isn't come free, exactly."

Hans surveyed the little lab, his mind boggling at the cost invested. "What do you mean?"

"I have a project I'd like you to work on for me," his grandmother admitted. "If you're interested."

He looked at her, curious. "What's that?"

"Did you know that sugar cane can be used as a renewable energy source?" she asked, watching him inspect the microscope closest to him.

"Sure. It's one of the cleanest burning possibilities to create bioethanol, far above white rice or even corn," he replied, impressed by the microscope's magnitude. It made the one Gretel had gotten him look like a child's toy. "It's one of the only truly renewable energy sources, because even the waste from fermenting it makes its own biofuel. Potentially, it could reduce gas emissions by seventy-five to ninety-five percent, at least compared to fossil fuels."

"That's right. You are such a smart boy." She patted his cheek, her palm as soft as tissue against his skin. "The only problem with sugar cane is the fermenting process..."

"Right." He nodded. He'd taken several environmental science courses already, as it was a particular interest of his. "They use genetically engineered organisms, don't they? But they've only figured out how to ferment some of the carbon sugars, not all of them. It slows things down a lot, I imagine."

"Exactly." She looked so proud of him it made him blush. "If we could genetically engineer an organism that would ferment all, or nearly all, of the carbon sugar glucose in sugar cane, we could increase production by 50% or more."

Hans gave a low whistle. "That would push sugar cane into the no-brainer category for use as the number one biofuel worldwide."

"Yes. Yes, it would," his grandmother agreed quietly. "Would you like to be the scientist who proved that to the world?"

His mouth felt dry when he responded. "What do you mean?"

"We have something close," she admitted, lowering her voice, although the door was closed behind them and Double was waiting in the hallway. "Very close. But our scientists have run into a wall. You're such a smart boy... I was hoping maybe you could take a look at our research for me?"

Hans stared as she pulled out a thick tome, reams of paper, from under the lab counter. He was practically salivating at the thought. How could he possibly resist such an opportunity?

"Sure, I can take a look," he said, trying to sound casual but feeling far more eager than he was willing to admit.

* * * *

Gretel ducked back into the laundry room, hearing someone coming down the hallway. She knew Hans was down here somewhere and she was determined to find him. He'd been coming down to the lower level for over a week instead of staying topside with her, snorkeling and swimming and sunning on the yacht's deck. He kept begging off, saying he was tired or didn't feel well, but she wasn't buying it. He felt fine—he was just up to something.

She heard voices, a man and a woman talking. "It's up here, I think."

Her grandmother had invited a boatload—literally—of people on board for an informal party. They were docked off the coast of Rockhampton somewhere, getting supplies, according to Drew. Gretel smiled in the darkness, a slow heat spreading through her at the thought of her grandmother's personal assistant and bodyguard.

After all, he was the biggest reason she'd agreed to the trip in the first place, she admitted to herself. She had found that talking to her "grandmother"—it was still hard to call the woman by that name or even think of her in that capacity—had brought her no answers and only more questions, but her stepmother and even her father had insisted that the two of them go on this little cruise with her, in spite of Gretel's misgivings.

Her intuition about the whole thing being a very bad idea had been so strong, she was nearly ready to stand up to them all, when Drew walked into the room and silenced her, at least externally. The man who had rescued her from the cold had turned out to be her grandmother's right hand man, and he would be going on the cruise with them to Australia. With that information revealed, Gretel had then found herself in quite a quandary.

It was his quick smile and that damned dimple that had done her in, she realized, waiting for the sound of the drunk couple to fade down the hallway before pulling open the laundry room door and slipping back into the corridor. There was something about him that made her knees weak and her tummy tighten every time they were in the same room. He'd been a fun companion, amusing and knowledgeable and attentive. And he'd kept her safely at arm's length so far, in spite of her varied and many attempts to get closer. Much closer.

She followed the curve of the hall to the right, finding the door without a label. It had a small window at the top but it was dark inside. This was where her brother had been running off to, working on some "project." But what, exactly, was he working on? She tried the knob but the door was locked. *Damnit.* Gretel cupped her hands and peered through them into the window.

"Well, there you are!" The sound of Drew's voice startled her and she actually screamed, jumping away from the door, her hand raised to the level of her heart. "You're missing all the fun."

"I got…lost," she said, breathless, as he approached. God he looked good, wearing tan slacks and a button-down navy shirt, the color almost matching his eyes. He was a button-down kind of guy, clean-cut and handsome, but not in the breathtaking kind of way that might have made him really stand out in a crowd. It was his smile that did that, the one that he was giving her now, a little naughty and mischievous, like he wanted nothing more than to find some trouble to get into. The problem was, so far, his intentions hadn't lived up to his smile.

"It's a big boat." He laughed, taking her hand and leading her back the way he'd come. "Come on, let's get back to the party."

They climbed the stairs to the main, or middle, deck, finding themselves in the corridor that led to both of their suites.

"I'm a little warm." Gretel slowed as they reached her room, pulling out a key card. The suite doors locked the same way hotel doors did, with key cards that slid into slots. "I think I'm going to change."

Andrew hesitated. "Do you want me to wait?"

"Why don't you come in?" She smiled over her shoulder at him, taking a deep breath and pushing open her door.

"All right." He followed her, shutting the door behind him.

"Have a seat," she called, grabbing a dress off the rack and heading into the bathroom. Of course, there was nowhere to sit but the bed, which was big enough for four people and covered in some sort of down duvet. She still hadn't gotten used to the luxury of this place, the breathtaking view, usually a vast expanse of ocean, out her window every morning.

"Sheesh, and I thought my suite was nice," he muttered. "You've got your own bar?"

"I'm not twenty-one," Gretel reminded him, and then cursed herself for doing so as she slipped her jeans down her hips. She'd left the bathroom door a little open so she could hear him and vice versa.

"Actually, the drinking age in Australia is eighteen," Drew called. "Mind if I indulge?"

"Help yourself." She undressed quickly, deciding to take her bra off as well as the sundress was strapless and didn't lend itself to wearing one. She turned on the light, kicking her discarded clothes into a corner, before slipping the soft, flower-print dress over her head, pulling a long curtain of red hair out from underneath and giving it a quick combing before she was satisfied.

"Did you find…" She trailed off as she came out of the bathroom, seeing Drew sitting with a drink in his hand, only she wasn't really seeing him—she was seeing his reflection in the mirror across from the bed. With the bathroom door cracked open, he could have seen everything, and from the look on his face, he most assuredly had.

"Here." He cleared his throat and handed her a shot glass. "Live a little."

She accepted it, already flushed, and the alcohol burned its way down her throat, spreading like hot fingers through her chest. *So he saw me naked,* she thought. *He's seen me in a bathing suit before. What difference does it make?* And hadn't she left the bathroom door open just a little on purpose, hoping…?

"Drew, can I ask you something?" She sat on the edge of the bed, holding her glass out and letting him pour some more amber-colored liquid into it.

"I'm sure you can." He knocked back another shot, making a face and pouring another.

She did the same, shivering, gasping, and then asking the question before she could lose her nerve. "Are you attracted to me?"

"Oh god, sweetheart…" Drew groaned, setting his glass and the bottle on the night table next to the bed. "Gay men would be attracted to you. How could I *not* be attracted to you?"

"Well then why…" She put her glass next to his, half-turning toward him on the bed, struggling for the words. "I mean, I think I've been… you know, pretty clear…"

He grinned. "Not at the moment, no."

Gretel gave up and kissed him, doing it without thought or reason. It was a purely impulsive act, something driven and beyond motivation, and it moved through them that way, like electricity traveling a livewire, shocking them both.

"Is that clear enough?" she breathed as they parted.

He swallowed. "Quite."

"Can we do that again?" She leaned in, this time with her whole body, pressing full against him, aching for more.

"It's probably not a good idea." He sighed, shaking his head and putting his hands on her shoulders to keep her at a safe distance. The look on her face prompted him to offer her more. "Because…because I work for your grandmother."

Gretel frowned. "So that's why?"

"That's why." He nodded.

"So your job is more important than me?"

He smacked himself in the forehead and fell back onto the bed with a groan. "Women!"

Gretel got up and went to the window, opening it so she could feel the night air. It was cooler than the heat of the day, but still warm, and the big boat rocked gently in the waves. She was far too full of longing, as if her body was too small to contain the feeling, her skin too thin to keep it all in, desire literally seeping through her pores.

She felt him approach, cautious, and she murmured, "The lights are pretty, but I wish we weren't docked. I like it better when we're in open water."

“We’ll be sailing back out tomorrow.” He was close now, close enough she could feel the heat of him behind her. “Your grandmother said we were stopping so your brother could pick up some supplies.”

“What is he up to down there in that lab all the time?” she wondered aloud.

“I like the open water best too.” Andrew’s arms went around her waist. She held her breath and closed her eyes. “Full moon reflecting off the water, dolphins playing in the waves. You feel so small and insignificant in the scheme of things, and yet a part of it all.”

“Yes.” She turned in his arms, tucking her head under his chin, a perfect fit. “I really like you, Drew.”

He hesitated just a moment and then she felt his lips against her forehead. “I like you too.”

“Please…” Her mouth had a mind of its own, finding his and making a small attempt to give him just a minutia of the feelings coursing through her body. He held back at first, letting her wrap her arms around his neck, her breasts pressed hard against his chest, her mouth searching for more, more.

Then she felt him give in, as if his whole body had exhaled. He even groaned a little against the press of her lips, his tongue finding hers, his hands groping her flesh, the sudden explosion of emotion so overwhelming that Gretel cried out from the pleasure, the pain of it. It was as if a switch had been thrown from “off” to “on” and her whole body lit up in response to his heat.

“Oh no,” he whispered against her neck, kissing and biting at her flesh, driving her backwards towards the bed with the lean muscles in his thighs. “We should so not be doing this.”

“I want an adventure.”

She let him tumble her onto the mattress, accepting his weight and curling herself around him as they kissed and fumbled in the lamp light. She closed her eyes and let herself be transported by sensation—the wet trail of his tongue across her collarbone, the hard throb of his cock against her thigh, the desperate grip of his hand over her breast, the nipple standing up for attention, begging for more.

She was so lost that when he stopped, still breathing hard, it took her a full minute to open her eyes to the realization.

"Gretel …" His smile was sad, a little sorry, and she hated it. She tried to kiss it away but he shook his head, rolling to the side of her, both of them staring at the ceiling now. "Sweetheart, wait. Let's just…stop…"

She took a deep breath, her limbs still tingling, cold now without him covering her. She wanted him back, she wanted the moment back, but part of her knew it was lost.

"Okay," she agreed, blinking at the white expanse of ceiling. "What do you know about my grandmother?"

Drew snorted a laugh. "Well that's a subject change if I ever heard one."

"Does she ever talk about my mother?" Gretel rolled onto her side toward him. "She won't tell me anything."

He reached out to smooth her hair, shaking his head. "Your grandmother is a very private person."

"You've been with her…how long?"

"Six years," he confessed.

"Does she ever talk to you?"

He shrugged. "Sometimes."

"What does she say?" she demanded, leaning in closer, searching for the truth in his eyes.

"Can we go back to kissing?" He grinned, only half-joking, she could tell.

"Do you want to?" She wasn't about to let the opportunity slip by.

"It seems safer." He smiled, accepting her arms around him, the soft press of her lips and, oh his tongue, exploring the soft recesses of her mouth. She slid a thigh over his, pressing it between his legs, feeling his instant response like a brand. Her dress was hiked up high, her panties soaked, the aching throb of her mound straddling the hard muscle in his leg, and she rocked like a wave against him again and again, whimpering her longing into his mouth.

He groaned, breaking the kiss and gasping. "Okay, I was wrong, definitely not safer…"

"Please," she pleaded, knowing she was begging and not caring in the least. "It's okay, I'm not a virgin. And I'm on the pill."

"Oh…well that's good to know." He blinked at her as he sat up on the bed, leaving her curled into a desperate, quivering ball beside him. "But that's not what I'm worried about."

Sighing, she sat up to face him. "What are you worried about?"

He leaned over to kiss her cheek but Gretel turned her face to him and he caught the corner of her mouth. She took full advantage of that, licking at his lips with her little tongue, lapping like a cat, her hand sliding behind his neck.

"You're going to be the death of me," he groaned and then got up, holding his hand out to her. "Come on, there's a big dance floor. Let's go use it."

Gretel wasn't giving up that easily. She stood too, wrapping her arms around his neck, letting the heat of her body sway against his. "We can do that here."

His breath drew in sharply when he felt her thigh pressing between his. "We can also get into much bigger trouble here."

"That's what I was thinking," she whispered into the shell of his ear, giving it a lick for good measure, using her fingernails to gently rake the hair at the back of his head.

Drew rested his forehead against hers with a sigh. "You're a very naughty girl."

"So spank me." She grinned.

"Come on." He turned, grabbing her hand and pulling her with him. "Before I lose the last thread of my sanity."

The dance floor was crowded. Their grandmother had decided the crew needed a little R&R—although Gretel suspected it was probably Double's request that had led her to the conclusion. She noticed him drinking at the bar, a woman hanging off each bulky arm, even smiling on occasion. Where all the people had come from, she had no idea. She recognized most of the crew, of course, the people who had been cooking their meals, making their beds, doing their laundry, but there were far too many unfamiliar faces in the group.

"Can you dance?" she asked Drew over the pound of the music but he pulled her against him, his hips answering her question, and she found her own body responding to his in kind. They rocked and swayed, rubbed and teased, grinding their hips together. She couldn't have asked for a better opportunity to continue seducing him. The music was too loud for words but their bodies spoke clearly enough for them both.

"You're driving me crazy," he managed to whisper into her ear as she rolled her hips, her behind grinding against his crotch. She could feel how crazy she was making him, the evidence rubbing up over her hip, and she wanted him to know he was making her just as insane.

Turning in his arms, she pressed her lips to his ear, whispering, "My panties are soaked." She heard him groan and smiled at the way his hands gripped her hips, pulling her close, as if he could get inside of her right there. The bodies pressed around them, everyone lost in their own sensations, the music keeping time, and Gretel kissed him, deciding to show him just how excited she really was.

Slipping a hand under her sundress, she hooked her thumb in the side elastic of her panties, yanking them down. They stuck wetly between her legs, but the buck and roll of her hips eased them down her slender thighs to her knees and from there it was as easy as letting them fall to the floor. The hardest part was getting down to retrieve them but the entire process, from wiggling her way down Drew's body, her cheek grazing the hard bulge in his trousers, to the triumphant slipping of her panties into his pocket, made them both breathless with lust.

"A present for you," she murmured, kissing his cheek before turning and weaving her way through the crowd, heading for the bar. She ordered a fuzzy navel, glancing over her shoulder and smiling to see Drew coming off the dance floor, inspecting the moist bit of material in his pocket.

"That's right, ladies, this key opens any door on this whole damned ship," Double announced, putting one arm around the blonde on his left, his other around the blonde on his right, the key card in one of his big hands. "Who wants to go with me so I can prove it to you?"

The girls giggled and teased him and Double bought them another round of drinks, probably in hopes he could get them both to go back so he could prove it, Gretel thought. She saw

Hans at the other end of the bar drinking a beer and waved. He waved back, giving her a brief smile. Then she saw their grandmother appear behind him, whispering something into his ear. She hardly ever saw the old woman without Double by her side, but she'd obviously given him the night off.

Her brother said something and nodded, turning on his stool and sliding off. She thought about going after him but then she felt Drew slip in beside her to order a beer. They drank together, both of them sweaty and hot, their clothes sticking to their wet flesh, eyes meeting over the rims of their glasses.

"How 'bout you, little one?" The rumble of Double's deep voice in her ear was loud even with the music playing over them. "I hear redheads are firecrackers in bed."

"Sorry." She turned and shook her head. "I'm taken."

He watched as Gretel took Drew's hand—he still had her panties clenched in his fist—and started leading him through the crowd.

"Where are we going?" he inquired, but she just smiled, leading him off the dance floor and onto the deck. They both gulped huge lungfuls of night air as they stood at the railing, both of them overheated and trying to cool down. The moon was full and bright, the ocean a simmering silver, the diamond tipped waves rising up to kiss the sky.

"I think these are yours." He slipped her panties into the side pocket of her sundress, giving her a kiss on the cheek. "I'm going to go to bed."

"Without me?" Gretel looked up at him in the moonlight, far too eager, but she couldn't help herself.

"I'm afraid so." He sighed. "Goodnight, sweetheart."

She watched his retreating back, resisting every urge in her body to follow. Instead, she waited until he was around the corner before weaving her way back through the crowd, finding Double still sitting at the bar. He looked up in surprise as she pressed herself against him, wiggling her way in between the two blondes.

"I think I'm looking for some trouble," she whispered, and he followed her like a puppy onto the dance floor. He was a wall of flesh, his meaty hands like hams on her hips, and any dancing being done was mostly by her. He just stood like a tree, swaying slightly as he watched her through half-lidded eyes. The two blondes didn't like her moving in on their territory and they joined them on the floor, the three women wrapping themselves around the bodyguard like vines, writhing together.

For Gretel, it couldn't have been a more perfect opportunity. She found his pocket without any trouble at all, slipping the key card out and pocketing it—sliding it next to her panties—before excusing herself to the little girl's room. He called after her, but the crowd was thick and the two blondes wrapped around his tree trunk legs prevented him from really going after her.

Drew's cabin was down the hall from hers, almost all the way to the back of the ship. Standing outside of his door, she contemplated the key card in her hand, wondering if it would even work. And did she want it to? She could just go back to the dance floor, put it back into Double's pocket, and stay out of trouble altogether.

Instead, she slid the card into the lock, turning the knob and pushing the door open. The room was dark and she stood for a moment, listening, trying to get her bearings. She had hoped she'd waited long enough for him to be in bed, asleep, but she didn't hear the sound of deep, even breathing, and now she wondered if he'd even come back to his room at all.

Then she saw the light under the bathroom door and heard the faint sound of water running. He was in the shower. She stood there, indecisive, for just a moment. Then she crept to the bathroom to listen. Hearing nothing but the shower, she turned the knob slowly, easing the door open just a little. He was standing in the shower, the curtain drawn, but it was the clear kind, giving her a hazy view of his flesh.

He probably would have seen her, or at least sensed her, but he had one hand braced against the wall above his head, and the other was busy between his legs, pumping his cock. Gretel watched him jerk off, the sound of his soft moans making her pussy throb in response, and couldn't help herself. Lifting her sundress, she slipped her fingers through the wetness, parting the curly red hair between her legs, easing her swollen pussy lips open.

"Oh god," Drew cried, pumping a little faster. "Oh yeah, baby, that's so good. Suck it. Suck it!"

Gretel whimpered, unable to resist his directive, slipping into the bathroom, out of her dress and into the shower before she could even think. Drew gasped in surprise at the intrusion but he didn't have long to process, because Gretel had him in her mouth, sucking him deep into her throat, her fingers already working between her own legs.

"Oh no," he groaned, shaking his head, closing his eyes as she knelt in the warm needle spray and worked him between her lips, running her tongue along the head, tasting him.

"Yes," she insisted, taking him in her hand, tugging as she stood, pressing him back against the tile. "Don't send me away again, Drew. Please."

She kissed him, her tongue drawing him out, his cock jumping in her hand like a livewire, and she felt him finally relent, his mouth opening to hers with a low growl, his hands finding her ass and pulling her in close. Neither of them could resist anymore.

Gretel sighed in triumph as he groped her breasts, her nipples hard and aching, pink twin peaks that welcomed the lash of his tongue. She arched and moaned as he made his way down her body, kneeling before her in the shower, hands cupping her breasts, tonguing her navel first, a delicious tease, before burying his face between her thighs.

The sensation was heaven and she wanted more, sliding her hand around the back of his neck and pulling him in further. Drew moaned against her flesh, pressing her back against the tiles, pausing only to assess their position and modify it slightly. There was a built-in ledge for soap and shampoo in the corner and he lifted her onto it—just enough room for her tailbone to rest on, but he took the rest of her weight, swinging her legs over his shoulders and delving back into her wetness.

The ache between her legs had gone from a dull throb to a steady, rising hum. She couldn't help the circles her hips began to make, searching for more of his mouth and tongue and fingers, as eager to find her own climax as he was to bring her to it. She looked down to see his gaze on hers, his eyes dark with lust, his mouth covering her mound, tongue working furiously against the sensitive nub of her clit.

"Drew," she moaned, her thighs quivering against his shoulders. "Oh yes! Make me come! Make me come in your mouth!"

And he did, focusing single-mindedly on her hot little clit, his tongue working back and forth at lightning speed, her whole body trembling with her orgasm, thighs clenching, pussy gripping his probing fingers as she let go completely, riding the crest of her pleasure like a wave.

Then he held her, folding her into his arms in the shower's wet heat, kissing her gently, her cheek, her jaw, her mouth. She could taste herself and she licked at his lips, sucking at his tongue, making him groan at her response. He gasped when she reached down and found the thick length of his cock, hers for the taking, stroking it lightly in her fist.

"Your turn," she murmured, sinking to her knees, grateful not to have to stand, still weak from her climax. His cock was fat and thick and she couldn't get all of it into her mouth, but she tried. Drew groaned appreciatively, his hand cupping her head, guiding her mouth, using the length of her hair to control her speed.

"Don't make me come," he gasped, looking down at her. She whimpered, feeling how swollen he was in her mouth, wanting to taste him. "I want to fuck you."

"Oh yes." She stood instantly, putting her arms around his neck. "Yes, please."

He laughed. "Not here."

They got out of the shower and Drew toweled her dry, spending a great deal of time rubbing her down, going over every inch of her with his hands and his eyes. She felt the heat growing again between her legs, a slow burn. By the time they made it out to the bed she was on fire for him again.

"Easy," he murmured as she straddled him, reaching for his cock. He let her stay in that position but slid further down on the bed so that her thighs were spread over his chest instead. "Play with yourself for me."

She flushed, hesitating. No one had ever asked her to do that before.

"Do it," he urged, watching her hands trailing over the hard buttons of her nipples, tickling down her ribcage. "Rub your pussy. I want to watch."

She swallowed, closing her eyes, and let her fingers go where they wanted, parting her swollen lips. Finding her clit, she began to nudge it back and forth, teasing herself, sending shivers through her whole body. And by the time she began rubbing herself in earnest, it felt too good for her to remain self-conscious. Drew moaned softly and the sound made her open her eyes and look down at him. His gaze focused between her legs, but he had one hand on his cock, pumping it slowly.

"You really like watching me?" she asked, seeing that dark, hungry look in his eyes, knowing he did. She was rewarded with another groan when she used her other hand to spread herself, showing him even more of her soft, pink flesh, giving him full view of her clit.

"Oh god," he whispered. "You're so fucking beautiful. I want you to come for me."

"Like this?" She rubbed herself a little faster, centering on her clit, a sweet wave rising in her belly.

"Just like that," he growled, watching as she began to rock her hips, her nipples standing up even more as she grew closer and closer to climax.

"Oh Drew," she moaned, the wet sound of her fingers rubbing her flesh filling the room, faster, faster. "So close…"

"Come for me," he insisted, grabbing her thighs and pulling at her. "Kneel up in my face and come for me."

She gasped at his rough grip but it sent her flying, her hips shoved forward, as if she could give all of herself to him, her body bucking with her orgasm. Drew grabbed onto her hips and ass, holding her as she came, hair flying, thighs clenching, tummy rolling, until she collapsed next to him onto the bed, still whimpering, as if in pain.

"Wow." He nuzzled her to her back, kissing his way over her shoulder, her neck, all moist from her effort. "That was pretty incredible."

She reached for him, eyes still closed, finding him even harder than before. “I want more.”

“Hungry girl.” He thrust slowly into her hand.

“You have no idea.” She gasped as she eased him down the length of her wet, swollen slit, wanting nothing more than to feel him inside of her, and this time Drew didn’t hold back. He let her position him before rocking his hips forward, giving her just what she wanted.

“Yessss!” She purred with approval, arching up to meet him, feeling the head of his cock buried deeply inside, almost to the point of pain. And still she wanted more. He stopped, looking down at her, searching her face and eyes for any indication and she encouraged him with her hips, rolling them in slow, wide circles.

“Oh Jesus,” he breathed, lowering his head to her neck. “Where did you learn to do that?”

“Summer camp,” she replied, closing her eyes and rocking.

“I shouldn’t have asked.” He laughed, his hips already taking over, his thrusts long and slow and oh, so very deep. She wrapped her arms around his neck, keeping him close, wanting to feel his delicious weight, the way his belly slapped against hers with every thrust.

“More,” she insisted, wiggling beneath him, spreading wider. “Oh Drew, please…”

“Harder?” he whispered, kissing her ear, her cheek. “Deeper? Faster?”

“Yes!” She gasped when he gave her what she wanted, driving her backward on the bed toward the headboard, slamming his hips into hers. His cock made a delicious wet sound between her thighs, the friction building to tremendous heights. Gretel moaned, her throat vibrating with his thrusts, her sounds a breathy staccato to match their motion together.

“Like that,” she managed, feeling the thick slide of his cock between her lips, stretching her so wide. “Yes! Oh, just like that!”

“You feel so good.” His breath was hot against her face, his lips soft, pressing into hers. “I don’t know how long I can do this.”

"Let's see if we can come together." Encouraged by his earlier urging, Gretel slipped a hand down between them, finding her throbbing clit. He propped himself up on his arms, watching as she rubbed herself off, both of them focused on the point where their bodies joined, his cock still easing in and out of her wetness.

"Oh fuck," he whispered as she began to rub herself faster, lifting her hips, her thighs spread wide, the muscles taut. "Oh fuck I can't—"

"Now!" Gretel felt her pussy clamp down over the swollen length of his cock, the sweet, rolling spasms clutching him again and again. He buried himself into her with a low grunt, feeling him filling her in thick, hot spurts as her climax went on and on, her pussy milking him with every contraction. He collapsed onto her in a sweaty, musky heap and she cradled him against her breasts, murmuring his name softly and kissing his forehead.

She didn't know how long it was before he lifted his head and asked, "How did you get in here?"

"I stole Double's passkey." She grinned at the shocked look on his face.

"You really are a naughty girl," he exclaimed. "Maybe I will spank you."

"Promises, promises."

* * * *

Hans was close, so very close. He'd easily recreated the experiments detailed in the report his grandmother had given him, with similar results. About half of all the sugar glucose molecules were being fermented in the process, but the rest weren't breaking down fast enough for the sample to be useful. There was a time factor in using sugar cane as a biofuel because the product only retained its properties for a short amount of time after being cut. It had to be fermented quickly or it was useless. Which was the real reason they'd been docked for nearly three days off the coast of Rockhampton—so he could have access to recently cut sugar cane.

He knew he was being obsessive, but he got like this when he was working on a project. His science project in eighth grade—making his own version of an electrical generator—had kept him in his room for over a week. Gretel had brought his dinner to him on trays because he refused to stop working. Of course, as his grandmother kept reminding him, the stakes now were so much higher than they'd been in eighth grade.

He'd spent a few hours mingling at the party, but he couldn't get his mind off the work. He'd thought about talking to Gretel. She didn't understand the science part of his babbling, but she was a good sounding board and asked interesting questions that got him thinking in different directions that usually helped, but she'd been dancing with Andrew. Although he wasn't sure what they'd been doing could be called dancing exactly.

"You bastard," Hans swore, holding up the Petri dish where the organism they'd already developed was currently residing. He had been able to reproduce this particular bacteria without much trouble, but it only worked so fast and no faster. They'd already tried everything from removing molecules from the sugar itself before the fermentation process—that had resulted in the artificial sweetener with the brand name Splenda—to splicing it with all sorts of DNA, from frogs to goats to soybeans, all with no successful results.

"We need to modify you, not the sugar, huh, guy?" Hans slipped a slide under the microscope and turned it on. They'd done that too, of course, slicing and dicing the bacteria, introducing all sorts of agents to see if it would increase its production, to no avail. He had a list four pages long of things they'd tried.

It had been Gretel bringing him a meal on a tray and sitting on a stool watching him that had given him the first breakthrough, although he didn't like to admit it. He'd refused the sandwich and she had sat and watched, picking at the little pieces of crust on the side and lining them up on the lab counter.

"Would you stop making a mess?" He'd been irritated at his lack of progress and short with her.

"Just making crumbs for the mice." She had nodded toward the three of them in their cage in the corner. "What are you doing anyway?"

"I told you—I can't tell you."

Gretel had pouted, sweeping the crumbs into her hand and then throwing them at him on her way out. He had been about to add something to the Petri dish and one of the crumbs had fallen in, contaminating the sample.

"Goddamnit, Gretel! You are such a pest!"

She'd just stuck her tongue out and left, slamming the door behind her. He'd set the sample aside and forgotten about it, but the next day, he'd remembered and had looked at it, just out of curiosity, before throwing it away, and had discovered something extraordinary—the organism was active. More active than it had ever been before!

But why?

The only difference had been the introduction of the bread crumb, but when he'd taken bread from the kitchen and tried to recreate the same experiment, nothing had happened.

Hans sighed, putting the Petri dish down and rubbing his eyes. He was tired, bone tired, sleeping only two or three hours a night. He felt like the weight of the world was resting on his shoulders. And maybe it was. He put his head down, going through the list of ingredients in his head—flour, salt, sugar, rye. It had been a Reuben sandwich, his favorite, piled high with corned beef and sauerkraut. He'd eaten it later, feeling guilty, and it was delicious, the bread toasted just the way he liked it.

"It's homemade. The cook baked it fresh today!" He remembered his sister saying, pleading with him. "Come on, Hans, eat something, please? For me?"

"Fresh!" Hans lifted his head from the table, eyes wide. "That's it!"

He had a feeling his little sister might have just solved the world's energy problem.

* * * *

"I'm sooo dehydrated." Gretel stuck her head out from under the covers, finding herself at the foot of the bed. She had no idea what time it was, but from the light coming in the window where Drew was standing, she guessed it was either early morning—or early evening.

"You need some more fluids." He came over to the bed, sitting on the edge. He had showered and looked rather fetching in his boxers.

"What a brilliant idea." She stretched across his lap like a cat, rubbing her cheek against his crotch.

He laughed. "That's only going to make it worse."

"Mmm, but it hurts so good." She nuzzled him some more, feeling his cock beginning to stir.

She was surprised he had any fluid left either. They hadn't left the room in two days. Drew had basically called in sick, having food left outside of his room for both of them. At least they had food and water. And as far as she could tell, no alarm had been raised about her disappearance on the boat. She'd wondered at that, but she knew Hans was busy doing—well, whatever he was doing. And her grandmother? The woman was shrewd. She probably knew exactly where her granddaughter was.

"You're such a little minx." Drew petted her hair, shifting to let her have better access.

"How long have you been awake?" she wondered aloud, unable to resist sliding her hand into his boxers. "How long have I been asleep?"

"A few hours." He nodded toward his laptop. "Trying to get a little work done."

His cock was only half-hard. She was going to have to work at it—but she was up to the challenge. "What time is it?"

"About dinner time."

She laughed, kissing the head of his dick, breathing in the fresh-showered scent of him. "I think we've got our days and nights mixed up."

"I think we need to forget days and nights altogether," he murmured, pressing her head down, groaning as she took him deeply into her mouth.

"Good idea," she said, but her words were mumbled, too full of cock for him to understand, and he wasn't paying attention anyway. She worked her tongue around the mushroom tip, flicking, teasing, finding the spot underneath that made him bite his lip and squeeze his eyes shut tight every time she rubbed her tongue there.

His cock was almost fully hard now but she wasn't done. Instead, she slid naked to the floor and he lifted his hips so she could take down his boxers, freeing him completely. She nibbled up the inside of his thighs, pumping him slowly in her hand, her tongue snaking underneath his balls, making his toes curl.

When she got to the head of his cock, he was leaking precum, and she licked it off playfully, round and round, her eyes never leaving his.

"No hands, just your mouth," he urged as she went down on him. "Look up at me. Oh god, yeah, like that."

She swallowed him nice and slow, taking as much as she could, even choking a little, her eyes watering, but he thrust up again anyway, aiming for the back of her throat.

"Put your hands behind your back," he instructed, his eyes full of hunger as she followed his direction, her breasts jutting forward with the motion, his cock pressing past the pink spread of her lips, seeking the heat of her tongue. "Oh god, what a sweet little mouth."

She practically purred under his praise, sucking him deeper, faster, whimpering as he fingered her nipples, sending jolts of pleasure straight down to her already wet pussy. She couldn't remember how many times he'd licked and fucked her, even just that morning after their breakfast in bed, yet she still wanted more.

"Stand up and show me your pussy." He leaned back on the bed as she stood, used to this already—he loved to see her touch herself. She parted her lips, showing him pink, sliding a finger down into her slit. God, so wet.

"On the bed," he said, his cock in his fist as he watched her. "Right over me."

"Drew," she protested, blushing, but she did as he asked, balancing a foot on either side of his body, moving her way up until she was standing directly over his head.

"Good girl." He smiled, reaching up to touch her himself, sliding two fingers into her wetness, making her moan softly. She loved his fingers, so much larger and rougher than her own. "Spread it for me. Like that. Stay just like that."

She bit her lip, flushing, holding her pussy spread wide for his gaze and his touch. He explored her moist pink folds with his index finger, teasing her flesh, avoiding the aching bud of her clit. Instead, he dipped his fingers into her, first two, pumping easily in and out. She whimpered and rocked with the motion, spreading herself even wider for him.

"Can you take more?" he wondered out loud, slipping a third finger in, making her howl. "Too much?"

"No," she gasped, getting used to the sensation, more like his cock than his fingers, stretching her wide. "It's good. Oh…god…"

"So tight," he remarked, working his fingers in and out of her wetness. "Christ, baby, you make me want you so bad."

"Me too." She smiled, glancing down to see his cock clenched in his fist, the tip seeping precum for her.

"Get on the bed."

She sank down to the mattress, letting him roll and move her the way he wanted, this time on her hands and knees, her ass high up in the air.

"Reach back and spread it," he whispered. She felt the heat of his cock pressing against her thigh and she couldn't believe how much she wanted him. "Both hands."

Her shoulders pressed into the bed, she reached back with both hands to spread her cheeks wide, showing him everything. Drew groaned, slapping the head of his dick against her pussy, teasing both of them.

"You make me want to fuck you so hard."

Gretel cried out as he entered her, losing her grip as he buried himself deep, driving her forward onto the bed. He grabbed her hips and pulled them back, lifting her to her hands and knees again, using his thighs to spread hers as he began to thrust.

"Oh god yes," she whispered, reaching underneath to rub her clit.

"That's a good girl," he urged, rolling his hips as he thrust, exploring every inch of her insides. "Play with yourself. Rub that pussy for me."

Gretel did, circling her clit with her finger as he fucked her. She lifted her ass in the air, giving him an even deeper angle, making him groan in response and fuck her even harder. Her pussy was swollen and wet, their bodies slapping together every time he pulled her back into the saddle of his hips.

"That's so hot," he murmured, exploring the crack of her ass with his thumbs. "You've got a sweet little ass."

"Drew," she protested, feeling his thumb pressing against her asshole. The sensation made her shiver. "Oh, no, not there…"

"I thought you were a naughty girl," he teased, pressing his thumb a little deeper, making her squeal and wiggle.

"Nooo," she wailed, burying her hot face against the covers.

"Easy…" He chuckled. "I won't put my cock in there. Not today."

She gasped at the thought, her eyes flying wide in surprise.

"But you can take just one finger, can't you?" he teased, pressing his thumb in deeper, to the first knuckle. She hissed and closed her eyes, but she didn't move away or protest. "Oh god, that's tight. So gorgeous. Such a hot little ass."

Gretel moaned into the bed as he began to fuck her again, this time with his cock, deep into her pussy, and with his thumb, in and out of her ass. The sensation was almost more than she could stand, her thighs trembling in an effort to contain it.

"You like that, don't you?" Drew's thumb was all the way in her now, moving in rhythm with his cock.

"Yes," she gasped, not wanting to admit it, but oh god, she did like it—she did.

"Tell me." He stopped thrusting, keeping his thumb buried deep.

"I like it," she admitted, feeling her whole body fill with heat. "Oh Drew, I love it. Please, don't stop—finger my ass while you fuck me."

He gave a low growl, driving his hips forward again, his cock swelling even bigger inside of her. Gretel cried out, her fingers rubbing her clit in fast circles, matching his rhythm. His thumb in her ass made her feel completely filled, her already swollen pussy hugging the length of his dick.

"Oh baby," she whispered, the feeling beginning to peak. "So close. So close."

"Yeah," he urged, his breath coming faster, slamming his cock into her. "Do it, baby! Come for me!"

"Ohhhh!" She let it come, her orgasm setting off a chain reaction in her body, her nipples tingling as they grazed the bed with every thrust, her clit throbbing, her pussy clamping down around his pistoning cock, and her little asshole clenching his thumb in a hot, steady rhythm.

"Oh fuck." Drew slipped his cock out of pussy and his thumb of her ass at the same time, making her cry out at the loss of him, but then he was bathing her in a white hot eruption of cum. He pressed the head of his dick against the hole his thumb had just vacated—not inside, just at the opening, fiery blasts leaking out around the tip and down the swollen pink folds of her pussy.

"Oh Jesus." Drew collapsed beside her on his belly, burying his face into a pillow. "Now I'm the one who needs fluids."

Gretel laughed, going to the bathroom to clean up. She opened a bottled water and brought one for him, too, finding Drew already snoring. She left the water next to the bed and went to the window. The yacht was moving again, out of port just that morning, into open water now. That made her think of Hans and she wondered what he must be thinking about her.

"Where are you going?" Drew asked as she pulled on her sundress. It was the only clothing she had to wear, not that she'd really needed any in the past forty-eight hours.

"Take a nap," she whispered, kissing his cheek and pulling the covers up to his shoulder blades. He was already snoring softly again.

The hallway was empty and for that she was grateful. Dinner had been left for them and it smelled delicious, but she ignored her growling stomach and continued down the hall. Her brother's room was next to hers and she knocked, waiting for him to answer, but not really expecting it. Instead, she used the universal passkey she'd stolen from Double to open the door and slip inside.

He wasn't there. The lamp was on and his bed was made and unslept in. Housekeeping came in to clean up, and even the clothes he must have discarded on the floor had been folded and left on a chair. There was no sign of him, or where he might have gone, but she had a pretty good idea.

Gretel made her way down to the lower deck, passing some of the crew. They just nodded politely, but a few of them gave her knowing little smiles that made her want to sink into the floor. So the whole boat obviously knew where she'd been the past few days. Great.

When she got to the lab door and saw the light on, she knew he would be in there. She knocked softly, glancing up and down the hall, still not sure she was even supposed to be down there.

"Hans?" she called, knocking again, a little louder. "It's me! Open up!"

His face appeared in the window, just his eyes, wide and alarmed. "What are you doing here?"

"Looking for you." She rolled her eyes. "Come on, open up!"

"I can't," he choked, more of his face filling the little window. "Gretel, she's locked me in."

"What?" She stared into his scared eyes, incredulous. "Who?"

"Our grandmother," he spat. She'd never seen him look so angry. "She's had me working on something for her company, and I've figured it out. Well, really, you figured it out for me. It was the yeast, Gretel. Yeast! I never would have guessed it. But it worked!"

"What are you talking about?"

"I should have listened to you about her," he lamented, leaning his forehead against the door. "She's awful. She's evil. I think she's going to kill us."

"Are you...insane?" She blinked at him. "Have you been sniffing something wonky in there? Now open the door!"

"I CAN'T!" He jiggled the handle and she looked down, remembering her passkey, but this door was different. There was no place to slide a card. This door opened with a real key.

"She's locked me in, from the outside. There's no way out of here."

"What's going on?" It finally occurred to her that he might actually be making some sort of sense, that what he was saying might, in some way, be true.

"Does anyone know you're here?"

She shook her head, glancing up and down the hallway, seeing no one. Not that it mattered. There were security cameras on either end, and if someone wanted to find her, they could.

"You have to get me out of here," he whispered.

"How?"

"I don't know." He sighed. "Gretel, listen. The thing I'm working on—it's an alternative energy source made out of sugar cane and it's worth a great deal of money. If I don't give it to her, she's going to kill me. But if I do give it to her, I'm afraid she's going to kill us both. You have to find a key and get me out of here."

"Okay." She nodded, backing away from the door. "I will. Tonight. I promise."

"Hurry!"

* * * *

He should have listened to his sister. The door had remained locked, and no food or water had been brought to him for twenty-four hours. His grandmother had come by only once, shadowed by the formidable Double, his big arms crossed, a new addition at his hip—a .44 magnum. Hans knew he was in real trouble when he'd seen that.

"Just give me what I want, Hans, and this will all be over," his grandmother soothed.

Yeah I bet, he thought, glancing at the gun. She had no intention of letting him go. She never had. The only thing she'd wanted was a solution to her problem. Even if he gave her what she wanted, he and his sister would be at the bottom of the Great Barrier Reef feeding the sharks and the fish.

"How can you do this to your own grandchildren?" Hans asked, hoping to distract her, looking for a way he might be able to grab Double's gun, maybe make a break for it.

The old woman scoffed, waving his words away. "Your mother was a whore and her daughter is no better. Your stepmother was certainly eager to get rid of you both, and I can see why."

Hans stared at her, trying to comprehend the words.

"She sold you to me, you know." The old woman laughed—more of a cackle really. The sound of it gave Hans chills. "Wanted to be rid of you entirely. Scuba accidents happen a lot out here, especially with such inexperienced divers."

Hans thought of Gretel, alone with his grandmother's other bodyguard, the one who had promised to teach her to dive—who said she'd be safe with him. Andrew was part of this, just as Double was, standing there with his big arms and his big gun, he knew it. Gretel wasn't safe, and he had to find a way to protect her.

"I'm going to get what I want," his grandmother insisted, her blue eyes turning to steel. "You might as well give it to me now."

"Then you'll just kill me," he said, stating the obvious.

"Oh Hans, are you so naïve?" The old woman looked back at her bodyguard and smiled. "Let's let's just say I'm not above using your sister as leverage. Double likes her. Really *likes* her."

"No!" Hans felt his whole body go cold and numb at the thought.

"Now, do you have something for me?"

He shook his head slowly, choking out the word again, "No!"

"Persuade him." The old woman stepped back and the big man stepped forward. Hans felt the first few blows—definitely the teeth-jarring one to his jaw, and two more to his kidneys after he'd dropped to the floor, but thankfully things pretty much faded to black after that and then, at least, there was no more pain.

* * * *

"Hans." Gretel whispered her brother's name, tears falling onto his bloody face. "Oh god, are you alive? Are you awake?"

He came to slowly, opening only one eye. The other was swollen completely shut.

"What did they do to you?" She mopped at the blood with the edge of her shirt but stopped when he winced and waved her away.

"How did you get in here?" he asked, although it sounded more like, "How dijoo gihn her?" from the mashed-up mess of his mouth.

"A key." She took his hand. "Drew is going to help us get out of here."

"He's in on it," Hans insisted, shaking his head. "Has to be."

"No." Gretel helped him stand, steadying him as he began to totter. "He has a plan. All the cameras are off right now. He gave me the key to come get you. He's waiting at the side of the yacht in a raft."

"He's going to take us out into the middle of the ocean and kill us," Hans hissed, bloody spittle flying from his lips, and Gretel took a moment to translate his run-together words.

"Trust me," Gretel insisted, poking her head out into the hallway, listening for voices. Her knees felt weak and she was shaking with fear. "Just trust me, okay?"

"He doesn't care about you." Hans turned his one good eye toward her. "She used him as your babysitter."

"Hans, stop it." She said the words to soothe both him and herself. She didn't like how much the words sounded like sense. "Drew is a good man. He's on our side, not hers. Please, just trust me."

"How can you be so sure?" he asked.

"Because he told me so."

Hans gave a choked laugh. "I guess a boat in the middle of the ocean is better than a locked room." He grabbed a Petri dish off the table, shoving it into his pocket.

"Shh," Gretel reminded him as they crept down the corridor, Hans stumbling beside her, holding his hand out to the wall for support.

She had memorized the way, back beyond the laundry room and through the darkened kitchen, up a back set of stairs to the main deck and then over the railing. There was a rope ladder waiting for them, Drew sitting at the bottom in a raft. If all went according to plan, they would be in it and rowing to shore in less than five minutes, before anyone even noticed that all the security cameras had gone oddly dark.

The kitchen was eerily quiet as they crept through, the glow of an oven clock illuminating their way. Gretel's heart was racing and she thought of Drew, what he was risking by doing this for her brother, for both of them. Hans might not trust him, but he didn't know Drew like she did. She knew he wouldn't do anything to hurt her—that all he wanted to do was protect her. When he'd been faced with the knowledge that the woman who employed him for the past six years had taken her own grandchildren captive and had every intention of killing them, he had believed her without a second thought.

And isn't that kind of odd, Gretel? Asked a little voice in her head. Why would he have believed her over a woman he'd known for six years? He'd hardly asked her any questions. Instead, he'd gone straight into action, formulating a plan to get them all out of there.

Hans grabbed her arm, pulling her body in close and clamping a hand over her mouth to keep her from screaming—and she was about to. Standing at the big, industrial-sized refrigerator was the hulking frame of their grandmother's bodyguard. It was three in the morning, but Double was fully dressed—and fully armed, Gretel noted in the bluish glow of the refrigerator light—as if he had been up and ready for action.

Now he was brandishing a long pepperoni like a sword, biting bits off the end as he hunted through, looking for something more satisfying. The two of them stood there, frozen in place, the bodyguard between them and the door to freedom. Hans began to slide slowly toward the floor, taking Gretel with him, until they were both kneeling behind the long metal countertop. Underneath, the cooks had various pots and pans stowed away, but she could still see Double's shadow cast across the floor in the light of the refrigerator.

A crackling sound startled them both but they managed to stay quiet as the bodyguard answered his phone in walkie-talkie mode.

"Double here."

"Security just informed me the cameras are down." The static burst of their grandmother's voice made Gretel's breath catch. "It's probably just a power problem, but I need you to check on my grandson."

"Will do," the big man agreed, closing the refrigerator. Hans gripped her hand, squeezing hard, shaking his head and holding a finger to his lips. Gretel tried not to move or even breathe as the bodyguard made his way up the center aisle, passing them on the other side of the counter, heading toward the door behind them.

"We don't have long," Hans warned, the adrenaline clearly moving him now as he pulled Gretel toward the other end of the kitchen. The door opened up to a back stairway and Gretel took the stairs first, Hans nudging her from behind, whispering, "Hurry! Hurry! Hurry!" The night air was cool against her face as she came up onto the deck, looking for the little red flag Drew had promised would be there on the edge of the railing, marking the site of the ladder.

"Where is it?" she whispered, not finding it even with the evening deck lights lit over her head.

Hans came up behind her, glancing over his shoulder, both of them listening for the sound of Double coming after them.

"Isn't he supposed to be here?" Hans grabbed the rail, leaning over to look below. Gretel did the same, seeing Drew secured in a raft next to the yacht, being towed in its wake—but there was no ladder.

"Where's the ladder?" Gretel tried to keep her voice low, calling down to him.

"Sorry—ladder was a no-go," Andrew apologized, waving them down. "You're gonna have to jump."

Gretel looked between the two men, judging the distance. It was a good twelve feet to the water—but it was dark, and she couldn't see what was *in* the water. Because they weren't just going to have to jump, they were going to have to swim to the raft, attached to the yacht, and get it in before Drew cut the line.

“Don’t be scared,” Hans whispered, checking the Petri dish in his pocket, making sure the lid was on and secure before shoving it back in. “It’ll be okay.”

“So you trust him now?” Gretel retorted, looking over the side again where Drew was urging them to hurry and jump.

“He’s our only possible way out of this.” Hans pulled a knife out of his other pocket. It was just a little steak knife, something he clearly picked up in the kitchen. “And if he tries anything, at least I’ve got this.”

“Oh my god, I should have left you locked in that stupid little room.” Gretel rolled her eyes, turning away from her brother and diving head first over the side. The water, even at night, was bath water warm, but still a surprise to the system. She came up gasping and swam toward the raft as Hans dove into the water beside her.

“Are you okay?” Drew grabbed her arm, hauling her into the little boat. “I’m sorry about the ladder. It wasn’t where I put it. I had to find another raft too.”

“It doesn’t matter.” Gretel hugged him close as Hans found the side of the boat, hauling himself up the side. “We’re all here and safe.”

Drew let her go to help Hans into the boat, giving a low whistle at the sight of him.

“They worked you over good, didn’t they?”

“Drew, hurry,” Gretel urged, looking up toward the railing. “They know the cameras are out and they’re going to find out Hans isn’t in his room.”

“Too late,” Hans wheezed, his gaze focused high above. Gretel followed his line of sight and saw Double running along the railing, heard him yelling something about “escape!”

“Get down!” Drew grabbed the back of her head, forcing her to the bottom of the raft, but even from that vantage point she saw him loosening the line, detaching them. And she saw the rising, white side of the yacht moving slowly away from them into the night.

“It won’t be long before they find out we’re gone,” she whispered, turning over in the raft to look up at Drew, noticing for the first time that he, too, was soaked. “Why are you wet?”

"Yeah, I had a little accident getting the boat." He gave her a sheepish sort of smile. "Good news: we got the boat. Bad news: my phone is dead. Which means we have no GPS."

"We're lost out here?" Gretel sat up, looking between him and her brother. She knew they hadn't left port too long ago, but they were still miles from even the sight of any land. "We're in the middle of the Pacific Ocean!"

"Yeah, I said it was bad news."

"It's okay," Hans spoke up. "We can follow the sea sparkle. Look." A long trail of glowing blue water stretched out behind them, caused by the yacht's forward motion through the water.

"Excellent." Drew gave Hans an appreciative look. "Let's hope they don't turn around. Can you oar?"

"Give me one," Hans said, holding out a hand, and Drew gave him an even more appreciative look as her brother, in spite of his physical condition, hooked the oar into its rest and positioned himself to row. Both men began without speaking, rowing them swiftly through the waves, and Gretel breathed a deeper sigh of relief as the white speck of the yacht began to grow even smaller.

"Drew, I have to tell you something." Gretel snuggled close against his back for warmth, feeling his muscles working as he rowed.

"Hm?"

"My brother has a knife in his pocket," she informed him. Hans stiffened and gasped, his oar slipping slightly. She stuck her tongue out at him and said, "Don't poke a hole in the boat with it, Hans, or we're all dead."

"That's okay, I have something to tell you both." Drew chuckled. "I'm not exactly who I said I was."

Hans swore under his breath, fumbling for his knife.

"Hey, hey, keep it in your pocket, hero. She's not kidding about poking a hole in the boat. We're dead in the water if that happens." Drew stopped rowing too, the raft floating on the waves. "The truth is, I'm actually a spy for a green nonprofit company. We've been following this research for years. They want your organism—and they'd like to give you a job."

"What do you mean?" Hans asked, pulling a cautious hand out of his pocket and putting it back on the oar.

"Just what I said," Drew replied, taking his own oar back, both men beginning to row once more, aligning them with the luminescent blue glow of the sea sparkle in the water. "We knew your grandmother's company was very close to finding a solution—but we also knew they intended to patent the organism and make it proprietary, so no one else could duplicate it. And then she intended to hold it as long as they could, until fossil fuel shortages maximized their profit. Our company wants to make it available now, to everyone, everywhere. It will drive the cost down and make it an affordable energy source for the whole world."

"So you lied to me." Gretel glared at him.

Drew sighed, continuing to row. "That's sort of a prerequisite of being a spy, sweetheart."

She leaned her cheek against his arm. "But you're one of the good guys?"

"I am. At least, I hope I am." He kissed the top of her wet head. "I try to do the right thing."

"Well I know one right thing we can do." Hans pulled hard on the oar. "We can get my sister home. The rest we'll sort out from there."

Drew smiled in the moonlight, looking fondly down at her. "Agreed."

With that, Gretel settled herself between her brother and her lover as they followed the gleaming blue streaks of light, stretching for miles across the Pacific Ocean, toward home.

Epilogue

"Are you okay?" Drew yelled. Gretel just gave him a thumbs up.

Part of her couldn't believe she was doing this—and another part of her couldn't wait. *It beats finishing school.* Grinning, she looked out the window at the patchwork of land below, wondering if she could see their house from here. A house that, in the past three months, had finally become a home again.

She smiled, thinking about her father, working again in a lab for the first time in ten years, this time alongside her brother. He had been so apologetic when they arrived home, certain that they would hate him for listening to their stepmother, but they'd both been shocked to hear that he had already kicked her out of the house and started divorce proceedings.

"An anonymous tip," her father told them tearfully. "I had the Coast Guard out looking for you both."

Gretel had looked pointedly at Drew, but he just rocked back on his heels and grinned and didn't say a word. But she'd been so thankful that she didn't have to see Vivian anymore. They could breathe in the house again. They could laugh and shout and joke around. No one knew what might happen to Vivian if the trial ever went forward. She'd been released on bond and no one had seen her since.

And no one would ever see their grandmother again, Gretel thought, sliding her hand into Drew's and feeling him squeeze it. The Coast Guard had caught up with the yacht, but by then the old woman had already collapsed. Heart attack most likely. She was seventy-nine, a good age to reach if you could get there, and although she'd clearly not done it happily, she'd died a very rich woman.

The will, which had curiously never been changed to reflect their grandmother's animosity toward her only daughter, was still in probate. Both she and Hans had agreed that, if the estate and company were ultimately turned over to them, they would use the money to further BioGen's mission. It was a good one, and they all had hopes it might work out in the end.

Hans was working and happy. Her father was working and happy. And Gretel… well, she was most decidedly *not* going to finishing school.

"Time to hook up!" Drew stepped in front of her and she put her arms around him as she'd been instructed. He fumbled with the belts and loops and buckles, hooking them where he told her to. He checked and double checked them as the co-pilot came back from up front. He triple-checked them before waving them out the open side of the plane toward Gretel's first skydive.

"Are you ready for an adventure?" Drew called back.

She squeezed him tight—her answer for yes, saying the words but not really expecting him to hear them over the noise. "Every day with you is an adventure."

But somehow he did hear, and he grinned back at her, that sweet dimple flashing in his cheek. "For the rest of our lives!"

Together, they jumped.

WENDY

"What in the world are you looking for?" Wendy bent to see under the shelf where the boy's lower half was still visible, his Keds kicking wildly as he groped underneath. She usually found this a quiet place to come and think, especially back by the "used book" shelves filled with old encyclopedias and out-of-print editions long ago forgotten.

"Mytingyrshaw," came the muffled response, followed by three quick sneezes in succession and a string of words that made Wendy's face burn.

"Your what?" she inquired again, squatting down this time to see. The space under the shelf was narrow, certainly too small for a man, perhaps even any full-grown adult, but just enough room for a lanky, determined teenaged boy.

"Let me look." A rough voice interrupted her and Wendy glanced up, shocked to see a tall blond in four-inch heels and a bright green mini-dress more appropriate for a street corner than a library on a Wednesday morning standing there with her arms crossed. The woman—and Wendy wasn't sure it *was* a woman—had more makeup on than Tammy Faye Baker at the breakfast table and in her heels, stood at least six-foot-four.

"I got it, Tink!" came the reply, followed by another string of sneezes and a hearty cough. With that, the boy appeared, his sandy curls tousled and full of dust, his face smeared with dirt. He waved a book with a black cover ."*Meeting Your Shadow*. Just where you put it!"

"I told you I did." Tink huffed, tucking her hair, cut short with dark roots showing underneath the blond, behind her ear. "I said I'd find it and save it for you."

"Good job, Tink!" The boy looked at Wendy for the first time, and when his gaze met hers, she felt her knees wobble a little. "Hey, who're you?"

"I'm Wendy." She introduced herself, holding out her hand, which the boy spontaneously used to pull himself up, nearly toppling them both in the process. "Wendy Dahling."

"Pete," he announced. "Peter Pann."

Wendy glanced up at the tall blond and Peter did, too—she towered over them both by at least a foot—making introductions. "And this is Tink. Say 'hi.' Tink."

The blond glared, but mumbled a sufficient, "Hi."

"What's so special about this book?" Wendy looked curiously at the cover. She didn't recognize the title or the author. It looked boring, probably non-fiction—certainly not light beach reading, which was her own usual fare.

"It's out of print." Pete slipped it behind his back, away from her prying eyes. "Very rare."

"Is it valuable?"

Pete shrugged. "It is to me."

"Wait... what are you doing?" Wendy went up on her tiptoes, trying to see behind Peter.

"What does it look like I'm doing?" He scoffed, pulling his shirt out of his pants and tugging it over the book he'd shoved down the back of his jeans.

"They're not free, you know." She pointed to the sign: *Used Books $1.00*

"What if I don't have a dollar?"

Wendy opened her little purse, finding a crumpled one-dollar bill at the bottom, stuck to a very dusty still-wrapped piece of Trident bubble gum. "Here."

Peter took it between his thumb and finger as if it might be diseased, but he smiled at her. "That's very nice of you."

"You're welcome." She snapped her little purse closed, already lamenting her generosity. "I can't really afford it either, but I'd rather give you my last dollar than watch you steal something."

The tall blond snorted a laugh. "How noble of you."

"Don't mind Tink—she's just the jealous type." Peter rolled his eyes.

"What's there to be jealous of?" Wendy looked between the two of them, thoroughly confused.

Peter linked his arm with her as if they were old school chums, leading her toward the front of the library, away from Tink. "So you're broke, huh?"

"You could say that." Wendy didn't meet his gaze, hoping the fall of her hair against her cheeks as they walked hid her flush.

"Shouldn't you be in school?" the boy inquired as they threaded their way through tables, a few patrons sitting and quietly reading.

"Shouldn't you?" she countered.

"I don't go to school." He sounded proud of this.

"How old are you?"

"Just turned eighteen," he replied. "How about you?"

Wendy glanced over her shoulder, seeing Tink following them. "I'll be eighteen on Friday."

"Friday! What a lucky break!"

She blinked at him. "Huh?"

"A birthday is good, but a Friday birthday is spectacular!" The boy's grin was infectious. She couldn't help smiling back. "What are you doing for your birthday?"

"Nothing."

"Nothing? No cake, no ice cream, no presents?" Peter looked truly aghast. "No parties, no fun, no wild overindulgences?"

"No." Wendy shook her head as they neared the library checkout counter.

"You're a boring girl." Peter dug the book out of the back of his jeans, slapping it on the counter along with the dirty dollar bill. The librarian took the offering, tucking it away in a drawer, and bagged the book.

"I am not!" Wendy protested.

"She is, she's boring, isn't she, Tink?" Peter looked over his shoulder for confirmation.

Tink obliged, quite happily. "Exceedingly. Let's go."

"I have to take care of my little brothers," Wendy protested as she followed the boy toward the door. The heat outside was oppressive—another reason the library served as a welcome respite. "I don't have time for parties or… or fun."

"No time for fun?" Peter turned to her, wide-eyed. "Now you've done it. You've gone and wounded me. That offends my basic sensibilities. Everyone has time for fun!"

Wendy swallowed, blinking back tears. "Not me."

"Even you." He leaned in to look into her eyes, and she knew they were brimming and she struggled to hold back. The boy named Peter smiled, his mouth curling mischievously at the corners as he touched his finger to the tip of her nose. "Boring girl."

"Peter, I have to be back…" Tink interrupted, wobbling a little on her dangerously high heels.

"Here, take the book." Peter didn't look away from Wendy, tossing the book behind him to the tall blond. She fumbled but managed to catch it.

"You want me to take it?" Tink looked from the book to Peter.

"You found it, didn't you?" Peter waved her away, his gaze still on Wendy. They were standing close, far too close for Wendy's comfort. She blamed the heat in her cheeks on the hot Florida sun. "Take it home and I'll meet you there."

"You trust me with it?" the tall blond inquired.

"Of course, Tink." Peter sighed, finally looking back at her. He smiled, that sweet, charming smile that made Wendy tingle all over, and she saw Tink brighten at his words. "You're my best girl. Now go!"

The blond hesitated a moment and Wendy noticed a necklace at her throat, a small silver bauble, but it was what appeared above it that mattered—the bob of a man's Adam's apple. Her suspicion had been correct—Tink wasn't really a girl after all. The blond gave one more glowering look at Wendy and Peter before following the boy's instruction, turning around to go home. Wendy watched her fly down the sidewalk, amazingly light on her feet in those heels.

Peter turned his attention back to Wendy. "So why don't you have any time for fun?"

"It's a very long story." That was an understatement. She didn't know if she wanted to share her life history with this strange boy.

But Peter grabbed her hand, swinging it as they walked. "I love stories!"

"Even terrible stories?"

His eyes widened. "Does it have lots of blood and violence and sex?"

"Actually… yes." She nodded sagely after considering his question for a moment.

"Then I'm sure I'll love it! You have to tell it to me," he insisted.

"You're a strange boy, Peter Pann." She couldn't help smiling at his enthusiasm.

"And you're a boring girl." He grinned back. "But you might tell an interesting story, and then maybe you won't be so boring. So tell!"

And she did. She didn't know why she told him—except that he was charming and persistent, pulling her to a seat under a shady tree on the library lawn—but tell him she did. For almost an hour they sat there while Wendy painted word pictures and Peter listened, laughing at all the funny parts (there weren't many) and sighing at all the sad parts (they were numerous), giving her all of his whole, undivided attention, something that she grew secretly to like as the story grew longer and longer.

Wendy told him a tale of three children without a mother ("I know what that's like," Peter briefly interrupted with a sad nod of his head) whose only support in the world was a very wicked man. Their mother hadn't meant to leave them with this man, Wendy assured him. She had died, quite suddenly, a car accident as swift and final as her last breath. With no mother to protect them, the wicked man had free reign to do whatever he liked, whenever he liked. And the wicked man liked, to no one's surprise, least of all Wendy herself, to do very wicked things.

Many of the things were so wicked Wendy couldn't even tell Peter that part of the story. His already wide-eyes would have bulged out of his head even more. So she skipped the really terrible, the most heinous, egregious offenses. But the little ones were awful enough.

"So I finally took the boys and we ran away," Wendy told him, pulling on a blade of grass poking up from under her bare feet. She'd taken off her shoes. "Now me and John and Michael live in a home for foster kids. Of course, I won't be able to live there once I turn eighteen. This Friday I will be effectively homeless."

Peter gazed at her thoughtfully, his chin resting in his hand. "That was a terrible story, Wendy."

"I know." She smiled wanly, wiggling her toes in the grass. "I told you it was."

He perked up, grabbing her hand and squeezing. "I have an idea."

"What?" She looked at him, startled, the press of his hand like a gift in hers.

"Come with me to Neverland."

She blinked at him, confused. "Where?"

"Come on, you'll see." He stood, pulling her with him so quickly she barely had time to grab her shoes.

"I can't," she protested, stumbling after him. "My brothers."

Peter stopped, frowning, and then brightened. "Bring them with you."

"Really?" Wendy perked up, turning the idea over in her mind. "I don't know if they'll let them go. We'll have to sneak out."

"We can do that," Peter assured, pulling her along again. "I'm good at sneaking."

"And stealing," she reminded him.

"And all sorts of things," he agreed with a wicked grin. "You bet. Come on, Wendy Dahling. Let's fly."

"Where is this place?" Wendy gasped, the stitch in her side growing as they hurried down the sidewalk.

Peter pointed somewhere into the blue sky above. "Second star to the right and straight on 'til morning!"

* * * *

John and Michael were asleep. Wendy had checked on them three times to be sure, but they were back to back in the little twin bed in a room more closet than anything else, with just enough room for a box spring and mattress on the floor and a small night table beside it. The boys didn't seem to care though. They'd jumped on the bed like monkeys and had torn through the place like it was a funhouse, running up stairs and opening strange-shaped cupboard doors, looking for the "secret passages" that Peter assured them did, indeed, exist.

Just ten and eight, the boys had suffered from their lack of parenting far more than Wendy had, and being the oldest, she'd assumed a great deal of motherly responsibility with them. If she didn't do it, who else would? Not their stepfather, to be sure. But she was questioning her choices now as she sat on her own bed in the room next to the boys', looking out the window into the darkness.

Outside, Neverland was still, except for the sound of crickets and bullfrogs and the occasion grunt of a 'gator to compete with the rustle of a breeze through the trees. It seemed like paradise compared to the shelter, this big old rambling house surrounded by fields and woodland and swamp. The boys loved it already. Peter had generously offered to let them stay indefinitely, but how could she possibly repay him for that kind of hospitality?

She had hoped something would come along before her eighteenth birthday, when she would be no longer welcome in the shelter, having reached the "age of adulthood." Whatever that meant. How could she take care of the boys then? She didn't even have a high school diploma, let alone a job. She'd gone to the library to look for resources, maybe find a job in the paper, to pray for a miracle… and then Peter had come along.

"Too much sad in your story, Wendy-girl," he'd said. "It's time to make some happy endings."

Maybe he was right.

"Wendy?" Peter poked his head in without knocking, seeing her sitting on the window seat. "There you are."

"Here I am," she agreed. There was something about him that made her smile.

"You have to come meet the boys."

"The boys?"

"I have boys too." He sounded rather proud. "I collect them. Tink does her best to take care of them, but of course, you can't really count on her all the time, especially when she gets into one of her moods."

"I bet." Wendy made a face, having already been subject to Tink's mood swings.

"What they really need is someone to look after them..." Peter explained, leading her down the stairs into the large living area off the kitchen. Wendy blinked and rubbed her eyes, sure she was seeing things. Everywhere she looked, young men were draped and curled and stretched out on the floor, the sofa, chairs, even one sitting atop the grand piano in front of a large door wall, singing at the top of his lungs while another boy played. Most of them were in various stage of undress—lounge pants or boxers with no shirts, a few of them in just briefs and a pair of socks.

Wendy gaped at Peter. "These aren't boys... they're... our age!"

"Well, technically, I suppose." Peter shrugged, waving to a boy who called out his name, steering Wendy into the room. The boys were looking at her, quite curious. "But they're all rather lost, you know. None of them can find their way."

"To where?" She frowned up at him, her brow knitted. Sometimes Peter seemed to talk in riddles.

"Anywhere." Peter slipped an arm around her waist as the boys started to get up, coming to find out who this girl in their midst might be. "So they stay here, at Neverland."

"Do they *all* stay here?" she whispered as they drew nearer.

Peter scoffed. "You thought I was all alone in this great big house?"

"I didn't know."

The boys were closer, looking, but not asking about her, not yet. The music was loud, probably too loud for any of them to hold a normal conversation. Even the piano-singer was having a hard time hearing himself over the noise.

"And no girls?" Wendy inquired, the display of masculine flesh around her a heady sight, like a smorgasbord of men.

Peter grinned. "Just you, now."

It was a prospect that made her dizzyingly uncomfortable, although not entirely in a bad way. Her thoughts were interrupted by the swing of a door and in came Tink, changed out of her green sparkles, trading that for red feathers and sequins, including a red and white boa wrapped around her neck that made her look a little like a tall, blond candy cane.

"Peter!" Tink blew the boy three kisses, leaving red lipstick prints on her big palms.

Wendy couldn't help but state the obvious. "I think Tink likes you."

"Of course she does," Peter agreed. "But I don't swing that way."

She would have asked which way he meant, but she had a feeling she knew, given what was happening already in the periphery, men kissing and touching and rubbing flesh through thin layers of clothing at the edges of the room. To Wendy, it looked like everyone here except maybe Peter swung that particular way!

"I have something fun for you, Wendy-dear!" Tink's voice dripped saccharine, the false sweetness leaving the girl feeling numb as the tall blond approached. "I made it up special, just for you!"

"Tink," Peter warned, frowning and starting to pull Wendy away as Tink opened the little tin box in her hand.

Wendy was too curious for her own good. "What is it?"

"Pixie dust." The blond leaned in and blew hard with her red-painted lips, the white stuff inside puffing up into Wendy's face in a cloud. She coughed and gasped and sneezed and Peter swore, but it was far too late for that. The world was already spinning, her feet going out from under her so fast she was hardly aware of Peter catching her and bringing her down to a sofa amidst a sea of concerned faces.

"Goodness," Wendy whispered, her eyes seeking out Peter and finding him. "That's… lovely."

"Wicked Tink." Peter grinned at the way Wendy stretched and smiled on the couch. "She's gone and given you a happy, hasn't she?"

"Is she really all ours, Peter?" One of the boys asked, eyes wide.

Peter nodded. "If she'll have us."

"I'm Curly," a boy with dark curls announced. "And this is Nibs." The boy beside him nodded a hello, his hair long and straight and dyed a deep, jet black to match the eyeliner and dark lipstick he wore.

"I'm Slightly." It was the boy from the top of the piano, his hair bright red, smiling down at her now with laugh-crinkles at the corners of his eyes. "On account of I'm just a smidge over slightly-too-handsome."

Wendy laughed like it was the funniest thing she'd ever heard, and maybe it was. Her body sure thought so—it was tingling, alive with good humor.

"His name is Edward Slight," Peter interrupted, making a face. "Oh, here are the twins."

For a moment, Wendy had thought she was seeing double, those two same faces and reddish-blond curls poised over her.

"There are far too many of you to remember all your names," Wendy apologized, half-sitting on the sofa now, seeing them all surrounding her. Twenty? Thirty? How many rooms did this house have anyway? Where did they all sleep?

"You'll learn us all," one of the twins assured her.

"Over time," the other twin piped up.

"Okay, let the girl breathe, would you?" Peter reached for her hand, pulling Wendy to standing. The world had stopped swimming, but now it was glowing, all warm and fuzzy around the edges. It was delicious.

"I love this song." Wendy put her arms boldly around the boy's neck and tucked her head under his chin. "Let's dance."

She'd never heard the song before in her life and didn't care, except that it was slow and pulsing and alive as they rocked together in the middle of the floor. They were the only couple for a moment or two, but then boys started to join them, twined together, limbs wrapped, hard flat bellies pressed together, navels kissing.

She thought she'd never seen anything so interesting before and she couldn't help staring as Nibs and Curly kissed each other like lovers, the pink flash of their tongues almost as much of a surprise as a glimpse of the pierced stud in Nibs' tongue.

"Are you shocked, Wendy Dahling?" Peter whispered, tucking a piece of sandy-blond hair behind her ear for better access. His breath was hot and it made her shiver.

"Terribly," she whispered back, nuzzling his neck, feeling him shift his weight in response. She was lost in the feel of him, long and lean, the way his hands pressed her lower back, but she noticed someone missing and couldn't help remarking on it. "Where did Tink go?"

"She's pouting." Peter's chuckled. "I think she wanted to dance with me instead."

"I can't blame her." She couldn't believe she was admitting it, but the way Peter's arms tightened around her alleviated any of her self-doubt. Why else had he invited her here? Wendy knew how the world worked, especially when it came to men—or boys, who were just slightly less mature versions of the same. She knew Peter would demand payment eventually. She hadn't expected any less.

"Let's go upstairs," she suggested, glancing around at the plethora of sex going on in the room. For some reason, it all seemed natural, the way the boys were mingled together on couches and bending over chairs, a cacophony of flesh, playing in time with the pounding music.

"We can't leave yet." Peter scoffed. "The party's just started."

What did he want? She wondered, still feeling wild and dazed as he led her over to a sofa. Curly and Nibs were on one end, oblivious to anything else but themselves. Slightly was on the other end with a boy Wendy didn't recognize or didn't remember, but she wasn't looking much at his face anyway, as the boy's considerable cock was out and being swallowed at great length by Slightly, who knelt between the unknown boy's thighs.

"Sit with me, Wendy-girl." Peter pulled her into his lap and she felt the evidence of his arousal through his jeans. So he *did* want something, she mused, wrapping her arms around his neck, feeling Nibs shifting behind her, giving out a low moan. Curly must have been doing something nice to him, although she couldn't see what from her vantage point.

"What do you want from me, Peter Pann?" Might as well just come out with it, she reasoned. Put all their cards on the table.

"Nothing." He shrugged, smiling.

She touched his nose with the tip of her finger like he had with her. "I don't believe you."

He opened his mouth to protest but they both heard the plaintive, "Wendy!?" call from the stairs. She jumped up and Peter followed, although by that time she'd already ushered eight-year-old Michael back upstairs, thankful she'd reached him before he could get around the corner and see what was going on in the living room—not that Michael and John hadn't seen worse, living where they had.

Wendy tucked him back in next to his sleeping brother, kissing him on the forehead.

"I had a bad dream about a giant fairy," Michael whispered.

"Did you?" Wendy blinked at him in the light of the nearly-full moon.

"She was scary." Michael's thumb went to his mouth. Sometimes he still did that, when he was very tired or anxious. "She told me she was going to eat me up if I didn't find you."

Wendy glanced behind, wondering where she might find Tink. "Are you sure it was a dream?"

"She had wings," Michael mumbled around his thumb, eyes closing already.

Shutting the door behind her, she found Peter sitting on the edge of her twin bed. How had he managed to find this room for her, with so many boys in the house?

"I'll take them somewhere else tomorrow." Wendy kept her voice to a whisper, sitting next to Peter on the bed. "We can't stay here and impose on you."

"You can't go." Peter's hand found hers in the darkness. The window was open and the sound of the swamp outside was night music. "I just found you."

She looked at the moonlit windowsill, felt the warm breeze on her face. "I'm just not sure this is the place for us."

"Where else is there for you to go?" Peter asked. The boy had a point. He squeezed her hand. "I promise, I'll make Tink behave."

"And what do you want in return?"

He shrugged. "I told you—nothing."

"You have to want something."

"Okay, then." He pulled the covers down, exposing the sheets beneath. "One thing."

She knew it. But she asked anyway. "What?"

"A goodnight kiss." Peter patted the bed.

"And that's all?" she asked, suspicious.

"Yes." Peter laughed, wrestling her around onto the bed and tucking the covers in around her. "Go to sleep. You've had a very long day."

She sighed. "I've had a long life."

Peter's mouth was magical, his lips impossibly soft, his breath like sweet nectar. Just one kiss, so very brief and tender. Wendy whimpered when they parted.

"I'm going to throw you a birthday party," he announced.

She smiled. "You don't have to do that."

"I want to." He sprang up from his spot on the bed, going over to open the door. She saw him framed in the light from the hallway. "Good night, Wendy-girl."

"Goodnight," she whispered as he closed the door behind him, not quite believing that he was going, that she was letting him go. But he was gone, back down to join the merriment, she imagined, and that thought had her wondering if she maybe needed to see a therapist as much as the folks at the foster care home said she did. What was she thinking, bringing John and Michael into this craziness?

Maybe it was just Tink's "fairy dust" that had her feeling warm and high and fine with everything. Maybe she'd re-think it all in the light of day, pack their bags, and go. But right then, with Peter gone and the lonely sound of crickets in the distance, she found herself very disappointed that she hadn't insisted that he stay.

* * * *

Peter had the house going mad, planning for Wendy's eighteenth birthday party. He'd had just a few days to put it all together, and he'd even enlisted Tink's help. The only thing that bothered Wendy was his plan for Michael and John.

"I'm telling you, they'll be fine!" Peter reassured her for the umpteenth time, helping her carry the boys' bags down the stairs. "Every little kid wants to spend the weekend at Disney World!"

Well, she had to admit, he was probably right. She just wasn't sure the twins were the right people to be taking care of them. It was like the blind leading the blind. Or the immature leading the immature. They were just boys themselves. How could the twins be responsible for her little brothers?

Of course, how could she? She was just a kid herself, really.

It was John and Michael who finally convinced her, popping up around her uncontrollably like Mexican jumping beans. They were desperate to go, Peter was paying—although she was afraid to ask where all the money came from—and there might not ever be another opportunity like it.

"You both be good." She kissed Michael's cheek, and he accepted that willingly enough, throwing his arms around her neck in a hug. John was more reticent, wiping her kiss away, but he let her kiss the top of his head without rubbing that off before he got into the car.

"And you two, too!" She hugged the first twin—Marmaduke—and then the other—Binky. She knew their names now but still couldn't tell them apart. "Take good care of my babies."

"We will!" They agreed simultaneously. One of the twins got into the driver's seat, the other in the passenger's side, and Wendy waved to the boys and they to her, out the back window, until the car disappeared around the corner.

"Okay, back to work." Peter ushered Wendy back into the house. "You go help Tink in the kitchen."

Wendy made a face. "I'd rather be slowly disemboweled."

“I’m sure she’d be happy to oblige.”

“Very funny.” She nudged him with her hip. “Where are you going?”

“I have more surprises to plan.” He gave her a push toward the kitchen. “Now go!”

The kitchen was the only room in the house that wasn’t simply lined with bookshelves. The living room, bedrooms, even the dining room, had wall to ceiling shelves crammed with books, books and more books. Only the kitchen and the bathrooms had been spared.

Tink was on her knees, rummaging through a cupboard and swearing like a sailor under her breath.

“Hi Tink.”

“Ow!” Tink swore again, holding her head where she’d banged it on the bottom of an open drawer. “Warn a girl, would you?”

“Sorry,” Wendy apologized, although she wasn't sure she was really sorry. “I thought I was.”

Tink straightened, still rubbing her head. “What do you want?”

“Peter said I should help you.”

“He did, huh?” Tink sighed. “Okay, here. Sit. Can you paint?”

Wendy snorted. “Paint by numbers maybe.”

“Oy.” Tink threw up her hands. “Okay, see these flower petals? Paint them all pink.”

“I can do that.” Wendy eyed the white pastiche petals doubtfully.

“Good.” Tink busied herself at the sink, rinsing and stacking dirty dishes. Tink seemed to be the only one in the place who actually did any housework or cooking. Wendy had offered to take some of the burden—it was the least she could do, she figured—but Tink had practically hissed and spit at the idea.

“So tell me something, Tink.” Wendy looked at the three-tier cake on the table, wondering if Tink might have poisoned it just out of spite. But of course, if she knew Peter might eat it, Tink wouldn't dare. “Why do you hate me?”

“I don’t hate you.” Tink was quick to reply but then she hesitated, frowning at Wendy. “I just love Peter.”

“I can understand that.” Of course she could. Peter was easy to love. She was halfway there herself.

“I don’t want him to get hurt,” Tink went on. Of course, that wasn't everything, and they both knew it.

“I don’t either,” Wendy agreed. “See, we’re really on the same side.”

Tink raised her waxed eyebrows. “I’m not sure I’d go that far.”

Wendy went on painting petals Pepto-Bismol pink. She didn't have the heart to tell Tink that she hated pink and she figured Tink probably wouldn't care. Or more likely, she would be secretly delighted she’d picked the thing Wendy liked least.

“How long have you known him?” Wendy figured they might as well talk about the one thing they had in common.

“Two years.” Tink had a secret smile on her face. “He got me off the streets.”

Wendy glanced at Tink’s outfit—a black sequin mini-dress under a flour stained apron. *You can take the girl off the streets, but...*

“And how long have you all been here?”

“At Neverland?” Tink shrugged. “About that long.”

“Did he get all the other boys off the streets too?” Wendy was thinking about the other night, the way the boys had touched each other, making out in all corners of the room, still not sure if her memory was clouded by her experience with Tink’s “pixie dust.”

“Most of them.” Tink lined up appetizers on cookie sheets.

“So what do they all do now?” Wendy sat back to admire her work. Painting flower petals wasn't rocket science or anything, but she thought she was doing a satisfactory job.

“They live here.”

Wendy looked at Tink, thoughtful. “But… how does Peter pay for everything?”

Tink didn't reply for a long time, arranging canapés on the tray. Finally, she said, “Maybe you should ask Peter that.”

The phone rang and Tink grabbed for it, looking relieved. It was the old fashioned kind that hung on the wall with a twisty cord attached.

"Hello?"

Wendy turned her attention back to the task at hand, smiling to herself at all the preparations Peter had undertaken just to give her a happy birthday. She could count on one hand the times she'd had a birthday cake, let alone a party. The last party she could remember was her tenth, and it had been a downright disaster, ending with her drunken stepfather sending all of her friends home and then doing unspeakable things to her while John and Michael cried in the other room.

"How did you get this number?" Tink's voice trembled, her face going white, the rouge on her cheeks standing out like fat roses. Wendy looked up, watching as Tink covered the mouthpiece, her eyes closing as she swore to herself, "Fuck! Fuck, fuck fuck!"

Tink put the phone back to her mouth again. "I'm sorry, there's no one here by that name, goodbye." She put the phone back in its cradle, resting her head against the wall, her breath coming so fast Wendy was afraid she was going to hyperventilate.

Wendy put her hand on the girl's shoulder—although she knew Tink's true gender, she still thought of her as a girl—and whispered, "Tink? Everything okay?"

"No." Tink lifted her head, blinking back what Wendy thought might be tears. "Definitely not okay."

"Who was that on the phone?"

"No one." She was clearly lying. "Nothing for you to worry about."

"Isn't there anything I can do?" Wendy asked, feeling helpless.

"I should go find Peter," Tink said faintly, wiping her hands on her apron and wandering toward the door. She stopped in the doorway, turning back to look at Wendy. "What was I doing?"

"Ummm…" Wendy frowned, startled by the blank look in Tink's eyes.

The timer on the stove went off and Tink jumped like she'd been goosed, grabbing hot pads off the counter and pulling a cookie sheet full of hors d'oeuvres out of the oven. She slid another cookie sheet in and set the timer again.

Wendy was curious about the phone call—she couldn't help it—but she thought it best not to mention it, given Tink's reaction. Instead, she went back to painting petals pink and watched Tink arrange more appetizers.

"That's a pretty dress," Wendy said, just to change the subject.

"Thanks." Tink smiled, tugging at the hem. It was very short and showed off her long, very shapely legs. "Oh, speaking of dresses—Peter had me leave a dress for you in your room."

"One of yours?"

Tink laughed. "You'd swim in one of mine, honey."

Well, that was true enough. Whatever hormone replacement she'd had, or maybe implants, had considerably blessed Tink in the breast department. She was tall, curvy, and large-busted. Wendy was far shorter, slight, and far less endowed.

"Peter picked it out for you." Tink's gaze swept over the smaller girl. "I'm sure you'll look adorable in it."

Wendy put down her paint brush. "I don't want to fight with you."

"Were we fighting?"

"Tink, I think you're a very pretty…girl…" Wendy started, a sort of peace offering.

"Why don't you go get dressed?" Tink waved her toward the kitchen door. "I've got this."

Wendy sighed but she went, giving up on trying to call a truce between them. It was impossible. Besides, she was far too curious about the dress waiting for her upstairs, and she wasn't disappointed when she unzipped the dry-cleaning bag. Peter had great taste, and although Wendy wouldn't have chosen it for herself, she had to admit that blue was her color, as bright as a cloudless summer day, pure silk, backless and barely to her knees.

She spent more than an hour pampering herself, shooing away several interruptions from the boys, but she knew there were other bathrooms in the house. For a little while, this one was hers. She shaved her legs, admiring them as she went. They weren't as long as Tink's, but they were shapely and smooth nonetheless. Her breasts weren't much more than a handful, but that meant she didn't have to wear a bra with the gorgeous dress Peter had chosen for her, a fact she wondered about as she dressed—had Peter considered that fact? The thought brought a slow, secret smile to her face as she used a curling iron to make long, fat blond ringlets in her hair.

She looked at herself in the mirror, feeling as if she'd been lost in a dream. One brief encounter in the library had brought Peter into her life and changed it completely in less than a week. It didn't seem possible—but it was real. She knew it for sure when Peter knocked on the bathroom door and gasped out loud when she opened it, the sight of her making his eyes light up and his mouth twist into a bemused smile.

"You clean up fine, Wendy-girl." He took her hand and led her down the stairs where guests were gathering, most of them she'd never even met, yet they all brought gifts for her because Peter had asked them to.

She saw Curly and Nibs standing together, each of them holding a beer, and was relieved to see a few friendly faces. Slightly was over in the corner, she noticed, his red head bent and whispering to the girl in his lap, but there were noticeably far fewer girls than boys present.

And of course, there was Tink, flitting around the room, refilling drinks and passing out hors d'oeuvres and smiling over at Peter, who winked and waved back. Wendy was the only one who saw her stick her tongue out when Peter wasn't looking. *There is just never going to be any love between the two of us,* Wendy decided.

"I want to introduce you," Peter said, pulling her more firmly into the room.

"To...?"

He smiled, hooking his arm through hers. "Everyone."

And he wasn't kidding. She knew most of the boys who stayed in the house, but there were many, many more, too many names to remember, too many faces to count. They all seemed glad to meet her, mostly because it was Peter who was doing the introductions. He drew people in like a magnet, without even trying. There was plenty of food, thanks to Tink, and music piped in through speakers in the ceiling with enough of a beat that a few people had formed a quasi dance floor near the piano.

Peter asked her to dance when a slow song came on and she followed him, just as drawn to him as everyone else was, glad to have a moment alone in his arms. He dropped his head and held her close, breathing her in, and they rocked slowly, as if it were only the two of them in the midst of a world of crazy.

"It's a lovely party, Peter, thank you." She tilted her face up to look at him. "No one's ever given me a party like this before."

"It's not over yet." His mouth curled into a slow smile. "I haven't even given you my present."

"You do realize how insane this is, don't you?" She couldn't help laughing at the way he raised his eyebrows and rolled his eyes. "I haven't even known you a week! And you've let me move in, you're giving me this elaborate party, and Michael and John..."

She paused, as if just remembering them, her brow knitted with worry.

"I heard from the twins," Peter said, guessing her concern. "They're all fine. The swashbucklers are having the time of their lives, in fact! The Pirates of the Caribbean will never be the same again, I'm sure."

"It's all so much." She brushed a sandy-colored curl from his forehead. She felt dizzy and flushed with him so very close. "Too much."

"It will never be enough," Peter protested, his face as serious as she'd ever seen it. "Not for you. A girl like you deserves this and far more, you know. I could give you everything in the whole world, everything I had to give, and it would still never be enough for my Wendy-girl."

"Your..." She blinked. "*Your* Wendy?"

"You are, aren't you?" he asked in earnest.

It was so hard to resist him, but she tried, not based on her feelings but purely driven by logic. “We've only known each other—”

His laughter cut her off and he swung her around in his arms, nuzzling her neck, disarming her completely. “You keep saying that, but it doesn't mean anything you know.” He whispered it like a secret in her ear. “The heart doesn't know any time.”

“Peter...” She tried to protest, but his lips were doing funny things to her insides, pressed to her throat like that.

“Say you're mine, Wendy-girl.” His lips found the hollow of her throat and her head went back, acquiescing.

“I am,” she confessed. It didn’t matter how long they’d known each other, how crazy her life had been before him or how crazy it was now. He was right—she couldn’t deny her feelings. “I'm yours.”

Peter kissed her squarely on the lips, his aim sweet perfection, and although Wendy had been kissed plenty of times before, had even been kissed once, albeit briefly, by Peter, it felt as if this kiss was the one she'd been waiting for her whole life. It was silly, ridiculous, far too romantic for her usually sensible sensibilities, but it was simply the unmistakable truth.

And she knew it completely when they parted, Wendy's head resting on Peter's shoulder, and she saw Tink glaring at them both.

“Peter.” Someone tapped on his shoulder, whispering into his ear, but Wendy paid no attention, lost in his embrace.

“Time for your birthday gift.” Peter’s voice brought her back to earth, back to the room around her. He led her out the patio doors, the crowd following, as if knowing just what was going to happen, although Wendy had no clue. She hadn’t been into the yard that day, but it was decorated for the festivities as well. Just how many people had Peter enlisted? She wondered, staring at the lights strung up high, the tent set up for a band to play.

“Sit here.” Peter situated her near the front of the tent, separate from the rest of the chairs that people were taking behind her. “Be right back.”

He kissed her forehead, squeezing her hand, before disappearing into the crowd. She looked around for a familiar face but saw none. The night was bright with moonlight and stars, the sounds of crickets and the occasional bellow of alligators from the swamp serving as background music for the laughter and conversation. She was all alone, and yet she'd never felt so happy, the anticipation of Peter's return still warm against her forehead.

When Peter appeared on stage, picking up a guitar, along with Slightly and Curly and Nibs and another boy she didn't know quite as well with the unfortunate nickname of Tootles, Wendy stared up at them in surprise. Tootles was tall and lanky, long blond hair falling in his face, but he disappeared behind the drum set as Curly picked up a guitar and Nibs a bass. Slightly positioned himself behind the keyboard as Peter stepped up to the mic.

"Hello." Peter's voice was soft as silk and the crowd broke into applause and cheers. They all knew him, loved him, and who could blame them? Certainly not Wendy. "We're *The Lost Boys."*

More cheers. Wendy blinked up at Peter in wonder, seeing him drop her a wink.

"I'd like to dedicate this next song to Wendy. I wrote it for her."

She couldn't believe her eyes—or her ears. The Peter she knew, the one she'd glimpsed, unfolded into a god on stage, his pouty lips and sultry eyes drawing her in. And it was all for her. The girls—and even some of the boys—instantly went crazy for him, crowding the stage, but his eyes were on her alone, singing his song for her.

"You sew my heart back together in the darka the night.
Bring my shadow back home so I can see the light.
You turn my lost boy into a found man
And you shine me back from my Neverland.

I would brave any pirate ship
Slay any dangers just to kiss your lips.
That kind of magic, girl, you make me fly.

Wendy, our love ain't never gonna die.

Wendy, no, we ain't never gonna die.
Long as our love lasts, girl, we're gonna fly,
Past all tomorrows to the starry skies.
Wendy, our love ain't never gonna die."

They sang more songs at the demand of the crowd, their music rising over the crickets and the swamp sounds, carried for miles on the wind, and Wendy sat entranced, so delighted with this Peter that she could barely breathe. When he came off the stage—under great protest from the audience—he went straight to her, reaching out for her hand and pulling her into his arms.

"Did you like your gift?" he asked in a whisper just for her and she nodded, unable to speak, not sure he could hear her over the people crowding around them, slapping him on the back, girls asking for his autograph—his autograph!—giving them their phone numbers along with kisses. The former he signed, the latter he rebuffed as much as he could, making his way through, leading Wendy with him by the hand.

"It was beautiful. I didn't even know you could sing!" She glimpsed Tink wending her way through the crowd toward them. "I bet there's a lot I don't know about you, Peter Pann."

"Probably." He smiled, squeezing her hand back. "Does it matter?"

"No," she confessed as Tink found them both, breathlessly grabbing Peter by the shoulders.

"Hey Tink." He greeted her as always, with a congenial smile.

"I have to talk to you." The tall blond dismissed Wendy with a glance, focusing all her attention on Peter. "It's important."

"Damned straight it is!" Curly clapped Peter on the shoulder, grinning from ear to ear. Nibs wasn't far behind, the two of them practically attached at the hip. "Guess who's here? Go ahead, guess!"

"I have no idea." Peter blinked in surprised, shaking his head. "The Pope? The President? Batman?"

"Far better." Nibs smiled, the silver hop piercing in his lip glinting in the light.

"Michael Corbett!" This announcement came from Slightly, appearing out of the crowd and into their conversation. "Fucking Michael Corbett! He wants to represent us, man! And I'm pretty sure we want to sign. Don't we, Peter?"

"Who's Michael Corbett?" Wendy whispered her question to Nibs, who happened to be closest.

"Only the biggest music agent in South Florida." Peter answered her question with a widening grin. "Guess we should talk to him, huh?"

"Come on!" Slightly grabbed Peter's arm, but Tink held onto the other, Wendy getting lost in the shuffle.

"Peter!" Tink cried. "I still have to talk—"

"Later, Tink!" He waved Tink away as *The Lost Boys* dragged him toward his future in the music industry, leaving both girls standing there, looking forlorn and forgotten.

"What did you have to talk to Peter about?" Wendy turned to Tink, but the blond was shaking her head, arms crossed.

"Never you mind." Tink huffed off into the house, leaving Wendy completely alone.

* * * *

She didn't follow Tink and she didn't follow Peter. Instead, she went for a walk, needing to clear her head, to breathe the night air away from the crowd. She wandered outside of the tent and down the pathway toward the swamp. Her heels got stuck in the grass so she took them off, walking barefoot, following to the sound of bullfrogs.

What had she gotten herself into? The thought kept recurring as she made her way across the edge of the water, her feet sinking slightly in the marshy soil. Yes, she'd been desperate to find a way out for herself and her little brothers. Yes, Peter had appeared as a guardian angel and had taken her, had taken all of them, under his wing. But things were so strange here, so otherworldly, surreal. And there was so much she didn't know about Peter, in spite of her growing feelings for him.

Did she trust him? She tried to be objective, to be smart, but the truth was, she did trust him. In spite of all the strangeness and everything she didn't know, there was something about Peter that made him guileless and loveable. But was she just kidding herself? Was her own aching, desperate heart leading her into trouble?

"Hello there."

The voice came out of the darkness and Wendy gasped, clutching her heart, suddenly jumping to life in her chest.

"You scared me!" Her eyes adjusted to the darkness, seeing a man standing in a motorboat on the water about five feet away. The moon was bright enough that she could make out a pale face, long dark hair, the flash of a bright white smile.

"I apologize," he said, giving her a strange little bow. He appraised her in the dim light, raising his eyebrows. "So you must be Peter's latest dish?"

Wendy frowned, taking a step back. "Latest…?"

The man chuckled. "He changes girls like most people change socks."

"Who are you?"

"No one important." He leaned toward her, resting on a pole stuck in the water at the side of the boat. "He seems quite taken with you."

She glanced back at the distant glow of the house, the white of the tent in the moonlight. "He gave me this party."

"Oh, aren't you sweet?" The man laughed, teeth flashing again. "But this isn't for you, dearie. This is all to showcase his band." The man snorted with disgust. "Don't let him fool you. This has been planned for months."

She looked from the man to the house and back again. The tent, all the food, all the people… was it possible?

She proceeded cautiously, still keeping her distance. "How do you know Peter?"

"Oh we go way back."

"Friends?" she inquired politely.

"You could say that." The man pulled something out of his pocket—a cell phone, its light bright in the darkness as he looked at it. "He's quite a catch, though. Hang onto him while you can. I gotta run."

He started to push off with his pole but Wendy rushed forward, her feet getting wet. "Wait! What else do you know about Peter?"

"Do you really want to know?" The man stopped in mid-reach, not starting the motor.

She swallowed. Did she? Did she really?

"Yes."

"Meet me back here at..." The man pulled a cord, the motor starting, a low hum. "Let's say... three a.m."

Wendy had to speak up to be heard over the boat. "That's awfully late!"

"The party should be over by then," he called, pulling the pole in. "It will be nice and quiet. Just you, me and the alligators. Then we can talk."

She hesitated, watching him sit down in the boat. "Why can't you tell me now?"

"I have a previous engagement." He waved and winked, turning on a light at the front of his boat. "But if you really want to know more about your new boyfriend, I'll be happy to tell you. Just meet me back here."

He revved the motor, getting ready to go, and she knew it was her last chance.

"Okay," she called. "Okay, I'll be here!"

"Good girl." He gave her a thumbs up.

"What's your name?" she asked over the sound of the motor.

"Hook. James Hook." He glanced over his shoulder at her. "And who might you be?"

"Wendy Dahling."

"Well, ta ta for now, Wendy Dahling!" With that, he was gone, disappearing into the swamp with just a shaky, hazy light to lead him.

Wendy returned to the party where Peter was still gathered with *The Lost Boys*, presumably talking to the agent. He had to be the one in the suit. Only Tink seemed to have noticed that she had gone missing, coming up to her with a deep frown, taking in her wet, muddy, bare feet, her shoes still dangling in her hand.

"Where were you?"

Wendy didn't answer. Instead, she asked the question that had been burning on her lips. "Does Peter know anyone named James Hook?"

Tink's mouth flattened into a thin line, her red lipstick all but disappearing. "Who told you?"

"Told me?" Wendy blinked in surprise. "No one told me. I'm asking you."

"Wendy!" It was Peter, coming for her, and in spite of Hook's warning, her heart soared at the sound of his voice. "Can you forgive me for leaving you?"

She smiled. "Of course."

He linked his arm with hers, grinning. "And are you ready to open all your glorious presents?"

"Ask Peter," Tink hissed, narrowing her eyes and walking quickly away.

But there was no time for that. First it was opening piles of gifts—clothes from jeans to shirts to dresses in just her size, plus a brand new iPhone (that's from *The Lost Boys,* Peter told her) and gift cards galore. Plus all those things you buy for a girl you don't know—bath salts and lotions and pretty bags and scarves. She thanked everyone for her gifts, and they all applauded her, but of course, she knew it was mostly for Peter, who stood grinning beside her, his arm wrapped tightly around her waist.

Then there was cake, and all sorts of other little dessert that Tink had painstakingly created, and more music and dancing. Wendy found herself in Peter's arms on the makeshift dance floor most of the time, the world around them shimmering like a dream.

The night faded away after that, people saying their goodbyes, some diehards setting up with booze and music and dancing in the living room. It began to feel a little like the night she'd first come to Peter's as people draped themselves across couches and chairs, limbs twined and lips locked.

"Come with me," Peter whispered into her ear, already pulling her away. Up the stairs they went, down the hall to the largest room in the house—Peter's room. She'd seen it once, just from the doorway, but she wouldn't have recognized it when he opened the door. The place had been transformed, twinkling lights strung up, criss-crossing the ceiling, gauze draped over the bed, the floor covered, simply *covered* in rose petals of all colors—red, yellow, white. They stuck to her bare feet as Peter led her into the room.

"Tink did this," Peter said, pushing the gauze aside and sitting on the bed. He patted the place beside him but Wendy couldn't stop looking around at the magic.

"She did it for you." Wendy smiled, taking his offered hand and stepping closer.

"No, she did it for you," he protested, slipping his arms around her waist, burying his face in her hair.

"And you did it for me."

He looked at her, his gaze soft, loving. "Yes, I did."

"Why?"

"Because I really, really like you, Wendy-girl." He kissed the tip of her nose. "And I've never met someone so in need of a happy ending in my life."

"With all the people living in this house, how can you say that?"

He chuckled. "You see, I'm the voice of experience."

His kiss broke her heart into a million pieces and put it back together, whole and beating and thick with blood, in an instant. She had never known anything like this, had never known anyone like Peter.

"It really is beautiful," she whispered as they parted, his hands in her hair.

"And so are you."

She flushed. "Stop."

"I'm just getting started."

He kissed her, softly at first, and then deeper, his tongue finding hers, sending electric shocks along her skin. There was no doubt about what they were going to do, and Wendy found herself welcoming him completely. He touched her gently, but he wasn't tentative. His motions were firm, sure—he knew just what he wanted as he pulled her onto the mattress, the gauze around the bed wrapping them in a hazy cocoon.

"Oh Wendy-girl, the truth is—I'm so in love with you," he whispered, pushing her dress up to her hips, pressing his lips against her navel.

She thrilled at his words and returned them without question, without thought. "I love you, too." It was impossible, but it was undeniable. "I want you. Please."

He lifted his head, where he was leaving kisses all over her flat, trembling belly. "Do you?"

"Yes." The word was breathless, full of longing.

Smiling mischievously, he cocked his head, eyes bright. "What if I decide to tease you for a while first?"

She whimpered as he traced his fingertips lightly over her skin, bringing her body alive with his touch. He explored her slowly and with relish, pulling the silk of her dress over her head and staring in wonder at her breasts as she stretched out on her back on the bed, her hands thrown over her head. She found herself giving in to whatever he wanted, letting him fondle and touch wherever he liked. He played her like an instrument, the notes rising higher, growing louder.

"Peter," she begged, wrapping her arms around his neck, her legs around his waist. They were both in their underwear, Wendy wearing a pair of powder blue silk panties and Peter just in a boxers. "Please, please, please."

"Please what?" He captured her nipple—it was wet with saliva, having enjoyed a long sucking just a few moments before. His eyes met hers and he grinned, his tongue making circles around her pink areola.

"I want you," she insisted, reaching down to find him. He was hard and she rubbed him, not inexperienced, and his eyes widened in surprise. Her hand slipped under the elastic of his boxers and she wrapped her hand around the base of him, tugging gently.

"Oh Wendy." He groaned, beginning to thrust in her hand. "That's so good."

"Is it?" She rubbed her thumb over the head. "Do you like that?"

"Oh god." He bit his lip as she stroked him, wiggling under him, wondering if she could just wish the rest of their clothes away. "You're a naughty girl, Wendy."

"I'm going to get naughtier." She was true to her word, sliding his boxers down his hips and seeking the heat of his cock with her mouth. Peter gasped, letting her roll him to his back and take him between her lips, sucking him slow and deep, moaning around his length.

"Oh girl," he whispered, his hand moving through her hair, his hips beginning to rock with her motion. "Oh god, girl, that's better than Disney World."

She giggled, licking the tip, tasting him. "Better than ice cream?"

"Uh-huh." He bit his lip, his eyes closing as she went down on him again, trying to swallow his whole length. "Better than sex… oh, wait."

She giggled again, nuzzling his belly, rubbing the wet head of his cock over her pert breasts. Her nipples were hard and rosy from all his attention.

"I want to go for a ride," she said, slipping off her panties and straddling him.

Peter looked up at her with bright eyes. "At Disney World?"

"It's better," she whispered, reaching down to grasp and tug at him, looking down to see him rising him against the flat of her belly.

"Oh yeah," he groaned as she slipped him inside of her for the first time. "Definitely better. Much, much better."

"Mmm hmm." She smiled, leaning in to kiss him, wiggling into the saddle of his hips, letting him fill her completely. They didn't move, just held onto each other, tongues and limbs mingling, their bodies finding a way to settle in, joining even more deeply.

"Wendy-girl." Peter swallowed, looking up, her hair falling around them like corn silk. "I'm sorry."

"For what?" she asked, smiling at him, bemused.

"I'm going to have to fuck you." He rolled her to her back in one movement, his cock shoved in deep, so very deep.

"Oh god." She wrapped her legs around his waist. "Don't ever apologize for that."

"No, I mean really…" Peter began to move, his eyes fluttering closed. "Really…"

"Oh!" Wendy cried out as his cock bottomed out inside of her.

"Really…" Peter drove in again, rolling his hips and pulling back.

"Ohhh!" She clung to him as he gave her more, more, rocking on top of her, the bed moving with the motion.

"Really fuck you," he panted in her ear.

"Yes!" She welcomed his weight, the buck and thrust of his hips, and begged him for more. "Don't stop! Oh Peter, yes! Fuck me!"

He groaned and dipped his head down to suckle at her breast, first one nipple and then the other, then knelt up between her thighs, spreading them so he could fuck her hard from that angle too.

"You're so beautiful," he murmured, looked down at her in wonder. "Fuck. Oh fuck. Ohhhh!"

She cried out in surprise as he withdrew, still thrusting, a rising stream of cum shooting over her belly. Grasping him in her hand—she couldn't help herself—she milked his throbbing cock as his climax shook his body. Peter moaned and thrust into her hand, showering her with cum, making her tummy and breasts sticky with it.

"Oh my," she whispered, rubbing the wetness into her body.

"Your turn." Peter grinned happily, shoving her legs back and burying his face between them. She twisted and writhed at his sudden attention, his tongue working magic against her clit. There was no escape. His hands grabbed her hips, mouth tight against her pussy, nose brushing the light, curly blond hair there, and when he slid his fingers inside of her, replacing the emptiness, she knew she was lost.

"Oh yes!" She rocked her hips up to meet him, her belly and ass clenched tight, giving him her orgasm with every thrust. "Yes, yes, yes!"

She was still shaking when he kissed his way up her body, leaving a wet trail. She tasted herself in his mouth when he kissed her, sticky and sweet.

"We need a shower." She traced the line of her jaw with her finger.

He shifted his hips, surprising her. "Not yet." He was hard against her thigh.

"More?" She raised her eyebrows and her hips, meeting him.

"Lots more." He rolled her to her belly, not letting her up to her knees as he spread her legs with his, his cock riding the valley between them, parting her flesh with his. Then he was inside of her, sliding in deep and hard and fast.

"Oh god!" she cried, grabbing into the covers in her fists as they rocked the bed. "Oh yes!"

"Touch yourself," he whispered, his breath hot in her ear. "Do it, Wendy."

She did, wiggling on the bed until she could get her hand between her thighs, finding that sensitive bit of clit and rubbing it. He encouraged her with every thrust, whispering in her ear, his breath short, panting.

"Faster," he urged, his cock like steel, impaling her, making her moan and arch against him. "Do it faster. Come on, girl!"

"Oh Peter," she cried, her flushed cheek against his as they fucked. "Oh you fuck me so good. Please!"

"That's it." He kissed her cheek, the corner of her mouth, their bodies slick with sweat. "Come for me. Come all over my cock."

She moaned and spread and gave him what he asked for, unable to hold it back for a moment longer. Her pussy fluttered and clenched at him as she came, her cries so loud she knew everyone must have heard them, but she didn't care. He growled and grabbed her, rolling and thrusting up, driving her toward the ceiling, and she had to hold on for dear life so she didn't topple right off.

"Oh god!" Peter groaned and grabbed her hips and ass, rocking with his own climax. "You're so fucking good!"

Wendy cried out, feeling him coming, the swell and surge of his cock bursting inside of her like fireworks. She glanced back to see his lips pursed with pleasure, his gaze rising to meet hers as he emptied himself completely inside of her.

"That was far better than any ride at Disney World." She laughed as she climbed off him and turned around to snuggle in his arms. "There's no way John and Michael are having as much fun as I am."

Peter grinned. "That was no Epcot Center tour, that's for sure."

"More like Splash Mountain." Wendy ran a hand over her belly, holding it up to show him the sheen. They were soaked with sweat.

Peter smiled, his fingers walking down past her navel, through the wiry nest of her pubic hair. "Definitely going to need to take another trip to the Magic Kingdom tonight."

"You're insatiable." She giggled.

"You have no idea." He took her hand and she gasped in surprised to find him growing hard yet again.

She lost track of the time—of the times and positions and rides and orgasms. She lost herself and found Peter and he found her, too, again and again. In the end, the gauze had been ripped from the bedposts, and they were covered in rose petals from head to toe. The shower washed most of them off but they giggled as they wiped them off their feet before snuggling back in bed together.

She'd almost forgotten her chance meeting and the man in the boat until Peter fell asleep, his breathing deep and even, but she was still awake, staring up at the cast of moonlight on the ceiling. It was in that moment she remembered and looked at a clock, finding that it was already a little after three in the morning. They'd been having sex for hours and hours.

She thought about staying, curled against Peter's sleeping back, but the call of the swamp and her own curiosity got the better of her. She only had her dress to wear—all her new clothes were still downstairs in their boxes—so she slipped it over her head and eased the bedroom door open.

The house was sleeping and dark. A few doors were cracked down the hallway, but only the sounds of snoring met her as she made her way, barefoot, down the stairs. Downstairs, the place was a mess, cups and plates and food littering every available surface. Obviously Tink had decided to clean up in the morning.

Wendy took a deep breath and slipped out the patio doors into the night.

The crickets greeted her with a rising hum as she made her way toward the water. She found him just where he said he would be, waiting in his boat, the motor silent.

"Hello there, Wendy Dahling."

"Hi." She stopped, hesitating, glancing back toward the house. "Sorry I'm late."

"Just a little past three." Hook glanced at his phone, a beam in the darkness. "I take it you had a good night, then?"

"Fine." She blushed, thinking of Peter, sleeping in his bed. "So… you said you'd tell me about Peter."

"And so I will." He patted the seat beside him. "Come on, let's go for a ride."

"Oh, I don't think that's such a good idea." She took a step back, glancing toward the house, and saw the flash of someone coming down the path. Her heart dropped, worried that it might be Peter, that he might be angry. Of course he would be. What had she been thinking?

"Can't talk here." Hook nodded toward the figure hurrying down the walkway. "See? Too many interruptions." He used the pole to push the boat toward the shore and held out his hand for her. "Besides, I want to show you something."

"What?" Wendy stretched a trembling hand toward his, hearing a familiar voice calling.

"Wait!" Tink shouted, her voice dropping at least an octave. "Wendy! Wait!"

"Come with me and find out," Hook insisted, leaning in to catch hold of her hand. She gasped at the strength of his grip. "Trust me, it will be worth it."

"And you'll tell me more about Peter?" she asked, hearing Tink yelling for her, panting, out of breath, running now.

"I promise!" Hook agreed, yanking her toward the boat. "Now hurry!"

She took a step up and he pulled her in, starting the motor in the next instant, leaving Tink standing on the shoreline, calling after them, her voice fading as they traveled through the swamp.

The last thing Wendy heard was Tink's cry, "You're making a big mistake!" and as she turned to face James Hook steering the boat through the darkness, she hoped that Peter's spiteful, cross-dressing friend wasn't right this time.

* * * *

"Thirsty." Water was all she could think of. It was all around her, the sounds of frogs jumping and splashing in it at her bare feet. Her tongue felt thick and dry. "Please. So thirsty."

"You look quite horrible, you know." James Hook smirked from his perch on the end of the boat. There'd been nowhere to go when he'd lunged for her, knocking her head against the side of the outboard motor, and as if that wasn't enough already to knock her out, covering her mouth and nose with a nasty tasting chloroform.

She'd awakened like this, tied to a post in the middle of the swamp on a tiny little island. More of a muddy hill really. He must have created it just for this purpose. She could see the lights of a cabin on the shore, the thing dilapidated, falling apart. She could see that much, even in the moonlight. She didn't know where they were, how far they'd come. Tink had been right after all. She'd made a terrible mistake.

"Please," she begged, trying to swallow.

"Oh save the theatrics for when your boyfriend arrives." Hook waved her cries away, using a very large knife to wedge the mud out of the treads on his boot. "That's when the drama will be useful."

"What do you want?" Wendy croaked.

"I want what's mine."

What did that mean? She didn't know. "I didn't do anything to you. I don't even know you."

"That's incidental." Hook slid the knife against the side of the boat, scraping mud off. "Peter will come for you. That's all that matters."

"He won't." She said it defiantly, although she knew it wasn't true. "He hardly knows me."

"Oh he will," Hook disagreed. "I've never seen him take to someone like I've seen him take to you."

Wendy went quiet. She knew it, even before she said it. "You lied to me."

"He didn't pick you for your brains, did he?" He laughed, shaking his dark head in the moonlight. "At least you're catching on."

"What do you want from Peter?" She was slowly working on the duct tape wrapped around her wrists. She was wet from the struggle from boat to pole and she was sweaty, the swamp air heavy and thick, making the tape nice and moist.

Hook snorted. "You want the story?"

"Yes." She wondered what she would do when she was free. Jump into the water? The Florida Everglades wasn't exactly the best place to go for a swim. She could hear the call of alligators in the distance.

"I suppose we can spend our time talking until your knight in shining armor arrives." Hook stepped off the boat, which he'd anchored to the pole, onto her little island. There was hardly enough room for the two of them and he pressed himself against her in the darkness. "Although I did have some other things in mind. Things that would really, really bother your boyfriend."

He used the knife in his hand to slit the shoulder of her dress in one swift motion. She hadn't realized the blade had touched her until she looked down, seeing her skin like silver in the moonlight, a dark line of blood running toward her nipple. The sight of it made her feel faint.

"You promised!" she reminded him, desperate.

"I make lots of promises." He leaned in and licked at her shoulder and she realized he was tasting her blood. She shuddered, horrified. What kind of man was this? "But I don't keep them."

"How will Peter know where to find us?" She tried to distract him. Clearly he wanted Peter to come after her, although to what end, she couldn't begin to imagine. "How could he possibly find this place in the dark?"

"He could find it blindfolded." Hook chuckled, his knife blade sliding under the other shoulder of her dress. She winced, feeling a sting, knowing he's once again cut her flesh. "He used to live here."

"Here?" She was too shocked by his words to register the pain, staring at the broken-down shack in the distance. There was nothing else up and down the swamp that she could see, no other lights. "When?"

"Poor little orphaned Peter." Hook drove the knife into the wood above her head and took a step back—as far as he could go without falling into the water, and looked down at her breasts. "He needed so much looking after."

"What did you do?" She stared at him, and would have kicked him in the groin and sent him flying into the swamp if her feet hadn't been secured to the post with duct tape as well.

"He was a good trained monkey. For a little while." Hook grabbed her breast, squeezing, fondling, assessing, his face impassive. "And he learned the trade well enough. All the boys did."

"What trade?" she asked breathlessly, ignoring his groping hand and working her own behind her back, hoping for a break.

"The oldest profession in the world."

"You… sold them? As prostitutes?" Her twisting and turning stopped. "You're nothing more than a pimp!"

"And you, my dear, are a whore." He twisted her nipple, making her scream in pain. "You'll make a fine profit for me too."

No! Her mind screamed even louder, faced once again with a man who wanted to use her for his own pleasure and profit. *No!* She wouldn't do it, not again, not ever again.

"Peter got the best of you, didn't he?" She spoke the words softly but clearly. "He beat you."

"He won a little battle." Hook sneered. "But he hasn't won the war."

"He did win," she insisted. "He's done just fine without you."

"Fucking bitch," he spat, pressing her up against the pole, the splintered wood biting her bare back. "So Peter took *my* boys and *my* money. So it's taken me five years to find him. *Now* it's time to settle the score."

Five years. My god, how old was Peter when he left, Wendy wondered. Thirteen? How long had this man forced him to prostitute himself…?

"It was you on the phone with Tink." Her realization made her stomach drop to her knees. He had found them—and Tink had tried to warn Peter. Over and over, Tink had tried to tell him. She'd even tried to stop Wendy from leaving with Hook.

"Got a little tip from a client." Hook grinned and she gasped, feeling him fumbling with the belt on his pants, knowing what was coming. "Music guy—talking about some new group, *The Lost Boys*, and their charismatic lead singer, Peter Pann."

"No," Wendy whispered, but his hand was under her dress, groping her between the legs.

"I never thought he'd settle so close to the old homestead," Hook mused, his fingers parting her roughly. "Oh stop that whining. I've got to fuck you to make it real. A man's gotta do what a man's gotta do."

"Please," she begged, trying to make herself smaller against the pole.

"Cap'n?" The voice called across the water and they both looked into the swampy darkness. The light from a flashlight bobbed along the shoreline.

"Smede!" Hook called. "Get in the house!"

"But I want to play with the girl!" came a plaintive protest.

"Later!" Hook called, his voice dropped as he looked at Wendy, his eyes glinting in the moonlight. "I'm going to play first."

"Cap'n?" Smede called again.

"Go!" Hook roared and the light bobbed again, heading back toward the house.

"Why does he call you captain?" Wendy asked, hoping to distract him. She heard a splash in the water behind them and hoped it wasn't an alligator. And then, when his cock was stiff against her belly, pressing her against the pole, she hoped it was.

"Because I'm the captain and they're my obedient crew." His breath was hot, rancid, and she turned her face away, feeling his fingers probing between her legs, looking for an entrance. It wasn't going to be easy, given her position. He could hardly spread her legs, but she had a feeling he was going to manage, even if he ripped her to shreds.

If he puts that in me, I'm going to kill myself. Or him. Whichever I can manage to do first.

"Damn, you're tight," he remarked, his fingers working their way in, making her cry out in pain. "Gotta fuck you up a little more. Make you really pathetic. It'll make him crazy to see you like that."

"Get your hands off me." Wendy's words had so much weight behind them Hook actually stopped, looking down at her.

"What did you say?" He blinked at her, bemused. She knew he was getting ready to hit her. She knew that look on any man's face well enough.

"She said, get your fucking hands off her." Tink's arms came out from behind Wendy as if they were her own, knocking Hook back into the water. He sputtered and flailed, and Wendy glanced behind her as Tink grabbed the knife out of the wood and quickly cut the rope tying the boat to the island, pushing it adrift. Then she bent to saw through her duct tape binding.

"Thank you," Wendy managed, trying to cover herself as Tink worked the duct tape at her feet.

"You bitch!" Hook was still flailing, reaching for the little island, but Tink had pushed him very hard and his movements had driven him further away. The boat was drifting in the opposite direction. "I can't fucking swim! Smede! Smede!"

Hook bellowed and splashed and both women stared at the spectacle, clinging to each other to stay balanced in the small space. Wendy was shivering, from cold and fear, and she let Tink hold her, the woman's breasts a wonderful pillow, a respite from reality. They were both wet and their body heat served to keep them warm.

"Now what?" Wendy wondered out loud, seeing a flashlight beam moving toward them from the house.

"The cavalry has arrived." Tink looked upstream and Wendy heard it—the sound of a boat motor. But would they be here in time? And did Smede have a gun? The thought made her even colder and she clung to Tink, trembling. "It's okay, Wendy. You're okay."

"Smede!" Hook's cries were growing fainter, his motions slowing. "Help! Help!"

They both heard the splash and Hook's cut-off cry. "I'm going to—"

"Cap'n?" Smede had shown up at the water's edge just in time to shine the light on Hook and see the rising reptilian head, the massive jaws snapping open and shut over the man's head. Wendy screamed and turned her face against Tink's not unconsiderable bosom, but the sound of the death roll splashing echoed through the swamp.

"Wendy!" Peter's voice called her back as the boat slid up beside them. "Wendy, are you all right?"

She looked down at herself, muddy and bleeding and half-naked, and then up to the woman holding onto her. "Thanks to Tink, yes. I'm fine."

"Thanks, Tink." Peter smiled as he helped them both into the boat.

"Cap'n!" Smede was still calling, his voice choked, the flashlight searching the dark, stagnant water.

"What happened?" Nibs asked, putting a blanket around Wendy's shoulders. Curly offered one to Tink.

Tink grinned, wrapping the blanket around her as Peter turned the boat. "Crocodile got him."

"Poor Smede." Peter handed the controls over to Curly, letting him steer as he gathered Wendy in his arms. "He was always dumber than a doorknob. I couldn't even get him to come with me."

"I'm sorry," Wendy choked, trying to apologize for everything at once—for not trusting him, for going with Hook, for what had happened to Peter as a child. And he'd said *she* had an unhappy childhood?

"No apologies, Wendy-girl." He kissed her forehead, smiling over at Tink, who wasn't glaring anymore. In fact, she was smiling, an expression Wendy had rarely ever seen on the woman's face. "We're all a happy family now."

"Is it true?" Wendy asked, looking up at him, his face pale in the moonlight. "Did you steal his money and escape with all the boys?"

"It was *our* money." Peter's jaw tightened, and so did his arms around her. "And yes, I took it. And the boys. And we made a new life for ourselves."

She shook her head in wonder. "How?"

"Thank god for E-Trade," Curly remarked with a laugh, guiding the boat through the water.

"Turned Hook's money—" Nibs started.

Peter reminded him harshly. *"Our* hard-earned money."

"Yeah," Nibs agreed. "Turned it into over a million dollars in five years."

"Don't forget my venture into the rare book trade," Peter reminded him. "That's netted us quite a pretty penny."

Wendy remembered the book Peter had been looking for on the day she met him, the walls of bookshelves lining every room in the house.

Tink took the blanket Nibs offered her, putting it around her shoulders. "Of course, Peter just kept collecting lost boys. And me."

"Aw Tink, you're still my go-to girl," Peter said, nudging her with one of his Keds. "Always will be. You know that."

"And me?" Wendy inquired, leaning back against him.

"You're my forever Wendy-Girl, of course." Peter smiled down at her, making her heart leap in her chest. She was his, and he was hers, and the future stretched out before them both, obliterating a terrible past. "I think it's time for our happy ending, don't you?"

Yes, Wendy thought, settling even more deeply into Peter's warm embrace.

Yes, it is.

ABOUT SELENA KITT

Selena Kitt is a bestselling and award-winning author of erotic fiction. She is one of the highest selling erotic writers in the business. With half a million ebooks sold in 2011 alone, she is the cream-at-the-top of erotica!

Her writing embodies everything from the spicy to the scandalous, but watch out-this kitty also has sharp claws and her stories often include intriguing edges and twists that take readers to new, thought-provoking depths.

When she's not pawing away at her keyboard, Selena runs an innovative publishing company (www.excessica.com) and in her spare time, she devotes herself to her family—a husband and four children—and her growing organic garden. She also loves bellydancing and photography.

Her books *EcoErotica* (2009), *The Real Mother Goose* (2010) and *Heidi and the Kaiser* (2011) were all Epic Award Finalists. Her only gay male romance, *Second Chance*, won the Epic Award in Erotica in 2011. Her story, *Connections*, was one of the runners-up for the 2006 Rauxa Prize, given annually to an erotic short story of "exceptional literary quality," out of over 1,000 nominees, where awards are judged by a select jury and all entries are read "blind" (without author's name available.)

She can be reached on her website at www.selenakitt.com

YOU'VE REACHED "THE END!"

BUY THIS AND MORE TITLES AT **<u>www.eXcessica.com</u>**

eXcessica's YAHOO GROUP
groups.yahoo.com/group/eXcessica/

Check us out for updates about eXcessica books!

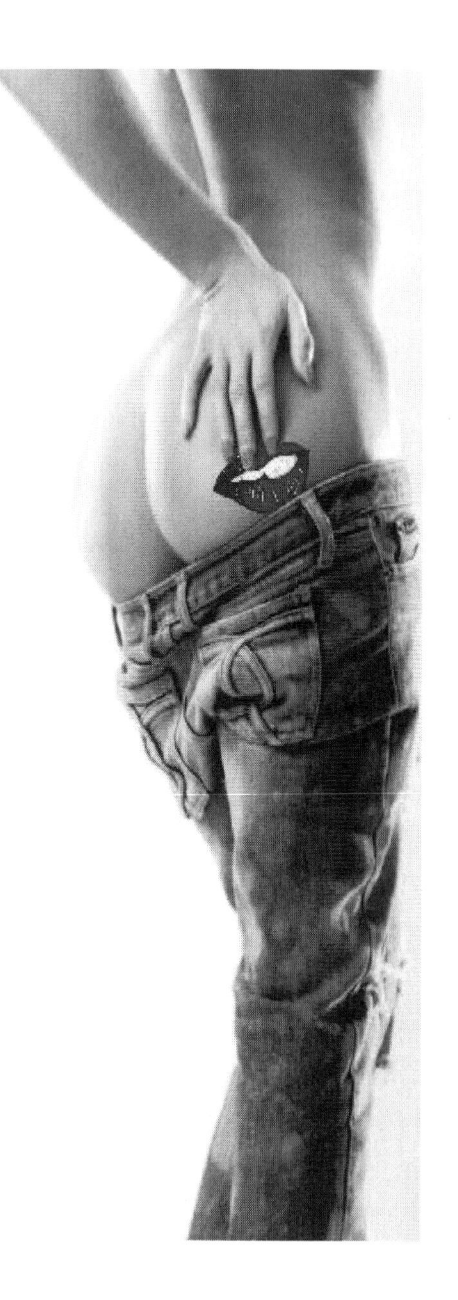

Made in the USA
San Bernardino, CA
20 February 2013